A DANGEROUS MAN . . . A
HEART-STOPPING MOMENT

Devon froze when she saw the long, beveled hunting knife appear in his hand.

"Your underskirts hold water and weigh you down," Gentry said. "You'll need to take them off."

Angry retorts filled her head, yet none flew from her tongue. "At least turn around," she said.

With a last warning glance, he did, his cavalry hat swinging to a halt between broad shoulders.

She turned also, and had one foot in the stirrup, pulling herself upward, before he whirled and clamped a hand on the horse's bridle.

"*Tskili!*" Witch. He sheathed the knife.

Devon felt his hands grip her waist and wrench her groundward. A small scream escaped her.

He pulled her close, hands gripping her waist with breathlessly tight pressure. Sweat ran a rivulet from his clean-shaven jaw, down his tanned throat to the unbuttoned neck of his shirt. A hiss of air rushed from between teeth clenched in anger.

After a long moment, Devon glanced up, prepared to face the ire his curse had promised. But there was more than anger in his face. Something as dark, but more controlled. A promise hot and frightening.

Slowly, his fingers relaxed. How fast the friction turned to fire. . . .

THE
SCHEMERS
LOIS WOLFE

BANTAM BOOKS
NEW YORK · TORONTO · LONDON · SYDNEY · AUCKLAND

THE SCHEMERS
A Bantam Fanfare Book / May 1991

*FANFARE and the portrayal of a boxed "ff" are trademarks of Bantam Books, a
division of Bantam Doubleday Dell Publishing Group, Inc.*

ISBN 0-553-28980-2

Published simultaneously in the United States and Canada

*Bantam Books are published by Bantam Books, a division of Bantam Doubleday
Dell Publishing Group, Inc. Its trademark, consisting of the words "Bantam
Books" and the portrayal of a rooster, is Registered in U.S. Patent and Trademark
Office and in other countries. Marca Registrada. Bantam Books, 666 Fifth Avenue,
New York, New York 10103.*

THE

SCHEMERS

PROLOGUE

Gentry

September 1853

Missouri

He touched her arm. Still warm. His wife's body lay on a bed of long, bent grass.

The wind blew stiff and chill across the knoll.

"Leave us!" he cried.

The onlookers behind him obeyed, straggling away in pairs and groups, their mumbling muted by the rasp of dry grass in the rising wind.

The ground was damp where Gentry knelt. A warm loam scent rose around him. Blood soaked the knee of his pants.

He could not move. Like a statue formed stone-cold and hollow in the dying sun, he was unable to turn away from his beloved's face. Long black lashes fringed the rise of her cheek, as in sleep. He yearned to place his ear to her parted lips, as if she would whisper his name. He brushed his finger along the smooth copper skin of her cheek, tracing the crease where her smile had so often lain against his chest, content in his nearness. He gently touched the curve of her nose. Her breath would no longer graze his neck in the darkness of their tepee, when the winter fire burned low and their robes moved sinuously like a spirit alive, seeking the rhythm only two could know.

His loss was great. Gentry's hand trembled as it withdrew.

Kai-ee-nah would not see her eighteenth winter. Soon the first dry snow would whirl in the air of the bluffs along the Missouri River, and the women in the small Sioux village there would hurry to stockpile wood for the evening fires. The storytellers would chant and the children would watch Kai-ee-nah carve flutes from summer reeds.

But the flutemaker would not be there to hear the testing songs hover above the warming fires. And the fault was his, for he had come home to make peace with his white father.

The pounding of a drum began somewhere in his head, insistent and strong, and he forced himself to look lower on her body. Her dress was a darkening mass of red.

He rose unsteadily and walked to his horse, searching numbly through the saddle pouch for a hatchet.

His anger was so great, he chopped through the first sapling in two vicious strokes. The second sapling took four, because he weakened suddenly. He could scarcely breathe. Slowly, more methodically, he hacked the small trunks free of branches and leaves, then split long sticks to make crossbars for the travois that would carry his wife's body.

Sweet, wise Kai-ee-nah. She had been so sure she could exorcise the demons of his past. You must honor your father, she had said.

Do not speak of him, Gentry had said. What honor did he? He sired a half-caste and abandoned my mother.

Kai-ee-nah, working at her pounding stone, had made a noise of impatience. She looked up, still grating dried buffalo into flake for the pemmican pot. Did your father not find you and keep you? she asked practically. Did he not refuse to marry, even to this day? And who is heir to his name? I wish to see this fearsome father-in-law, a wealthy man, you say. I wish to see Teague Morgan. He reached into a basket of chokecherries. I will tell you whether he is deserving of your forgiveness. Her stone ground an uncompromising rhythm in the hollow of the rock.

In time, Kai-ee-nah had convinced Gentry to make the long journey south. They had arrived with gifts for his father's house—skins, a carved flute, and a sable-colored pony.

Kai-ee-nah had worn her elk-skin wedding dress with its yoke of a thousand beads. But by dinnertime she had changed diplomatically to a blue cotton gown with a long apron that hid the shape of the growing child inside her. It was a simple gesture of courtesy to conform to the lodge of her husband's family, and she had worn the strange garment regally, with quiet pride, for she, too, was the firstborn of a man honored by his people.

All had gone well, until today, when abolitionists and border ruffians skirmished in the river bottom near Plain Shade. Gentry had fought at his father's side, in a hail of cross fire, until the border raiders were driven off.

Afterward, a begrudging pride had filled Gentry's soul, for he had shot well and drawn enemy fire while the defenders found position, and he had envisioned how Teague Morgan might boast of his son's courage.

But feeling one with the white man had always exacted a price, Gentry thought bitterly as he pulled cord from the pouch and began to lace the cross sticks to the two long saplings. Now, he had paid the dearest price of all, for the woman who made him a whole man was dead.

There on the knoll, overlooking the battle site, she had watched him fight. Then someone had shot her through the heart. A merciful assassination, before ungodly mutilation.

Gentry's eyes closed, for how long he did not know. He blinked back the shameful burn of tears. The pain leached nakedly from his heart. He was again half a man, half a breed. Kai-ee-nah—

The dry grass on the slope warned of someone's approach. He turned and rose in defensive stance, his hatchet in hand.

His father crested the rise and paused, then moved slowly closer.

Gentry looked away. He did not want Teague Morgan to see the unmanly grief in his eyes.

"Son?" Teague said.

On his father's lips, the word held the same uncertainty Gentry had sensed in the six years he'd lived in Teague's house. He didn't answer him.

A tall, broad-built man, Teague walked past him to the body of Kai-ee-nah. He stopped cold. His face contorted suddenly. He bent and turned away.

Gentry had nothing to say to this proud, lone man, this tough and temperamental Irishman whose delight in Kai-ee-nah and the child she carried had been evident to everyone in the household.

Gentry dragged the travois to Kai-ee-nah's horse and began to fasten the sapling poles to each side of the saddle.

"The marshal will catch the bastard," Teague said hoarsely, blue eyes shining.

Gentry was silent, knowing that the death of a Sioux

squaw mattered nothing to a U.S. marshal beset with warring factions of his own race.

Across the valley a wolf howled, a lonely warning that
night was falling in the rustling grassland. Gentry walked
past his father and knelt beside Kai-ee-nah. The wind was
colder and stronger, ruffling the thick hair at the end of her
braids.

He lifted her hand, then slipped his arms under her back
and legs and lifted her body. He cradled her against him as
he rose, stumbling, unnerved by her laxness.

His heart welled until it seemed to press against the wall
of his chest. He clutched her closer. Her stillness was so
complete. He carried something empty, but it took all his
strength to bear the weight.

Gently he laid her in the carrying frame that would be her
funeral bier. He would be the only one in the procession, for
their village and Ton-weya were too far away.

"Gentry?" His father's voice came from close behind him.

He swung into the saddle atop his white, piebald stallion.
Leaning down to seize the reins of his wife's bay pony, he
spoke to his father without turning.

"The child would have been a boy," he said quietly.
"Bury it."

He started the procession toward the red sun, the blunt
ends of the travois marking the trail of his last journey with
Kai-ee-nah.

Devon

September 1853
Berkshire County, England

"Shuh-shuh, shuh-shuh." Devon whispered the words
against the window. She didn't want to wake up Nanny,
who would scold her for being frisky.

Devon was riding the train to London. She mimicked the

rhythm of the powerful engine, hoping she could wake her older sister, Bertrice.

"Shuh-shuh, shuh-shuh," Devon said louder.

Bertrice's elbow felt like an arrow in Devon's side. It hurt, but Devon kept silent because she was lonely and wanted someone awake, even bossy Bertrice.

"Go to sleep," Bertrice hissed, then rolled over in her seat like a big sour plum and sat with her back to Devon.

Devon tried to comply. She brought her knees up to her chest and attempted to nuzzle comfortably against the seat. But the cracked leather made little tracks in her cheek. She pulled back to look at it. It was the color of the wood in the outbuilding behind their house in Devon. And there was something funny about the smell, something secret, like the parts on a puppy Nanny said not to touch. Devon slid her cheek along the seat back, sniffing. She came upon a slick spot of hair tonic that smelled like medicine; she had to rub against Bertrice's shoulder to get it off her cheek.

Bertrice shrugged and Devon sat up, bored. She wriggled off the seat to find her pencil and tablet. They were beside Nanny. Devon sneaked them away without tugging on Nanny's best wool traveling cloak—the one with two moth holes in spots where no one could notice.

Then Devon saw the lady across the aisle.

The lady smiled at her.

Devon carefully smoothed the new double-breasted piqué princess dress Cook's daughter had sewn for her. It was powder blue and stiff, with scratchy lace on the collar, no fun to wear. But Nanny said Devon looked just like a catalogue picture in it, and besides, Aunt Margaret had sent the money for it.

"Lord knows you'd best learn to please yer aunt Margaret," Nanny had said.

She said that a lot. And Devon hadn't ever even seen Aunt Margaret. She wasn't a bit keen to go to London to live with her, but she had to.

With a directness she hoped would not be too bold, Devon crossed the aisle and sat in the seat across from the lady. The lady was old with gray hair. She had skin that looked soft and loose like bread dough. Her smile was nice; her eyes crinkled.

On impulse, Devon opened her tablet and held it up so the lady could see.

"What a fine house you drew," the lady said.

Her voice was warm, like an open blanket to climb into.

"And what's that in front? A pony?"

"A cat," Devon said.

"Of course. How could I miss the whiskers?" The lady smiled. "You're going to be a grand artist someday."

Devon's heart skipped. That was exactly what her mother used to tell her. Devon wanted to move closer, but it wouldn't be proper. She bit her finger in indecision.

"Would you like to sit here and show me some more?" the lady suggested, patting the seat beside her.

Devon scrambled up on the seat and opened her book to her most favorite drawing.

"Who's this?" the lady asked, pointing. Her hand had huge brown freckles on the back.

"My mother," Devon said.

"It's easy to see where you get your angel looks. Does your mummy have pretty blond hair like you do?"

Devon shook her head. "Brown hair. But it got wet." She pulled at a thin spot in her white stockings.

"Wet?" the lady asked.

"Mummy and Papa were in a boat. It sank. Then they went to live with the angels, and Bertrice and I went to live in a flat with the Toddsons on Bradford Street. I didn't like it there. Too much cabbage."

"That can be tiresome," the lady agreed.

Devon was quiet awhile. She wanted to ask the lady questions she was afraid to ask Nanny. Couldn't the angels let Mummy come back just to say good-bye? And maybe Mummy was only lost in the water swimming home and hadn't found the edge yet. She could still come home then, couldn't she?

"How old are you, darling?" the lady asked.

"Eight."

"And what's your name?"

"Devon Cheritt Picard. Cheritt was Mummy's last name and I'm going to keep it." She frowned fiercely. "We'll live with Aunt Margaret and Uncle Arnaud, but I'll keep my whole name."

"Of course," the lady said.

"They're very, very rich," Devon said doubtfully. "I've never even seen them before."

"Rather scary, isn't it?"

Devon nodded.

"Exciting, too, what with all new things to see and do."

Devon shook her head forcefully and bit her lip. All of a sudden she was horribly frightened.

"Well, I know something that's exciting," the lady said quickly. "We're about to pass the horse."

"What horse?" Devon whispered, holding a giant sob in the back of her throat. It hurt terribly because she couldn't let it out.

"Come sit on my lap, lovey, so you can see out the window. It's the Uffington horse, and it's the biggest one you'll ever see."

Devon clambered onto the soft lap of the gray-haired lady and held on to the window ledge.

"All that green out there, that's Berkshire Downs. And underneath all that green is chalk soil. White, you know. And long ago, in the time of King Arthur, a very great, very secret artist started scraping away the grass, bit by bit, day by day, until finally he was done. And do you know what he made?"

"A horse."

The lady smiled. "Not just any horse. A grand horse, a hundred and thirty yards long. A skinny sort of creature with a long, long neck. Primitive, you understand. But it was his horse and no one has ever made another one like it. We'll be passing it soon enough. Lie back and rest, and I'll let you know when to look."

Devon relaxed against the lady's big breasts as if they were cushions. Closing her eyes, she pretended she was in a big closet. The lady's clothes smelled like things that had been there a long time.

Devon let her head loll while the train jostled them gently toward the horse. The lady began to hum, and Devon could feel the high-pitched buzz against her cheek. It tickled.

"I know a nice song," she said in a small voice.

"What's its name, darling?"

" 'Barbry Allen.' "

"Ah, yes." The lady smiled. "Would you like to sing it with me?"

Devon shook her head. "You sing it."

" 'In the mer-ry month of May, when green buds were a'swellin' . . .' "

The lady's voice was high and soft, quivering in spots as if it were fragile and might break. But the song was there. Her mother's favorite song.

Devon was careful to cry only with her eyes, because if the lady heard her weep, she would stop, and Devon might never hear her mother's song again.

The train rumbled *shuh-shuh, shuh-shuh.* The lady sang all the verses she knew.

Devon held herself as stiff and still as the chalk horse on the hill, tears washing the starch from her new lace collar.

ONE

August 1864

Virginia

Its firebox hot and the coal tender filled, the boiler engine harrumphed a warning to the twenty South Side Rail passengers.

The travelers reluctantly left the shade of the station's lean-to roof. They pressed toward the train car, jostling carpetbags and haversacks, maneuvering around the young woman who had stopped in the middle of the small boarding platform.

Devon Picard stood fast against the tide, rising on tiptoe and craning to see beyond shoulders and hats. Her twill-brimmed bonnet was slipping, pulling a pinned cluster of golden hair with it. She grabbed it with one gloved hand, holding it in place.

"Aunt Margaret?" she called as she tried to back out of the crush. Her silk skirt was caught under the toe of a soldier's mud-caked boot. She grasped a flounce of the long skirt and jerked her hem free.

"Perce!" Devon waved with relief as she spotted the blue bonnet of Mrs. Perce, their maid. "Where's Aunt Margaret?"

"She went looking for a facility. And she never came back, miss," said Mrs. Perce, the hairy mole on the tip of her chin quivering.

Devon took Perce's hand to calm her. "Get on board then and find our seats. And don't worry." Devon forced cheerfulness into her voice, for the elderly servant was growing more frightened with each mile traveled.

Devon was sure Mrs. Perce knew nothing of their real reason for leaving London. But since beginning the last leg of their journey here in Virginia, behind the lines of the Americans' civil war, Mrs. Perce's chin had become a trembling bellwether of her distress.

Maybe Perce realized they were being followed, Devon thought. She smoothed one hand along her stomach, hoping to quiet the knot of fear tightening there.

Aunt Margaret still was nowhere in sight—and neither was the dark, silent passenger who had been observing them so closely throughout the trip.

The man was black-haired and sun-darkened. He wore the butternut-brown uniform of the Confederate Army. His rolled-brim hat marked him a cavalry soldier. He had been their shadow since the train left Rappahannock Station south of Manassas, although he never sat near enough to be obtrusive. Still she had realized she and Aunt Margaret were always in his sight. His was not the sly, offensive awareness of a man eyeing the swell of a breast or awaiting a glimpse of stockinged leg. This man's scrutiny was different. He witnessed without watching, slouched in his seat, most of his face hidden by the crown of his hat. Each time she attempted a low-toned dialogue with her aunt, she felt his senses warm to her.

The man had invited conversation from no one during the long run through the Shenandoah, nor during the change of trains at Lynchburg. There, civilian passengers, attendant slaves, and a few soldiers on leave boarded the only coach car on the South Side Rail line. It was a cramped cabin that looked more like a trolley cab; it had two rows of unyielding wooden benches, all facing front, as inviting as church pews awaiting penitents.

When everyone had debarked at the small, isolated rest stop, Devon had watched the dark-haired stranger disappear in a clearing of outbuildings where a solitary tree spread a canopy of shade. She could only pray Aunt Margaret hadn't taken the same path.

Devon stepped quickly off the platform in the direction the cavalryman had wandered. As she hurried around the corner of the lean-to, she nearly bumped into a petite woman in a blue gown.

"Aunt Margaret!" Devon said breathlessly, steadying herself against the building. "Where have you been? The train is about to—"

She stopped. Behind her aunt loomed broad shoulders.

In the awkward silence, the tall man tipped the brim of his cavalry hat higher, a barely polite gesture. His cold blue eyes met Devon's. In them she saw no mask of social courtesy, only a boldness she could challenge—or ignore.

Shocked, Devon summoned what she hoped was a dismissive look and returned her attention to Margaret. "We must hurry," she said.

Amazingly, Margaret turned and gave an appreciative nod to the tall cavalryman. "Thank you again, Mr. Morgan."

Then Margaret walked away, tucking her baby-blue gloves more tightly between her fingers.

Devon hurried to keep pace. "Who is that man?" she whispered in her aunt's ear.

"Gentry Morgan, he said his name was. From Plain Shade, Missouri. Not a very talkative chap in any regard."

"Why would you speak with him at all?"

"He was standing there pulling some leaves off that big tree and I felt compelled to ask him why he was denuding a limb that gave perfectly good shade. He handed me a leaf. They have an extraordinary flavor. You suck on the stem and it tastes spicy, like cider that's gone a bit off or something. Sassafras, he said. Good for a cough, I should think."

Margaret opened her small damask reticule. Inside, Devon was dismayed to see a crush of green. Her aunt's purse was stuffed with mitten-shaped leaves emitting a pungent aroma.

She hurried her aunt along. Margaret Picard had always been a woman of rash judgment and strong will. But Devon feared the hardships of the trip were beginning to wear on Margaret's good sense.

It was not her aunt's fault, of course. God knew, Devon herself had contributed to the difficult burdens Margaret had to bear. But it was the powerful friends of Devon's uncle, Arnaud Picard, who had added criminal risk to their journey.

Devon had thought clearing customs in Philadelphia would be the most dangerous hurdle. Everything had gone smoothly there, however, and Devon and Margaret had emerged from the Federal offices with papers that allowed them to visit relatives in secessionist territory. But they had not boarded a truce train, as instructed. They had found Confederate transport and were now traveling through the countryside where bands of Confederate guerrillas and scavengers frequently skirmished with Federal soldiers. God willing, they would reach Wilmington, North Carolina, without incident.

The train whistle shrieked its final warning, and Devon urged her aunt up the platform steps.

"I think that man is a spy," she whispered.

"I think that's ridiculous," Margaret said sotto voce. "He's a Confederate soldier. We're on the same side. Now please stop whispering. It's not dignified."

Across the landing, five black women in linsey-woolsey shifts stood silently, waiting for the last white people to enter the coach.

The slaves did not watch Devon and Margaret approach. Their eyes were cast down or focused respectfully low. Devon felt a strange unease tingle her conscience. She had long enjoyed a genteel life that depended on the deferential industry of a servant class. But slavery was different. What these dark, stoic people waited for was entirely different.

"A servant chooses to submit; a slave chooses nothing." The staccato comment of her liberal friend and publishing mentor, Damien James, echoed in Devon's thoughts.

She supported Margaret's elbow on the step up through the narrow door, then glanced behind her. The cavalryman, Gentry Morgan, had gestured for the black women to board, then left.

Devon quickly found her seat and looked with hope out her window. But her spy was not leaving the train.

The tall cavalryman loped along the tracks, past two rusty boxcars, a flatbed filled with supplies, and a slat-sided stock car loaded with wounded. He waved all-clear to a sooty man leaning out the window of the front engine.

The big driving wheel on the locomotive whooshed with the pressure of the boiler, like a whale clearing a blowhole, and the train lurched forward.

The cavalryman waited alongside the track.

Devon watched as her car slowly rolled closer to Gentry Morgan. He grabbed the handrail and swung up into the front doorwell. He did not look at Devon as he passed down the aisle.

Other passengers seemed unduly aware of him. Devon saw averted glances and heard quiet mumbles. It seemed her fellow travelers had drawn a quick conclusion about his dark skin and startling blue eyes. "Breed," she heard a matron behind her whisper.

He chose a vacant seat beside a young mother holding a baby. The spot was across the aisle and three rows behind Devon and her aunt.

Too close for comfort. Devon sat stiffly, facing forward, dipping her head occasionally in the direction of her aunt's chitchat. But Devon wasn't interested in the churlishness Margaret had encountered in the new gardener at Langley Place.

Devon preferred discussion of art or politics, and her aunt only tolerated one and abhorred the other. Though reasonably well-educated, Margaret held to the theory that intelligent womanhood was a state that should be sought solely by the plain. Ladies blessed with beauty, as Margaret had been in her youth, and as Devon was now, shouldn't be too clever, lest they appear challenging or indecorous.

Devon had lived with her aunt and uncle for eleven years and had yet to hear Margaret challenge Arnaud on any matter that affected family or finances. Perhaps she should have, Devon thought grimly. Arnaud Picard's investment decisions over the past two years had created a terrible drain on the finances at Langley Place. And Arnaud, of course, hadn't even been home in two years to assess the problem.

That had made Devon's conduct with the earl's son all the more crushing for Margaret. Devon had ruined Margaret's chance to share the easy status and gratuities of old money. This American journey was an attempt to let the scandal die for lack of Devon's presence to feed it.

To Devon, the chilly disposition that her aunt had shown since leaving London was quite understandable. But then, Margaret never had been a woman of sunshine and warmth.

That Margaret had agreed to the current charade at all was a measure of her desperation to see her husband. It had been a difficult life, Margaret had oft assured Devon. So confining for the former Margaret Granville, fifth daughter of an English baronet, reared in a whirl of social engagements. Childless, she had spent long years in the role of military wife to a dashing French sea captain who kept garnering higher positions and more distant postings.

Then Devon and her sister, Bertrice, arrived, orphaned by the death of Arnaud's brother and his wife. Devon could never remember a day that Margaret did not have appointments—for visits, fittings, introductions, and teas. Even in her letters to Devon and Bertrice at school, accounts of social events filled the pages. Margaret was a tireless manager. And now she had managed this trip to the warring United States, for Admiral Arnaud Picard had been posted by his emperor as a consultant to the Confederate Navy.

The train car was beastly warm, even with the windows down. Devon wished she could remove her hat. But Aunt Margaret would find it undignified.

"We must make a trip to New York before we board a ship home," Margaret was saying. "I want to get something special for Sarah and Cyril. That blockade's a terrible nuisance, you know. In his letters, Arnaud says there's hardly a luxury left in Wilm—"

"Indeed!" Devon interjected quickly, before Margaret blurted out their destination to everyone within earshot. "I'm sure the children are expecting a large package the next time they see you," she added.

Bertrice's children was an inexhaustible topic for Margaret. They were like grandchildren to her, and Bertrice like a favored daughter. Bertrice, after all, had had the good sense to accept the match Margaret had arranged with a pious and wealthy squire who had an estate near Coventry and a London three-story not far from the Picards'.

Throughout their childhood years at Langley, Bertrice had always done the correct thing. Whenever Devon looked to her older sister for guidance, she was counseled in obedience and gratefulness for the generosity of Margaret and Arnaud. "If not for them, we would not be well bred," Bertrice had said often.

"What are we? Horse stock?" Devon would tease.

"Don't be literal! Your tongue's always got you in trouble."

"But they're only questions. Why must questions get me in trouble?"

"Because they're rude and show you don't have the proper attitude. Don't upset my life, Devon. Just don't upset anything until I'm married and gone. Then ask all the questions you want."

How scared her sister had been, Devon mused. Afraid that the good circumstances in which she had landed would be snatched out from under her. But then Bertrice had known more about the iconoclastic life Papa had led than Devon. Bertrice had spent her years at Langley fleeing the taint of her dead father, Frederic Picard, and Devon had spent all that time seeking his shadow's shape and texture, and searching for the face of her mother. There were no pictures of Prudence Cheritt Picard at Langley Place. Devon could remember the feeling of her mother, but the warm, embracing figure had no face.

Bertrice, the practical one, had quickly transferred her loyalties to the stern, petite Aunt Margaret. And she was justly rewarded. There had been a grand wedding fete, for which Margaret had demanded Arnaud come home from his posting. And then there had been four pregnancies in three years, two of them live births, two lively sparkling children whom Devon adored. While Bertrice and Margaret remained in the sitting room judging samples of drapery and poring over the latest advice from *Godey's Ladies Book,* Devon would play in the nursery with Sarah and baby Cyril. How many sketches had she made of those cherubs, their faces so pure in antic joy or utter despair?

Devon loved life in the nursery. The children were either happy or unhappy, their play either safe or unsafe. There were no agonizing choices, only easy questions to ask and to answer.

Devon looked at her aunt beside her, lolling loose-jointed in her seat, rocking with the rhythm of the rails. Margaret was not a woman who entertained difficult questions or vague expectations.

Devon knew, to make up for her mistake, she must show uncommon loyalty in this furtive affair—even though her conscience was uneasy. Perhaps her resourcefulness might finally be of use to Margaret, who had always considered Devon's ingenuity an irritating obstacle on the road to refinement.

The miserable temperature and humidity had extinguished conversation throughout the car. A baby whimpered. Devon turned in her seat, attentive. It was an excuse to monitor the man who monitored her.

Suddenly, iron wheels locked tight against the rails with an earsplitting screech. Passengers were flung forward. Leather satchels, brocade bags, and gaily striped hatboxes skittered down the aisle like litter before a wind.

The forward momentum pinned Devon to the bench in front of her. Margaret was thrust to the floor, one shoulder twisted against the leg of a seat. Devon clamped a hand on to her aunt's arm to keep the small woman from falling farther into the aisle.

The high-pitched cry of metal-on-rail jarred Devon's equilibrium more than the awkward position. Unable to breathe, she glimpsed fragments of hats, shirt cuffs, and frightened faces in scattered array.

Slowly the wail of the brakes receded. Windows rattled in their frames as the train came to a ragged, jarring stop.

Devon grasped the stained oak window ledge above her with one hand and used the leverage to lift her aunt to the safety of the seat. A bedraggled figure in a serviceable cotton and broken blue bonnet rose from the floor. The timid Mrs. Perce smoothed her rumpled bodice and pressed a handkerchief to her trembling chin.

"It's all right, Perce," Devon whispered quickly.

Beside her, Margaret expelled a pent-up breath. "It is not all right," Margaret said in a low voice, tugging her silk shirt straight. "We should not be stopping like this."

"Are you hurt?" Devon asked.

Margaret ignored her. Instead, her fingers fumbled with the hatpin at the crown of her blue bonnet. She had worn the lined, ash-weave hat every day since they'd left England. Now she lifted it from the chignon of her graying hair.

"Trade bonnets. Quickly," Margaret said.

The urgency in her aunt's voice belied the calm manner she practiced, and a cold chill of certainty spread through Devon's breast.

They would be discovered. Pray God by Confederates, for if the Federals deciphered the message . . .

Without a word, Devon slipped off her brown hat. She smoothed back the wavy strands that had been jostled loose and tucked soft, gilt-streaked curls into the simple bun high on her head. Then she donned her aunt's small woven bonnet and quickly tied the white satin ribbons under her chin.

With a coolness she did not feel, Devon placed her hands in her lap, curbing an impulse to look behind her. She knew that Mr. Gentry Morgan of Plain Shade, Missouri, noted sassafras expert and cavalry soldier, had carefully noted the exchange.

All about them, ladies in long, flared skirts crowded the aisle in search of lost bags and reticules. The few men in the car were trying to squeeze through to the door when shots rang out.

"Yankees!" someone shouted.

A sudden hush fell in the car as scuffling noises from outside came closer.

"Throw out your guns," a man yelled. "Or the engineer dies!" The voice was gravelly and deep, an orator sure of his audience.

The coach suddenly filled with competing waves of anxious voices. Few of these beleaguered Southerners had guns, but those who did wanted to hold fast to them, their hatred of Yankees as solid as a battle shield.

"They can have my gun—when I'm dead," said a feverish Confederate soldier two rows in front of Devon.

"Throw 'em out now!" shouted the enemy outside.

From her window seat Devon heard the click of the hammer of a gun cocked, undoubtedly, she thought, for the hapless engineer. She fixed her gaze on the stubborn soldier in front of her. He was placing defenseless citizens—including Aunt Margaret and Perce—in danger. She must convince him to give up the gun before he caused a bloody melee. She hurriedly stepped past her aunt to reach the aisle.

But she stopped cold when she saw Gentry Morgan striding toward her, gun in hand.

He approached slowly, filling the aisle with his solid, muscular body. His jaw was clean-shaven and free of the anxious sweat that stained the collars of other men in the coach. His head was bent to clear the low ceiling, and his long black hair fell forward, grazing his jaw.

Sun-burnished, he seemed to heat the air as he neared. The warmth consumed the fuel of her anger, emptying her bosom and stilling her breath. Blue eyes commanded hers with a message breathtakingly fierce and natural.

Heart racing, Devon obeyed and moved quickly out of his path.

Gentry Morgan reached the gun-wielding soldier in front of her. "The Yanks don't need prisoners or dead civilians," he said. "They're after something else. Best not make things bloody."

He turned his revolver muzzle-first into his palm and tossed the weapon out the nearest window, then waited for the feisty Rebel in the seat to do the same.

The boy stubbornly kept his silence. But his seatmate, a soldier who'd lost an arm, let his revolver slip over the dusty sill.

Reluctantly following suit, the angry Rebel thrust his rifle butt-first out the open window. "You better be right, scout," he spat at Morgan.

The narrow door at the front of the train car burst open. Two Federals in dark blue uniforms entered, pushing passengers out of the way.

The first man was short and trail-grimed, with a wrinkled jacket that drooped low on bony shoulders. He held a revolver in each hand and a plug of tobacco in his cheek.

The Federal officer behind him stood pompous, lanky, and clean, his long-nosed Colt extended. He wore a braid on his hat and lieutenant's stripes on his sleeves.

"Get'em to settle down, Lyle," the lieutenant said.

"Move!" the short soldier barked, and he prodded his gun in the stomach of a frightened matron.

Devon watched Gentry Morgan ease back to the end of the aisle and lean against the wall. His hat slid off his thick hair, dangling below his shoulders on a rawhide lanyard.

When the passengers were quiet, the bony Lyle returned to the front of the car and scratched his cheek where his chaw puffed out, firm as lead shot.

The lieutenant holstered his revolver and reached under his coat to hook a thumb in scarlet suspenders. Methodically, he scanned the passengers, the expression on his long face intent and critical. His gaze rested for endless moments on Margaret.

Slowly he walked down the aisle, the flaps of his coat brushing Margaret's arm as he passed. "You folks, relax," he said, high-necked collar holding his chin high as a preacher's. "We just need a few supplies. And we'll be questioning any foreigners you have aboard."

Margaret stiffened in her seat. The lieutenant strode back to the front of the car, and Devon watched as he passed. Although brushed and clean, his uniform reeked with a sour smell. Even the silver, embroidered lieutenant's bar on the epaulet was lackluster.

He nudged his bony cohort and gestured at Margaret and Devon.

Margaret raised her chin, refined and defiant.

"Your name, ma'am?" the lieutenant demanded softly.

"I don't speak with irregulars," Margaret said in her iciest London clip.

He gave a small, humorless smile. "I figured you were English. Step outside please."

Devon stood quickly, her gloved hands folded primly around her small purse. "You have no right to detain us. Our papers are in order."

"We know," said the lieutenant. "Outside, ma'am," he repeated to Margaret.

Devon's hand tightened around the derringer secreted in her bag. "Don't go," she told her aunt.

"Pretty stupid, refusing a man with a gun," said the little soldier, Lyle, moving closer.

Without warning, he spat a short, derisive stream of tobacco juice across the heads of several seated passengers. The dark drippings smacked expertly on the window glass next to Devon's seat.

Margaret's mouth dropped open, speechless at the vulgarity.

Devon looked directly at the soldier, whose lip dribbled escaping juice. "Superb manners—for a wretched little cricket."

A tense quiet filled the coach.

"Will you be doing a little hop for us too?" she asked.

"High-nosed bitch." Lyle's thumb jerked up to set the hammer on his gun.

"Lyle! Not now!" the lieutenant commanded sternly.

"Not now? Then when, Lieutenant?" Devon asked, her voice rising so everyone could hear. "When do brave Federal soldiers shoot unarmed women and peaceful citizens?"

"Probably when they don't shut up."

The deep voiced warning rose close behind her. Gentry Morgan had inched forward during the angry exchange. High spots of color marked Devon's cheeks as he moved past her.

The lieutenant's small eyes narrowed, suspicious, as he studied Morgan. Slowly he relaxed. "Damn. Posters don't do you justice, scout."

"Pleased to recognize your face, too, 'Lieutenant,'" Morgan said.

The lieutenant sucked his teeth for a long moment. "I guess maybe you should step outside with us," he said.

"Guess so," Morgan replied.

"No more fussin'," the lieutenant said impatiently, gesturing for Lyle to herd Devon and Margaret off the train.

"I wouldn't struggle, ma'am," Morgan said to Margaret as Lyle pulled her from her seat.

"I would if I were your size," Margaret said, looking up at the cavalryman.

"There's a time for spit and grit, and a time to build an alliance."

Margaret froze at the word *alliance,* but only for a moment. Lyle gave her a rough jerk to get her moving.

Devon had also noted the strange use of the word. Uneasy, she raised a hand to the brim of Margaret's blue bonnet, pretending to tuck in a stray curl. Then she helped the terror-stricken Mrs. Perce from her seat.

Devon exited with as much grace as she could muster in the circumstance. Her skirt gave a silken whisper as she gathered it hastily in the narrow stairwell of the train.

Gentry Morgan was right behind her.

TWO

Devon squinted against the glare of the early-afternoon sun.

The train had stopped on the ridge of a high embankment. Iron rails radiated the foul, acrid burn of braking metal. The dirt shoulder that skirted the rails was wide. It sloped gently down to a kidney-shaped clearing bordered on the far side by dense pine woods. Bobbing white crowns of Queen Anne's lace grew in knee-high clusters at the edge of the woods.

Looking along the line of the train, Devon saw that the only Federals wearing uniforms were the two who had boarded their car. Far down the track, near the engine and coal tender, three other men were unloading the boxcars and packing crates onto mules tethered nearby. Their colorless, rough-weave shirts showed dark half-moons of sweat under the arms. Down in the clearing was a sixth man tending horses.

The lieutenant helped a livid Margaret down the rocky railroad embankment. Lyle nudged Devon with the nose of his pistol, and she step-slid down the slope, barely keeping herself upright in heeled shoes.

Poor old Perce stopped cold at the top of the incline and had to be carried across Morgan's shoulders like a sack of feed.

The women were led across the clearing, close to the pines and near to where a sinewy old soldier held the reins of six horses.

"Why do you harass us?" Devon asked, hoping she sounded more outraged than scared. The information sewn in the lining of the hat weighed heavily on her.

The lieutenant ignored her.

"What about the mail?" one of his men called from high on the tracks.

"Don't need it!" he yelled back as he unbuttoned his blue uniform. "But put a little bag of that Virginia ham on my saddle. I wanna doctor up that hog slop Corley calls beans when we make camp tonight." The lieutenant's accent had suddenly acquired a lazy, natural drawl.

They acted more like a gang of bandits than a band of soldiers, Devon thought. She stole a glance at the silent Gentry Morgan, who, apparently, was a wanted man. As if he had patiently been waiting for her to make the connection, he nodded carefully in the direction of the horses. The elderly man had long since dropped his hot Federal jacket in the dirt.

She turned away to hide her confusion. Could they really be bandits? Did that mean they weren't after the alliance message? But they clearly had orders to detain Aunt Margaret.

And why had Gentry Morgan offered mention of the alliance like a password? Didn't he know the code phrases linking all alliance contacts?

And for what crime would his dark, brooding face grace a reward poster? She watched him, wondering. And that name, Gentry. Curious bequest to a half-white savage.

She averted her eyes when he caught her looking and turned her thoughts to a better question. How quickly could three women disappear into the thick woods on her right? The pines started just a few yards beyond where she stood.

She moved closer to Margaret, aware Morgan was watching her.

"So you know my face?" the bandit leader said to Morgan.

Morgan nodded. "They had a picture in the *Richmond Dispatch* once. Story said Reg Landry's awful particular about his clothes."

Devon glanced at the bandit's carefully brushed coat and polished boots.

"Besides," Morgan went on, "I know there're no Federals east of Stoney Fork right now."

" 'Cause you just got out of a Yankee prison and you keep

track of them bluejays, don't ya, Gentry Morgan?" Reg
Landry asked, laughing.

Landry was leader of a ragtag but efficient band of rene-
gades known throughout the Shenandoah. His raiders would
sometimes engage a detail of blue-coated Federals, but most
of their forays were for scavenging and stealing from uniforms of any color.

"Hear you killed two guards escapin' from that prison in
Delaware." Reg pulled the stub of a black cigar from a vest
pocket.

"They didn't want me to leave," Morgan said.

Reg grinned, pinching the stub between yellowed teeth. "I
reckon not." He took the wet-tipped cigar from his mouth
and leaned closer to Morgan. "Let me ask your advice. I
gotta choice. You can ride with us, or I can shoot you here
and collect the reward the Yankees posted on the Rappahannock. What you think I should do?"

Morgan shrugged. "Depends."

"On what?"

"How bad you need a scout. Word around Richmond's
pretty embarrassin'. Says Reg Landry sets pickets so green,
they take hits broad as a barn board."

The bandit leader shrugged off the criticism. "Wartime.
Gotta take what you get." He stuck the black stub back in
his mouth.

Morgan looked down and scuffed a rock with the toe of
his boot. "I won't be scoutin' for Jeb anymore."

"Too bad about General Stuart," Reg agreed. "Heard he
promoted you to head scout." The bandit leader thought a
minute, shifting the cigar to the other corner of his mouth.
"Listen. You train a couple of my boys, an' I'll divvy up
things even as pie—keepin' in mind we ain't never split with
a breed before," he added, his smile generous.

Morgan was quiet. His eyes took on a stony set, but when
he spoke, his voice betrayed no emotion. "I need a horse and
my gun." He smoothed hair back from his brow and set the
rolled-brim hat on at an angle.

Reg nodded. "Get them for him," he told Lyle.

The little bandit Lyle spat a vehement stream of black
juice into the dust. "I don't trust him," he said, not budging.

Reg stepped in front of Lyle, towering over him. "We
need 'im. Now tell the boys to stop loadin' and get that train

on its way." The words held a warning for the stubborn
Lyle.

Lyle scowled, hitched up his trousers, and strode up the
embankment.

Devon's heart raced. Time was running out. She looked at
her aunt. Margaret was unnaturally subdued. The heat had
flushed her small face a fierce, unhealthy red.

"What are you going to do with them?" Morgan asked,
indicating the three women.

Reg smiled. "Got a friend close by who wants to pay 'em
a visit soon as the train leaves."

Morgan smiled and half-turned to Devon, as if savoring
the thought of a visit with a pretty young blonde like her.
But she noticed how he looked beyond her to the scrub pine
dappled by afternoon shadows.

She had no time to lose. "You can't leave us here!" she
cried suddenly. She swept a finger across her cheek as if
wiping a tear, then reached into her purse for a lace-edged
hanky—and the derringer. Her index finger slipped neatly
around the trigger of the small gun.

"Please," she added with a sweet sniffle, moving closer to
Reg Landry as she pulled her hand from the bag.

Reg smiled indulgently. But his grin froze when he saw
her snub-nosed pocket pistol, aimed at his jugular.

"Tell your men to saddle up and leave, Mr. Landry. You'll
be our 'guest' on the remainder of a rudely interrupted journey."

Aunt Margaret exploded with relief. "Bravo, Devon!"

Mrs. Perce raised one eyebrow in halfhearted hope.

Morgan didn't move.

Devon held the gun out straight, sighting it high, as her
friend Damien had taught. And she remembered to keep a
safe distance so Landry could not grab the gun.

"Don't be a damn fool," he said.

"Don't be a dead outlaw," she replied softly.

The steam wail of the train whistle rent the air.

No! Devon glanced up the embankment. The train was
leav—

Gentry Morgan's hand came out of nowhere to envelop
her wrist. He twisted as he jerked her gun arm skyward.

Crying out in pain, she resisted his wrenching, but he
spun her around and she found herself backed against him,

her left arm pinned at her side. She struggled wildly as she felt his arm snake tightly across her waist.

"Drop the gun." His mouth was close, right by her ear.

"When hell freezes," she hissed, trying to twist away from contact with his groin and thighs.

"Then keep moving." His voice was intimate, intense. "It feels good."

She froze.

Cautiously, he released her left arm.

She sagged against him, as if swooning.

He shifted his hold to support her—and she jerked on her gun-hand, pulling down with all her might, almost freeing the gun from his grasp.

She heard him curse softly, then felt his steely grip take control of the gun and its aim. As she tried to wriggle free, he leveled her arm as if she were a stiff puppet. His finger squeezed atop hers in the small trigger guard of the gun.

Reg Landry was laughing at the struggle when the gun suddenly discharged.

The small bullet scored the knuckle of the old bandit holding the horses. He yelped and flailed backward, striking one of the horses across the nose.

The big gray reared with an outraged squeal, reins free. His hooves pummeled the rump of a chestnut mare, and in an instant the ground erupted with a dry, dusty cloud of thumping horseflesh and animal squeals.

The wounded bandit rolled free of the commotion, and the spooked horses broke, galloping headlong for open, rocky ground.

"The horses!" Reg yelled, hailing Lyle and the three bandits who were guiding mules down the embankment a hundred yards away. The three men scattered down the slope to try to head off the horses while Lyle stayed with the mules.

Devon felt Morgan rip the gun from her hand. He gave her a shove. "Run!" he growled.

But she backed away from him, spent and scared.

With an angry shake of his head, he rushed to join the bandits in the dust of the panicked horses.

"Go, Devon!" Margaret was suddenly at Devon's elbow, pushing her niece toward the woods. "Get help!"

"I couldn't leave you!" Devon cried, glancing down the line of track. Lyle, and a .60-bore shotgun, watched from a distant post near the mules. But then she saw him turn his attention to the men chasing the skittish horses more than a quarter mile away.

"Don't be silly," Margaret said. "They're not going to hurt two old women. And we simply can't allow them to infiltrate the alliance. It means everything to your uncle Arnaud, and to his precious Confederacy. Here," she whispered. She urgently pressed a piece of folded foolscap into Devon's hand.

Another message! Devon's heart sank in exasperation as she tucked the foolscap down the neck of her gown.

Margaret pushed her insistently in the direction of the woods.

"I can't leave you!" she repeated. A feeling of dread, as tangible as an icy bath, spread through her body, numbing her legs. Her fear of the bandits was negligible. It was the thought of willfully abandoning the only mother she had ever known that terrified her.

"Come with me," she said, reaching out her hand to Margaret.

"Don't be a baby! For goodness' sake, run!"

From his post atop the embankment, Lyle sent a warning spray of buckshot into the dirt a yard from Devon.

Instinct flared with the sting of rock at her ankle. With a parting glance at her aunt, Devon bunched her heavy skirt and petticoats over one arm and raced through wildflowers toward the thicket at the edge of the woods.

"The girl!" Lyle called. He shifted his chaw to the other cheek and fired again.

The shot shredded a tall clump of Queen Anne's lace between Margaret and the woods. But Devon had already disappeared into the stand of long-needled pines.

She ran recklessly through natural gaps in the trees, over ground heady with the scent of dried cedar. Laurel bushes pulled at her skirt. Her heart hammered at the breakneck pace.

Finally, she could run no more. Chest heaving, she stopped on the approach to a small gully and hugged a tree trunk for support.

Rest. Just for a moment.

A gunshot cracked the air, close, thunderous. The rough

bark of the tree splintered near her hand. She stifled a scream.

"Hold it right there."

The measured Southern voice came from a stand of saplings behind her. Devon turned, terrified, then sank wearily to the ground, her back against the trunk of the tree.

The gunman slowly stepped away from his hiding place.

He was a bandit she had not seen before. His white shirt was cut of fine broadcloth, with sleeves uncuffed and rolled halfway up his forearms in deference to the heat. His hat was black, the brim a shadow for his eyes; a black kerchief covered his nose and mouth. He moved with a tensile grace natural to lean-framed men, but his strangely refined gait seemed out of place in the wilderness.

Devon felt a distinct chill as the stranger advanced. It was more than the five-shot revolver he had trained on her. It was his leisurely approach, as if he would have all the time in the world for her.

"Expected that plucky old woman," he said. "Not a pretty young thing like you."

His muffled voice was a hoarse whisper now, his original tone already a distant memory for her.

He stopped and tilted his head as he studied her. "I don't quite know what we're going to do with you," he said softly.

Her eyes slowly widened, then closed to keep the gunman from seeing the hope there—hope in the form of the man who silently stalked him from behind.

Gentry's rifle butt caught the masked man sharply on the back of the skull. The gunman's revolver slipped from his fingers, and his body pitched sideways, over the lip of a grass slope.

"Damn!" Gentry swore as he tried to stop the body and grab away the mask. But the bandit rolled heavily down the gully.

Gentry quickly picked up the masked man's gun and turned to the girl.

She had not moved. She sat like a child, knees to her chin, shock curling a warm, comforting shell around her.

Damn her anyway, he thought. He hadn't planned to interfere so openly. His job was to infiltrate. But she had forced him to act, she with the indelicate tongue and too small gun that could have gotten them all killed.

Yet she was important. She was courier for the secret Confederate alliance.

Soft white woman, raving in high temper like the virtuous or the untried. Trouble in the best of circumstances. In a war zone, playing at spy games, she would be the kiss of death.

Gentry breathed deeply, steeling himself. He hated blond women. And if she didn't have information about the alliance his boss needed, he would hate her even more.

He reached down and jostled her.

She raised a face of fine lines, well-apportioned features. Brown eyes were set wide, dark as a deer, moist as earth turned deep, harboring secrets. And her skin, cream smooth, porcelain pale.

"Get moving!" He towered above her, impatient. "Landry's coming."

"Is there a difference, him or you?" she asked.

Gentry grit his jaw painfully tight. But it was the tightness she incited elsewhere that enraged him.

"The difference is this," he said. "I'm going to Wilmington, North Carolina."

She stiffened. The name had meaning for her.

She began to rise, her hand grasping along the tree trunk for support. "On the contrary," she said. "I think where you're going is hell."

"What luck that I have such fitting company." He grabbed her arm and pulled her behind him into a lush, cool canopy of green.

THREE

In Washington, D.C., Gentry Morgan's boss was feeling the heat.

Pinkney Dobbs's second-floor apartment on Madison Avenue was stifling. The mustached chief of the Federal secret service threw off the flimsy cotton coverlet. "For God's sake, Lilly, move over. We're sticking together like salted fish bellies."

Buxom Lilly playfully punched the stocky fifty-four-year-old man on the arm and scooted down to the foot of the brass bed.

"I swear, Pink," she said, using the crumpled sheet to wipe sweat beads from between her breasts, "if you were any more romantic, I couldn't endure the ecstasy of your company."

Her voice sashayed up and down the scale like a child on a seesaw. It had always tickled him, that blueblood Virginia drawl and the upbringing of a dirt-poor tenant farmer, all rolled into a body curvaceous enough to make a Baptist run for the river.

"I think you're worried 'bout something." Her chin rested on her shoulder as she looked back at him. "You better tell me 'bout it, or it's gonna eat at your insides like a ball of pinworms."

Dobbs smiled. She fished for information as indelicately as she made love. It was one of the things he liked most about her.

He shrugged, buying time to think of a smoke screen for his troubled thoughts. "Something's going to break this week on those Reb-loving bankers in Baltimore," he lied, reaching for his trousers as he rolled slowly off the bed.

"Really?"

"We've got a good lead on where they're hiding the contraband." He grimaced as he sucked in his belly to button his fly.

"How do you think they're getting gold past the checkpoints?" Lilly asked, idly swinging around the footpost, one arm extended.

He shook his head and walked around to the foot of the bed. "Lilly O'Callahan Frith," he warned.

She swung right up against him, her breasts flattened against the gray hair of his chest.

His voice lowered to silky suspicion. "If I didn't know you were a loyal Unionist, I'd wonder about all those questions you ask."

She pulled away, brows drawn in a frown over her hazel eyes. "You grizzly ole bear! I'm just trying to help you get trouble off your mind. 'Cause you know what happens when your mind's somewhere else. Everything's somewhere else." Her fingers traced the inseam of his crotch.

Dobbs smiled. She was real quick sometimes. Still, he didn't want her to think he was that easy to fool. He struck a sharper tone, one that meant business.

"If you need a younger man, get one. Or two. The point is, you agreed not to poke your pretty nose into my business. Remember that promise. I wouldn't want something to happen to one of your more becoming appendages."

She backed away from him, wrinkling the complimented nose. "I've got lots better parts than that and you know it."

"Maybe you'd be happier showing them to someone else."

They both knew he was not bluffing.

Nervous, Lilly backed away. "But I like you," she said in a small, strange voice. Tousled brown hair veiled her profile.

There was a plaintive hesitancy in her answer, something vulnerable and honest. Dobbs sighed, because he liked her too. Only he was older and knew the importance of implying it rather than showing it.

"Then go downstairs and bring up a pitcher of fresh water. I need to wash up before dinner."

She shrugged on a scarlet robe. "Will you be suppin' with

Secretary Stanton and the President tonight?" she asked slyly.

"Lilly!"

"Just kiddin', you humorless son of a bitch," she said lovingly. She shut the door softly behind her.

Dobbs controlled his exasperation and ran a cupped hand across his mouth and unshaven chin. He was grateful for the privacy. Lilly was perceptive enough to know he was deeply worried about a project. But it wasn't contraband couriers, Army deserters, or arms smugglers. It was a reluctant double agent named Gentry Morgan. The fate of too many —including President Lincoln—depended on the progress the half-breed was making behind the lines in Carolina.

Dobbs's hand raked through the thinning layer of steel-gray hair atop his head. He was getting too old for this job. Too old to get a message from the President saying the Rebs had a secret plan to break the blockade. Instead of registering as one of the greatest secret service challenges of his career, the news had left him stiff and silent as a pallbearer. It had taken three bloody years just for the North to find a gutsy general like Grant who could lead an 850,000-man army. Three years to build the biggest navy in the world. Three years to systematically destroy Rebel supplies and resources.

Now, a coded message from Lincoln's ambassador to England warned of a monied alliance of Southern sympathizers there, a conspiracy that was international in its operation.

Dobbs's stomach roiled. A little pool of bile rose to the back of his throat.

His solution to the threat was a man he had wronged eleven years ago.

He jerked open the medicine drawer of his rolltop desk, then pulled out a bottle of whiskey and poured himself a jigger.

He was taking a huge but calculated risk with Gentry Morgan. The mercurial Rebel was the only high card Dobbs held—and only luck had dealt him that one. Luck and a stint as marshal in Missouri where Gentry's dad, Teague, owned the biggest farm in the state.

Dobbs took the whiskey in one swallow and screwed his eyes shut as the fire dug a trough to his stomach.

Gentry Morgan's name had turned up with a sheaf of

routine desk correspondence. The captured scout was on a roster of Rebs being brought to prison barracks in Delaware.

Gentry was Dobbs's direct link to a known alliance contact on this side of the Atlantic, Confederate Army Colonel Miles Brant.

Brant was Gentry Morgan's brother-in-law.

Given the half-breed's stormy family history, Dobbs knew there was no love lost between Gentry and the Brants of North Carolina. Prisoner of war Gentry Morgan was the most obvious wedge he could use to pry a board loose in alliance plans.

He had presented his offer to Gentry three weeks before in a worm-rotted shanty outside the stockade.

The tall, shackled prisoner had been silent a long time— long enough for doubt to churn up the acid in Dobbs's stomach.

Finally, Gentry had turned away from the shuttered window. "I'll do it, but only if you find my wife's murderer. And prosecute him."

Dobbs stared at the long-haired half-breed with disbelief. Ten years of history and neglect had buried the case of the Sioux woman Kai-ee-nah. The killer had never been found. Dobbs knew, because as marshal he had investigated the slaughter.

But not well enough, Gentry's unforgiving eyes told him.

"White man's justice for a white man's crime," Gentry said.

"Fair enough," Dobbs agreed warily.

In his bedroom, Dobbs poured another draft of whiskey, a finger high. Investigation had started with a guard at the prison where Gentry was being held, an old farmhand from Teague Morgan's place. Then interviews in Plain Shade with those who'd fought in the skirmish with border ruffians in '53, and research of back issues in offices of the *City Star*.

Yesterday Dobbs's detectives had reported back. They gave him the name of a man who had high motive and a lie for an alibi. A man Dobbs had had no reason to interrogate eleven years ago.

Dobbs's hand shook a little as he tossed the liquor down.

Gentry knew.

• • •

South of the Carolina border, the sun sent bloody streaks across the skyline. Gentry jerked his frothing horse to a halt near a river fork. He held his breath so that he could catch the sound of the yellow-hair's horse. Breaking brush at a cautious canter, her mount was a few minutes behind, following the path he had made.

Gentry knew Reg Landry's men were poor trackers, but he had taken no chances. More than once he had sent the yellow-hair off alone on a forest path while he doubled back to confuse the trail or hide tracks. At last sighting, the two most persistent pursuers were headed toward Rickbow Mountain, victims of a trail he had baited with a shred of hat ribbon. The rest of Landry's posse should be reporting back to the raiders' camp by now.

Stroking his horse's damp neck, he unconsciously uttered the Sioux words of thanks for the hard work of his "legs." The roan had performed well, surprising him, as had the yellow-hair.

But then, he had not expected much from her in this escape. Her obstinacy had cost them precious time in the beginning, when Reg Landry's bandits were still horseless but starting to surround the woods in search of her.

Gentry had hidden a mare from the spooked herd, and he had pulled the yellow-hair roughly through the brush until he found the thoroughbred hidden by the masked gunman. He had bent quickly to cup one hand and help the yellow-hair mount the mare.

She had backed away from him, eyeing the saddle. "Astride?" she'd whispered.

Fighting fury, he'd run his cotton sleeve across the sweat on his forehead. Then he'd grabbed her around the waist and boosted her roughly onto the horse he had taken from Landry's herd. "Astride."

He'd known the bandits would fan out in a south-spreading pattern to search the woods. The best escape route lay in riding north and doubling back.

The time-consuming ruse had worked.

Now, as Gentry watched the red sky darken toward night, he allowed a smile to curve one side of his mouth. The yellow-hair had kept him in view during the pounding ride, but just barely. She was not used to riding astride, taking hilly terrain at a hard gallop, nor being pursued by bandits hell-bent on her capture.

His tricks to obscure the trail would work until tomorrow, when Reg's masked client would no doubt hire good trackers. Then the chase would begin again in earnest.

He turned in his saddle as the mare crested the rise above the river. The yellow-hair reined roughly to a halt beside the roan.

Both rider and mare had kept the pace, but at a price, Gentry saw. The lady's face was tight with fatigue. Her delicate cheek was sweat streaked and dusty. Slim shoulders hunched forward over the pommel. Hair the color of goldenrod at dawn hung loose about her shoulders, a soft, tangled pillow of swirls and waves still half-pinned at the crown of her bare head.

The bonnet. He had monitored the safety of the stiff-brimmed hat ever since it had slipped down her back in the first hour of their escape. Held by long, white ribbons now dust laden and dark, the hat nestled in the curve of her waist, protected.

She caught the direction of his glance. He saw her shoulders straighten.

"How far behind are the bandits?" she asked as she edged her horse away from his.

He shrugged. "Far enough to let us make camp in an hour and sleep until dawn."

" 'We' will not make camp. I must find a farmhouse and get my bearings."

"Easy," he said, as much to her as to the horse that danced under him, impatient to get to the river for a drink. He could not allow the Englishwoman contact with anyone until he had the message she carried. "Whoever took the trouble to hire Reg Landry will be asking for you in every town from Stoney Fork to Wilmington."

"I have to get help for Aunt Margaret and Perce."

"Reg's got no reason to harm your aunt," Gentry said truthfully. The plans of the masked man who had hired the bandits were another matter. "Didn't your aunt tell you to deliver the message as soon as possible?"

She avoided his eyes. "You're very good at implying a knowledge of business that doesn't concern you. I think you're a man who guesses well when he knows very little."

He gave her a hard smile. As tired and vulnerable as she was, she was drawing a line. She needed a sign that he was a genuine contact for the alliance. And Dobbs, damn him, had been able to give Gentry few hard facts beyond the name of the courier.

"I could be a pretender," he said. "Then again I could be your protector, sent by people who care a lot that certain news reaches the Brant plantation."

The name registered. Her eyes narrowed a little and held his.

"I'm Miles's brother-in-law," he said.

"And I'm his cousin," she said, "but I wouldn't know him from a powder monkey, just as I don't know you."

Her suspicion of him was as solid as a wall between them. He gambled on a point he had heard the masked man confirm.

"Look at it from my point of view." He smiled thinly. "You could be the pretender. Your aunt's the messenger. You're not even supposed to be here. Who changed the plan, Miss Picard?" He said her name playfully, with an exaggerated French slur. "And when?"

Unexpectedly, the questions made her blush and she looked away. "Fate changes everyone's plans, Mr. Morgan," she said, uneasy. With a too harsh kick of her heel, she urged her horse forward, down the knoll to the edge of the river.

Gentry made a note of the sensitive nerve he had struck. Then he dismounted and allowed his horse to wander down to the shallow water of the river fork. He stayed on the hill to backtrack their path, checking the dry clay soil for telltale prints.

Devon's horse walked straight into the rocky shallows and bent thirstily. Rounded river stones glistened in the dying light, each smooth, brown face an oasis in eddies of rushing water.

Devon hesitated, every muscle in her body cramped with complaints of the bruising ride. She had dreaded this, the moment of dismount. Her legs had braced against the pounding pace for hours. They felt numb, barely part of her. She was not sure she could stand upright, but she was too thirsty to care whether she drank with dignity or fell face first.

Slowly she swung her right leg around, eased herself up, and held tightly to pommel and mane as she slid ground-ward. Thank God she was not as petite as Aunt Margaret; she did not have so great a drop.

She leaned unsteadily against the mare's shoulder a moment, then sighed with joy when she found she could straighten her legs and take small steps. But then she had always been the more athletic of her aunt's wards. While Bertrice had excelled at sneaking sugar plums, Devon had sneaked Marney Street urchins inside the garden walls of Langley Place to play shuttlecock and tag.

Devon suspected Bertrice still had to use stealth in her quest for sugar plums. The stern squire she had married valued parsimony as the gateway to wealth—and matri-mony as an outlet for masculine health. Or so said poor Bertrice.

The water beckoned, and Devon waded away from the horse to the center of the ripples. She stooped and cupped her hand in the cold, rushing current. The water was clear as fine crystal. She sipped slowly, savoring, then stopped. The wetness coated her empty stomach like a chill bath. She had not eaten since dawn.

The noisy rush of the water obscured the splash of his bootsteps, and she felt rather than heard Gentry approach. She turned and rose, waiting for him to berate her for allowing the winded horses to drink so long. But he merely grabbed the horses's reins and offered each mount a sheaf of fresh grass.

She studied the man's profile, his hair thick and black as a skein of burnt satin, some strands falling forward to hide eyes the color of a brilliant day. With an artist's perception, she took in the whole scene, the contrast of shadow and light, the linear slope of the horse's head, and the clean, inward curve of Gentry's throat as he looked up to follow the homeward glide of a hawk. She saw tension as he glanced back to the hill, and an unthinking tenderness as he stroked the horse's cheek.

She liked the converging angles, the contrasts and brood-ing light. Perhaps she could re-create them if she was ever reunited with her pencils and chalks. But the tools of her avocation would arrive without her at the depot in Wilming-ton. Uncle Arnaud and safety awaited her at the home of

Miles Brant. But she was lost in a wilderness with a volatile half-breed—and wanted killer—as her guide.

She looked away as he waded closer, pulling the two reluctant horses behind him.

She did not want him to see through her mask of certainty, where childish fears overwhelmed years of genteel tutoring, leaving her painfully aware of how alone and unskilled she was.

She stooped to cup more water in her hand, not caring that the train of her beige silk gown had grown a soggy dark brown. She bent over her water, a prisoner without privilege, a world away from art museums and the fine tile etchings she had created for the publisher of a children's book. A world away from the private scandal she had created for her family.

Never, Devon had told Margaret. Never would she marry Roger Bivens.

Well, Margaret had said, perhaps the rigors of an American journey would put life with an earl's son in perspective.

Gentry's boots appeared before her, breaking her reverie. Dusty, wavering lines marked the depth of the water on the brown, tooled leather. "We have another mile to go," he said.

She straightened, trying to hide her dismay at the thought of riding farther on horseback.

"We walk," he added, a vague hint of a smile around his eyes. He handed her the horses' reins. "We'll wade the river to the deep bend before the light dies."

She took the reins and gentled her mare with one hand. Warily, she watched Gentry reach along his belt. The leather of his sheath was so worn and smooth, the blade didn't give a whisper of warning as it was drawn.

She froze when she saw the long, beveled hunting knife appear in his hand.

"Your underskirts hold water and weigh you down," he said. "You'll need to take them off."

Angry retorts filled her head yet none flew from her tongue. If he touched her, she wanted all her energy focused on fighting him.

"If there comes a time to worry about my conduct, I'll give you fair warning. Right now, we have to hurry."

She swallowed hard.

"Waste any more time and your modesty won't have a thread left to hide behind," he said.

Her words came out breathy, but full of conviction. "One day, if God is just, you'll be a prisoner in my world."

"On that day I promise to disrobe much more cooperatively than you have for me. Petticoats. Now."

Neither she nor his blade moved for a long moment.

"At least turn around," she said.

With a last warning glance, he did, his cavalry hat swinging playfully to a halt between broad shoulders.

She turned also and had one foot in the stirrup, pulling herself upward, before he whirled and clamped a hand on the horse's bridle.

"Tskili!" Witch. He sheathed the knife.

Devon felt his hands grip her waist and wrench her groundward. A small scream escaped her as she landed upright with a splash in the shallows. She was whirled around to face him.

He pulled her close, hands gripping her waist with cruelly tight pressure.

Sweat ran a rivulet from his clean-shaven jaw, down his tanned throat, to the unbuttoned neck of his shirt. A warm hiss of air formed a word, "Tskili."

After a long moment, Devon glanced up, prepared to face the ire his curse had promised. But there was more than anger in his face. Something as dark, but more controlled. A promise hot and frightening.

Slowly, his fingers relaxed. His thumbs swept low across her abdomen, unerring explorers, and marked the rise of her pelvis with a delicate press.

Devon grew still, her breath slow, uneven, afraid that any movement would fan the tightening knot of warmth inside her. She wanted it to stop. Her eyes warned his. It must stop.

Gentry released her suddenly and backed away, wary. Slowly he reached for his knife. "Do not move," he told her.

He bent and picked up the dripping bottom of her skirt. His left hand wrung the fabric roughly, flinging small streams of water against his leg.

He pulled the skirt higher to reveal the waist ties of her crinoline and flounced petticoats.

Devon closed her eyes. She felt the flat edge of the knife

slip inside the waistband and jerk outward, snipping the ties. The knife ripped down, tearing a line through the cotton flounces, waist to hem.

The heavy underskirts fell to the water behind her, revealing long, lace-trimmed drawers.

She choked back a sob of fear and pulled away, jerking the skirt of her gown down to cover her. But his hand clamped hard on her arm, a warning to stay still.

He scooped up the fallen underskirts and pushed them into her hands. Then he sank low on his haunches in front of her and yanked the bottom of her silk skirt taut. The knife pierced the fabric with a tearing sound that stilled her. She felt the weapon's pull, until it had slit the damp hem.

Two flaps fell free against her ankles.

"Turn around," he said.

Numbly, she did, then felt the rip as the knife jerked a path down her skirt parallel to the one in front.

Gentry reached inside a small pouch at his belt and drew out a thin piece of rawhide. He cut it in half, then sheathed the knife. Quickly, he gathered the split bottom of her skirt around each ankle and tied it, creating loose, ballooned trousers that would allow her to walk free and fast.

He rose and took the petticoats from her, buckling them across the backpack of her saddle. Without a backward glance, he picked up the reins of the roan and waded toward the center of the stream.

"Keep your shoes on," he said. "The rocks are sharp."

Devon looked down at her mutilated gown. A moist film collected in place of the clear-eyed demeanor she had hoped to project.

In a small, shaky voice she called to her horse, then pulled the stumbling mare forward, down the center of the shallow stream, her tears a hot, coursing counterpoint to the chill water around her calves.

Ahead, the half-breed and his horse blurred quickly in the dimming light. She stopped a moment to clear her eyes, and Gentry looked back at her, then beyond to the shallows where they had entered the stream.

He turned suddenly, handing off his horse to her as he walked past. Alarmed, she watched as, with a careful stride, he backtracked their steps. What had he seen? Reg Landry's trackers?

He stopped and bent beside a large, exposed rock that had been overturned by her horse's hoof. Already the water had washed away the muck from the bottom of the stone, leaving a startling two-toned marker. A sharp line divided the exposed, sun-bleached top from the dark, mud-seated bottom. With one hand he settled the stone aright, then waded back to her.

He worried that they would find a stone turned in rushing water, she thought. Dear God. How doggedly he expected them to pursue her. The cold drawl of the masked man echoed in her mind. He was a man who expected compliance. He would demand the courier and her message. Would Aunt Margaret tell him all that her niece carried? Would he—?

"Will he hurt her?" She blurted the question out loud as Gentry passed. Her hand clutched a fistful of shirt to stop him.

He looked down at her. "I think your aunt's a resourceful woman. She'll tell him enough to keep herself safe."

Devon released his shirt. She turned away. "And you," she said. "Now they know you helped me escape."

Gentry watched the yellow-hair fight to control her fear for her loved one. He phrased his reply carefully. "They will know I was sent to protect the courier."

Now would she believe his story and come to trust him?

When she turned to face him, her regard was cautious, a vigilant searching for clues. Her lips parted as if she would question him, and he noticed how her upper lip was modest and defined, the bottom full and dark and the unspeakable pink of a woman's soft shadowlands.

"*Tskili,*" he whispered to himself in warning.

Soft, arrogant, pale-faced woman, symbol of a culture that despised and destroyed his own.

Hatred welled inside him, hatred for her white, inviting skin, for hair that flaunted purity of parentage.

Hatred for her willfulness, for she would demand much from him before offering confidences, or caresses.

Just as Kai-ee-nah would.

He looked down at the rushing water.

The memory of his dead wife was sudden and painful, her spirit rising beloved but unbidden beside his thoughts of the yellow-hair.

Kai-ee-nah. He had known no woman more beautiful, and allowed no other woman so close.

Trancelike, his hand moved slowly toward Devon's face.

The faint scent of horse and musk, leather and leaves, reached her long before she felt his thumb sweep gently along the ridge of her cheekbone, under her eye. His touch smeared the wet salt of tears across one cheek, then the other, mixing dust and water to a dark, diagonal streak.

He stepped back and appraised her. Then he held out his thumb, showing the soiled, wet smudge he had used for painting.

She watched as he smeared a thick, faint line under each of his own eyes. The message was clear.

War paint.

"To remind each of us," he said softly.

They were enemies.

FOUR

Just before dark, Gentry veered out of the water and up the bank of the stream. He held out a hand to help the yellow-hair up the steep slope.

She was trembling with chill and hunger.

He led the way through a narrow trail thick with rhododendron. Water squished softly in the yellow-hair's shoes. For half a mile they fought the insistent thwack of small branches. Tendrils of green caught at the ribbons of the bonnet hanging down her back. He glanced back often to make sure she held the hat securely.

The brush-beating path ended suddenly and they emerged in a clearing. Tall maple and sparse-limbed hickory rose like guardians of the open space, and the night crickets buzzed furiously in the woods around them.

The tired mare snorted as she pulled a resistant clump of grass from a rhododendron thicket. A loamy, fertile scent of damp leaves and earth hovered like heavy perfume beneath the boughs.

Gentry looked at the sky. Sunset had left an intense crescent moon that would light the way of any night-stalkers.

He walked across the clearing, but the yellow-hair didn't follow. She moved to a cluster of saddle-sized boulders and placed a hand on one stone to brace the descent of her sore body.

Sitting was such a relief that a soft cry escaped her lips.

He gave a small smile, for he was no stranger to the exhaustion of the hunted. He knew he could force her no farther that night. Still, they were not far enough from the water. This campsite would be on the perimeter of an easy search pattern for an experienced tracker.

Gentry considered. He would get little sleep tonight—but he would get the message of the alliance, and it would help him decide his next move.

He abruptly left his horse and strode over to retrieve the mare. "Gather firewood," he said as he passed the yellowhair.

Bent protectively over the bonnet in her lap, she glared message of her fatigue and his inconsiderateness.

"Keep moving. You'll be warmer," he said less harshly.

She rose slowly, fueled for the moment by her resentment.

She had a stronger constitution than he had thought, Gentry mused. Later he would see just how much strength she had in reserve.

The hansom cab turned sharply onto Alderon, moving through Liverpool's market district at a quick clip. The onehorse coach dipped left with the centrifugal force of the curve.

List starboard, you blue-nose whale, the driver silently admonished the passenger in the cab. Standing on his perch in back, the driver tsked and pulled back lightly on the reins to slow the horse and straighten the course. The horse clopped down the three-block stretch of gaslit cobblestone crowded with evening revelers.

At 32 Alderon Circle, the driver stopped the cab in front of an unusually wide brick house. A two-story oak staircase jutted from the building's facade like a giant crooked nose. The steps were painted plum red with white, whorled banisters.

The stairs made a dogleg turn at a landing and rose ostentatiously to the second-story entrance of the building. On the rooftop, a gingerbread-trimmed widow's walk perched in the lee of a Gothic turret.

While the outside decor of the house called to a gaudy crowd, the ornate stairs boasted liveried servants who waited impassively at the foot and crown. It was a contrast the patrons of The Damson Club loved, for the gin palace was famous for poking fun at its own pretensions. It was a joke, of course, that only the very rich and their lucky attachés could afford.

The hansom cab creaked and sank right as its portly passenger stepped out with surprising grace. Harcourt Bivens,
Earl of Grayshire, tugged the lapels of his elephantine jacket
straight under a flowing greatcoat. Then he dug a thick,
bejeweled finger into a vest pocket, withdrew a sixpence, and
dropped it into the driver's hand.

Lord Grayshire turned and walked away with a brisk,
solid step.

Behind him the driver tsked and flicked his whip in solemn judgment on rich men who exhibited too much chestnut pudding and not enough gratuity.

The earl took the steps at a semblance of a run, his gold-
knobbed walking cane a nimble third leg. As he approached
the top landing, the modest, brass-handled door was opened
for him. He stepped across the threshold into a grand-scale
entrance hall with a frescoed ceiling, kentia palms, and
tufted settees upholstered in plum-red silk.

The butler bowed and took the earl's overcoat. Lord
Grayshire glanced at the six-foot-tall cabinet clock in the
hall. "God's ramparts, I'm late! The little Arab's going to
skewer me. Out of my way." The earl threw his top hat over
his shoulder and strode down the entrance hall, past Grecian urns and arched doorways hung with bulbous drapes.

The earl nearly collided with a giggly young lady in taffeta
who emerged at a run from behind a set of curtains.

"Oh! Excuse me, Bivey!" The little tart's apology was respectful, but Grayshire stiffened at the diminutive of his sur-
name. The short form of "Bivens" had become much too
familiarly exchanged by much too common a sort in the
confines of the club. He harrumphed the bosomy little chit
out of his way.

God knew he'd love to have time for such child's play.
But dalliance was for ineffective fops and purposeless drunk-
ards. Lord Grayshire had a political dream he was making a
reality.

Near the end of the hallway, across from the servants'
stairwell, an alcove led to a narrow set of gaslit stairs. Lord
Grayshire took them as swiftly as he could and arrived at
the top with an annoyed wheeze. Another corridor lay
ahead, a dark but homey hallway that smelled of fresh cigar
smoke and stale port.

The earl slowed down to catch his breath and compose

himself. The meeting tonight was important and he didn't want to look ruffled.

He fished in his jacket pocket for the noose. Damn, where was it? He slipped an anxious finger inside the pocket of his vest and closed his eyes in relief as he found the knotted cord. God help him if he ever lost it, because he couldn't remember how to tie another one.

"Bivey, any common sailor can tell you how to tie the monkey fist," Khaled had told him laughingly some eighteen months before when the whole enterprise began. But Grayshire would swim a running sewer before he sought help from a smelly deckhand. The thought strengthened the earl's composure, and he knocked on the door, three sets of three short knocks.

A short, dark-skinned servant in formal serving coat opened the heavy door. Lord Grayshire handed over his knotted cord and the servant stepped aside.

"Bivey!" The combined admonition and greeting came from across the room. A darkly handsome man of average height and dressed in a wine-red smoking jacket rose and tapped the face of his gleaming pocket watch. "We were getting worried about you."

The words were solicitous, but Lord Grayshire knew that behind the facade was a very annoyed Arab. Khaled al-Sayed Dexter ran alliance business by the clock. It was the reason so much had been accomplished in a year, but Lord Grayshire still considered it déclassé to be so absorbed by schedules and deadlines.

"Thank you for your concern, Khaled." The earl took off his coat and handed it to the dark servant. "I trust our Frenchman is already here?" He crooked an arm back to receive the sleeve of an elegant smoking jacket the size of a haberdashery awning.

"Beaumond sent a message from Dover yesterday. His crossing was delayed. He arrives by the London train this evening."

"Then he is late," Lord Grayshire said with a small smile.

"Like you." Khaled smiled back. "But the Quincy brothers are here. Quite prompt."

"Merchants always are," the earl said, and clenched a newly lit cigar between his teeth.

The servant opened double doors to a sideroom of master

proportions. Wing-backed chairs with horsehair seats and gold-fringed trim ringed an ebony table.

Khaled watched as Bivey greeted the Quincy brothers. The fat old fox always hid his dislike of the enterprising commoners for the good of the cause. Tad and Clarence Quincy were shipbuilders and charter members of the Alliance of the Monkey Fist. Their contacts had been essential to outfit the fleet that, in one month's time, would rupture the Union blockade.

Khaled sat casually, one leg crossed over the other, and pulled an ivory cigarette case from his vest pocket. A servant held a small candle to the slim teak-brown cigarette he placed between his lips. Khaled exhaled leisurely. He loved this room. Like all private meeting chambers at The Damson Club, there was no monied vulgarity here. On a drop-leaf table at the end of the room, a Bristol glass fountain rose four feet high. White glass birds with ruby-red wings perched on the glittering, hand-blown geyser.

Along a wall paneled with Moroccan leather, giant oils of famous clipper ships hung grandly in one long row.

Khaled smiled. It was a fitting room for the weekly meeting of The Savannah Sound Men's Society, an obscure fellowship of aristocrats and boating enthusiasts planning a yachting expedition to the Caribbean.

With Allah's grace, they would set sail within the week.

Absently, Khaled twisted his ring, a gold scarab enhanced with rubies, which he wore on his left hand. It was the only sign of nervousness the elegant Egyptian allowed himself.

He laid his cigarette in a dish and took a deep breath. Then he crossed the room and dutifully joined the earl, the use of whose ships and money Khaled ordered in correspondence each day.

As he talked, the sacred golden beetle with ruby eyes twisted round and round his finger.

Hidden by falling darkness, a thick column of smoke whirled up from the tinder bed, and a flicker of red-orange singed the pile of dry twigs.

As the fire finally took hold, Devon felt like crying for joy. It had taken so long. Gentry had unsaddled and tended the horses while she gathered wood. Then he'd cleared a fire ring, marked it with stones, and shredded a square of her cotton petticoat for tinder.

From the small pouch at his waist he had drawn two flintstones. He'd struck them together quickly, rhythmically. Sparks had sailed like lights into the tinder bed. He'd bent swiftly to blow life to the smoldering spiral.

Devon had watched each step, fascinated, in case she should ever find herself alone with only flintstones and a forest for warmth. The process was so much easier when you had Perce to stack tinder, lay a fire in the grate, and carry in coal for the scuttle. Good Perce, Devon thought sleepily. She wouldn't dare take the maid's efforts for granted when next they met.

Devon sat with knees bunched to her chin, her feet and legs as close to the fire as she dared. The flames were dancing and she watched until her eyes began to close. If she weren't so hungry, she could sleep sitting up, right there, right then . . .

"Dinner is served." The phrase she wanted to hear, but the voice was slightly mocking, and very close. She opened her eyes warily.

Gentry waited on one knee beside her, a meal of hardtack and beef jerky in his palm. She was so hungry, her hand shook as she reached for the meager fare.

"That's mine," he said. "This is for you." He handed her a small bundle wrapped in grease-stained linen.

Devon smelled the sweet, meaty aroma of ham as she unwrapped the parcel in her lap. The sight was more beautiful than she had dared hope: three slices of cured ham and a pile of crumbled corn bread.

She took a deep breath for control. "We must share," she said, handing it back for him to divide.

"I've had mine," he said. "The man who shot at you kept a nice pantry in the saddlebag."

She looked at the dry biscuit and tough twist of meat he'd claimed for himself. "If you are still hungry, you must take more." She picked up the largest slice of ham and carefully laid it atop the hardtack in his hand.

There was a solemn quiet between them.

Gentry took a small bite of the sweet meat. She, too, began to eat. Famished, she finished her meal quickly, with

only a semblance of delicacy, picking at each crumb of corn
bread until the linen was bare.

Gentry watched her as he methodically chewed the
leatherlike jerky. She had offered him the meat out of politeness, he knew, or perhaps because she'd guessed that he had
lied. He had not eaten. But Gentry sensed more in her gesture. He'd grown up in a culture where men and women
showed respect in definite rituals. An Indian wife fed her
warrior first.

This pampered Englishwoman was showing mixed instincts, and they were a little too intriguing for his physical
comfort. He moved to the other side of the small fire to put a
safer distance between him and the long golden hair he
wanted to touch.

She also seemed uncomfortable. "I'm sorry," she said finally, apologizing for rudely devouring the food.

He shrugged. "Understandable. You missed tea today."

"Yet another insult?"

"Or a tease to make you smile," he said. "Which do you
need?"

The question held a quiet sympathy. She said nothing. A
tear burned its way over the ridge of her eyelid.

Gentry did not look politely away as the droplet sped
down her dirty cheek. "My grandmother told me woman's
tears are strong medicine. They're bad spirits escaping the
good."

"And what are men's tears?" she asked in a strained
voice.

"Invisible. We must hold bad spirits inside, to fight with."

She tilted her head to wipe the wetness from her jaw.
"Then you assume I'm weaker now?"

"No." He watched her as he swallowed his last bite of
biscuit. "I think you will always fight."

The words were quieter, more potent than they should
have been.

"Mr. Morgan—" she began.

"The alliance message," he said, brushing crumbs from
his hands.

She rose stiffly, still sore from the day's ride. "We must
talk. I have no assurance you are—"

"Just pass the hat."

The crickets' wild song filled the air in the clearing. Devon hesitated, knowing he would jump her if she did not comply. Slowly she slipped the loop of mottled ribbon over her head and swung the ash-framed bonnet across the fire to him.

The moment he grasped it, Devon made a dash for the saddles stacked at the edge of the clearing. She had already relieved the bonnet of its precious note. And she knew he would explode with rage.

Breathless, she reached the saddles lying on the ground and pulled madly at the stock of the rifle that protruded from one. Behind her, she heard the slow, measured crunch of boots against dirt.

She whirled.

Gentry advanced slowly, bonnet in hand, its ribbons trailing over rocky ground.

"Stop!" she warned.

"What did you do with it?" he asked, slipping his hand inside the already ripped lining of the delicate frame.

Her gaze never wavering from him, Devon hurriedly shoved the rifle's loading bolt closed. The metallic clack broke the stillness of the night. The shrill crickets stopped abruptly.

She quickly raised the gun to sight.

Gentry halted, eight feet away, the rifle bead sighted at his chest.

"It's a message for my uncle and none of your concern." Her voice was breathy, uneven.

"I'm escort to a courier with a pack of mercenaries on her tail. If you're captured, I need to carry it on."

"That won't do, Mr. Morgan. I need a sign. If you were sent by the alliance, you know the password."

He gave a small, indulgent smile. "In England rich men may play at spy games and secret words. Here we are at war, and you trust only what you see and feel, not what is said."

"Exactly. You say we're on the same side, but I feel you're an enemy. If I trusted my instincts right now, you'd be claiming a bloody bedroll at St. James infirmary."

The heavy gun had sagged out of position. She was straining to hold the sight.

"If I were you," he said, "I'd worry more about completing your mission."

"That's a lie," she answered softly. "If you were me, you
would already have shot a presumptuous intruder for the
spy he is."

Gentry was silent a moment, choosing his lie. "Listen to
me!" he said suddenly. His tone was edgy, as if he were
losing his grip on his patience. "I'm the second soldier chosen to guard the courier. My predecessor was killed yesterday before he could pass on the words that would ease your
mind. All I know is that President Davis in Richmond got a
request to see the Picards safely to the Brants'. And that
there would be trouble along the way."

"You should thank me, Mr. Morgan. The longer we talk,
the better your story grows."

"That's it!" He flung the hat away and started for her.

"Stop! I know how to shoot!"

"At a flushed quail? A fox cornered by the dogs?"

"At any wild beast in front of me!"

Unheeding, he continued walking toward her.

A slow hammer pounded on the wall of Devon's chest.
She would have to shoot him or give up the message her
uncle needed.

Less than six feet away now.

An angry tremble began in her arm.

Five feet.

Her trigger finger tensed.

He was nearly in arm's reach of her.

Suddenly she jerked the gun right, off target, and fired.

Click.

He halted. Slowly he drew two brass-capped cartridges
from his shirt pocket.

"You vile, black-hearted bas—" She stopped herself. With
a cry, she grabbed the gun barrel and swung out at him.

He dodged the blow and jerked the rifle from her hands.

"I could have killed you!" she cried.

The realization shook her as much as his precaution of
taking the bullets, he thought.

"I believe you," he said, watching as her body stiffened
with the need to contain her anger.

If she were a man, he would have a fight on his hands. But

she was a woman, so she bewitched the fight and embedded it in his blood, making conflict within himself.

He studied her, knowing that a man must walk wary of the quicksilver in such a creature or be confused by her strength and her weakness, by hot words and chill silence, by the courage in a warm, red heart and the fear in a lithe body of supple flesh, cupped and curved to seek the mold of a man.

Awareness of her was strong, stirring need, an affirming warmth in his veins. Gentry tried to curtail his appraisal of her, but she was so well formed, with a proud bosom curving high and full over a slender frame. The torn skirt tied at her ankles pulled the garment tight along her torso. His gaze swept down the clean inward curve of her waist, then lower across a flat abdomen to a dark fold of skirt draped like a curtain to hide entrance to a secret room.

Slowly, she backed away, stealing the locus of his gaze.

It was her right. He did not move.

She receded, until the distance between them was farther than he could ever reach that night, until he could again see that she was white, a means to his mission, a woman frightened of him.

Devon stumbled against a flap of stirrup on the ground. She steadied herself against the carapace of the empty saddle and turned her back. Shaken, she summoned disdain for the arrogant savage and his vulgar stare.

But her mind did not obey her heart. Instead, the languid visage of Roger Bivens appeared in memory's mist as the object of her contempt. Heavy-lidded eyes, slim pinch of nose, and lips sliced in a smile. Swine. Swine in swan's mantle. He wore a mask. Aunt Margaret, did you know he wore a mask?

Devon closed her eyes and banished Roger's smile, banished the shame of that night. She searched deep in the sphere of loathing for the dark face of the half-breed Gentry.

He was not there. She had to open her eyes and turn around to find him, to see him waiting in firelight, too hard-hewn and real to enter the tenuous chamber Roger had built.

When he spoke, his words were offered from safe distance, from a spirit schooled in patience.

"It's good to follow your instincts. Instinct told you not to

kill me. The journey's long and you might yet have need of
me. You may still have to kill, though, to preserve something dear—your life, or your cause. Our cause."

She gazed wearily at the fire. His cause was not hers. She
could muster no loyalty to the scraps of paper she hid from
him. In this conspiracy, she was a prisoner of family loyalty,
not of her beliefs. She abhorred slavery. Indeed, abhorred
dominion of any man over another without right of compromise and consent. It was a truth she had never had the
courage to voice to her aunt, lest Margaret see the ghost of
the democratic Frederic Picard rising in his daughter, de-
spoiling her, giving her political ideas, bequeathing her the
only wealth an indigent poet had. And if Aunt Margaret and
Uncle Arnaud learned of the anti-slavery meetings she'd attended in the last few years with Damien James—

Devon suddenly felt drained. Fatigue and silence had consumed the ire that fueled her. It was late. She felt her senses
softly overtaken by inconsequentials, the scent of a blossoming bush deep in the thickets around them, and the moonlight, shadowing his face and gentling the bold line of his
jaw.

She was aware, too, of his moving nearer, so that soon he
would be within arm's reach of her. If she wasn't careful, his
strong hands would begin a willful search of her for the
piece of parchment he wanted. He was capable of taking
what he wanted, as Roger was.

Her knees weakened. She sank slowly to the saddle behind
her. "All right, Mr. Morgan," she said. Numb and exhausted, she fumbled at the laces of one high-topped shoe.

Gentry knelt on the ground and loosened the laces
quickly. He pulled the damp shoe off her small stockinged
foot, and a piece of watermarked parchment fell to the
ground.

"You win," she whispered, her aunt's square of foolscap
lying safe and warm under the lace of her chemise.

"With you, ma'm'selle, I am never sure," Gentry said
absently as he unfolded the small note.

In that one French word Devon heard an accent correctly
slurred, and she wondered who he was and how well he had
been schooled. She watched him frown as he read the note.
She had memorized the brief words on the page.

Loyal friend,

Beware the seventh monkey fist. The traitor bleeds us dry.

In place of a signature, Devon knew, the note ended with three strange insignias—lengths of rope ending in large round knots. It was the knot of the monkey fist, symbol of the alliance—and the password Gentry Morgan lacked.

He looked up. "Do you understand it?" he asked.

"Would I tell you if I did?"

"This cannot be all," he said, frowning. "It is only a warning. Where are the details, the orders?"

A cold wave of apprehension spread upward through her chest, enveloping the note hidden there. But she shrugged off his question. "Perhaps there is another courier."

"Or another message." He quickly untied her other shoe and slipped it off.

He found nothing, and hung her shoes on a branch to dry.

As he worked, Devon slipped slowly off the edge of the saddle to the ground.

"I'm tired," she said, settling on dew-moist grass.

She watched as Gentry crossed the clearing, then returned with her slit petticoats in hand. The campfire popped weakly, devouring the last rods of dry hickory as he knelt before her and spread the undergarments as her camp bed. He did not rise.

She laid her head back against the saddle, baring her slim white throat to the moon's ghostly light. Dark gold waves of her hair pillowed softly against the leather.

"Mr. Morgan?"

He was silent.

She swallowed hard and went on. "I don't . . . I'm not sure how to say this. I realize my reputation will not be intact after an unchaperoned night in the woods . . ." She paused.

"But you expect the rest of yourself to remain so?"

"Yes." It was a whisper, a breath.

In the shadowy moonlight, he could not see her well, but he sensed the heat of her unease and the blush that would darken her face. She had good reason to be wary. The dim light had softened his image of her. He could no longer see the pale, pampered symbol of an unjust world. Somehow she had darkened and taken his cast, welcoming rather than fearing the gentle cloak of night that shielded her body. He saw a woman tired, a woman who had no choice but to take him at his word.

"Your sleep will be safe," he said, the words softer than he intended.

"I want to rest here," she said, her eyelids heavy.

He nodded.

She turned her head, exhausted, and placed her cheek against the cool, hard leather.

Gentry rose, silently, and hovered over her. She did not move.

He waited, watching her, until her breath came soft and even, and until the smoldering fire had safely died. Then he slowly bent toward her. He laid the back of his hand against a wavy tendril of her hair. He meant to touch her only for a moment, just so he would know that the flaxen strands had the feel of silk, so that he would not wonder tomorrow. But the moment grew into a long minute, until he withdrew reluctantly, the delicate-scented nest springing up as he released it, and silky stragglers lingering in his fingers.

He had not craved such delicacy in a long time. He had had no reason to. Even now, the moment had to be stolen, but the yellow-hair surely could not mind the trespass.

It was so little to ask on a night when he had promised so much.

FIVE

The heavy jangle of saddle gear startled Devon awake.

It was still dark. At the horizon, the sky filtered to a gray fog at the treetops, hinting at rising light. Across the clearing, Gentry was saddling her horse.

Devon uncurled slowly, stirring a vague scent of rosewater from the petticoats Gentry had cut away the day before. She pushed herself upright and sat with her back to the horses.

Her clothing was bedraggled. She checked the fastenings and found them intact. Her corset bit persistently into the soft skin under her arm. She pressed a hand to the valley between her breasts. A folded edge of the foolscap shifted with the pressure.

She closed her eyes in relief. The alliance message was still there.

Hearing the sudden gritty scrape of a shoe nearby, she scrambled to her knees as the legs of Gentry's dark gray trousers appeared beside her. She quickly covered the glimpse of leg and white pantalette bared by the slit in her gown.

"You scared me," she said, and stood up slowly. "Must you sneak about like a thief?"

"You mistake caution for stealth," he said.

"You mistake my brain for cow dung," she retorted, jerking her mutilated skirt straight.

Between them, the air was moist with dew and already warm, the temperature rising quickly to the promise of a sweltering day. The morning larks broke the tense silence with a cheery call.

Gentry gazed down at the yellow-hair, who glared back, ready to run from him. "It's time to move out," he said impassively, as if he had not seen her gently probe her bodice for something hidden there, as if he did not know she carried a second communiqué, the important one. "Fold your bedskirts tight and buckle them to your saddle. You have fresh water in the canteen. I'll cover the fire." He walked past her as impersonally as if she were a soldier under his command.

He removed the ring of stones around the fire, carefully scraped the burnt refuse onto a slab of tree bark, and dumped the ashes into a thicket. Then he sprinkled the fire spot with dry soil and leaves. It would not fool a Lakota Sioux, who would sniff disturbed ground to find a campfire, but it might buy some time.

With a branch, he swept the area until footsteps and traces of activity were obscured. When he turned to the horses, Devon was already in the saddle.

She sat the horse better that morning, he noted, but unnaturally stiff, the grip of her corset choking freedom of movement. She bowed to the dictates of fashion like any docile woman made for parlor games and parasol strolls, a creature of rigid gentility. But she was not docile, he knew now. Not made for shallow pleasures in public rooms.

She was young, harboring a sensual honesty he had not expected. And reckless, attempting escape in the stream. Yet so vulnerable when he held her. He had watched a luminous curiosity appear in her eyes, just for a second, before her wanting turned to warning for them both.

Walk with care, he told her silently, yellow-hair, Dalonika, waiting now in half-light, cool and silent in gypsied clothes and tangled locks and terrible temper.

How much safer if he could dismiss her as a useless bauble. But the woman damned herself, showing persistence and a foolish courage, instincts that ennobled her.

Gentry mounted his roan quickly, before his mind could acknowledge the certainty he felt: If he spent another night alone with this woman, he would compromise two things of value—his mission and her virginity.

His horse bounded forward and she heeled her mare to follow.

Though hungry and aching, Devon felt a more pressing

need. Escape. At the first sign of civilization, she would try to find her cousin's plantation with the help of more conventional soldiers, men in the field who cared nothing of international conspiracy, men who simply followed orders as she did.

She was an agent of delivery, nothing more, ignorant of the contents of the message, though privy to the personalities and conflicts within the powerful inner circle of the alliance, thanks to Margaret.

Her aunt had quite obviously been relieved to share the burden of secrecy. From the first, Margaret had hated the fact that wifely duty made her a bedfellow of Arnaud's pet intrigue. He placed her in a vexing position, outside the rules of law, beyond the credos in *Godey's Lady's Book*. She could gain comfort only from the self-assurance that she was obeying her husband in a matter of importance.

Devon had gathered that the alliance leadership was small in number and centralized in decision-making, thus easier to hide in a maze of contributors and suppliers.

Secrecy was no small achievement in the political climate of London, where there were many Confederate sympathizers and a Yankee spy for each, aching to report to the American ambassador's office.

It was conceivable that an ambassadorial report had notified the Federals that Margaret Picard carried a message from the secret alliance. But wouldn't the Federals have simply intercepted her when she arrived in Philadelphia? They wouldn't hire bandits for a charade. Nor would Confederate leaders in Richmond. They had sent Gentry to head off such trouble, or so Gentry said. Who else would know that Margaret Picard carried crucial dates and battle plans for an alliance attack? If it was someone within the alliance network there in the South, why would he have to steal information?

Questions were never-ending. And it would have been a diverting puzzle, Devon thought, if she weren't one of the lost pieces being packed across country in sweltering heat without food or comforting companion, entrusted to a man who made her uneasy in a way that had little to do with secret notes and war plans.

It was his boldness, and his disdain for the simplest of

social graces. She felt adrift in a world without signposts, no etiquette, elders, furnishings, or finery to guide her.

She was left to her instincts, and they roamed rich and free, sensitive to the most primitive detail. Dew gliding from the laurel. The graceful flick of a horse's tail. The rawhide lanyard dangling from Gentry's chin. The generous timbre of his voice. The tension in his shoulders when he'd hefted the saddle to the broad back of her horse, a man of animal grace, sure of his strength.

Such thoughts triggered a softness in her shield against him. Perversely, she felt safe standing in fear of him, or confronting him. Simply to consider him invited risk. There was too much she wished to know, and the curiosity created a deep well of warmth inside her. It rose sometimes when he neared her. If he touched her, it would overflow and take her breath.

It was tempting to let her thoughts play in fields of the flesh, where the artist in her marveled at texture and shapes, the tones and templet of the human form; where mystery was sketched in a shadow, dark as her desire to touch and know.

Devon had spent a lifetime learning to rein in the intensity of her emotions to the level proper for her class. Aunt Margaret had always been diligent in teaching restraint. When Devon romped too exuberantly in the nursery, when she sneaked a cuddly pet into bed, when she spent days at the country house sporting and running the hounds with Damien James—each time she grew too passionate about people or pastimes—Aunt Margaret would admonish, "Lady Wild visiting, is she? Send her off, spit-spot. This is no home for her."

Yes, Aunt Margaret. Always yes. Excited Lady Wild would flee in the face of her aunt's disapproval.

So Devon had turned to her sketchbook to contain the exuberance. Her creativity seesawed, though. If Lady Wild overtook her, all structure was lost. When discipline reigned, it was rigidly evident and her work lost fluidity and grace.

She had achieved a marriage of opposites, however, in the tile cuts she'd created for the book, a whimsy and humor that offset the severe rules in *Lilah Peckingham's Guide to Wholly Acceptable Behaviorism in Children.* Damien James, a magazine publisher, had helped her prepare the illustrations under a pseudonym.

But after publication, Aunt Margaret had discovered the real identity of the secretive young artist whose "fine commercial debut" was acclaimed for "fresh, original style."

Dear God, what a tizzy it had induced. Margaret had buzzed about like a mad little wasp who smelled smoke in her nest.

She had summoned Damien and issued an ultimatum: either he stopped supporting crass tendencies in Devon, or he would no longer be invited to Wednesday cribbage and family holiday in Windermere. Margaret made it clear that she had long appreciated Damien's fatherly attention for Devon and Bertrice, especially since Arnaud was rarely at home. But she could not accept such an egregious mistake in judgment.

Apologetic but unchastened, Damien had adjusted his wire-rimmed spectacles. "You are making a mistake to hide the child's talent."

Devon had sat on the horsehair davenport, silent as instructed, aching for her old friend. Damien was more a father to her than Uncle Arnaud had ever been, and Damien had always cherished her abilities, herding them into the public arena with an editor's crusty recognition of high craft.

Aunt Margaret was appalled. "Devon can draw for her family, she can draw for her friends, for amusement. But I warn you, Damien. I've spent eleven years grooming this child for life attendant to her class. And I won't allow her to jeopardize her future selling services like a Gypsy."

Damien's bald pate shone rosy pink in the firelight. "Margaret, you are overwrought and showing your shortsightedness. Devon can be a respectable—"

"Wife and mother!" Margaret interrupted angrily. "This has gone too far, Damien! You have gone too far, filling her head with middle-class delusions, treating her like the daughter—and son!—you never had. Gun play, indeed. The servants report on your target contests, you know. And your teasing at last Sunday dinner. Devon will *not* be 'the prettiest correspondent to illustrate the *Times.*' Utter nonsense!"

"You've already set the standard for nonsense, Margaret.

Saddling Devon with a piddlewit like Roger Bivens. No appreciation of art or of intelligent womanhood!"

"Aha!" Margaret squared her small shoulders. "There's the tiff, isn't it, Damien? We didn't consult you on a match for Devon."

Damien curtly jerked a kerchief from his breast pocket and mopped his prominent forehead.

Devon felt a pounding in her ears, the pulse of her silent rage, for she was sick of being a well-behaved chattel. Look at my pictures! she wanted to cry out to her aunt. Do you not see? Children who sit correctly at the table, with bibs askew. Children who twist their hair as they listen politely to scripture. They are not "wholly correct." Neither am I. God help me, neither am I.

When Damien continued, restraint was evident in his voice. "I realize Roger's father, Grayshire, is an older family friend than I. But as a matter of courtesy, Margaret, you could have consulted me. I am concerned for Devon's future."

"Are you implying I have not found a good enough match for this child?" Margaret was incensed. "The son of an earl is not a prize? You're outrageous!"

"Roger Bivens has wealth and title. But where is his character? Where is his integrity?"

"In his lineage," Margaret said, biting off each word. "I cannot abide your tasteless democratic attitudes, Damien."

"I've never expected you to," he shot back. "But I do expect you to respect Frederic's legacy."

Margaret gasped in disbelief at the mention of Frederic Picard, Arnaud's brother and Devon's father. "A dissolute ne'er-do-well leaves nothing worthy of respect!" she blurted.

Margaret's handkerchief flew to her lips, but too late. She fell silent.

Damien tensed and turned away.

"Aunt Margaret," Devon said.

"I misspoke," Margaret said quickly.

Devon rose and approached her aunt. It was an effort to walk slowly. She was close to hearing truth from Margaret, the truth obscured in sassy taunts at school where the decorous taps of the mistress's shoes echoed in the halls, and the teasing of provincial classmates lurked in the shadows.

"You play false with my father's memory. Why?" Devon asked.

Margaret nervously smoothed her hair back, the palm of each hand pressing sleek gray to the side of her head. "It is nothing. I am beside myself."

"She is afraid, Devon," Damien said quietly, tucking his large handkerchief back into the breast pocket with deliberate strokes.

Margaret stiffened. "Don't, Damien. It's too painful."

"Ignorance is painful, Aunt Margaret," Devon said. "And lies more so. Have you lied to me?"

Not answering, Margaret sought an armchair and unsteadily lowered herself to its support.

"Margaret is afraid," Damien said, "that you are showing the social sympathies that haunted your father. And that further contact with me will create the same independence of thought that estranged him from his family."

Devon turned to Margaret. "You told me my father was a respected writer and professor of history, hardly a social destructionist."

"Frederic Picard was never more than a book clerk at United Services College in Devon," Damien said gently. "But he was a brilliant man—"

"He was a misguided fool," Margaret said tightly.

"He was a champion for the poor, the deranged, a strong voice against slavery in the colonies long before it was abolished."

"Tell the truth, Damien!" Fury hardened Margaret's voice. "Frederic was a penny pamphleteer and ale was his inspiration!"

"The truth?" Damien's angry gaze fixed on Margaret. "Two brothers went separate ways. Arnaud, the older, succeeded dashingly. Married the daughter of a wealthy baronet, much to the delight of his family in France, those aristos who nursed each new generation on bitter milk, so that the noble sons of France would never forget the bloody horror of revolution, the horror of permitting power to the people.

"But Frederic, the younger son, the temperamental one—he fled the family, the mean politics. And he sank dismally under the weight of his questions about the ruling class. And he was never forgiven the sin, was he, Margaret?"

"Neither did Frederic forgive!" Margaret's voice shook with outrage. "Especially those who deserted him! His fine chum Damien for one. A fair-weather friend who accepted Arnaud's investment capital over Frederic's worthless rhetoric."

Damien looked pained. "I failed Frederic once. I will not fail him with Devon."

"That reverent tone is ridiculous. Frederic was no saint. He descended into a fanatic's hell and took his family with him."

Devon kept quiet. Margaret's enmity called up the shadowy ghost of her father, animating the thin, frozen face in the daguerreotype on the mantel. Devon looked to see if something flashed behind dark eyes fixed so blankly, if something disturbed the slick tonic's hold on his blond hair and let a strand fall forward in fevered disarray.

But all she saw were the spindly, black-stockinged legs of the Edmond sisters running ahead in the school's cavernous halls. All she heard was their singsong refrain: "One pence and half for makin' 'em laugh, A shillin' for showin' her tail. Home to the guv'ner who surely did luv her, As long as she brought home the ale."

Devon calmed herself with a deep breath. "My mother was not a minister's daughter from Wight, was she?"

"Not exactly," Margaret admitted. "She was a Shrop Street . . . er, artisan."

"A what?"

Margaret dabbed her handkerchief along her pursed upper lip. "An actress, I suppose. An entertainer."

"She sang," Devon whispered. Something caught in her throat. Her mother sang.

"And danced, God be merciful."

"She was poor?"

"Quite," Margaret said. "But talented, Frederic assured us. Now let me say, in no uncertain terms, Prudence Cheritt was a wonderful soul, a tenacious provider for her children. Taught you manners as she could. But she worked in those little theaters on Shrop Street. Appalling places. She had to paint up, you know. Your father had a strong head but very poor lungs. Arnaud and I sent money. Many times. And each time it did not buy medicine for your father, nor food and lodging for you children. It went to the printer for another treatise, or to the pub for another pint. Finally Arnaud refused to send another shilling. So your mother convinced Frederic to cross to Cherbourg and ask help of his father. Their ferry overturned and—"

They died. Devon closed her eyes. "And left us dependent on your charity."

"Arnaud and I have worked hard to wipe the disgrace of your parents from your past," Margaret said wearily.

"Yes, you have," Devon replied. "And you erased me in your zeal. Parts of me are now so faint I'll never see them. I have been consumed by your charity."

"You've been fed, clothed, guided, and loved," Margaret choked.

"A child's heart takes what a mother's gives," Devon said. She took Margaret's hand. "I'm no longer a child."

"I'm not—I'm not a—" Margaret was weeping.

"You are the only mother I've ever known," Devon assured her. "And you know that I must be free to know my father, to read his work."

Margaret had wept long that day. But that night Perce had appeared at Devon's door with a carpetbag full of pamphlets and articles and sheets of foolscap filled with manic scrawl.

Devon had spent the night sifting public remains for a private glimpse of her father.

How distraught Margaret had been, Devon mused, and how sad she herself had felt for her aunt. To fear a dead man's ideas, Frederic's flirting with Chartism, his fervent belief in the equal rights of man, his admiration for a rational idealist such as the American essayist Emerson, whose work she herself had—

A strange howl rent the air. A wild dog? Devon's horse pranced nervously and she had to stop and rein tight. She looked ahead, worried.

Gentry glared back at her. He had uttered the call in warning, to bring her mind back to the world of heat and thickets and foothills of ancient oaks ahead on a canopied ridge.

He pulled the stop from his canteen, and his gesture silently demanded she do the same.

The yellow-hair had hovered too long with the dream spirits that day, he thought. Perhaps she was only tired, as he was. Rolling his shoulders to loosen their cramp, he took time to check the detailed map Pinkney Dobbs had supplied.

The best route for escape lay through wooded hills well west of a direct line to Wilmington. But the farther west they strayed, the more chance of encountering a battlefront.

Cavalry units of Federal troops had been raiding the region for months. It was just such a troop that had captured him and a band of Confederates a few months after a skirmish near Lynchburg. Gentry had been separated from his squad during relentless pursuit across the North Carolina border.

The memory caused a bitter smile. He would still be free if he had not stopped to water his horse in the cove of a river called Hiwassee.

It was the land of his Cherokee ancestors. He had not been there since he was two, when his mother's tribe had been forced to join others in a massive march of exiles. President Andrew Jackson had uprooted the Cherokees and all Eastern tribes to resettle them in barren land across the Mississippi.

The Trail of Tears had begun there long ago. Gentry's spirit had grown heavy as he'd dismounted at the edge of the river. He was so tired of the running, so long without a home.

He had knelt and opened the deerskin sac that hung at the neck of his shirt. One by one he lay the sacred tokens by a ring of fire stones—an eagle feather, a sliver of buffalo hoof Kai-ee-nah's mother had studded with beads, the razor claw of a badger he had killed, a wolf's fang, a mottled charm stone, and a tiny tendril of black hair.

The lock was wispy dry, no longer shiny as when he had cut it from his beloved. He closed his eyes and began the chant, his voice hoarse and uncertain. It had been so long.

His words grew stronger when he looked up and called the name of the Apportioner, Une-lanu-hi, and the prayer name of the river, for he was going to the water to cleanse his spirit.

"You have drawn near to hearken, O Age-yagu-ga. This man's soul has come to rest—"

A warning shot stung a stone beside him.

Ambush. Federal troops pursuing him had been lured by

the fire. He was captured like a fool amid white soldiers' mockery of the sacred words.

Though he had suffered in the weeks of his imprisonment, the spirits had also been kind. They'd given him a sentry he knew, a man who had fought the border ruffians with Gentry the day Kai-ee-nah had been killed, a man who had seen Gentry's brother-in-law Miles Brant leave the fray and return—with blood-soaked knees.

Had Miles knelt in Kai-ee-nah's blood? Had his butchery spilled it?

Gentry would know when he and the yellow-hair got to Jasmine's Reach.

Finally, he would know.

SIX

In the paneled chambers of Liverpool's Damson Club, Khaled al-Sayed Dexter glanced at the jeweled Roman numerals of his watch. Two hours.

The earl, Lord Grayshire, had been orating for two hours.

With his thumb and forefinger, Khaled pinched the bridge of his nose, pressing hard to counteract the throbbing in his head.

Lord Grayshire had propped himself in a high, wide armchair styled in popular Gothic Revival. No hint of the green velvet padding of the seat and arms could be seen; Bivey's bulk covered it all. Pairs of twirled Gothic spires and quatrefoil behind the earl's head looked like a crown and gave him a porcine resemblance to Henry the Eighth without the robes. And without the sexual proclivity, Khaled suspected.

Finally, Khaled interrupted gracelessly. "Forgive me, Bivey, but you've made your point eloquently. True, I should have monitored the money more closely. True, also, Miles Brant has played us for fools. Our task now is to assess how much damage has been done to the fleet. We'll worry about retribution later. The rendezvous date is too near. What do you want me to do? Send an avenger to Wilmington to rifle Colonel Brant's pockets and demand payment?"

"If the truth be told, we need Brant, thief or no." His words were loud, his French accent staccato and precise. Count Valerie Beaumond tipped his wineglass up and downed the last of the burgundy. "Miles Brant is master of ordnance for the biggest port city the Confederacy still holds, correct?"

Khaled nodded. "He has control of blockade goods and transport lines."

"So. When the alliance fleet breaks through, we need him to direct transfer of munitions and supplies to battlefronts."

"But the blackguard has dishonored his uniform," fumed Lord Grayshire, his thick fingers curling around the base of a snifter. He swirled the purplish-red plum liqueur, a sweet treat the club served its tenured members. "Why would the alliance empower men who steal?"

"Because they are smarter than the men who don't!" the count spat. "Would you entrust the heart blood of a new republic to the zealots surrounding President Davis? The idiots! To blunder in battle is forgivable. But they shoot themselves in the foot before a cannon is fired! Holding on to their cotton like arrogant provincial brats." The slim Frenchman angrily gestured to his attaché, and the count's glass was quickly refilled.

The earl pursed the lips under his walrus mustache.

Khaled knew Bivey ached to retort, but the French count was right. When the War Between the States began in 1861, Confederate leaders felt they held all the cards in the world cotton market. They hoarded cotton and put an instant stranglehold on the supply so the price would go up. Instead of kowtowing and rendering diplomatic recognition, though, import countries found alternate sources of cotton or went without. The south lost the chance to establish a cooperative, international supply line that would neatly have armed, fed, and clothed the Confederacy throughout the war.

"Their leadership has made miscalculations," the earl muttered into his glass. "But you cannot denigrate their military panache and brilliance. They fight like tigers, like true cavaliers."

"I agree," the count said. "That's why we must help them begin the new order in the hands of experienced militarists—"

"But no thieves!" the earl thundered. "What do you think this war's about?"

Khaled and Count Beaumond exchanged glances as Lord Grayshire rolled his bulk forward to get out of his chair. The Arab and the Frenchman knew exactly why the ruler of Egypt and the Emperor of France were involved in the conspiracy. Unlike the principled English earl, their rulers placed politics firmly before ideals.

"I'll tell you what the war is about!" Lord Grayshire said. "The death of all we hold dear!" He paced around the meeting table. "The rights of birth are at stake. We are salvaging what is left of the aristocracy in that democratic abyss. Free the slaves and you doom generations of fine families to a classless existence. Estates will perish. And the rights of men will die!"

Flushed and emotional, the earl paused.

Seeing Count Beaumond hide his disgust in a sip of wine, Khaled tried to soothe Lord Grayshire. "We are all working to preserve that, Bivey. But first we must mobilize the alliance fleet, rupture the blockade, and—"

"—and shake the Union's faith in its great homely leader," the count finished curtly. "Lincoln must not be reelected. Colonel Brant can help us prevent that. He is a sworn member of the alliance and has the confidence of Admiral Picard."

"Then my good friend Arnaud is trusting a snake," the earl said bitterly. "And I have told him so."

An uneasy quiet fell on the room. "When, Bivey?" Khaled asked.

"I sent a message with Arnaud's wife, Margaret."

"Was this note in high code for Arnaud's eyes only?"

"Of course not! I don't play foppish games with nooses and bloody books." The earl untied the sash of his smoking jacket and signaled for his evening coat.

Count Beaumond moved slowly toward him, his thin, elegant frame tensed as if he were stalking the earl. "The need for secrecy is critical, milord," he said. "It is the only reason we have armed and positioned more than twenty fighting ships without having war declared against our respective countries. I am surprised you consider survival a dandyish game."

Lord Grayshire held the count's gaze for a moment, then shrugged his coat straight. "I will survive. I have more at stake than anyone in this venture. Fourteen ships. Half of my Orient packet line diverted in a cloud of paperwork to serve a greater cause. And contributions. Have you any idea how many of my associates in Parliament have monetarily professed sympathy for a liberated Southern republic?"

"Your contracts and resources have been invaluable, Bivey," Khaled began, "and we—"

"But where would your ships be without French foundries to cast the rifled cannon?" Count Beaumond interrupted. "Without gunsmiths working round the clock to arm Maximilian's peasants in Mexico, and our own alliance mercenaries in the islands?"

"The partnership of France is vital," Khaled said cajolingly.

"The fact remains," Lord Grayshire said, yanking a white cuff free of his coat sleeve, "I cannot condone the actions of a thief, no matter how valuable he is to our goals. Colonel Brant is trouble. And we will pay for it."

Fingers spread, the earl patted his girth in search of the chain of his pocket watch. "It is late, gentlemen. Until we cast off for the islands, adieu."

He abruptly left the meeting room. Khaled accompanied him to the door, knowing he must placate the rotund nobleman whose textile constituents and partisans in the House of Lords had contributed hundreds of thousands in currency and gold, and whose East Indian fleet of well-maintained passenger steamers was the foundation of the entire alliance assault.

"We are all a little edgy," Khaled apologized. Beside them, a servant in jacket and tails held a knotted cord in his hand.

The earl looked at the rope and sighed.

Khaled smiled. "The monkey fist is a sign of our unity and our commitment to save the noble Confederacy from—"

"I know." Lord Grayshire snapped the cord from the servant's grasp. "It's a knot to tie off a heaving line you're tossing overboard. An appropriate, though disgustingly named, metaphor for salvaging a cause." Irritated, he stuffed the monkey fist in his pocket.

"Be of good cheer," Khaled said. "You will use it only twice more. When we set sail for Nassau, and when we toast the gathering of the fleet."

"You've done a masterful good job, my boy," the earl said, not noticing how the Egyptian's shoulders stiffened at the diminutive. "I hope you never question my appreciation —nor that of the men I represent."

"Of course not, Bivey. Good night."

The earl left. Khaled stepped back from the door and breathed deeply to prepare himself for the debriefing with the French count.

The diplomatic young Arab had too often found himself the peacekeeper for needled British and French factions of the alliance.

Dear Allah, he prayed, keep me patient and clever, and my reward appropriate to the task.

By noon the sun had burned away the heavy haze above the foothills. Gentry's roan cantered to the edge of an open space between two ridges, then snorted as Gentry jerked the reins taut.

Everything around them seemed quiet. A woodpecker rapped tentatively for grubs in the bark of a slash pine.

Gentry shifted in his saddle, slipping his hat off and rubbing the sweat from his face with a shirtsleeve. Ahead a half mile of open vale lay between them and the safety of dense woods. The sight made him uneasy.

He turned in his saddle and regarded the yellow-hair. There was little of the gentlewoman left in her appearance— a limp froth of lace at her cuff, stubbornly shiny bodice buttons of polished bone. She had donned her bonnet to control the tangled waves of hair that tumbled down her back. But her mutilated gown was wrinkled and smudged, and her face was beginning to reflect the lean cast of too many miles without food. He had to find time to hunt before nightfall.

He pulled the canvas-covered canteen from his saddle bag and lifted it in a questioning salute. She nodded at the silent invitation to drink.

Out of the corner of an eye, he watched her, gauging her energy reserve by how smoothly and carefully she retrieved her own canteen. There was no clumsy lethargy in her movements . . . yet.

He took a long swallow of the tepid water.

"Are we being followed?" she asked quietly.

"Did you see something?"

"No. But you've got that hunted look," she said, capping the canteen. "If you had hackles, they'd be bristling."

"A woman takes a chance seeing the beast in a man," he teased. "Makes him want to rise to the expectation."

She flushed light pink under the tender burnished tan she was acquiring.

She knew more than a proper lady should about a man's bed and body, he thought. He made note of the discovery and tucked it in the back of his mind. His collection of information and insights about her was slim, and he wanted it to stay that way. He had already begun to wonder who she was and how she'd become a partisan for the South. To know her, in any way, would place them both in danger. A gruff, gap-toothed general who had taught Gentry at West Point phrased it best: "Once you see a person where an enemy stands, your ass is good as gone."

That was a long time ago, when he had gone to the Academy to please his father. A wasted gesture of obedience, for when Gentry had left the Academy in disgrace, his father had been more displeased than ever.

He capped his canteen and gave the yellow-hair curt instructions. She was to cross the open space as quickly as she could, then enter the woods downslope. He would be splitting off to head uphill and find an outlook.

"Head into deep cover, then follow the easiest path to the bottom of the hill," he said. "I'll meet you there."

Devon had no time for questions. He gave a sudden "Hah!" and the roan lurched forward. She was alone on the narrow trail amid pin oak saplings and myrtle bush.

She heeled the mare out into the open. After glancing worriedly uphill, she bent low, hugging the saddle as the mare found her stride and angled downslope.

After so many hours on hilly trails, Devon felt vulnerable and exposed in the sunlit swale. A tall pin oak with a forked trunk loomed ahead. The mare slowed and Devon ducked into the safety of the woods, patting the horse's neck.

She let the horse wander through the wide-spaced pines until the edge of the woods was far behind. The stringent pine scent closed around her in the stillness.

As the path became rockier, she dismounted and led the horse past an outcropping of sharp-faced rock. Farther down, she heard a faint roar of rushing water. The sound grew to tumultuous rumbling as she reached a mountain stream at the top of a narrow waterfall.

She stepped on slabs of dry gray slate along the edge of the fast-running stream. Water swirled and spumed as it ran toward the lip of the falls. The white-frothed curtain dropped forty feet to a shallow pool, then eddied swiftly around high rocks to another drop.

Devon kept an eye on her horse as the mare drank between the stones. Still pools of water collected there, safe harbor for skittish crayfish that darted backward with a flick of their tails. Tiny black minnows shifted in unison like a single fleeting shadow.

Devon cupped her hand to the fresh running steam. The water escaped down her chin as she drank. She turned her chin to her shoulder to let her gown soak up the cool drops as she glanced up the wooded slope.

She saw no sign of Gentry. She could hear nothing but the roar of the water.

Above her, a spacious canopy of oak and maple shielded her like the vaulted ceiling of a church. She had visited the cathedral at Troyes, had sketched its turrets and balconies. But the serenity of this haven was sweeter, its offering simple —a moment of rest and safety in a life gone awry.

To a woman in her position, it was a priceless gift.

Up the hill, far from the stream, overlooking dense woods and steep gullies, Gentry climbed an embankment to a rock at the top of the ridge. There he lay flat-bellied on the warm gray stone. He faced the swale they had crossed and had a good view of the woods they had traveled. Farther east, beyond a low-lying pasture, he could see a small farmhouse and blackboard barn.

A quiet minute passed. Gentry began to relax in the sun. Then he saw a lone horseman stop at the edge of the brushy trail he and the yellow-hair had followed.

Gentry lay still, thankful for the rock-grime color of his clothes.

The horseman who tracked them had a rifle sling on the rear of his saddle and a pistol snug in a leather holster along his thigh.

As Gentry watched, the black-bearded rider set off down the slope, tracing the yellow-hair's path. He had obviously seen her enter the woods, and he would find her within minutes.

Gentry quickly crawled to the edge of the rock and felt

for a toehold in the embankment that flanked the jutting stone.

A sixth sense set the hair on the back of his neck tingling. He paused, heard the snap of a pine twig. . . . Gentry rolled immediately to his right as the slug of a .44 stung the granite beside him.

A second tracker, dammit. He scooted off the opposite side of the rock and drew his pistol. Squatting low, his back against the moist earth, he listened.

Nothing moved. He reached for a small rock with his left hand and tossed it far down the slope ahead of him.

The rock tumbled in the dry pine needles.

Silence. The gunman was not fooled into wasting a second rifle shot. He would shoot only when he had his quarry in sight. The instincts of a soldier used to hoarding ammunition, or the steely control of a hired killer who never wasted his effort.

Gentry had no option but to draw fire. He could not lie there and force the gunman to search for him. There was no time. The other killer would soon find the yellow-hair.

He dove for cover behind the nearest tree. The rifle crack sounded even before he made it to the broad trunk. Gentry rolled to his feet. He had a precious minute while the gunman reloaded.

He ran a course roughly parallel to the top of the hill, an erratic path that darted up and down slope. Another shot, a miss that bit the bark of a sweet-gum tree two yards away. Not a good marksman on a moving target. There was hope.

Gentry ducked behind a boulder. A bullet hit the rock dead center. The ricochet smacked a layer of pine needles farther down the slope, near a stand of trees where Gentry's roan was tied.

He dared a quick glance above the boulder and saw the nose of a rifle withdraw from the crest of the ridge. The man had a deadly vantage point. Gentry would have to retreat painstakingly until he was out of gun range.

Down the slope his horse, within easy rifle range of the marksman, stomped nervously.

Gentry grabbed a handful of pebbles in his left hand and took aim with his right. He was out of pistol range, but he wanted to draw fire. His revolver cracked once.

The gunman obliged with a slug that stung the boulder at

the rounded edge near Gentry's head. He ignored the flecks of granite that peppered the brim of his hat and immediately threw two rocks in quick succession at the rump of his horse.

The spooked animal whinnied and reared, pulling on the reins looped across a slim branch. The reins held. Gentry threw more pebbles, measured assaults that insistently pelted the horse's neck, forcing the scared animal sideways.

The reins slipped off the end of the branch, and the horse loped downhill, away from the barrage and into a more densely wooded area.

With the horse safely out of range, Gentry took a deep breath and began a saw-toothed run down the hill, darting left and right.

The rifleman stopped firing after three more misses. By that time, Gentry was panting in deep brush nearly out of range. Running low, he continued straight down the hill. His horse, as he'd hoped, had not gone far in the crowded woods.

Gentry mounted quickly and rode out of the trees and into the open swale. He headed down toward the oak with twin trunks where, not long ago, he'd seen the yellow-hair ride confidently into the dark woods.

If she could hear the shots, she would know the danger.

In the haven of the clearing, Devon could hear nothing but the soothing roar of the waterfall. She bent over the stream, scooping cool water to wash the grime from her face and neck. She pushed up her lace-trimmed cuffs and washed her hands and forearms. What she wouldn't give for a proper bath.

The call of the rumbling water was incessant. She knew she had wasted time there, but a few moments' wait was not much to ask of the stern, dark man she rode with.

The hand gripped her arm suddenly, savagely, and she screamed.

The crash of the water muffled her terrified cry. Only her attacker heard, and a quick backhand across her mouth warned her not to issue another one.

She stopped struggling and faced the man whose arms clamped hers so tightly. He was taller than she, but not much. Pink, puffy lips protruded vulgarly from the center of a black curly beard. His eyes were small, like a bird's, and as sensitive as those of any creature with a small brain. The little beads narrowed at the sight of her.

Devon could see a decision growing firm—a glazed, unarguable plan that made her heart pound with alarm.

She began struggling again, and he smiled and thrust her away from him. Stumbling on the uneven rock bed, she fell. He reached down and yanked her up. She scratched the side of his face and kicked at his shins. Her kick connected, and she heard his foul curse. At the same time, she felt the material at the front of her gown give way to his tearing.

She collapsed suddenly, twisting out of his grasp, and crawled, then ran to the grassy bank, gasping in pain and fright.

She slipped, crying out as she fell to her knees. At that instant his rough hand grabbed her shoulder, wrenching her over onto her back.

He was on his knees, straddling her. The nose of his revolver was icy cold against her flushed cheek. "Time ta lay still," he said.

Devon didn't move.

His hand fumbled with the buttons of his pants. He looked down to unbuckle his belt, and his gun swung wild for a moment, straying from her head.

A shot rang out from the laurel brush nearby, and the bearded gunman recoiled as the slug rammed his chest.

Devon felt him right himself, still straddling her. A tremor began in his gun hand.

The hidden gun fired again, and the bearded man jerked backward. As soon as she felt his weight fall away from her, Devon scrambled backward up the bank. Dry leaves crackled and gathered at the small of her back as she inched away from the lifeless body, away from what he had wanted from her.

From behind, the rough cotton of a trousered leg brushed her hand. She screamed, preparing to flee.

"Daloni-ka," Gentry said quietly, knowing that the roar of the falls would drown his name for her, knowing, too, that words were unimportant. The stark fear in her eyes wavered, then departed as she recognized him.

He knelt beside her, not touching her. He ignored the flap of silk torn from her shoulder and kept his gaze high, away

from the creamy swell of breast her attacker had exposed.
Slowly, as to an untame creature, he extended his hand.

There was doubt in her gaze, then desperate need. Her
hand reached out and clenched his shirtfront. His hands
closed on her arms and they rose together.

She breathed in jagged bursts, as if the air trapped in her
chest was too sharp to expel.

Locked an arm's length away from her, he gazed down on
a face painfully young and beautiful, a face radiant with
disbelief. He had not held such an innocent in a long time.
He loosened his too tight grip on her arms.

"We must go," he said, watching the yellow-hair fight for
control. She licked lips dried by the uneven passage of air.
She swallowed, choked. There was no moisture to coat her
throat.

The air was heavy with fecund scents and unseen, ever-
present spores. Gentry studied the woods over her shoulder,
then glanced quickly behind him. The setting was too open.
He and the yellow-hair were clear and easy targets as they
stood on the shady bank near moss-covered rocks and ferns.
He frowned as he listened for signs of the marksman from
the ridge, but the falling waters swallowed all sound.

Gentry clasped the small fist still knotted in his shirt. Her
smooth skin was chill. How cold she had grown with her
fear, but he could make no move to warm her, or she would
fear him too.

He pulled her hand away. "Another man follows us," he
warned. "We cannot—" He stopped, his senses on guard.

Damn the noise of the water. An intruder would have to
be very close for him to hear brush breaking, and there was
no way in hell to hear the creak of a rifle stock—

He gripped Devon suddenly, irrationally, as lifelong instincts took hold. As he scanned the woods behind her, a
movement registered at the corner of his eye. Instantly, he
swung Devon away from it and cradled her to him as he
dived to the ground.

The gun thundered before they hit the earth, and Gentry
felt the searing path of the bullet as it tore through his side.

Teeth clenched, he swore silently.

Devon lay under him, breathless but unhurt. He had blan-
keted her body in time, but he would not be able to protect
her any longer if the rifleman reloaded and shot him again.

"Tell him I'm dead," he whispered quickly in her ear. "Scream! Hurry!"

He rolled off her suddenly, as if he had been pushed. His head lolled against a rock, and he prayed the yellow-hair had heard him and understood. His right hand lay under him, finger curled around the trigger of his six-shooter. He had three shots left.

Unsteadily, Devon sat up, her face as white as the froth in the rapids nearby. She placed a hand on Gentry's arm and jostled him.

When he didn't move, she got to her knees and crawled frantically across his torso, pressing close to his face. "Are you hurt?" she whispered. "What did you say?"

He didn't respond.

"Tell me!" She scrambled off him and grabbed the front of his shirt. Her wrenching ripped the worn fabric from his shoulder to his waist, and at his waistband her hand met the warm, wet stickiness that had soaked the back and side of the shirt.

Devon screamed and backed away, rising on shaky legs. She held up the hand coated with Gentry's blood and shook her head. "No." It began as a whisper and grew to a sob she could not control. "You cannot die and leave me here!" she screamed.

"He ain't got a choice." The hard voice came from behind her.

She whirled and saw a tall, trail-dusty man with cat-green eyes and two broken front teeth. He walked toward her slowly, his pace eerily calm and unhurried, a professional who never took death for granted.

The gunman stopped beside Gentry's body, stilled in an awkward sprawl. He quickly pressed the nose of his rifle under Gentry's chin. "You killed my buddy, you son of a bit—"

Gentry's hand made a lightning grab at the barrel of the gun and wrenched it up, away from him. The jerking movement caused the gun to fire and the gunman caught the recoil. He grunted as the rifle butt thudded sharply against his chest.

Gentry leaped to his feet like an animal freed from a trap, swinging his Colt into position as he rose. But he had no time to fire.

The barrel of the single-shot rifle cracked squarely against his wrist. Hissing against the pain, Gentry barely managed to hold on to his pistol.

The gunman quickly turned his gun stock-first and swung it at Gentry's head. Gentry ducked, then lunged from his low crouch. The green-eyed gunman was knocked to the ground, and his rifle landed with a clatter on the rocky shore of the rapids that fed the falls. Gentry scrambled to straddle the downed man. Breathing hard, he sank the nose of his Colt deep into the soft flesh below the gunman's ear.

The would-be assassin froze, his eyes bright with animal fear.

"Don't move," Gentry said, teeth clenched together with the effort of holding his guns steady. The damaged muscles in his right side sent stabbing protests.

He sensed the yellow-hair drawing near. Folds of silk rustled softly behind him.

As he eased backward off the gunman's chest, Gentry reached over him and unhooked the flap of the cartridge box on the man's belt. He gathered a handful of shells for the rifle, then raised slowly to his feet. Not looking away from the gunman, he extended his fist to Devon. She cupped both palms together as he dropped rifle cartridges into her hands.

Feeling a tremor of weakness, he glanced at the rich, wet darkness that had spread over half his shirt. "Get his rifle," he told Devon.

As she hurried down the bank, he gestured for the hired killer to stand.

The man rose cautiously. His build nearly matched Gentry's, and his thin lips drew back to bare a black gap of lost teeth.

"Who are you?" Gentry asked.

"Name's Bloxie Taft."

"Who hired you?"

The green eyes held Gentry's. "Landry."

The shot from Gentry's revolver caught Taft by surprise. The gunman yelped and jerked his shoulder back as the bullet neatly grazed his arm. Eyes narrowed and hate-filled, Taft slowly eased his shoulder forward. His left arm crossed his chest to clasp the shallow wound.

"You lie," Gentry said. "And the next shot, you die. Who hired you?" The masked man who'd employed Landry's raiders was a missing piece to the alliance puzzle, and Gentry wanted his name.

"Someone who'll pay three thousand when he sees your scalp," Taft said, licking dry lips and stalling for time. "The girl can die quick. But not you."

"Who wants me dead?" Devon asked. She kept her distance from both men, kneeling on one knee as she pulled open the loading bolt of the Henry rifle and slipped in a cartridge.

Taft smiled, his knobby gums red and revolting.

Devon looked at Gentry, seeking reassurance.

At the moment Gentry's eyes shifted to her face, Taft made his move.

SEVEN

Taft leaped for the gun, clamping a broad hand over the muzzle and ramming Gentry backward.

As Gentry fell, the assassin wrestled his way atop him and raised an elbow high for a sharp right jab. Gentry's forearm blocked part of the blow, but he felt his grip on the pistol weaken.

Moist, dead leaves crackled beneath them, belying the desperate energy of the scuffle. Gentry's heels fought for leverage in the earth and finally carved a gritty hold. He heaved upward, nearly crying out at the pain, and pitched himself downhill at the same time. The two men tumbled down the sharp slope of the bank, the roar of the rushing stream louder and closer with each roll. He somersaulted sideways to break the tumble, his gun hand finally wrenched free—but so was the gun, spiraling on a low arc uphill.

Sickeningly aware that the more he fought, the more blood he lost, Gentry took a deep breath. He groped for the hunting knife sheathed at his waist, but Taft dived at him again, jerking him into a body roll that sent both men tumbling over the earthen bank to the rocky shallows at the edge of the stream.

Gentry landed with a near-blinding flash of pain on the rock bed. Beyond the shallows, the water swirled in a deep, fast-moving current that washed around exposed stones and sent rivulets rushing off the edge, down the jagged cliff face of the falls.

He had barely staggered to his feet when Taft was on him. He swerved out of range, but that put him in swirling, knee-high water. Fighting the leaden pull of the current, he rushed forward, ramming the tall gunman in the stomach and hoping to fight on more solid ground. But Taft wrestled him into deeper water, close to the angry, rushing center of the stream. Taft slipped suddenly on the algae-covered streambed and pulled Gentry down as he fell into the rushing water.

Taft rode the current a moment, then fought his way back to shallower water. Exhausted, Gentry grasped an exposed rock as an anchor. He held tightly in waist-deep water, the cold current streaming through his torn shirt. The white froth that eddied behind him turned a light pink.

With one hand he reached for another rock, trying to pull himself out of the tow, but he was instantly wrenched away and carried four feet downstream, just beyond Taft. Dazed, he groped for a handhold in the wash.

Taft picked up a thick oak bough caught between two rocks. Stepping knee-high into the turbulence, he raised the club in a swing that would crush Gentry's skull.

A shot exploded.

The lead buzzed past Taft's ear and hit water within arm's length of Gentry. Taft ducked instantly and turned toward shore.

Devon was no more than eight feet from them, rifle stock tucked under her arm, pulling frantically at the breech chamber. She had to reload.

Taft splashed out of the running water, holding the heavy limb like a javelin. Desperate to stop him, Gentry forced his feet to dig a purchase in the rock bed.

Onshore, Devon slipped a cartridge home, rammed the chamber shut, and hoisted the gun—but it was only halfway to her shoulder when Taft heaved his club.

The bough struck her arm broadside and the rifle discharged as she fell.

Taft jerked to a stop. Blood dripped down his cheek. He cupped a hand to his scalp, then staggered forward.

"I'll break every goddam finger you got," he vowed.

He reached down and grabbed her arm, jerking her upward.

From behind, a heavy river stone rammed down on the base of his skull.

Taft crumpled to the rocks beside Devon.

Biting back a cry, she crawled away from the body.

Hands still above his head, his chest heaving, Gentry let the huge stone drop.

Biting back a groan of pain, he curled his arm downward to cradle his side. The thin fabric of his shirt lay plastered to his chest and back. Water cascaded from his trousers, sending rivulets down his boots.

Breathing unevenly, he rolled Taft's body, one kick at a time, to the edge of the water. There, the swirling eddies lapped and pulled hungrily until the body was lifted and carried to center stream. Gentry watched until the current swept it over the edge of the falls and out of sight.

Then he turned to the yellow-hair. She sat on the soft grass of the bank, gingerly rubbing her arm and staring blankly ahead.

Hair matted and dripping, Gentry made his way to the grassy embankment. He eased down beside her, silent, and lay on his left side with his back to her. God, it felt good not to move. He closed his eyes against the throbbing in the wound.

He sensed the yellow-hair's withdrawal as she rose and walked away from him.

Long minutes passed and his consciousness faded, carried to the edge of a Darkening Land, taunting the Raven-mocker from the bank of a terrible river. He knew the black-winged spirit could not cross. Not yet. The yellow-hair stood beside him, strong, guarding.

Gentry stirred. Bent blades of grass unfolded against his cheek, prickling.

Where was she? Was there yet another sniper to fear?

A faint drumskin in the ground carried her steps to him, soft and hesitant in approach. She was afraid, he thought.

She laid the bundle of crinolines from her saddle near his head, jostling a cloud of rose scent from hidden seams.

He felt her tug gently at his shirt, freeing it from his waistband. The afternoon breeze roamed his back with a cold, clammy hand.

The yellow-hair was silent. He knew she was examining the bullet holes. There was more than one; he had already probed to make sure.

Two blood-darkened, irregular slits marked the entrance and exit, a three-inch tear through his flesh. The wound still bled weakly, but the chill water had cleansed it and helped staunch the flow.

Devon tore a strip of clean cloth from her frilled white underskirt and folded it. Her movements were mechanical, distanced. She was grateful to have a purpose for her hands, a focus for her thoughts, for memory threatened her with the weight of the black-bearded man across her stomach, the animal grunt of the green-eyed assassin as he fell harmless by her side.

She pulled Gentry's shirt higher and pressed the bandage against the swollen wound in his back. His skin was so cold. She spread her fingers across his ribs, waiting for breath to expand them. His breath was too light for one so strong.

In that moment, a feeling of aloneness swept over her like a drowning tide. "Will you die?" she asked, wondering if he'd hear. He was so still.

"Are you hoping?"

He answered. Thank God.

The muscled ridge of his back tautened under her touch as he tried to stir.

She wiped a streak of wetness from her cheek. Eagerly, she rose and stepped over him, her hand still holding the cloth over his wound.

His face was pallid, drained by blood loss and exhaustion. His eyes, though, held a stubborn vitality.

"Obviously, a man who can jest about death is not near enough to it," she said, hiding her relief in testy reply.

"And a woman who fights so fiercely has a long life ahead," he said, grimacing as he raised on one elbow to face her.

The exertion and pain had left a dry hoarseness in his voice. She should have brought the canteen, Devon thought. She looked up the hill where her horse was grazing peacefully near the body of the bearded gunman. The dead man sprawled faceup, the paunch of his belly a rigid prop against the loosened tongue of his leather belt.

Without warning, hot tears welled and spilled slowly down her cheeks. Her face felt hard and waxen, as if she were a doll with stony stare and empty chest.

She took Gentry's hand and placed it on the bandage to keep pressure against the wound. "I should bring you some water," she said, starting to rise.

He stopped her. "Get my gun. There are two shots left."

She was relieved to find strength in his grasp. "Are we no safer now? Two men are dead."

His gaze dropped to her bosom where the alliance message lay hidden. "As long as you wear a target, you draw fire."

Self-consciously, Devon pulled the torn flap of her gown higher to cover her bared shoulder. Her uncle's precious alliance was no longer a diverting puzzle. It was a killer's game. And the wounded man in front of her had known it from the beginning.

She turned away, her voice pained. "Mr. Mor—"

"I am Gentry."

"Gentry." His name fell softly and tentatively from her lips, as if it were an intimate accessory she wasn't sure she should bare. "It is time I saved us both a struggle."

Gentry watched as her hands raised slowly to the row of polished buttons that held the remains of her bodice across her breasts. She slipped the buttons from their loops, one by one.

He did not pretend to look elsewhere. He could not, for the beige gown parted to reveal a chemise of eyelet trim, a swatch of white that was fresh and startling. The lace clung to the swell of each breast, enhancing rather than masking the shape of firm, rounded flesh underneath.

He watched as she slid two fingers in the shadowed crevice, where warm curves met and hugged each other, overflowing the space allotted them by the lip of her corset.

Her fingers emerged with a tightly folded square of paper. She extended her hand, drawing his eyes away from her bosom to the note. "This is what you want so badly," she said.

The missive, so warm and moist, lay pale and lifeless in his palm. He felt a curious emptiness. He knew her gesture was more practical than trusting. She would no longer carry the bait for him, or any other conspirator, to attack her.

"Now, you are the courier," she said, brushing a strand of hair from her eyes.

"And you?" he asked.

"I am Devon. A freer woman." She began to button the tattered remnant of her gown. Each loop reunited with its button seemed to tighten her reserve and make her secure.

Devon. He voiced the word once in his mind, like an incantation, one to be uttered cautiously until its power was revealed.

They had shared the sweat and dust of hot pursuit and a rocky night under the stars; he had helped her escape a kidnapping, ambush, and rape; and at last, they were formally introduced. He wondered if each step toward civilized behavior with this woman was as demanding.

He lay back on the grass, unfolding the coded message. There were no words on the sheet, only numbers, rows upon rows covering half the sheet of crude printing paper. Coded.

Devon awaited the question she knew would come. As she tore more strips from her crinoline, she allowed her gaze only one sweep of Gentry's hard chest exposed between flaps of his shirt, one glance at the dark abdomen that wanted to lead her curious eyes astray, below the band of his trousers.

"Do you know what's written here?" he asked.

"A courier's only a dumb beast of burden."

"I need a straight answer: Can you translate the code?"

She ripped a length of cotton and methodically folded it into a thick pad. "I think you should worry more about patching holes in your body than deciphering gibberish. Can you sit up?" She kept her distance as she held out the thick, clean pad he could exchange for the bloodied bandage lying low on his side.

He rose slowly, leaning left. The stained bandage fell to the grass as he suddenly reached out to grasp her forearm. His grip, like his voice, was firm and demanding. "Only an amateur demands more finesse than honesty in a partner. I've lost too much time and blood to do a pretty little prance around the truth with you. Now where's the codebook to translate the letter?"

She pulled her arm free. "It's in a safe place! That's as honest an answer as you'll get until we're in Wilmington. Then we'll get at the truth of this 'partnership.' Your help has been far too convenient to be believed!"

He took a deep breath, as if pain were threatening to overwhelm. Devon didn't know whether the pain came from his wound or from her. But he was angrily fighting the sensation.

She ripped more strips of bandage and tied them together,

then gathered the ribboned strips and dropped them in a pile beside Gentry.

"I'll need your help," he said. It was not a request.

She nodded warily and settled closer to him, careful that her knees did not touch his outstretched leg. He laid a length of cotton across the darkening bandage at his side. She began to smooth the strip across his torso. She had to lean very close, and her arms created an awkward embrace as she wound the strip behind his back and around to the front.

She sank back on her heels, the bandage trailing from her hand.

He did not move.

She leaned over him again, widening the embrace so that her arms would not hug him so tightly. The bandage smoothed around him, and her soft cheek grazed the center of his chest, a solid, bronzed plane of skin warm and openly male.

She withdrew again, hotly aware of a savage heritage that spoke physically, primitively through his flesh. Her breath grew shallow, hovering high in her throat, as if to prevent her inhaling too deeply and taking in too much of him. The wet musk of river water that dampened his skin, the fresh liquor of grass rubbed into his shirt, the sheen of sweat that glistened above lips drawn taut with watchful patience.

Her pause grew long and awkward.

"You are doing well," he said in a low voice.

She shook her head and could not look at him.

Knowing he shouldn't, he glided a finger along her jaw, testing its softness and curve. She froze like an animal sure she was caught, yet not certain of the strength of the snare. Her eyes were the night brown of his people trapped within skin the wrong color, but the same warmth, the same yield. His finger made a filmy sweep across her lip, and she finally escaped with a small turn of her head. He could not pursue across her refusal to look at him. The chasm was deep and dark, filled with generations of warning.

"Finish." He was so weary, he whispered the request.

Cautiously, she resumed the dip and sway of winding the bandage around him.

"There's a farmhouse about two miles east," he said. "We will stay the night there." Thumb and forefinger at his temples, he massaged hard. Trauma and blood loss had begun to drain his concentration.

"You know the owner?" she asked.

"We're in secessionist territory. We'll be treated as friends. But even if we were Yanks, a farmer would have no choice but to help us."

She tied off the last length of bandage, bending her head close to him to start a tear in the fabric with her teeth.

He eased back when she finished, away from her, weary of the long day, anticipating a feverish, pain-filled night, aware that among the many aches in his body was the desire to slide his fingers through the strands that had lain for a moment like exotic fur against his stomach.

She clenched her hands in a fold of her gown, long, fine fingers with sensitive touch, hands chafed by leather reins, scented with gun oil, stained with his blood.

She was troubled. "Two men died horribly for a ridiculous piece of paper."

"They were murderers," he said. "Their deaths can not be on your conscience."

"Can they be on yours?"

He tried to smile. "There is no room for them."

A rubbery weakness and chilling cold were beginning to take hold throughout his upper body. He struggled to a sitting position and slowly, awkwardly, rose to his feet. He had to lead the yellow-hair to the farm he had seen from the top of the ridge, before nightfall—and before the healing spirits gripped his cold body and bathed it in the sweat of their fight.

"By now, Bloxie Taft should've sent my brother-in-law to a smelly buffalo hut in hell." Colonel Miles Brant impatiently shrugged his butternut frock coat off one shoulder as he entered the frescoed chambers of the Trieste Room. His valet, Victor, grasped the coat by the collar and eased his master's arm from the chevroned sleeve.

" 'Course, I don't count Gentry as blood family," Miles added quickly as he loosened his black cravat. He lowered his slim body into the black-lacquered armchair that faced the balcony.

It was a western exposure, one that allowed the eye a gentle dip over a trim grass hillock to the lush oaks and willows below, silent gatekeepers planted sixty years earlier when Miles's grandfather was still master of Jasmine's Reach.

"Gentry Morgan's just a breed that got lucky," he went on. "Got himself sired by an Irish potato-back who just happened to turn out richer than a mountain of Midas's manure. Teague Morgan's a sentimental fool if he thinks he can leave it all to that breed."

Miles narrowed his gaze on the garden below and willed himself to relax. He had taught Victor to skin back the filmy gold-chintz curtains just so, and to gather the crimson brocade drapes in an artful swag each day at this time, so that the baroque privy garden below became a living, gilt-framed tableau. He drummed his fingers in a measured gallop on the oakwood armrest, harder and harder, until he had tapped the Morgan bastard into a less urgent compartment of his thoughts. Now the garden could work its magic.

"Brandy," Miles ordered softly, his gaze on the intricate beds of ornamentals he had designed: sweet periwinkle bordered in a flowing scroll of santolina; a sunken, royal-colored quadrant of ageratum, begonias, and petunias, imprisoned like herds of winged fairies within walls of crepe myrtle and clipped dwarf yaupon.

Rising above the bordered flower beds, near the high back wall of the garden, an alabaster Venus stood in a cold stone gown. She was the regal, white-eyed hostess in a domed pavilion of trellised walls wild with yellow jessamine and ivy.

He sipped from the snifter Victor had brought, feeling the brandy roil on his tongue like the acrid bouquet of a fine cigar. Venus had never been his favorite goddess. Miles preferred lesser immortals who offered something more stunning than beauty. "Goddesses with grit," he whispered pensively. A striking face and figure made it too easy for a woman to love herself first, her man second.

Best if a woman didn't love herself, nor her man, too freely. Security bred predictability, and a lovers' relationship needed a certain tension to be gratifying.

Sad to say, he had never experienced any such gratification with his wife, Regina. She so thoroughly hated her identity that she had surrendered it to him readily, placing her feminine essence gratefully in his hands, to be cast and molded and used.

Certainly she was a model wife, but Regina's main attraction had been family inheritance: Her adoptive father, Teague Morgan, was an ambitious land baron and horse breeder in Missouri.

"Now that's where I belong. Dammit!" Miles slammed the glass down on the arm of the chair. West, far west, in wilder country where rules were flexible and empires were new. Index finger rigid, he pressed hard into his right temple, God, how tired he was of playing by fools' rules. It took so much effort, and lately he'd felt his creativity losing ground to the daily necessities of covering his tracks.

Last week there had been questions about the dry goods unaccounted for when a blockade runner jettisoned cargo in the reef at Lockwell's Folly. Now, General Farwell was questioning the skimpy documentation Miles's department had submitted on firearms brought in on the previous day's tide.

"The old horsehead's on my back ag'in, Victor." Miles shook his head, trying to forget Farwell's latest diatribe. Miles's commanding officer had an irritating voice, one that rattled in his head like dry peas in a pot. In the past three months the general had blustered about the cannons Lee needed in the field and whined like a woman for some Sharp's set-lock, double-trigger carbines like the Federals were using.

How in hell could Miles get mortars when privateers were running the blockade with flintlock muskets, four-bore cartridge pistols, and crinoline hoops in their holds?

Miles blamed it all on the disorganization and lack of diplomacy in Richmond. The Confederacy couldn't just go out and order carbines, twelve-pound howitzers, or hundred-pound rifles. They had to take what they got through the blockade or capture what they needed from the Federals.

They ought to trust his judgment instead of questioning it, Miles thought, downing his brandy. As chief of ordnance, he had sent most of the muskets to a Tennessee sharpshooters' regiment where they could be effective, and where they had a smart commander.

The Tennessee officer had had the good sense to send Miles two gold coins, a twenty-pound bag of flour, and a bolt of flannel last time he'd been in Wilmington. It wasn't much, but it was a helluva sight better than the $1,000 in Confederate bluebacks anted by a Kentucky cavalry captain. The Kentuckian had shown a heart full of patriotism and a head full of horse-hocky. The South's currency was only worth a penny on the dollar now.

Miles sighed as he raised his left leg and laid it across the brocade top of a footstool. Victor bent to unbuckle the thin leather straps of the metal brace that caged Miles's leg from ankle to knee, but his master waved him away impatiently.

"Leave it on. I've got a meeting with General Farwell."

Unfortunately, the general was a Carolina blue blood who didn't drink, command, or fornicate with enough passion to be blackmailed for anything. Farwell was one of those aging cavaliers who floundered in war, men whose lack of vision had allowed The Great Rebellion to suck the economic life-blood of the Confederacy dry. They did not know that wars —like empires—were won by strategically creating and crushing partnerships.

That was what had appealed to Miles about the alliance. It was a partnership of complex order. Each faction—English, French, Egyptian, and Confederate—had secret designs within the grand partnership.

Miles had never been to one of the alliance meetings in Liverpool, but he had paid his informant well to give him details about The Damson Club room where founding members Khaled Dexter, the Earl of Grayshire, and the French count Beaumond convened each week.

Miles had heard about the *de rigueur* elegance of The Damson, the leathered walls, spun-glass sculpture, and paintings of clipper ships that bedecked the meeting room. Miles had also paid for personal tidbits about the alliance leaders, how they looked, what they drank, the kinds of women they favored.

Miles had learned that Khaled the Egyptian possessed a gift for planning and collating details. Eminently practical, he sometimes entertained young men when he was far from his wives in Cairo. The earl, Grayshire, was a shrewd investor and idealistic blowhard who could raise more money than a shame-slinging preacher on Easter Sunday. The count, Valerie Beaumond, was an elegant, sanctimonious minister of the French emperor who demanded age in his cognac, maturity in his women, and perfume in his bath.

It had been much easier than Miles had thought to distinguish himself in the secret society. His distant cousin, Arnaud Picard, had arrived in Wilmington the past year as French advisor to the Confederate Navy. Arnaud was a charter member of the alliance, and Miles had quickly become the perfect, loyal protégé of Rear Admiral Picard.

After three months, Miles had enough information about the buildup of the secret fleet to know when, where, and how to divert alliance monies into his special postwar nest egg, the Brant Heritage Trust. The trust was based in a St. Louis, Missouri, bank. There, agents painstakingly bid for small parcels of land that abutted Teague Morgan's estate, because when Teague died, his holdings would be willed to Miles's wife, Regina. The inheritance would not be questioned. Regina's brother, Gentry, was—or soon would be—quite dead.

Miles tipped the snifter to his lips and found it empty. Victor, decanter in hand, was waiting beside him.

"Did I tell you Taft's going to bring me that half-breed's scalp? I love the irony." Miles smiled, swirling the rich amber in the bowl of his glass.

He felt good. The liquor spread its tingling warmth, and Miles languidly ran a hand through his honey-brown hair, brushed back from his forehead in obedient, flattering waves. It was a blessing to be able to relax. The past two months had been awful.

First, Miles's relationship with the elderly Arnaud had grown strained. Arnaud was jealous because the alliance's inner circle had adopted Miles's innovative battle plan over the conventional strategy proposed by Arnaud.

Then Miles's informant had sent an emergency message in June: The alliance had discovered that Miles was embezzling funds.

Miles had fumed for weeks, not knowing whether he would be assassinated or censured. Then came the good news, something he could act on. A message was being sent to Arnaud. The message might reveal Miles's diversion of funds, or it could relay the final plans for the rendezvous of the fleet.

Miles never gambled when the odds were fifty-fifty. He devised a plan to intercept the alliance communiqué.

That was when he hired Reg Landry. Then he requested a special leave to study General Early's armament needs in the Shenandoah and headed north to supervise the kidnapping of Arnaud Picard's wife, the courier.

But Margaret Picard had apparently been a decoy. Miles couldn't be certain, because the old girl had fallen apart during questioning the night of the kidnapping. The only coherent thing she'd offered was that the letters were safe with Devon.

And Gentry Morgan, dammit, had come out of nowhere to rescue Devon Picard and the messages. Gentry's presence was suspicious, as if someone in the alliance knew there would be an attempt to waylay the information. But why pick Gentry?

Only God knew. But, clearly, it was Miles's chance to be rid of Teague Morgan's heir and to get the alliance communication that might brand him a traitor. Miles had hired Bloxie Taft for an exorbitant sum, with payment contingent upon delivery of Gentry's bloody forelock.

Miles stretched his arms in a long, graceful arch above his head. A pity the girl had to be killed. She was lovely. Willful and talented, too, from what he had heard. But what he remembered most was her startling face, with skin like porcelain. How her face had flushed with anger when he'd fired on her in the woods, then paled with shock as he got closer to her, a black-garbed avenger in his bandit mask. How dashing he must have looked.

Miles smiled into his glass. He hadn't realized who she was at the time. Devon Picard, ingenue turned strumpet, the orphan who had privately blackened the reputation of her guardian family with a single, bold stroke. Miles knew everything, because the distraught Arnaud had stoically confided the details, amid apologies for any ensuing shame on the family. Miles had reacted with appropriate largesse and sympathy, but secretly he found it amusing, and fascinating.

It seemed that Devon Picard had been discovered exiting her fiancé's bedroom one morning, wearing Roger Bivens's good silk shirt and nothing else of note. Servants swore she exuded breath highly scented with sherry and her hair had been in considerable disarray.

Roger, Miles thought, had reacted nobly for a man whose chief attributes seemed to be drinking gin and teasing tarts. He had requested marriage immediately, but to both families' surprise, Devon had refused.

She was obviously a woman of independent thought. Or perhaps, Miles mused, she had embarked on a simple quest for knowledge. Whatever her motives, he was intrigued.

He sighed and bent to straighten the leather knee collar on his brace. He loved a curious intellect in his women. He would have enjoyed hosting Miss Picard at Jasmine's Reach, for when a young woman's virginity was gone, so was her reason for saying no.

He stood, suddenly aware of a wistfulness. He slipped an arm into the freshly pressed sleeve of his jacket.

The liquor's heat had engulfed his belly, a swollen tide that spread its warmth ever lower, until it lolled comfortably against the firm memory of the Englishwoman. Miles closed his eyes a moment in homage to the heady, sweet demand. He would need help to answer it tonight.

Victor held the door and gave a small bow as Miles left.

"Have Portia here by midnight," Miles said.

The gilt-inlaid door clicked shut.

Only Victor remained in the room, his massive shadow cast into a corner, its angle broken, half-looming. Slowly he unclenched the fist that had curled tight and tremulous.

Portia.

His eyes squeezed closed, and he molded the flat of his broad black hand against the door, pressing silently, forcefully, until the wood relinquished a long, sorrowful groan.

EIGHT

The roan and the mare ambled across a field of high yellowing grasses.

On a knoll a half mile away, Devon saw the steep roof of a weathered-gray house. A giant willow drooped its parasol of green across high eaves, and a blackened, clapboard barn hulked nearby like a sentient guard. A mongrel ran to the edge of a sagging split-rail fence and began to bark a warning of the riders' approach.

Gentry halted the roan.

Devon drew up, facing him. His eyes were hidden in the shadow of his hat brim, but his face seemed drawn and drained of color.

He had let her take the lead on the path, a sign of confidence that they were not being followed—or a clue to the intensity of his pain. She could not tell whether his wound still bled. The side of his shirt was a stained, dark sheath.

"We are almost there," she said, trying to comfort.

He nodded. "You must pretend to be my wife."

"You're out of your mind!" she exclaimed, stunned.

"You're arrogant," he said, giving his horse rein to graze.

"Me, arrogant? You mannerless son of a—"

"Vulgar too."

"The cheek!" she exploded. "I refuse to take part in a marital farce and I'm a snob? The only despicable conceit here is yours!"

Gentry gingerly cradled his right arm to his side and bent forward. "A good touch. We will arrive fighting, like real husband and wife."

He signaled the roan forward, but she grabbed his reins.

"Why must you always bait me?" Her voice trembled as she tried to control her outrage.

He slid the brim of his hat higher. "As far as I can tell, anger's the only warm feeling you and I can exchange safely."

She slowly drew back. Inside, a knot of physical awareness hardened. He knew. She released the reins of his horse and made her face into a guarded mask. He knew the conflict inside her, how she fought a growing passion to explore, quite beyond the bounds of virtuous conduct.

"Why not try a logical question instead of an assumption about my baser instincts?" he asked. "There are reasons to arrive wedded. Foremost is safety. I carry the alliance message, you hold the key to translating it. It's dangerous when we're separated. Secondly, the only woman who'd accompany an Indian scout on his escape from prison is his wife—or his whore. The choice is yours."

The restless roan began to dance and pull at the bit. Gentry hissed as movement awakened the pain in his side. He swore at the jolting horse and impatiently swept his sleeve across his forehead, jostling his hat into a backward glide on thick black hair.

Devon had a close view of pain and determination etched in the creases around his eyes. Though his cheeks were darkened by a day's growth of beard, she could see the ashen cast of his face and the tensed muscles at the edge of his jaw. A bead of water rolled down his temple. Fever.

It would make no difference which role she chose. He could not take advantage of either that night.

"All I know is your name," she said, hesitant.

"There is little else of importance. I am Cherokee, the only son of Calla Summer Sky, an honored woman of the village Hiwassee, and I am bound by blood and kinship to the Teton Sioux. The rest of my life, dear 'wife,' is yours to create."

Devon's mare started forward with a clear snort of reluctance.

A half mile ahead, inside the gray, three-story farmhouse, a girl's shrill voice broke the sunset stillness. "Miz Selliger! Quick! We got company!"

Magda Selliger dropped the ladle back into the pot on the hearth, wiped her hands on her stained apron, and reached above the mantel for the .44-caliber Henry in the gun rack. With the breech-loading rifle at her side, she leaned her ample bosom over the pastry table and cautiously pulled aside the drab chintz that hung at the window. Two riders were approaching—and one of them was a woman!

As Magda shook her head in disbelief, she spied a raisin on the edge of the pastry table, a precious sweet that had escaped the egg bread she'd made for Sunday dinner. She pounced on the raisin as if it could scurry away, then bit into it thoughtfully, pondering the last time she'd enjoyed polite conversation with white womenfolk. Must have been seven, eight months ago when she'd made the long journey into Charlotte.

She looked again at the travelers who had halted outside the fence. The man wore Confederate colors and needed a haircut. The girl looked more like a wildwood Gypsy than a parlor visitor. Magda pursed her lips and gave a little sniff of resignation. Strangers meant trouble, no matter what colors they wore.

At that moment, Plaidy ran into the kitchen, out of breath. She was a sprite and pretty fourteen-year-old with caramel-smooth skin light as a pecan shell.

"You lock up the chicken house?" Magda asked.

Hand at her throat, Plaidy panted, "Yes'm."

"You put ole Lieber in the side stall?"

"Yes'm," Plaidy said, and started turning away.

"Hide yourself then," Magda said as the terrified girl fled. Magda knew Plaidy would scuttle into the storm cellar under the barn and hide with the piglets. Last year when visitors came, the girl had found herself one petticoat shy of being violated. A Confederate regiment had stopped for water and food, and a few of the men had decided they needed something else when they saw Plaidy.

God had been merciful that day, because Magda's shot hadn't killed the walleyed Mississippi infantryman who had pinned Plaidy to the ground.

Gott, she thought, if only her Heinrich had been there. He would have whipped the eggnog out of that soldier—and shamed the lieutenant who bred such lack of discipline in his line. But Heinrich Selliger was a battery sergeant on the move with heavy artillery caissons in Virginia, and he hadn't been home in two years.

Two years. *Mein Gott.* Magda sighed and bent across the pastry table. She tucked the rifle under her arm and laid the nose of the gun on the flour-white windowsill. With a calm born of experience, she leaned her cheek against the rifle stock and drew the tall rider into her sights.

Outside in the yard, Plaidy's brother, Eben, waited patiently for the riders to dismount. He was a strapping thirteen-year-old whose job was to throw his shoulders back, look as big as a man, and greet visitors with a pitchfork planted upright at his feet.

Gentry hailed the boy. " 'Day, son," he said quietly, nodding once.

Eben returned the gesture. "Suh." He nodded, eyes respectful but unreadable.

Gentry turned his gaze to the window beyond the boy's left shoulder, where one side of a yellowing curtain had been pulled askew. In the gritty half-light of dusk, he more felt than saw the barrel of a gun aimed at him. "We mean no harm," he said to the shadow in the window.

There was a flatness in his voice even he could hear.

"Please," Devon said to the boy. "He's wounded." She slid to the ground.

Beside Eben, a skinny mongrel hunched his shoulders and growled at the sudden motion. "Hush, Boog," the boy said.

Gentry began a slow careful dismount, easing his right leg over the saddle and bending to coddle the pain in his side. He landed, bit back a gasp, and braced himself against the saddle. A searing flame swept higher and wider along the curve of his torso.

He leaned his head on the saddle and waited, eyes shut, for the fire to subside.

"What can I do?" Devon asked anxiously. She placed a hand on his arm.

After a long minute, he shook his head. "Wait," he said, then turned to face the porch of the pine-frame house. He did not move until the gun-wielding occupant appeared at the threshold.

Magda Selliger was a tall, broad woman, clothed in a shapeless workday dress that fell straight as a box from her shoulders. She had thick gray hair streaked on each side with a swath of brown, all tightly pulled back in a brownish bun that perched low on her neck. With a stern nod that was not a greeting, she tucked the butt of the rifle against the side of her breast like a recalcitrant child she would just as soon turn loose.

Gentry walked slowly forward.

The woman on the porch seemed to dismiss him. Her gaze was on Devon, who had not moved. Gentry could feel judgment and suspicion of the yellow-hair waft accusingly across the yard.

The yellow-hair wore a gown unrecognizable as clothing, hair that had not seen a comb in two days, fine leather shoes plastered with mud. And she was an Indian soldier's woman.

He paused and half-turned to Devon, warning her with one tired glance that it was time to confront the woman's moral suspicions.

"You could give me some help," he said, raising an arm.

Devon stepped forward abashedly and slipped under his outstretched arm. He could feel how tentatively her own arm lay across his back, how she stiffened her shoulder to keep the side of her breast free of contact with him.

By the time they reached the bowed steps of the porch, Devon leaned passively against him, outwardly supporting in a wifely manner. Inwardly, her caution had given way to a heady awareness of the strength embodied in the man she embraced.

Stopping at the steps, she met the hard hazel eyes of the woman in front of them. "My husband has been wounded," she said. "Can you help us?"

Devon sensed the woman's scrutiny of every disheveled detail of her once-fine clothing.

"Bring him inside," the woman said finally.

She led them through a small entrance hallway dank with the humid air of summer, past a formal parlor with cameo-back chairs and a deep crimson Turkish rug, past a kitchen that percolated the smell of something meaty and hot. Devon's empty stomach churned with hope, and a touch of nausea.

"I'm Magda Selliger." The introduction came over the older woman's shoulder as she rounded a corner of the hall-way, just beyond the kitchen.

"My name is Devon Picard . . . Morgan," she added haltingly.

The bend in the hallway became the short leg of an L. At the end was a bedroom door that creaked a stiff-jointed protest as Magda opened it wide.

The two windows in the room were thickly draped. Devon could barely see the tall, spindled knobs of the bedpost in front of her.

Gentry, though, moved directly toward the ladderlike shadow of a chair near one of the windows. She heard the hissing intake of his breath as he sat down. A candle flame wavered in the gray gloom of the hallway and moved into the room.

"Light the lantern, Eben," Magda said. "Then get Plaidy out from under the barn."

The round cheeks and serious brown eyes of the black boy were highlighted as he bent to the table near Gentry. The candle flame latched hungrily onto the wick of the coal-oil lantern. Eben lowered the flame and replaced the glass flue.

The warm glow lit Gentry's face; his brow was wet with perspiration.

"Gunshot?" Magda asked.

Gentry nodded.

"I have a salve that—"

He shook his head. "Go to the willow," he said to Eben. "Skin away a piece of bark. Cut deep, to get the inner skin that's moist. Mash the pulp, and bring it to me."

The boy looked to Magda for approval, and she nodded. "Choctaw?" she asked Gentry.

"Cherokee," Devon answered softly for him.

Magda turned to her. "Do we have to get the bullet out?"

"No. The wound is clean, but the bandages should be changed."

"I'll bring some warm water—" Magda began.

"My wife will attend me," Gentry interrupted quietly, eyes closed.

Magda sniffed, shifting the rifle to carry it barrel up. "Who is it you ride with?"

"Jeb Stuart," Gentry said, his uneven breathing making speaking difficult. "Lead scout for him. Until May. Sheridan raided Yellow Tavern, and Jeb was wounded. We lost him two days later."

" 'Fraid our side's losing too many of the good ones,"

Magda said. "Come, Mrs. Morgan. I'll get you some bandages, and maybe some food. You both look starved."

Devon began to walk away with Magda.

"Wife."

The possessive tone brought a touch of warmth to her cheeks.

"I need boiling water, and a cup to steep the willow bark," he said.

"What you need is to lie down," Magda said. "You won't be the first soldier to bleed on those sheets, nor the last. I'll wait for you in the kitchen, Mrs. Morgan."

The stilted congeniality in the farmwoman's voice told Devon that something else would await her in the kitchen—questions.

What can I tell her? she wanted to scream at Gentry. But he seemed unaware of her. Like a man in a trance, his blue eyes glistened in the lamp glow, coolly fixed.

"Lie down," she said with resignation as she turned down the musty patchwork quilt on the bed.

Gentry lay on his side, facing her. She turned quickly to leave the room.

"Devon."

Her name on his breath spoke of something intimate and knowing between them. She walked away from it, breath caught in her throat, unable to respond. She paused near the door, but did not turn around.

His words came softly. "The best lies are those that are half true. Just be careful which half you reveal."

She closed the door with a timid click.

When she entered the kitchen, Magda was at the hearth, swiveling the black iron cooking hook outward, away from the fire and toward the hearth bricks.

"Ingenious," Devon said, complimenting the cranelike contraption. Magda did not respond. Devon waited patiently in the silence, knowing that before she could be offered any dinner from the potbellied kettle, a payment of information would have to be rendered.

"My Heinrich is good with metalwork," Magda said at last. She wrapped a blackened towel around the iron-bale handle and hefted the big kettle off the hook and onto the bricks. "Your husband is good with a gun?"

"Yes."

"Then how was she shot?"

"We were ambushed by thieves, men who dressed in Federal uniforms. Gentry recognized their leader, a guerrilla mercenary named Landry. They chased us."

"Why?"

Devon paused a moment. "Money. Gentry is wanted by the Federals. He killed two guards when he escaped prison."

Magda pulled a smaller pot from a cupboard and stepped outdoors, propping the kitchen door open with her body. "Where are you from?"

"I was born in Devon, England. My father was—he was a professor of history there."

Devon heard the wooden lid of a barrel give a hollow scrape, then came the slap and slosh of a dipper filling the empty pot with rainwater.

"My parents died crossing the Channel to Cherbourg," she continued. "My sister and I were very young. My aunt and uncle in London took us in."

"You must feel like an orphan again," Magda called through the door. "I take it you lost all your belongings?"

Devon's hand rose to the torn shoulder of her gown where the bearded man had grasped her hungrily.

"I was attacked by one of the thieves. Gentry saved me, and was shot."

Magda frowned from her post at the door, sympathy rising, but her question was stern. "Why isn't your husband with his regiment?"

"He is on special leave because of me." The combination of truth and fabrication came much more easily than she'd expected. "We were on our way to Gentry's family in Wilmington, so that I could stay there."

Magda swung the pot of water onto the cooking hook and laid two hefty chunks of split oak in the grate.

Devon watched the smoldering char underneath embrace the new wood with smoky enthusiasm. She crossed her arms under her bosom, nervously clasping a hand to each elbow. "You see, I was waiting in Richmond for permission to travel north to see Gentry," she said uncomfortably. "But then he escaped, and he came to me instead."

"Must have been a surprise." Magda walked over to a tall cupboard built into the wall and pulled out a neatly folded stack of rags.

"My husband is a master of it," Devon said.

Magda gave a sudden hearty laugh, and Devon blushed.

"You've been married a short time?" Magda asked.

"Two weeks."

"Your family approve?"

"They disowned me," Devon said quietly, her tone of sorrow genuine. With less gracious guardians, she might have found herself in social or financial exile for renouncing her pledge to marry Roger Bivens.

"I see." Magda tsked. "So you are alone in America?"

Devon met the older woman's gaze. "I have Gentry," she said firmly.

"As long as he lives. But a soldier's life is not always a long one." Magda's voice softened a little. "Why have you chosen this path for yourself?"

Devon was silent. The older woman was asking for the history of an English city-dweller's love for the half-breed Cherokee she called husband. Devon closed her eyes. Erratically, as a dream unfolds, she found words to create a past for her and for Gentry.

"Last year," she began softly, "I was visiting with my uncle. He is a consultant to the Confederates. I went out alone to make sketches of the hillside around Richmond. I do illustrations for my family. My nephew in London wanted a picture of army cannons. I saw an area of tents, and I sat on the hillside and sketched. Then I heard explosions and gunfire nearby. I panicked and ran into the woods to hide."

Magda tsked. "The woods? Where the mortars fall? *Mein Gott.*"

"I was fortunate. One of the Confederate scouts found me in the melee and escorted me home."

"Your husband?"

Devon nodded. "We conversed on the way home, and then"—she paused—"we met the following day."

Magda energetically ripped a length of bandage. "Bold of you." She pursed her lips below a nose that was hawk sharp.

Devon was uncomfortable. "He's a man who incites bold actions," she answered, eyes down. "He's also an educated man, well-spoken when he chooses, trained in military maneuver at academy, an excellent scout and loyal soldier."

She looked up to face the breech of morality in Magda's

accusing eyes. "When I left for London, he wrote to me, and I to him. I told him my dream of becoming an illustrator. He told me his plans to settle in the West, far from the belittling judgments of people who look at the color of his skin and the cast of his eyes and call him a half-breed bastard."

Magda's eyes widened in disbelief at the directness of Devon's words.

"We pledged our love," Devon continued more gently, "and marriage, and when my aunt found out, she sent me to Bristol to be supervised by family friends. I ran away and boarded a boat for America. When I found out Gentry had been taken prisoner, I requested help from the English consul to see him."

"That's how he knew you were in Richmond?"

"In truth, Mrs. Selliger, my husband would have found me anyway. I never underestimate his abilities."

"And I never underestimate what a woman will do for love." Magda shook her head with judgment, yet also with a wistfulness that let Devon know she had struck a romantic chord in the German farmwoman.

"Your wedding was small, I assume," Magda prompted.

"And quick. In Bristoe Station." Devon picked the name of the town where she and her Aunt Margaret had boarded the train.

Magda tsked sympathetically.

"Do not feel sorry for me. A ceremony is only a public mark of a private pledge. The gathering is for family, and my family cannot be with me in this."

"You know your children will bear the weight of your decision," Magda said.

Devon blushed at the thought that she would bed and produce heirs for the stranger in the bedroom. "Children bear gracefully what their parents bear proudly," she said somewhat defiantly.

Magda smiled and shook her head once more as she spread the wood with a poker to dampen the blaze. The water in the pot was boiling. "You are right. Strong willed and stubborn, but right. I feel for your family. They must be dying with worry. But I feel for you too. I left Germany with my Heinrich when I was fifteen. So young, so long ago. I knew nothing. He taught me everything."

A black girl entered the kitchen door and flattened shyly against the wall, her eyes wide at the sight of the disheveled blond woman who talked with her mistress.

"Plaidy, set the table for one and make up a tray of bread and broth," Magda said, bustling from hearth to sideboard. "We have a sick soldier in the house. This is Mrs. Morgan. Her father was a professor. You know, I was a teacher, too, in Philadelphia," Magda continued, warming to her captive audience now that her questions were answered. "Then we came here to farm. We were going to build a dairy herd, but times got hard. Plaidy, tell Eben to hurry up with that willow bark."

"I got it right here," Eben's voice sounded from the narrow hallway by the kitchen.

"Then take it to Mr. Morgan," Magda said.

"Here, suh," Eben said instantly, still in the hallway.

The words gave Devon a chill of apprehension. She slowly turned to face the open kitchen door and saw Eben extending a moist bundle wrapped in burlap. A familiar sleeve of bloodstained cotton reached to take the gift. Gentry stepped into the doorway of the kitchen, his feverish eyes finding Devon's astonished face, but revealing nothing of what he might have heard.

"I need my rifle and saddlebag," he said to her.

"Eben can get that," Magda said. "Get back to bed."

With a nearly soundless tap of boot sole on oak planking, Gentry returned to the bedroom. Devon's heart pounded painfully. How much had he heard? And how much would he glean from the half-truths and pretense she had created? Her cheeks warmed as Magda Selliger returned to her monologue.

"We were good and hardworking people here in the South, but more and more laws came from Washington, telling us we cannot do this with our property, our crops, our people. We should not have to endure the hatred of our own nation. Now we die for the right to stop the persecution, and to survive."

"You die for the right to hold slaves," Devon said simply.

Magda looked at her. "We have no slaves. My Heinrich fights for respect, and laws that let us prosper. Eben and Plaidy are free Negroes. I have their mother's freedom papers."

Magda turned to Plaidy. "And when you are grown, you will leave! And Heinrich and I will be poorer still, for who will help us with the farmwork?"

"I won't leave you alone, Miz Selliger," Plaidy said, clinking bowls and cutlery.

"You'll soon want a life of your own." Magda sighed and took a chipped porcelain basin from a cabinet. She used the hem of her apron to protect her hand as she tipped the hot pot of water toward the basin.

"We'll let this water cool," she said, then poured boiling water into a clean tin cup. "This will be for soaking the hard bark. It makes an infusion, a good drink for fever and pain. My grandmother did the same in Heidelberg. The old medicine is sometimes the best."

Plaidy set a steaming bowl and shank of bread on the plank-wood table near the doorway. Devon, famished, sat quickly on the table bench, suddenly aware of how weak she felt. Her hand shook as she lifted a spoonful of rabbit stew to her lips.

Magda crossed the threshold into the hallway, bandages under her arm, the basin of hot water in her hands. "I'll tend your man right now, Mrs. Morgan. You'll need your strength for the fever tonight."

NINE

"Miz Morgan?"

Devon felt a small, hesitant hand on her shoulder.

"Miz Morgan, your bath's ready," Plaidy said.

Devon raised her head from her arms and stared blankly at the wall in front of her. She had fallen asleep at the table, her hand curled around the soft, yeasty center of a piece of bread.

"Bath?" she said groggily, shading her eyes from the lantern in the girl's hand.

"Yes'm. Miz Selliger says ladies can't stand to go to bed dirty as you are. She says I gotta help you undress, 'cause ladies don't do it by themselves."

Devon followed the shape of the girl's faded calico dress down the hallway to the bedroom.

Plaidy set the lantern on a burl-walnut table near the bed. The smoky glow gave an aura to the faded roses that climbed the damask wallpaper. The room had a dark pine floor and the smell of a closed trunk, its vacant air awaiting body scents and movement to dissipate the neglect.

Gentry lay with his face in shadow, his body still, one bare arm and shoulder atop the quilt that covered him. Devon felt oddly unnerved to see his fierce intensity at rest. It was an unnatural quiet that seemed more ominous than peaceful.

"Is he asleep?" she whispered.

Plaidy shrugged uncertainly. "He's *your* husband."

Devon tiptoed close to the bed. Gentry's face was dark against the white pillow, his lips parted and dry, his breathing shallow. Strands of thick black hair draped forward across his cheek. On impulse, she smoothed the long hair back from his face. His cheek was damp with perspiration.

The gesture was far too personal, but permitted of a wife, Devon knew, and it was a necessary test. The straw ticking in the mattress would crackle a warning with the slightest shift of his weight if he were awake.

She waited, aware of the length and breadth of this body in the high bed. She wondered how a woman's hand would regard his flesh, so solid, like a curving plane on a block of new clay, smooth, allowing scant imprint, submitting to the dip of fingertips coursing the surface. But beneath was the living shield of sinew and muscle that shifted with motion and set itself taut against the play of his skin.

The shield slept now. She could consider him in safety, watching the barely perceptible rise of his shoulder as he breathed. The white border of the blanket was drawn low across his chest, a contrast of color and dimension where the smooth, flat quilt met hard, concave muscle along his belly.

Too warmed by wondering, Devon turned to Plaidy and began to undress.

Plaidy, who was nearly Devon's height, quickly loosed bodice buttons from their loops. Devon slipped the top of the gown off her shoulders.

Plaidy stooped to help remove Devon's shoes. "Lord Almighty," she said when she saw the rawhide thongs that tied Devon's split skirt to her ankles. "Miz Selliger told me you got attacked, but she didn't tell me 'bout no torture."

"Only my clothes were tortured," Devon said. "My husband did it to make them like trousers, easier to ride with."

"He does like things his own way," Plaidy said, untying the gown and pulling off mud-caked shoes. "But he finally let us get him cleaned up and bandaged. He's lucky, ma'am. That bullet hole go any deeper and he'd go deeper—into the ground, Miz Selliger says."

"Please," Devon begged, "the corset."

Plaidy's nimble fingers went to work on the hooks. The corset was pulled away, leaving ridged imprints on the white chemise underneath. Devon groaned softly in relief.

She glanced at the bed as she stood in bedraggled chemise and pantalettes. Plaidy had laid a thin cotton nightdress, toiletries, and extra blankets on the chair by the window.

A small oval tub sat on a braided throw rug beside the

fireplace, the kind of tub meant for stand-up bathing. It was hip high with a rim the size of a rain barrel.

The prospect of shedding trail grime was enticing. Devon skimmed the tepid water with her fingers.

Plaidy pointed to a cup on the tiny, three-legged stand near the bed. "Miz Selliger made more o' that willow tea. Smells like turpentine to me, but she says he'll need it tonight. There's clean water in the pan to wipe him down with." The girl moved quietly to the door. "Miz Selliger's room's upstairs, if you need her. 'Night, ma'am." The door clicked softly shut.

With the self-assured girl gone, Devon felt her own confidence fading. She waited, unmoving, listening. Leaves rustled in the warm breeze outside the open window. A barn owl's throaty hoot carried distantly across the knoll. Crickets chirruped below the window, a buzzing serenade to the crescent moon's brightness.

There was no sound of movement from the bed, no sign that Gentry was awake. Devon took a deep breath. She did not know whether she was motivated by extreme fatigue or foolishness, but this moment was the closest semblance of privacy she'd had in two days, and she decided to act on it quickly.

Spirals of black smoke played inside the bulb of the glass lantern as she turned the wick lower, lower, until only a tiny flame burned determinedly at the edge of oil-fed cloth. Its glow barely reached beyond the tabletop. She walked into the shadows by the tub and lifted the cotton chemise over her head. Then the pantalettes slipped silently to the floor.

She stood motionless a moment, unsure in her nakedness, fearful, as if the room had suddenly discovered her presence. A light draft of air coursed the sensitive dip above her buttocks, and the poplin curtain billowed, alternating shadow and moonlight across the bare mantelpiece in front of her. Her feet sank softly, pliably, into the knobby braid of roped rug. Her body grew attuned to the unseen elements of air and space that dominated the room, and she felt as if her skin were being subtly explored.

With her back to the bed and her cloth and soap in hand, she stepped into the tub. The slosh of disturbed water reverberated in the silence, and she paused, her chin turned to her shoulder, concentrating her senses on the bed behind her.

Ten feet away, all was still.

Nonetheless, an uneasy vulnerability gripped her as she began to wash, rubbing the hard lye soap against the cloth, squeezing rivulets of water across her skin. She swept the washcloth along her extended arm and cupped water in her hand to rinse the soft skin that curved under her breasts.

She stopped a moment, looking down on her bosom, two exuberant, overflowing handfuls destined to be cupped and corseted into a shape not their own. She had secretly tried to sketch them once, sitting at her dressing table in a locked room, her young breasts in gravity's free grip, firm mounds that lay like thickened cream dropped from a ladle.

She had been only fifteen then, and though she drew their outline accurately, creating gentle curves and a center of pale, ridged nipple, the portrait was anatomical and flat, without the wonder and forbidden feel of a woman's breast. Lovemaking and a man's lingering hand would create awareness in the secret curves of her body, she thought.

Scant months ago, at nineteen, she had tried to attain the knowledge she wanted, that terrible night with her fiancé. But she had felt no depth or blossoming from Roger's touch. He had groped and squeezed with hands that moved as lovingly as a Yorkshire farmer clearing brush before his lunch got cold.

The memory brought a warm flood of shame to her face. She stood with her arms crossed to her shoulders, suddenly anxious to hide her bosom.

Behind her, the dry crackle of straw rose from the bed.

Devon held her breath. Her heartbeat slowed.

The pine floor creaked once, close by.

She whirled defensively, the water churning in a rush around her legs.

Gentry stood there, facing her, solid and feverish, his broad shoulders blocking the feeble light of the lantern. There was nothing between them but darkness—and the hot cry of fear she choked back.

His hand grasped her arm, and the other her thigh, steadying her, touching her bare skin without right or apology.

He was cast in shadow, as she was, his skin bare to the waist. She could see the muscled cords of his upper arms outlined against the light. The bandage rode low on his abdomen, a ceremonial belt around his tight, flat waist. His hair nearly reached his shoulders, lending savage emphasis to angular planes and high cheekbones.

She willed herself not to move, frightened that his hands would then have cause to roam and deepen her shame. He had a gentle hold along the back of her thigh; his other hand relaxed on her upper arm. His thumb nested in the soft crevice where her arm and breast met.

Their moments marked passage on a clock outside the face of time, so Gentry did not know how long he stood there, his spirit stilled by a strange calm. He could hear the pounding of his heart as he studied her. Alabaster as a statue, her surface felt distant and cool. Inside, he knew, her groin was knotted with the fear of being touched, the dread of being seen, and the shame of wanting both. She was a woman sure and unsure, innocent but breathtakingly curious, a chaotic mixture guaranteed to feed any man's desire.

Her hunger had to be nursed carefully, if at all, he knew. So much of his life hung in the balance each time he approached this woman—success of the espionage against the alliance, his pact with Pinkney Dobbs, the case against Kai-ee-nah's murderer.

In the silence he deliberately summoned the memory of his wife, to stem the craving he felt for this proud white foreigner whose hair lay angel light, like corn silk, across his hand. But Kai-ee-nah's spirit, her dark, heart-shaped face, did not rise in his thoughts. Instead, his hand moved of its own accord, the thumb sweeping an arc of wetness from the warm, sensitive crease of Devon's arm to press delicately on the cream-soft breast she had tried to cover.

The movement broke her frightened trance, and he felt her stiffen as he lifted her hair, smoothing it back behind her ear.

"Stop." She was panicky, her arms futile guardians across her breasts.

"When I can," he whispered, bending toward her, cupping her head in his hand and pulling her frightened body closer.

The hand that gripped her thigh spread fingers wide to encompass as much of her skin as possible. Devon felt the tingling pressure of each finger gliding in unison up her trim leg, each fingertip dipping delicately inward where her buttocks met her thigh.

She trembled at the boldness of his trespass. His hand found the small of her back, and he suddenly pressed her harder toward him. His lips fell warm and firm on her mouth.

When she tried to twist away, he held the back of her head in a grip that allowed her no freedom, and his mouth against hers allowed her no voice.

She gave a strangled mew of distress as his lips tightened with an insistence that confused her, for when her mind sought anger to keep her lips firmly closed, her body sent a gentle moan that parted them instead. When her mind cried out in fear of her second assault of the day, her groin convulsed with a heat more womanly than she had ever known.

Worse, she knew he felt the chaos within her. He nurtured it with a kiss that probed and teased between her full lips, again and again, until her mouth pressed hungrily against his in a rhythm set by desire shared.

Satisfied, the hand imprisoning her head relaxed.

She wrenched her mouth from his, free of his kiss but not released. She laid her head on his chest and felt the fever beneath his skin raging hot and dry.

"Let me go," she said softly. Deliberately, she allowed her crossed arms to fall free of her breasts. His body straightened against her, his chest hardening with held breath as her nipples raked him bold and bare in the darkness.

When his hand slipped away from the small of her back, she immediately pushed away from him.

The water swirled awake from its reverie.

Gentry purposefully backed away from her, allowing her space to escape the tub and stand dripping on the braided rug. He stopped beside the walnut table, blocking her access to the toweling on the chair.

Her words emerged angrily between shuddering breaths. "I will not accept such common, vulgar treatment!"

He watched her a moment. "You have intellect enough to know that what you felt is neither." He turned the key to the lantern wick, winding it higher until the flame fed light to half the room.

Shadows fled, and her body was fully revealed to him,

defiant and vulnerable, virginal and womanly, her long hair
hiding the swell of her breasts. But it was another curtain of
gold his eyes sought, lower, below the dark jewel of her
navel. There, a thatch of light hair curled wet against her,
feeding droplets of water like teardrops down her thigh.

"Have you not shamed me enough?" she whispered.

"I see no shame, only beauty," he said, knowing she
would not understand. He had needed to see her completely,
so he would no longer be driven to imagine.

He smiled, pensive. " 'No beauty she doth miss, when all
her robes are on; but beauty's self she is, when all her robes
are gone.' " The madrigal lyrics, long strayed from his memory, slipped softly from his tongue, as if just yesterday he'd
sat among the yellowed pages and book dust in his father's
library. He had spent secret, late-night hours there, adept at
exploring the treasure, but careful to hide his enjoyment of
this white man's pleasure. His mother had taught him to
read and write English, knowing that someday his father
would return from the white man's world and take his Indian son.

"How did she know?" he whispered to the frightened yellow-hair before him.

Devon frowned at the irrational question, and the poetry
that preceded it.

The acrid smoke of newly fed flame stung Gentry's nostrils and he backed away.

Devon's gaze fixed on the bare torso she had never before
seen so clearly. A high sheen of fever made his broad chest
glisten. But it was the flesh below each shoulder that drew
her eye. Two ragged scars lay like cruel mistakes on the
tight, perfect skin of his chest, wounds where flesh had
healed in a sunken mottle of pink and russet whorl, a painful
design and primitive reminder of hurt endured.

As he turned from her and sat stiffly on the bed, she felt a
lull in the air, a vacuum of emotion, as if he had suddenly
withdrawn the threat of a storm. She quickly donned the
thin, worn nightdress Plaidy had left. The garment had lost
its cross-lacing at the neck, lying open to a V appropriate to
a lover or husband, but not to a fevered enemy who assumed
the rights of both.

Uncertain where to go, Devon wrapped a blanket around
her and walked to the other side of the room.

As he watched the yellow-hair retreat to a safe distance, the comforting image of Kai-ee-nah finally answered his summons. The yellow-hair clutched the blanket at her throat as Kai-ee-nah had her buffalo robe each winter, and Gentry remembered how his wife had paced in her fur, trying to quiet the kicking child who disturbed the food in her stomach. "Come," he had called to her. "I will rest my hand on your belly and rock that rude baby."

His beloved had knelt on their pallet beside him, eyes bright and mocking. "Your touch is not quieting to me, husband." She had smiled.

Gentry opened his eyes, quickly, before the warm reverie could turn to bloody memory.

Across the room, the yellow-hair watched him strangely.

Had he said something? Gentry slowly unclenched his fists. The fever was rising. He knew because his head felt light and separate from his body, as if his consciousness were being lifted aside to allow the healing spirit control.

He shook his head sharply. "I will sleep outside," he said in the silence. "It is too hot." He stood, grimacing. His desire for the yellow-hair no longer substituted for the pain that spread low along his back.

Clutching the blanket, Devon walked toward him. "You must stay here."

"Neither of us would have to leave if you had not taken the light," he said softly.

She shook her head. She didn't understand.

His conscious mind hovered safely distant from the fever, but too far from his words to explain things clearly to her. How to tell her the importance of light? A change of light was the prisoner's signal of mornings lost and found, the marker of work's progress, the silent clarion of punishment begun and ended. He had spent eight weeks in the stockade, and five days in the "crate," an isolated wooden cell without windows.

Tonight he had awakened almost fearful, thinking the door to the crate had closed like a coffin lid on him again. But he'd found it was only the yellow-hair dimming the lantern before her bath. She was bent over the light, in an undergarment, white and loose enough to allow the lamp's friendly hue inside eyelet rim. Her breasts were firm, sweet mounds, taut-skinned testimony of her youth.

Now the yellow-hair approached him with a large tin cup, interrupting the fine musing. "Drink this and lie down," she said.

The willow brew was bitter, but he sipped until it was gone, one hand on the footpost of the bed to steady himself. Then he lay down, as stone still as when he'd first awakened watching her, his eyes focused sharply as an animal's stalking night prey, following her into the shadows where she felt safe.

He remembered how the moonlight had wrapped her naked body intermittently with long, transparent scarves of light, here illuminating the profile of a full, perfect breast, there tucking a shaft of light inward along the curve of her waist or across her tight, intriguing belly. And there was a moment when she paused before getting into the water, when her buttocks were held in sudden highlight. Then, too quickly, the high-flying poplin curtain fell exhausted to the window, protecting her nakedness once again.

He had heard the water trickle in hidden, glistening trails, the washcloth slap gently against her skin. He'd visualized the swirl of water at her thigh, the stream of rinsing wetness across her protruding breasts, the sheen of it gliding across her abdomen.

And he could wait no longer. He had risen from the bed, not knowing he would touch her so quickly. But when she'd turned, she had seemed to falter. His hands had found their place instinctively, a sovereign right of possession granted by circumstance, and by her naked daring of fate.

She liked to tempt the wheel of fortune, this goddess. Did she know, as he did, that claiming good fortune meant also embracing bad? With such an understanding, he could revel in the grace of holding her body against him and tasting the glide of her tongue against his, even if briefly. These things were one spin of the circle of fate, and his fever-racked body was another. "Such is my nature," said the Roman goddess Fortune rising from the musty pages in his father's house, "and the game I play continually."

The sound of splashing water entered his dreamy half-world and led him back to the edge of consciousness.

He turned his head against the pillow. Gradually his senses awakened to the smooth surface of the linen against his cheek, the sharp odor of feathers moistened by his sweat, and nearby, the soft hiss of a cloth compressing air and water from its pores.

He looked up and saw the yellow-hair in her protective blanket come near and place a basin of water on the stand by the bed. She sat beside him and laid the cloth against his face, absorbing the heat and moisture of the fever. He knew he could not reach out for her; she would flee. To hold her presence, he would have to lie fevered and weak, an easy task.

"Do you wash me for my shroud?" he asked.

"I won't have to. Your body bathes itself," she said tiredly, wringing the cloth into the basin.

He tried to focus on her, but his eyes closed of their own accord, although not sleepily. He was comfortably aware of her weight on the bed.

"Where does an English lady acquire her skill as a nurse?" he asked.

"In the nursery. I have watched the nannies tend my niece and nephews."

"And where does she learn to tend a man?" he asked softly.

The cloth suddenly stopped its soothing glide across his chest. She began to remove her hand, but he neatly grabbed her wrist.

"I am sorry," he said.

"No. You are not," she said.

His palm was warm against the thin, delicate skin of her wrist, and he felt her pulse quicken.

"Why do you provoke me?" she asked. "After two hours of watching you thrash, listening to your nonsense words. Two hours of padding out to the rain barrel for fresh water to keep your bloody body cool!"

A silent alarm sounded, and his grip on her tightened. "Nonsense words." What had he said? He slowly raised to one elbow, pulling her nearer. "What did I say?" he asked.

His apprehension must have been tangible to her, for he watched her expression change, grow self-assured, as she searched her memory for snippets from his delirium with which to bait him.

"You spoke of many people," she said, looking at her wrist still gripped tightly in his hand.

He released her and waited. She would not be in a hurry; she was in control.

"You talked often of Dobbs and the medicine."

At his temple, a throbbing tension pulsed. Pinkney Dobbs was a name well known to the Confederate hierarchy. Dobbs was a civilian detective who had professionalized the U.S. secret service, making it as effective an espionage agency as Lincoln would allow. Dobbs was known for running double agents. And dear God, what had he said about the medicine? It was part of his pact with Dobbs. In return for Gentry's discovery of alliance contacts and battle plans, Dobbs would not only find and prosecute his wife's murderer, but also send precious medical supplies to the Sioux. Kai-ee-nah's tribe was being wiped out by smallpox. Medicine was vital, and nearly impossible to come by in wartime.

"Enough," he muttered, furious at the weakness his body had displayed, and at the yellow-hair for understanding the importance of his ramblings. "Dobbs was a scout, a friend, killed on the Kanawha last February. What I said doesn't matter."

"I agree." Her mocking eyes said the opposite. "I'm sure it was all nonsense."

The silence between them was barbed with the threat of sharp words unsaid. Devon moved away.

Gentry lay silent. The yellow-hair now had names and bits of information that someone like Miles Brant could put to good use. The chill gripping his spine spread throughout his body, or perhaps the fever was breaking and his body would soon shiver with the change in temperature.

There was nothing to do except let his body rest. And keep the yellow-hair in sight. He could not allow her to escape, with or without the alliance papers he had tucked in the false lining of his boots.

"I apologize," he said finally. "But there are ghosts in my past, and I'm not eager for someone to breathe life into them at the wrong moment."

She nodded. He knew she did not believe him. But the deep shadows under her eyes and the forward droop of her shoulders bespoke a day—and night—under siege. She was tired of fighting.

"You're exhausted," he said. "Come to bed now."

She looked at him strangely. "Where will you sleep?"

"Where I lie. There is room for you." He gave the pillow on the other side of the bed a pat.

Devon considered. In all her life, she had never known such a bodily ache for sleep. The alternative was the floor, or the davenport in the parlor, which would indicate to Mrs. Selliger that the true-love marriage Devon had described was indeed more bold than blissful.

"I can't trust you," she said challengingly. She felt oddly secure, protected by the half-sentences and strangled words he had uttered. She could make her shield last until they reached her cousin's plantation.

"Nor I you," he said. "But I give you my word, as I did last night."

It was against her better judgment, but her better judgment was as badly in need of sleep as the rest of her.

"Douse the light," he prompted.

She did, then felt her way around the bed to the other side. Blanket drawn around her like a cocoon, she lay down close to the edge, biting back a cry of relief as she relaxed her aching body into the straw ticking.

His voice came softly from the blackness. "Good night."

She lay with her back to him, the harsh straw crackling at her ear, the linen rough against her cheek. She huddled tensely, until she was sure he would make no move to violate the flimsy boundaries of her privacy. Then fatigue fell over her like a sodden blanket, and she felt heavy, drained of strength, as if she were shrinking under a great weight. After triumphantly facing terrors and rigors for which she had never been prepared, Devon felt a strange helplessness fill her heart. It was as if she were a child. An irrational homesickness jolted her to tears. She was a world away from the soft, rose-scented cotton of her skirted bed in London. She was isolated from all things familiar, working to defend a cause not her own, partnered with a man whose lips seduced too vulnerable truths from hers.

Tears slipped silent and hot into her pillow. She kept the sobs clenched deep in her throat, to hide them from the man beside her.

But Gentry could feel the fear that curled her body so tightly, he could hear the irregular breaths she drew. And he knew the cry of mourning. It could be wailed loudly and piteously, as from Kai-ee-nah's sisters, or be locked silent and tight in the chests of lost souls.

He knew the yellow-hair cried. He was connected to her, for he had drawn her breath when they kissed, and she had taken his in return.

He rose in the darkness and gently slipped his arm around her curled body. She shook with the effort to control her sobs.

"Truce," he whispered, and gingerly gathered her unprotesting body close. His hand guided her head to his shoulder, and the silken wetness of her cheek shocked his fevered skin.

She moaned.

Awkwardly, tenderly, he cupped her cheek to his shoulder.

She began to sob outright, lying with arms clasped to her body, but molded now to him, protected by him.

Gentry savored her warmth as he pulled a coverlet over them both, for chill would soon replace his fever. He listened in wonder as her breathing slowed, and finally, all that was left of her sadness was a tear pooled in the sensitive scar below his shoulder. The honored scar of his pledge to the Sun Dance, when the pain made him one with the Maker of Breath briefly, so briefly.

The salt of this white woman's tears lapped innocently at the mark of his heritage, and he suddenly knew how dangerous she was.

He embraced his enemy and turned his head to rest his dark cheek on her hair.

TEN

Above him, the crescent moon gleamed like an imp's crooked smile. Colonel Miles Brant reclined in the seat of his open carriage, hat over his eyes.

Near the entrance gate to Jasmine's Reach, moonlight filtered through a stand of poplars. The horses clopped eagerly toward the glow of oil lanterns on each side of the estate's spired gates.

Miles gave a perfunctory salute to the infantryman who had drawn picket duty that night, and the carriage and its contingent rolled along the dirt road winding around the esplanade to the manor house.

Miles removed his hat and let the scant breeze from the momentum of the carriage stir his light brown hair. Here, inland, the air was still in the humidity of August. But oceanside, the wind had insolently whipped the skirt of his frock coat straight up when he bid good-night to General Farwell outside the keeper's log house on Lighthouse Point.

Miles smiled at the memory of a discomposed General Farwell, who had very early in the evening unbuttoned his jacket and unhooked his collar to compensate for the hot flush generated by Miles's French brandy. As the general had stepped outside the keeper's cabin, his loose coat had inflated like a balloon across his back. The few strands of gray hair plastered to his balding pate had flapped rigidly to attention in the stiff breeze.

If he ever aged to such a lackluster degree, Miles had thought as he'd amicably bid the general good-night, he hoped he'd be put quickly out his misery. By the grace of fine brandy and some falsified reports, he had convinced the general that no muskets were missing from the latest load of blockade cargo. By the time the real discrepancy was discovered, Miles would have new supplies in the ordnance pipeline to cover for those that were "lost."

The paperwork was intricate and tedious, but thoroughly worthwhile, Miles thought, grasping the leather trim of the seat back for balance as two wheels dipped into a rut. There were so very few ways for a battlefield hero such as himself to make money from this godforsaken war.

The buggy drew to a halt under the white portico of the manor house, and he rose impatiently from the seat.

Portia awaited upstairs in the Trieste Room. The prospect never failed to invigorate him.

He curved his palm around the cool marble head of his cane and carefully maneuvered the step down from the carriage. His attendants knew better than to offer help.

The metal brace on his left leg clanked as his foot met the ground. Miles had made it a policy never to accept aid when climbing steps or mounting a horse so his dignity and stoicism would be all the more obvious.

He dismissed his men. The carriage horses eagerly jerked forward, turning off the main drive behind an arbor of wisteria and making their way to the rubdown and fresh hay that awaited in the carriage house.

Miles mounted the red brick steps slowly, making a note to talk to the groundskeeper. Someone had taken a brush to the griffins. The winged backs of the Brant family emblems rose garishly on each side of the entrance alcove.

Griffins. God rest the overreaching bourgeois soul of his father. Big Josey Brant had loved anything that sent a message of grandeur—statues, cobblestone drives, coffered ceilings, fresh flowers on tall plaster pedestals. But that was because Josiah Brant was nearly illiterate and always trying, to no avail, to produce evidence of his cultural acumen. Miles's grandfather, Jebediah Picard Brant, had been a genteel farmer with quiet, continental tastes, but somehow he had produced a son whose sole talent was spending money. It was genuinely propitious when Big Josey died six years earlier. If he had lived any longer, Jasmine's Reach would have been in a decline hard to reverse.

As it was, Miles had had to reduce feeding and maintenance costs on the six-hundred-acre plantation. He'd traded and sold a quarter of the slaves who worked the cotton and indigo fields of Jasmine's Reach. Then he'd diversified production, planting tobacco so that he could have a small piece of the growing domestic market. He'd mandated higher food-crop yields from his tenant farmers. And he'd hired a known bastard of an overseer to make sure both slaves and tenants achieved productivity.

Tom Creel had cost Miles more in overseer salary than he wanted to pay, but the soft-jowled Louisianan had been worth every penny. Within two months the plantation hummed like a spinning wheel dawn to dusk. Slaves moved quickly from pallet to field in the murkiness before sunrise. Long-legged children milked cows, dragged baskets of cleaned cotton to the spinning shed, and scattered feed for the chickens. House slaves, seamstresses, and cooks dressed in clean calico labored more efficiently than ever before, because they knew Creel had the ear of Marse Miles and would not hesitate to suggest they be made field hands to learn how to work harder.

Ah, Creel. The man had actually been a passably educated soul. He had worked as a trapper in the bayous. A slave hunter and dog trainer, he knew instinctively when to be cruel to set an example.

Once, on the way to a day of backbreaking picking, a field hand had lagged behind, then refused to respond to a question with, "Yes, sir, Marse Tom." Creel immediately decked the tall black with a rifle butt. In full view of everyone, he then cut off the slave's ear with a bowie knife.

When the field hand came to, Creel spoke only a few quiet words. "I reckon I got your ear now, boy. Next time, I take your tongue, 'less you use it to talk respectful."

It had been a masterful stroke of motivation, Miles thought. The slave was not incapacitated, yet his mutilated profile in the field, bending over the prickly cotton bolls, was a constant lesson of obedience.

Though Miles had never invited the overseer inside the manor house, he had often called Creel to join him on the L-shaped veranda that ran the length of the house in the back, facing Miles's garden. The dark, hairy Louisianan would speak in the joyless voice of a church elder, his righteous eyes gleaming as the whiskey loosened his tongue. Liquor was Creel's only visible vice—though it had been Creel who called Miles's attention to the burgeoning, prepubescent qualities in Portia.

To each his own, Miles had thought, sipping a dry sherry while Creel slugged another shot of bourbon and continued a monologue on the secrets of success. "Don't use a lot of words when you speak to niggers and women," he would say. "Don't explain nothin'. Just say 'Pick the south field by sundown' or 'Put your hand right here.' Just tell 'em what to do, and what you're gonna do if they don't."

Crude man, Creel. And effective as hell. Miles missed him.

The large entrance door to the manor house opened as Miles approached. He paused and lifted a boot to the cast-iron scraper bolted to the floor. He ran his sole across the beveled bar, leaving a crust of Carolina clay on the floorboards.

Evaleen, the housekeeper, waited patiently by the door, and Miles crossed the threshold into the spacious wainscotted foyer. It was actually one of the tasteful spots in the house because Big Josey had left it alone. Miles's great-grandmother had hired a local artist to paint a latticework mural of yellow and white jasmine in the ceiling inset. The effect was airy and elegant, gracefully Southern.

"Marse Miles," Evaleen greeted him, extending her hand to take his hat and coat.

Her skin was the rich, dry color of a roasted coffee bean. Dark blue veins rose in bas-relief on the back of her hands. She was thin as baling wire and twice as strong, despite her age. Evaleen had been a slave in the big house ever since Miles could remember. And for just as long, Evaleen had hated him. As a child, Miles had told a lie that made Big Josey beat her bloody. Though there'd been a stage in Miles's life when he had actually thought about apologizing to Evaleen, he never had. Too much time had passed. The lie and its punishment stood oddly final and comforting, like a chasm over which neither had to bother reaching out to the other again.

Miles walked slowly down the pine-plank hallway, his leg brace jangling. As he passed the downstairs parlor, he checked for the dust-mottled cobweb that drooped atop a Doric column. He had forbidden anyone to clean away the cobweb. It was essential that Jasmine's Reach look suitably bedraggled by the effects of the war.

Although Miles had too few slaves for the planting he wanted, he had held on to more of his human property than any other gentleman farmer in the region. With his access to blockade goods, his family was also well situated with staples of coffee, flour, and sugar, as well as wartime luxuries such as silks, hat frames, bolts of worsted, and bottles of wine.

His wife had perfumes, too, for his black-market friend Beque Trouvier was a dapper Frenchman who appreciated the cultural importance of sweet-smelling women. "When your wife wears this, you will forget war and remember man's higher duty," Beque had said as he showed Miles the etched scent bottle.

Damned if the skinny frog hadn't sold him the outrageously priced perfume. But it wasn't for love of his wife that he'd bought it. It was in deference to future business dealings with the crafty Frenchman who had the stature of a string bean and a brain that stored more profit margins than a silo. With a trademark felt bowler plopped like a basin on his head, Beque captained his "gray ghost" with a pirate's elan, bluffing his battle-gray blockade-runner past Union gunboats in the predawn mists.

Miles paused as he approached the curved staircase and placed a hand on the newel post. He had noticed a musky, closed smell in the house these days, the gaseous mixture of heat, dust, and humidity trapped in dank passages.

But the scent of entrapment was everywhere. Atlanta was mortally threatened. The Yankees were tightening their siege of Petersburg. Sheridan outnumbered Early in the Shenandoah. And the Federal Navy . . . Dear God, what gunpower afloat.

Autumn could break the Confederacy. The surprise appearance of the alliance fleet was crucial to save Atlanta, to revitalize the South's war, and to cripple Lincoln's reelection campaign.

The alliance—and his status within that secret confederacy—weighed on Miles's spirit more than he wanted to admit. Headquarters had just received word from Margaret Picard. She had been stranded near Raleigh but would reach

Wilmington in three days. Her niece, of course, could never arrive, but her contraband would, via Bloxie Taft.

Miles ached to hold in his hand the couriered message that labeled him a traitorous thief, for when he saw the charges against him, he could mitigate them. Slipping away from culpability had been a lifelong gift of his intellect. With luck, Bloxie Taft would bring him the alliance message tomorrow, along with a scrap of carcass that had once been Gentry Morgan's scalp. Bloxie might even bring a lock of the blond woman's hair. But Miles doubted it. Assassins rarely showed a flair for sentiment.

He began to climb slowly, rising one stiff-legged step at a time, his cane tip a quiet counterpoint to the jangle of his brace. He was bathed in the glow of silent Evaleen's lantern, carried precisely two stairs above him. The only sounds in the quiet house were the hollow ticktocks of a pendulum clock and the light clank of his steps and cane. He watched his shadow advance to the landing, looming right as he leaned hard to pull his braced leg up. He was not ungainly in his impairment, for he had practiced to create a fluidity in his limp, like a dancer's lift, working the muscles of his torso, hip, and thigh in careful unison.

Miles paused at the landing, not because he was tired, but because it made Evaleen wait. He tested her, as he tested them all. All waiting, he thought. Victor in the dressing room, Portia in the bedchamber of the Trieste Room, his wife, Regina, in her bedroom, all aware of the halting rhythm of his approach. Because he could no longer surprise anyone with his presence, he was content to let his attendants anticipate it.

Miles and his shadow leaned forward to step up, and Evaleen's shadow rose slowly as on cue.

What must they say to each other in that room? Miles wondered as he neared the top of the stairs. Victor and Portia, father and daughter, both intelligent, educated Negroes forced to comply with the simplest request. No choice for Victor but to be the perfect valet in his buttoned, black broadcloth jacket and starched white shirt, never misstepping because he knew the cost. No choice for Portia but to act the perfect mistress in pale lavender flounced twill, as Miles had ordered, the skirt tiered wide with crinoline hoops to a dimension appropriate for ballrooms.

He smiled thinking of Portia's body. Her shoulders bared by the ballgown would not show the exotic, yellow-tan skin of a mulatto. Portia was rich with the ebony of her ancestors, dark as shining heartwood, with skin supple and soft, and a firm, black bosom that rose sinuously from the low-sweeping neck of the gown. And her hair, cropped dramatically short, befitting a proud princess of the Ashanti, for Miles knew that Victor, against plantation law, kept a vestige of his language and traditions alive in furtive ways.

Perhaps it was this distinct difference and separateness of race that made Portia the most enticing of the young slave women he had tried. When he elicited response from her, whether in conversation or in lovemaking, it was an exotic triumph. Her movements, her words, her spirit, were rooted across the ocean in a primitive time and place, and when he reached inside her, he felt like a giant with feet planted in two great spheres.

Ahead of him, Evaleen stopped at the door to the Trieste Room, the lantern's light on the brass doorknob. In the dark corridor beyond her, even though he couldn't see it, he knew the door to his wife's bedroom stood ajar, like a half-open eye. But he would ignore the invitation this night, as he had every night since his return from the battlefield a year before. He had done his duty and begat one child with Regina. He respected the role of his wife and provided for his household, but he'd be damned if he felt compelled to endure Regina's martyred, submissive love.

" 'Night, Marse Miles." Evaleen backed away as Miles opened the door. He smiled at her haste. Few slaves had been inside the Trieste Room, but many had heard stories about what went on there, and none wanted to be called to enter Miles's sanctum.

And to think he had been worried he could not keep his secret when he returned wounded from the attack on Charleston. The Trieste Room, formerly an upstairs library, had become a private chamber of therapeutic ministrations for his scars of war. No one was welcome there, not even his wife and daughter, unless he granted permission.

The antechamber visible through the open door was a wide entry hall. The sole decoration was a tall walnut reading stand, its pedestal an ornate carving of a childlike angel.

On the tilted podium lay a gilt-edged copy of the Bible, unread, for there was no light in the antechamber.

Victor appeared at the entrance to the Italianate dressing room and gave a half-bow.

Miles sensed that Victor's politeness was offered under unusually tight control that night. His handsome black face was a rigid mask betraying nothing as he caught the uniform jacket Miles tossed him. But as Victor came close to unhook the gilt cuff buttons of his master's sleeves, Miles could see cords of tension in the black man's muscular neck. His head gave the impression of being pulled downward, his tight shoulders creating a defensive hunch, a stance for fight—or flight.

Miles smiled sympathetically at Victor's quandary as the slave hung the Confederate jacket in the wardrobe.

Bare from the waist up, Miles stood in front of his full-length mirror. The mirror was a hinged, tilting masterpiece, with a carved wood frame of grape clusters and vines.

Miles scanned himself critically, admiring the tight, concave muscle of his abdomen, the rolling curve of his biceps. Although slim of stature, he held to a regimen of sport that kept him, at thirty-six, well developed. The hair of his chest lay in a nicely shaped triangle of burnished brown curls that swept to an apex below his navel.

His eyes narrowed as he bent close to the mirror and ran a hand over the day's growth of beard on his cheeks. He pursed thin lips. He need not shave. Portia would not complain. And the honey-dark cast of his beard lent a hollow, desperate edge to his comely face.

He carried the fair-haired genes of generations of Carolina Brants, and his long face, wide steel-gray eyes, and inviting smile were trademarks of his family. From someone in his past came an uncharacteristically weak chin. He did not mind. It lent his face a kindly mien.

Behind Miles's image in the mirror, Victor was visible as he withdrew a velvet smoking jacket with gold-tasseled sash from the armoire. He approached his master, eyes carefully averted from the gray ones that watched him in the mirror. He held out the jacket; the satin lining whispered slippery friction as Miles's bare arm eased inside the sleeve.

Miles tied the sash himself. Behind him he could hear the sound of glasses clinking on a tray, the painful scrape of a cut-glass stopper leaving the neck of its cruet, then the healthy splash of sherry against crystal.

"Sir?" Victor's query came soft behind him.

Miles turned, realizing that it was the first word between them since he had arrived. There was always a solemnness on the nights he took Portia.

Victor held a brass-inlaid tray that carried a glass of sherry. Miles took the drink and sipped delicately, savoring the burning, fruity dryness. He downed a larger sip as he turned away from the brocade drapes that shielded the doorway of the bedchamber. The time was drawing near, and he was getting less patient.

His leg brace clanked as he moved to the tufted leather sofa against the wall. He sat down and Victor knelt, unlatching the leather straps and spring hooks that hinged the leg brace around Miles's ankle and below his knee. The brace fell open like the jaws of a toothless trap.

Victor began to massage the firm calf muscles, but Miles shook him off and rose, downing the last of his sherry.

With deliberate steps, but no limp, he strode across the room, then jerked the curtains aside. His gaze flew immediately to the window on the far side of the huge room, for she always waited there beside swagged gold drapes banded with blue.

Perhaps it was because the shadows gathered there, escaping the brightness of ornate torcheres that stood in each corner of the room. The high, Circassian-walnut ceiling was dark, as were the walls of gilded leather, and it took extra lanterns to meet Miles's need for adequate light.

Portia had not moved when the curtains opened, as if her cue had not yet come. She stood calmly at the open window, her head cocked to listen to the night sounds of horse harnesses and rustling leaves.

"Portia," he said quietly.

The serious, ebony-skinned seventeen-year-old turned to him, and he motioned her closer. Her soft, violet gown caught dips and swirls of lantern light as she gracefully swayed the hooped skirt forward.

She tipped the flounced bell sideways and maneuvered around him, swaying to a stop at the blue-curtain barrier to the dressing room.

"Go now, Father," she said quietly to Victor, her face creased in a gentle smile.

The tall black turned as if in pain, then bent to light a candle from the lantern wick. The torn, knobby remnant of his ear was presented in garish, harsh light.

When Victor closed the door to the hallway, Portia turned to Miles.

Her smile, as he expected, was gone.

ELEVEN

In half-sleep, Devon grew aware of the morning. Sunlight warmed one shoulder bared above the yoke of her night-dress. Sparrows chirped busily in the eaves above the window. She turned her back to the shaft of dawn light, and the straw tick crackled, an immediate warning that she was not in her dust-ruffled four-poster at home.

Uneasy, she slipped down off the edge of the high bed and looked around the room. Gentry was gone, along with his boots. But his gun stood propped by the bed. The door to the room was ajar. In front of the hearth, the oval tub stood like a cold bronze monument to her foolish judgment the night before. Self-conscious, she gathered the blanket around herself and cautiously walked out into the hall. Morning sounds drifted from the kitchen—the *thwomp* of a wooden spoon against a kettle, the gentle clash of crockery being gathered.

Devon padded barefoot down the hall and peeked around the doorframe. She caught the rich, oily aroma of ground coffee beans and traced the fragrance to a cast-iron coffee mill perched on the pastry table near the window. A scorched tin coffeepot sat on a cooking plate above glowing embers in the grate.

The boy Eben was eating breakfast at the rough oak table. He poured thin, bluish milk into a bowl of corn mush and dunked a wedge of bread into the paste.

Plaidy was ironing near the hearth. She picked up the flat iron from its heating brick and spat lightly against the black-ened triangular plate. The moisture bounced off with a hiss, and she quickly pressed the iron to the inseam of a light blue poplin dress.

Magda Selliger had an old cane basket of vegetables tucked under her arm and was transferring snap beans and cabbage onto the sideboard for cleaning when she spotted Devon.

"Good morning, Mrs. Morgan." Magda set her basket on the floor and wiped her hands on her apron. "Did you sleep well?"

Devon nearly blushed. "Yes, thank you," she said quietly.

"Heard you knocking around the rain barrel last night. Was his fever bad?"

Devon nodded, holding the blanket at her throat. She looked longingly at the fresh dress Plaidy had just finished pressing.

"Your silk was ruined," Magda said. "This one should fit pretty well, though." She handed Devon the garment.

"Where is—my husband?" Devon asked.

"On the porch. He was up early, writing. Found him at the desk in the parlor, using my good ivory pen." Magda arched an accusing eyebrow at Devon, as if she should have taught her husband better manners. "Said he had to post a letter to your relatives as soon as you two found a town. But I have to warn you. He wrote it on a crumpled piece of scrap paper instead of using my writing pad, so your family won't be too impressed, even if he is educated enough to write. He said you're leaving today. Is that true?"

"I would guess it depends on Gentry's health." Devon frowned and turned to go. To whom had Gentry written? And what? Could he have copied the coded letter? If so, he was acting far beyond the bounds of bodyguard and escort. It made him a courier. For whom?

"Mrs. Morgan?" Magda said hesitantly.

Devon glanced back.

The older woman cast her eyes awkwardly to the floor and cleared her throat. "Your husband also said he would be paying us for any supplies and inconveniences—in gold." She paused, as if the statement were a question.

Devon did not know whether Gentry's superiors had supplied him with gold specie for his mission, but she was sure of two things. "Gentry doesn't make idle boasts, Mrs. Selliger, and he always keeps his word."

In her room, Devon found a hairbrush and faded satin ribbon on the table. She dressed quickly in the blue poplin dress, made of the same material as the curtains. The garment, obviously Mrs. Selliger's, had hastily been modified for Devon. It was a ribbed cotton twill, unworn and pungent with a cedar closet scent. The dress fit snugly along the torso but was loose in the sleeves. Mrs. Selliger had not guessed well on the length of the hem. Devon's slim ankles showed immodestly beneath the simple, full skirt.

Her hair required many patient pulls from the hairbrush. She stroked until her arm ached, then rested her hand in her lap, her thoughts as tangled as the filaments of hair trapped in brush bristle.

The memory was shockingly vivid—her nipples straining against his fevered skin, his hands exploring with a certainty that roused a curiosity as strong as her instinct to flee.

How quickly virgin's confusion had turned to woman's longing. The feelings, and the bold freedom they represented, frightened her, perhaps even more than Gentry did.

What could they have in common—a Confederate scout reared in the shadow between two worlds, bred to fight and kill; and she, reared a gentlewoman in wealth and refinement, bred to be a parlor ornament?

Bric-a-brac for the Lords Bivens' drawing room she was not. And Gentry, she knew, was no cold-blooded killer.

Neither the lady nor the scout were what they seemed. Still, their uneasy pretense was the wrong path to an intimacy that could topple her already shaken reputation.

The American journey with her aunt had offered blessed respite from the conflagration with Roger. And it provided a means for Devon to redeem herself in the eyes of Uncle Arnaud.

She was such a poor spy, though. She had already relinquished her contraband to a man whose only proven link to the alliance was the bullet he had taken saving the life of its courier.

Truthfully, she had no wish to help a government that needed slavery to fuel the quality of its economic and social life. She had even attended abolitionist meetings in London, with the help of Damien James.

Damien had always been eager to awaken her to liberal affairs, as if he could rediscover his ideals through tutoring

hers. And he was an unstinting supporter of her talent in
art. She had illustrated *Lilah Peckingham's Guide* under the
pseudonym James D. Frederic, paying tribute both to
Damien and to her father.

Though her drawings had been hailed for their verve and
style, Devon knew her work had a provincial quaintness and
limited scope. Her spirit could sometimes soar with a touch
of the exuberant Lady Wild, but her body and mind had
been firmly sheltered in Langley Place within the walls of
Aunt Margaret's expectations.

And now?

This journey had placed too much of life within her grasp.

If only she had her sketchbook. She could have contained
the fear and hardships of the past two days on one somber
page. And there, too, on paper she could define and make
real the man whose heart held a pool of alien experience she
could never hope to understand. Which nation did he call
home, Indian or white? Or had he been orphaned, like she?

With a tense sigh, Devon pulled her hair back and secured
it with the ribbon. It was time to face him—and to mask
somehow the discomfit of having shared his kiss and his bed.

She stopped in the kitchen, and Plaidy offered her a small
tray of soft bread, shiny with a Spartan film of butter. "This
is the last of our coffee," Plaidy added as she upended the
pot into two pearl-colored mugs. "Miz Selliger was saving it
for special." Delicate feathery designs beneath the glaze
marked the heavy pottery as mocha ware, favored by Euro-
pean countryfolk such as Magda.

"I'm grateful. Could I have cream?" Devon asked, sniffing with pleasure the steam that swirled up from the thick,
heavy brew.

"Eben has some milk left over," Plaidy said. "How does
Mr. Morgan want his coffee?"

Devon was silent a moment. "He'll take it black," she
said.

She found Gentry on the narrow, weathered gray porch,
reclining on a bench swing, his legs stetched along the seat.
A patched denim shirt was buttoned down his chest. She
stooped beside him to set the tray of bread and coffee on an
upturned bucket. As she handed Gentry his cup, she stole a
glance at his face. He looked warm and weary, but the

ghostly pall of his skin was gone, and his face wore a health-ier bronze cast.

"I see you also wear a contribution from the Selliger fam-ily closet," he said, breaking the awkward silence.

She nodded and backed away from him to lean against the banister and sip her coffee.

To the side, just beyond the porch rail, the open window of the kitchen emitted the muffled scrapes and bangs of Magda's preparing the kettle for day-long simmering.

"Mrs. Selliger says we are paying in gold for what we need," Devon said quietly, eyebrows raised.

"Don't worry. We have enough." He smiled as the kitchen sounds halted. "Remember what I said on our wed-ding day?" His smile deepened, mocking her. "I promised to provide well for us, Devon, and I will."

She turned her head from his teasing glance and noted that a knife had resumed its methodic, hollow chops on a board. All in all, Magda Selliger's unseen presence was reas-suring. Devon did not relish being alone with Gentry.

"Should the dressing on your wound be changed?" she asked.

"Mrs. Selliger has done me the honor, inasmuch as my wife is a lady used to sleeping late."

Gentry carefully eased himself upright, feet to the floor. "Perhaps our visit will help Mrs. Selliger save for a cooking stove," he went on, voice raised for their listener. "It's sad that such a good cook is without one." The chopping stopped. Without warning, Magda's head poked through the bedraggled chintz.

"I'm doing just fine," she said, "so watch your imperti-nence!" She frowned. "Besides, my first range was an Ober-lin with isinglass panes, and I'm prepared never to see its like again. So don't you dare get me thinking about it!" She withdrew her reddened face.

Gentry took a sip of the strong, scalding brew while a cupboard slammed emphatically in the kitchen. "All loyal Southerners have turned in their iron to be smelted for rail-road ties or cannonballs or rams for ships' prows," he ex-plained quietly.

"Then why do you tease her?" Devon asked. The outside door to the kitchen clattered open, then shut.

"So that she knows I recognize the high price she has

paid." He turned his head to watch Magda's boxlike body
march determinedly toward the barn, then looked back at
Devon. "And so that she would realize we know she's an
eavesdropper and leave us alone."

A chill gripped Devon. She pivoted quickly and saw the
retreating figure of Magda Selliger join Eben and Plaidy outside the barn. A dust-heavy mist hung stubbornly in the
sunlit valley beyond them.

"So, Devon Picard . . . Morgan," Gentry said as he
placed his coffee cup on the tray. "You yearn to be an artist?"

He must have overheard everything she'd said to Magda
yesterday, she thought. "I am an artist. I yearn to be free of
you and this intolerable circumstance."

He rose from the swing with a slow, stiff effort. "What do
you draw?" he asked, offering her the plate of bran-flecked
bread.

"Why this sudden civilized interest in who I am?" she
asked as she warily slid a piece of bread onto the flat of her
hand.

"It's foolish for a man not to know his friends, and dangerous not to know his enemies. Besides, I confided in you
last night. Now, you must return the gesture."

"Your tongue was loosened by delirium, not by a desire to
be social." She set her cup on the weathered rail.

Gentry did not answer.

He studied her, struck by how fresh she looked after a
late, embattled night. She seemed so young when she slept,
like a child, trusting the night to be safe and comforting. He
was older, at least ten years her senior, and he had learned
to trust the darkness with an owl's cunning, stirring awake
instinctively to sweep the night with his senses. And so he
had awakened intermittently to find the woman-child's
cheek against his chest, or the bare, delicate length of her leg
touching his. Nothing about a woman's body was new to
him, yet her presence was too promising, too needy, too
satisfying, to be commonplace.

He had dozed fitfully until just before dawn, when he
found that the pain in his side blazed healthily, properly in
its place. The radiant fever sickness was gone.

He'd turned to the yellow-hair in the dim half-light. She
lay facing him, tucked on her side, fine locks of hair like a

loosened skein of silk across her neck, her gown a shifted sea of white, billowed and rumpled. One breast fell forward in overflow, eclipsing the full cup of its counterpart underneath, a bold weight that created an achingly firm crest.

He had risen from the bed, stiff with need, fleeing the impulse to transgress her sleep with an intimate touch. He had left the room with silent steps and a heartbeat that seemed to thunder in his chest.

Here, in the boundless presence of sun and earth, it was easy to subdue the wish to touch her. She had crystallized in the daylight as a shelled creature, protected. She was a groomed white woman of means, her hair tamed back to show the symmetry of her cheeks, her small ears bared like a schoolgirl's sweet surprise, a gift bred for presentation to her mirror mate, a groomed white man of means.

He saw she was growing nervous under his scrutiny. She smoothed a wisp of hair behind her ear and tried to shift past him.

He grasped the rail, forming a barrier with his arm. "We must begin to speak honestly," he said. Devon looked away. How fearful she found the opportunity to voice her thoughts —and face them.

"We are foreign to each other," he went on, "curiosities, nothing more. There is nothing in the night to be feared, nothing to regret. And nothing to repeat."

She pushed against the arm that blocked her way. "You are much too . . . direct!" The word caught in her throat. "Let me go."

"I have questions," he said.

"You grant absolution from supposed sins and then become the Grand Inquisitor?" she asked hotly. "I question your assumption of godliness in this matter, Mr. Morgan."

"A more mannerly woman would have remembered the Christian name of the man she slept with."

She swung angrily at his face, but his forearm blocked the blow. His left hand neatly grasped her wrist.

"Save your outrage for a less pretentious moment, if ever you experience one," he said. "And listen to me! For the sake of the alliance and your family, listen."

She stopped struggling.

Still holding her wrist, he pulled her closer to the bench swing. "Sit."

Devon bit back a retort and yanked her arm away, lowering herself to the creaking plank seat.

He began hesitantly. "The alliance has been betrayed." He had to bank on half-truths and hard bluffs to pry details from the yellow-hair for his report to Pinkney Dobbs. "The fact that you and your aunt were attacked shows that secrecy has been breached, and President Davis suspects the danger comes from inside the alliance."

"From whom?" she asked coldly.

He shrugged. "Whoever hired Landry's raiders to kidnap you and your aunt. The masked man who shot at you in the woods, maybe. Or someone who is privy to the code," he added, fishing carefully. "Who in Wilmington knows how to translate the symbols in the letter?"

"My uncle. And don't you dare imply he's a traitor. He's a champion for the South, a navy consultant and emissary from Napoleon the Third. He's been working for the Confederacy for two years and—"

"—he would have no reason to waylay his wife and niece," Gentry finished. "Off duty, he stays with Miles and Regina at the plantation manor, Jasmine's Reach?"

Devon nodded slowly, and Gentry could see suspicion growing in her eyes. His questions were too detailed.

"Could the danger to my family not come from Yankee infiltrators?" she asked. "Perhaps it really was Federal agents who attacked the train."

He shook his head. "As far as we can tell, Lincoln's people don't know much, only that there's a Confederate plan afoot to break the blockade. But even if they knew about you and your aunt, the Federals wouldn't be stupid enough to use Southern mercenaries to steal a Southern war plan."

"Who would they have used?"

He paused, meeting her eyes. "Probably a single agent."

"One who would follow us, gain our trust, and take the messages?" she asked quietly.

He was silent a moment. "You and I have already crossed that bridge. If I were a Federal agent, I would be gone. I have the letters."

"You are wounded. Or had you forgotten?"

Her tone incited a faster throbbing in his temple than in his side. "No, I have not," he said, his hand abruptly grasping the rusty chain that supported the swing. "Let me help you distinguish between the motives of a loyal patriot and a Federal spy." His voice grew harsh. "A spy would woo, would pose gentlemanly compliments until you rose giddy to the bait, and then he would play false on your feelings to get what he wanted. Perhaps that's what you'd prefer. But a Confederate treats a compatriot more honorably, with honesty and—"

"—unbearable frankness," she interrupted. "Well, let me respond in kind. I am not your compatriot. I am trying to fulfill an obligation to my family, and so far, I haven't done a very good job. And as to how a man treats a woman, I think that has more to do with his personal kindness than his allegiance to country. You can't excuse your behavior last night as a patriotic gesture."

She tried to rise, but he stopped her with a hand on her shoulder.

"Wait."

She sat still, the nerve-bright stillness of a woman waiting for assault or for release.

His hand opened, and his thumb slid inward to encompass her throat, a hold that was gentle and lolling and a mistake. It was a mistake to touch her.

Yet Gentry found it hard to withdraw his hand. Logic demanded that he use her, for his pact with Dobbs and his pact with the past. When he arrived at Jasmine's Reach, business would take precedence over wordplay and dalliance with a curious virgin. Serious business.

But here and now, her flesh, her secrets, and her wit lifted the bitter weight of revenge from his shoulders. For that respite he was thankful—and angry. He backed away from her.

"I'm afraid I lack good manners to question a lady gracefully," he said quietly.

" 'Defect in manners is usually the defect in fine perceptions.' " She spoke haltingly, quoting Emerson, as she hurried to a space of safety behind the swing.

"Actually, I perceive quite well. You're very agitated. Didn't Emerson say a lady must be serene? 'Coolness and absence of heat and haste indicate fine qualities.' Perhaps you, too, have a defect in manner." He smiled. " 'Every natural function can be dignified by deliberation and privacy.' "

She looked away. "Actually, I much prefer his treatise on politics. Are you familiar with his views on the equal rights of man?"

He nodded. " 'A man has the right to be employed, to be trusted, to be loved, to be revered.' "

She was silent.

"The teaching is not so different from that of my people," he said, and moved a step closer. "You must realize your family is entangled with mine, in ways you must help me understand. If you do not, your uncle may not survive to play his part in the battle of the blockade."

"What in God's name are you saying?"

"That the masked man who tried to keep your uncle from receiving the alliance letters will have an alternate plan when his hired murderers don't return with my scalp and your messages. Your uncle may be killed."

"You're speculating," she said.

He paused, waiting for her worry to mount and muddy the logic of her thoughts. "Think. Who besides your aunt and uncle knew your travel schedule?"

"Perce, my mother's maid. The earl, Lord Grayshire—" She stopped abruptly, uneasy.

Gentry waited.

"The executive committee of the alliance knew, of course," she continued cautiously. "And Miles's family, possibly."

"Miles is the only other alliance contact in Wilmington?" Gentry asked.

"The only other one my aunt is aware of. Are you accusing him?"

Gentry avoided the question to raise her suspicion. "Remember the short note, the warning about the seventh monkey fist? That may have been more important to the traitor than the coded letter. Who wrote the warning to your uncle?"

"I don't know."

"There are times you don't lie very well."

"You're perilously close to depleting my meager store of facts about the alliance." She abruptly turned away.

He made no move to stop her as she walked to the door. "Soldiers are on their way. See the haze in the valley?" he asked.

She gave him a puzzled look.

"It's been a dry summer, but it takes more than a division or two to raise a cloud like that." He stepped down into the yard. "Caissons. Supply wagons." He watched the bend of the scrub grass in the yard and raised his hand to the wind. "Wind from the northwest. It's blowing dust ahead."

"Are they Confederate or Federal?" she asked.

"Who knows until they get here? They could be reinforcements for Sherman's campaign in Georgia. Could be part of Hill's corps, Confederates who were defending Weldon Railroad south of Petersburg about the time Landry stopped your train."

"What will we do if they're Federals?" she asked.

What would he do if they were Confederates? he wondered. They would question his unauthorized leave after an escape from prison. He hoped the Confederate transit papers Dobbs's office had prepared had an up-to-date CO's name forged on them.

"Answer my question," she said. "What if we're captured by Federals?"

"In that case, I'd give the letters back to you. They'll be safer under your skirts, for a while."

"And you?"

"I'd go back to prison, until I was hanged."

"And what would happen to the other letter?"

"What letter?"

"The alliance letter you copied. Mrs. Selliger said you were writing this morning."

"It was a report to President Davis."

She was quiet a moment. "There are times you don't lie very well."

He smiled. "Sometimes I don't lie."

Devon whirled to leave, then stopped. She walked over to the tray she had brought from the kitchen and picked it up.

"Nice of your ladyship to remember," he said.

"Quite low of you to point it out," she said regally, and disappeared into the house.

TWELVE

In the kitchen Devon set the cups and plate in the sink. The pump handle gave a great iron squawk as she wrenched down hard, but no water trickled out for her as it had for Magda that morning.

She heard Gentry close the door to the front porch.

Devon pumped hard again and touched her finger to the mottled iron tongue of the pump. It was dry.

"You need to prime it when the well's low," Gentry said. She turned. He stood in the doorway. "Would help if you pumped instead of slamming it like a whiskey press."

He stepped toward her. With his presence the farmhouse kitchen took on a curious intimacy. It was a room of things shared—work, food, talk, hopes.

"We have to pack and leave, real soon," he said. "Can't let the Army find us staying here, pretending to be married." He was beside her now, and Devon held herself very still.

He reached around her to get a small cup of water sitting in the window above the sink.

"Here," he said, handing her the cup. "Pour it into the top."

The water trickled down, a forlorn, hollow sound deep in the funnel-shaped top of the pump.

Gentry gave the handle short, swift tugs. The water gushed upward and out the tongue.

Devon stepped back away from the splash. She felt cool droplets touch her face—and Gentry's hands encircle her waist.

He turned her slowly to face him.

She did not struggle. She waited. And she watched his expression become tense with concern.

"You'll soon be safe," he said, almost to himself. He pulled her closer.

She knew he would stop if she resisted, yet she felt no wish to be farther from him, no desire to quiet the readiness that tautened her body, no need to stop the soft parting of her lips as his drew near.

His lips moved against hers with a sucking gentleness that lulled her mouth pliant and open. Then a sudden sweep of his tongue gave her a taste of deeper hunger. He tore his mouth away and pressed his lips to her hair, nuzzling gently.

He trailed kisses from her ear to the soft crease of her neck. And he stopped there, waiting.

She felt his warm breath. She leaned her cheek to his, unwilling to leave, afraid to continue.

He let his arms slide free of their embrace.

"You would be damned, and I the cause," he said.

She pulled away and looked down, gathering her skirts. Then she walked slowly to the door.

"Perhaps, just perhaps, I am already damned," she said.

"Then I offer a prayer. Run fast, run far, Daloni-ka. And pray God you travel far from me in spirit, or neither of us is safe."

In Washington, the gala was only an hour old and already the tea roses in the table garlands were bowing to the heat in the crowded room.

The Petit Danse was the smaller of the Willard Hotel's two ballrooms and had hurriedly been readied by a miffed manager and his white-uniformed staff. President Lincoln's supporters had initially booked the grand ballroom on the second floor, but as the gala date drew near, it was apparent that many influential Republicans would not be attending to hail Lincoln's try to win election for a second term. He'd been nominated as the party's presidential candidate just two months before at the convention in Baltimore. But it was a hard won fight and Lincoln's popularity was at a low point. Thus, the smaller salon was engaged, so that the room would look full instead of half-empty.

Pinkney Dobbs graciously took his leave from a gaggle of businessmen and moseyed over to a fern whose giant fronds trailed halfway down a tall pedestal. Glossy, hump-backed frogs on a ring of lily pads danced around the belly of the hard-paste porcelain pot. Dobbs turned as if to examine the intriguing amphibians, then quickly yanked his ill-fitting vest lower to cover the firm paunch protruding above his waistband. Jaw jutting forward, he swung his head left and right, trying to free a wattle of skin from the prison of his high, starched collar. Dobbs was a field man, and he eschewed formal evening dress almost as much as he avoided the types who wore it.

He looked longingly across the room at the balcony nearest him, but the crowd vying for fresh air was daunting. Round hoop skirts compressed to ovals as elegant ladies in ruffled gowns shared footage inside the towering French doors, their jeweled fans fluttering frantically like the iridescent wings of trapped insects.

The sky-blue coffered ceiling reigned high above the crowd, its deep soffits accented with elaborate rosewood trim. At each end of the room, a gas chandelier suspended three tiers of painted white globes, and Dobbs felt as if the glare was deliberately seeking out his thinly covered scalp. His young tease of a mistress, Lilly Frith, told him he was too sensitive. "My black mammy always told me, 'The more hair a man lose, the more shine you gonna take to 'im,' " Lilly had drawled last night.

It bothered him, how her voice echoed in his ear, even when she was absent. He had left her, pouting and ranting, in her frilly apartment, because he could not risk bringing her to the gala. He'd told her point-blank that her painted face and unladylike reputation would incite an apoplectic rage in the President's wife.

Lilly had grown quiet. "I can wash my face, Pink," she'd said with that readiness to please that made Dobbs feel ancient and fatherlike. But he was beginning to question the saucy simplicity of Lilly's reactions. She was a Confederate informer, inexperienced but willing to give her all to get tidbits for the Confederate secret service. Dobbs himself had no compunction about demanding her all, and giving her little in the way of reward. He had a lifelong habit of self-protection, so it was easy to be careful, ridding himself of papers, keys, and telegrams before he visited Lilly. His own boarding room was carefully bereft of personal items other than clothes. He justified his relationship with the beautiful Southerner because she was a valuable conduit. He regularly funneled baited or outdated information to the Confederates through Lilly. No matter how expert his handling, though, Dobbs knew better than to allow the charming spy social access to the government's high and mighty.

Lincoln's most staunch supporters had turned out this night. Cabinet members rubbed long, starched coattails with monied merchant Republicans from the Eastern Seaboard. Dobbs saw a Connecticut banker and a Senator arguing in a far corner, each drawing a kerchief from his shiny broadcloth jacket to catch the perspiration dripping down salt-and-pepper sideburns. The President's renomination was literally a hotly debated topic.

" 'Scuse me." A stiff-shouldered lady in dark blue angled past the fern Dobbs was using as an observation point.

It was the President's wife. Dobbs sucked in his stomach and smiled. " 'Evening, Mrs. Lincoln."

"Mr. Dobbs." Mrs. Lincoln nodded in acknowledgment, interrupting the nervous twisting of her fringed fan. She stopped before him, the wide bowl of her crinoline skirt swinging like a muted bell.

Dobbs cleared his throat in the awkward silence. "Warm tonight," he said to the flushed First Lady, who appeared to be steaming in her heavy, taffeta-trimmed gown.

"Not as warm as it is for my husband, is it, Mr. Dobbs?" she said, stone faced, and took her leave.

Though Mary Todd Lincoln was renowned in Washington for her spending habits, unstable temperament, and deranged outbursts, she could send words flying straight as arrows sometimes. It was indeed a hellish night for the President.

A black servant walked by with a drink tray, and Dobbs reached quickly for a glass, even though he knew, with Mrs. Lincoln's blessing, the fruit punch would be as potent as a shot of cider. At least it was wet, he thought.

"Think that punch could use a quick right jab?" Secretary of State Seward asked over Dobbs's shoulder.

"Be much obliged." Dobbs turned, not surprised at the secretary's presence. He had kept Seward in sight for the last half hour.

Seward sedately pulled a flat gold flask from a hip pocket and poured a healthy slug of whiskey into Dobbs's glass.

"To the end of the war." Dobbs raised his glass in a sober salute and took a grateful sip.

"Pray soon," Seward added grimly. "But we've been praying that for three years." He took a quick swig straight from the flask and grimaced.

"If these are the President's friends, I'd hate to meet his enemies," Dobbs said. "These people look as loyal as fleas at a dogfight."

Seward shrugged. "They're just nervous. So am I. I'm nervous about this conspiracy the ambassador discovered. That'd really be a gut-twister, Pink. Foreign intervention could break the blockade. Resupply the Rebs. Helluva possibility. The President agreed to see you tonight. Room one twelve in an hour. He's aching for some good news from that Cherokee of yours."

Hell, join the club, Dobbs swore silently. He downed the fruited whiskey and waited for the burning tide to bubble up to the back of his throat and remind him he shouldn't be drinking.

Room 112 was one of the Willard's cheapest cubicles. It was nicely furnished, but looked out over a dank, unlit alleyway. Dobbs sat waiting in the dark to the right of the open window, his cigar tip glowing red. All he could hear was a tomcat's high-pitched yowl as he protected the choice strip of real estate below.

Footsteps outside. Pine planks groaned beneath the fringed hall-runner outside the door.

The door opened. "Pink?" The voice held an honest, Midwestern twang, unmistakably Lincoln's.

"Here, Mr. President."

"Can smell you better'n I can see you," the President said."Put that stogie to good use and light the lamp."

"Move back away from the window." Dobbs garbled the words as he puffed up a firestarter for the kerosene wick. "Where's Taylor?"

"He's holding my drink while I heed the call of nature," Lincoln said. The lamp glow rose to highlight the tall, gangly figure of the President as he began to unbutton his evening coat.

"Some bodyguard, that Taylor." Dobbs spat a fleck of

tobacco off his tongue and made a note to fire the boy the next day.

"Easy on him, Pink. I like it when you pick one naive enough to let me break away once in a while." Lincoln hung his jacket over a straight-backed chair. "Got my eye on that comfortable armchair over there and don't want to crimp these bodacious coattails. People got enough ammunition tonight. Don't need to give them something socially criminal to add to the list." He folded his length into a stuffed rococo chair in the corner. "Can we get down to business? Heard anything from that agent of yours?"

"No, sir."

"Expect to anytime soon?" Lincoln asked quietly.

"Yes, sir." Dobbs felt his innards cramp.

"You think you can trust him?"

"Believe so, sir."

"Pink, for some reason the confidence ringing in your answers isn't sufficient to lighten my heart."

"I expect you're looking for a little relief right now."

"Relief!" Lincoln shouted, then lowered his voice when Dobbs frowned at him. "I'd feel better with a two-ton rock on my chest!" He slapped his palm flat against his heart.

"I know the situation, sir."

"Do you, Pink? Let me lay it out in black and white, like I see it every day, in hell-raising letters scattered all over my desk. Grant's in for a long siege of Petersburg and Richmond. He's going to lose a lot of men. I'm looking at another fall and winter of death rosters and war bills. You realize the dollar's only worth thirty-nine cents now? The bankers are chewing my tail over that. Shippers are asking where the hell's the Navy when one Confederate cruiser takes thirty-one merchant ships in three weeks. A passel of savvy politicians tells me point-blank I can't get reelected in November, and you know something, Pink? I'm beginning to believe them. Even my Cabinet members are looking like pallbearers to me."

The President paused, then thumped his fist on the plump arm of the dusty horsehair chair. "But I won't run from a fight! I'll wrestle long as I can, with all the deals that I can. 'Cause if the Democrats got McClellan in, he'd make peace at any price. We'd be the Divided States of America, a half-slave, half-ass democracy."

Dobbs said nothing, but bit harder into his cigar.

The President's voice slowed to a quiet, even pitch. "But there's a catch, Pink. There's no reason for me to spend all this energy scrappin' for reelection if the Confederates have a half-even chance of breaking the blockade." Lincoln paused. "I rattled my war club at England and France, and they didn't recognize the Confederate republic as a sovereign nation. But you and I know there's rampant sympathy for the Rebs in Europe. All we got is a whiff of this alliance, and it sure smells like a bigger animal than I can deal with before the election. So I've got a real bad case of the jitters, 'cause a lot's riding on a Rebel soldier you're not sure about."

"What do you want me to say?" Dobbs flicked the fat cigar out the window. "Gentry Morgan's a blasted one-man army and he's going to break up the conspiracy with a pinto pony and a tomahawk?"

"Not asking for tall tales, Pink. Just a little hope," the President said, expelling a sigh that indicated he expected none.

Dobbs was silent for a moment. He stood up, paced four steps toward the President and plunged his hands in his pockets. "It's not all on Gentry's shoulders. Our consul in Liverpool is looking for signs of shipbuilding activity, and I've got two men headed for Bermuda, one already in Nassau, and I'm running a double at Fort Fisher—"

The President interrupted with a shake of his head. "I read your reports. I want to know more about Gentry Morgan."

"You want a long or a short story?"

"I want to know why you think you can trust him."

Dobbs pursed his lips. " 'Cause what we want him to do jibes with his one goal in life."

"Namely?"

"To find his wife's killer and bring him to justice in a white man's court. I promised him I'd reopen the investigation of his wife's murder."

"That's all he wanted?"

"It's quite a lot. To get a white man convicted of killing an Indian squaw? Lots easier said than done. Second part of what he wanted was simple. I promised to send some medical supplies out to a Sioux camp where Gentry's in-laws live. Smallpox got'em dying like flies."

"But where's his allegiance? Why's he willing to be caught and shot as a Confederate traitor?"

"Confederate and Union labels are paper allegiances. They don't mean much to people like Gentry. Personal loyalty is another matter, and Gentry rode for Jeb Stuart because he respected the man."

"One good general's the only reason he enlisted with the slave states?"

Dobbs shook his head. "His wife was killed when some fanatic abolitionists raided a slave-holding town. This was back in '53 in Missouri. Crazy times. Burnin', shootin', and lootin'. I was marshal there. Death of a Sioux squaw just got lost in the mess." Dobbs's voice deepened. "I had my hands so goddamned full."

Dobbs walked to a chair and sat down, facing the window. "Tell you the truth, I didn't want to think about that murder. See, someone cut her open." He cleared his throat again, uncomfortable. "She was about six months gone. People said the baby was . . . Well, I never went to see. Couldn't. But Gentry saw. And he screamed out this war cry that scared the bejesus outta people. Just raised his face to heaven and yelled at God, they said. He yelled and yelled until his lungs were raw, then the wolves started in. Christ, what a night ... ." His voice trailed off.

The President blew out a breath and gave a worried smile. "Eleven years is a long time to be hearin' wolves, Pink."

Dobbs nodded. "The other reason Gentry signed up Reb was to rile his dad. Ever hear of Teague Morgan?"

"Yes. Big abolitionist farmer and cattle breeder in Missouri, Union to the core. This Reb's his son?"

"And heir. Gentry and his dad haven't seen eye to eye since Teague took the boy from a Cherokee resettlement camp."

"If this story gets any longer, I'm going to go get my drink from Taylor and come back and light the fire," the President said, raising an eyebrow. "I haven't heard a thing that makes me want to trust him, Pink. He sounds mixed up as hell."

"No. Like a fox. Had one of my detectives go to St. Louis last week, pretending to be a newspaper writer, to do some preliminary sniffing out. He interviewed some of Teague Morgan's farmhands and looked at back issues of the *Westport Border Star*. Found a discrepancy in the family stories about the day Kai-ee-nah—Gentry's wife—was killed." Dobbs paused. "Motive's pretty solid, but evidence will be scarce as hell."

"I'm afraid to ask who's your suspect."

"Brant," Dobbs said softly. "Colonel Miles Brant."

There was silence. Finally the President spoke. "Do you think Morgan will kill Brant before he gets the information we need?"

"He might, but I don't think so. Gentry wants a public spectacle, a proper trial. And I'm guessing he'll want to strike back at Brant by scuttling the alliance network, assuming the alliance is something dear to Colonel Brant. I met the glorious colonel once. A real charmer. So disarming I was patting my watch pocket when he left. He's in ordnance in Wilmington."

"Wilmington's the Confederates' last port," Lincoln said. "Farragut's sewing up Mobile Bay right now. The writing's on the wall. You'd think the Confederacy would give up."

Dobbs stood and retrieved the President's coat. "Would you, sir?"

Lincoln shrugged the tight broadcloth jacket over his shoulders. "Hell, no. And that's the reason the Rebs have lasted so long. Jefferson Davis is as bullheaded as I am."

Dobbs stopped the President as he headed for the door. "I just want you to know, sir. Gentry will do his job. He gave me his word, man to man. He swore."

The President gave an incredulous laugh. "On what?"

Dobbs looked down and used his toe to smooth a wrinkle in the carpet. "We didn't use a Bible, sir. I had his sack of medicine charms. Indians wear them like amulets, for protection. He didn't have much. A buffalo hoof with little beads in it, some charm stones, a little lock of hair."

"So he enlisted in the Union Army by swearing on a buffalo foot? Lord, you're in a savage business, Pink. I got no more room in my worry box for this one. I'll have to trust your judgment—and your agent." The President opened the lacquered walnut door.

"Sir?" Dobbs fished in his vest pocket for another cigar.

"You'd best say your good-byes to Taylor tonight. He won't be posted as your guard tomorrow."

The President smiled. "One little slipup and he's gone? Would you be as harsh with this scout of yours?"

Dobbs didn't smile. He looked down at the cheap Virginia cigar he rolled between thumb and forefinger. "Gentry's in a little bit different situation. One slipup and he's dead." Dobbs bit the tip off his cigar and spat it into his palm.

The President turned to go.

"Savage business. Sir," Dobbs said.

THIRTEEN

From the top of the slope, the young Confederate could see the road to Jasmine's Reach. A stray breeze rippled the wildflowers in the field below; tiers of scarlet-purple bells jostled on slender stalks of foxglove. The soldier urged his horse cautiously down the knoll and hailed the bearded infantryman standing guard at the gate.

"Think they'll spare us a meal or two?" the boy shouted as he passed the sentry.

"They got plenty of everything at the big house." The guard worked his lower lip to resettle the wad of snuff in the crease below his teeth. "Ole 'Contraband' Brant keeps his nest feathered better'n anybody's."

From her upstairs window Regina Morgan Brant noticed the lone soldier riding up to the portico. It wasn't Miles. Uninterested, she returned to the vanity mirror so Tulie could work on the half-finished plaits. Regina prided herself on the sleek, classic braids Tulie pinned in an elegant figure eight at the back of her head.

Finally, Regina rose from the stool and Tulie straightened the drape of her mistress's yellow-print gown over tiered hoops of crinoline.

"Sure is a pretty new dress, Miz Brant," Tulie said. "Bright like sunshine."

Regina smiled at the compliment as she glanced back at the tall antique mirror that hung beside her chifforobe. It was Regina's ritual, this over-the-shoulder look of personal inspection before she left her room.

The mirror, her mother's, had always been Regina's friend, reflecting over the years a gracefully maturing woman, handsome and strong. She had never allowed sunlight to darken and toughen her fashionably white complexion. At thirty-five, she had one distinctive streak of gray in her chestnut hair, a tidy badge of matronhood that she felt appropriate.

The mirror had miraculously survived her family's trek westward in a wagon train twenty years ago—as well as the Indian raid that had left Regina an orphan.

She had refused to give her parents' clothes to the surviving members of the train. Instead, she had swaddled the precious mirror in her father's long johns and her mother's underskirts, and she'd traveled southeast to Missouri. There at the rambling, one-thousand-acre farm of her father's old friend Teague Morgan, she had settled in a room all her own, in a house with eight fireplaces, and carefully unwrapped the large, oak-framed mirror. It, like Regina, hadn't broken. Now she lived with genteel folk in Carolina, in a house with fewer fireplaces but more rooms. Many were empty, though. The war had transformed the halls of Jasmine's Reach into eerily lifeless corridors. Miles had lost his family. As far as Regina could learn, he had only one young cousin left—and he was battling typhus in a Mississippi infirmary.

That made Regina's job all the more important. She had to make sure her daughter, Grace, had a superior upbringing, even with the socially stultifying impediments of war. Nine-year-old Grace would someday inherit Jasmine's Reach.

"Tulie, mind those woolens in the storage trunk! They're going to need airing out," Regina called as she maneuvered her skirt through the narrow anteroom of her bedchamber. "Autumn's just around the corner, thank goodness." Her hand closed on the embroidered handkerchief clipped to the cuff of her gown, and she gently blotted the beads of perspiration above her lip as she descended the stairs.

On the landing Regina stopped. Evaleen, the housekeeper, was admitting a young soldier through the front door.

"What is it, Evaleen?" Regina asked.

Evaleen backed away so the soldier could speak directly to her mistress.

"Sergeant Morgan told me to ride ahead and tell y'all that Miss Devon Picard is safe and on her way here."

A little chill took hold in Regina's chest, below her diaphragm, shortening her breath. "Thank the Lord Miz Devon is all right," she said. "Evaleen, go to the sickroom and tell Miz Margaret and Admiral Picard the news. They'll be so relieved. You said a Sergeant Morgan sent you?"

"Yes'm. Jeb Stuart's best scout," the boy said. "He's ridin' with us just temporary, though. Your brother has leave to visit y'all."

The cold rose higher, a solid feeling so heavy she bent forward. She placed a steadying hand on the banister. Gentry, she thought. Gentry. Here. She felt hardened to the spot, like a snail that had wept its glue and disappeared in a shell.

Evaleen walked quietly up the steps, on the way to the upstairs guest room where Admiral Picard lay ill. She paused on the landing beside her mistress.

"Well, hurry on up, Evaleen," Regina said sharply. "Didn't you hear the boy? We got 'family' coming."

The small contingent passed through the entrance gate and wound slowly around the bend of the manor road. Gentry rode on ahead of the wagon.

Even though his sergeant's chevrons were on the sleeves of a coat lost on his way to the Delaware prison, Gentry was still ranking officer in the ragged escort detail. Three foot-soldiers from Henderson's Fifth had been assigned to accompany him and Devon, in hopes the soldiers could take supplies of food and clothing back to their regiment. The infantrymen were young, but each had a tense, seasoned squint around his eyes, creases that came from straining to draw a bead on the battleline of an army that had bigger and better guns pointing back.

It had been easier than he'd thought to step back into the role of army scout, even though his commander and protector was dead. Not even when thinking of Jeb did Gentry feel like a traitor in his mission to infiltrate the alliance.

The Federals were not his enemy. Kai-ee-nah's killer was.

A sprawling two-story house came into view, a red-brick mansion with Gothic dormer windows and two high red chimneys at either end of a lightly pitched roof. A white-columned portico jutted over a bricked drive.

Regina's house. He had never seen the place, and he knew he was not welcome.

He chanced a glance back at Devon riding in the wagon. She looked worried, as if Jasmine's Reach would hold personal demons for her too. Doubtless he was one of them. Before bounding ahead, he tugged his hat brim in polite farewell.

Devon avoided Gentry's eyes and gave a nod, as defensive and distant as on the day they had been found watering their horses in a stream miles from the Selliger farm. During the four nights around the campfire with their escorts from Henderson's Fifth, she had perfected a careful reserve.

Devon held tightly as the buckboard rounded a turn. Looking ahead, she saw that Gentry had already dismounted under the portico of the manor house. He was addressing a dark-haired woman. The woman stood above him on the steps of the house, crinoline supporting the primrose-yellow scallops in her skirt. Gentry stood wtih a casual slouch to his shoulders. His hat lay lanyard-length down his back rather than respectfully in his hands.

A movement caught Devon's eye, and she saw a tiny bird of a woman tiptoe down the manor steps, holding her lorgnette aloft like a tightrope walker's umbrella.

Aunt Margaret! Devon nearly cried out her name. Aunt Margaret was safe. Devon wanted to scream her relief.

She watched as Margaret rushed to confront Gentry. The tiny woman boldly grasped his hand. As the rattling of the buckboard sounded closer, Margaret perched the long-handled spectacles atop her nose.

Devon waved.

Margaret's right hand rose to her throat as if catching her breath. She remained in the middle of the road waiting, until the wagon was nearly upon her "Devon!" she cried as the wagon rattled to a halt with echoes resounding under the portico roof.

"Devon! Thank the Lord you're here!" Margaret clasped Devon's hands in hers with a fearful intensity. "Come now! Quick." She propelled her niece up the stairs, urging her toward the door.

"Aunt Margaret! Perhaps I should meet—"

"Of course, forgive me," Margaret said with a flush of anxiety in her cheeks. "This is our very gracious hostess,

Regina. Regina, I'd like to present Devon, who is more daughter than niece to me and who is actually quite stunning when she is not untidied by importunate circumstances. Now please come, Devon. Arnaud is—" Margaret's voice cracked. "My precious Arnaud is . . ." She faltered.

"Your uncle is very ill," Regina interjected.

Regina's round face registered the proper sympathy, but something in the calm of her voice made Devon uneasy. Was this what Gentry had suspected? Had her uncle already been assaulted by an alliance traitor?

She put her arm around Margaret's shoulders. "We will see him immediately," she said.

"I'm sure you would rather compose yourself first," Regina said, her hazel eyes roaming the wrinkles and soiled patches in Devon's ill-fitting gown.

"Perhaps I would," Devon said. "But it is much more important that I attend my uncle. I'm sure you understand."

"Of course," Regina murmured, her tone cognizant of the priority Devon placed on proper deportment.

Still hugging Margaret's trembling shoulders, Devon turned to face Gentry. He seemed more a stranger to her at that moment than when they first met. His long hair hung to the neck of his shirt, sleek and straight, emphasizing his Indian heritage. He was guarded, a gaunt tension in his face and dark shadows of fatigue under his eyes.

Her own face must reflect the same hunger and exhaustion of the week-long odyssey, she thought.

He pulled his horse's reins from a servant's hand and prepared to mount.

"Mr. Morgan," Devon said quickly, stiffly. Regina's scrutiny was unnerving. "Thank you. I am very grateful to be reunited with my family."

"My goodness, yes, Mr. Morgan," Margaret said. "We shall always be in your debt, Arnaud and I. Always."

Gentry gave a small smile and exaggerated bow. "Duty incurs no debt," he said.

"Spoken like a gentleman." Margaret sniffed into her handkerchief. "So like my Arnaud . . ."

Hardly masking incredulity, Regina pressed her lips into a thin line.

Gentry mounted.

"We will have the pleasure of my brother's company for

only a brief while," Regina said coolly. "Gentry must return to the field very soon, is that not so?"

"I have my orders," he said, as if a bargain had been struck. "I will see the men bivouacked." His horse whinnied at he wrenched the reins hard to the right.

Regina watched him ride out of sight.

Quickly, Devon urged Margaret forward toward the open door, before the frigid chasm yawning between brother and sister spread its chill to all on the periphery.

Devon followed her aunt up the wide staircase. "Is Perce well?" she asked, surprised that the elderly maid was not there to greet her.

Margaret stopped. "Mrs. Perce has gone to her reward," she said quickly, as if it were a litany she had memorized.

"Perce? Gone?" Her aunt's lifelong maid, her long-suffering companion. "The bandits? Did they—?"

Margaret took slow steps upward as she spoke, her breath growing markedly short. "We had to spend a night in the wild. Then we walked a great distance to find shelter. Mrs. Perce took a spell of pleurisy that night. She worsened in Raleigh and she died there."

She died there? It could not have been so simple, Aunt Margaret, Devon thought, her eyes brimming. Death was not so simple. Did you comfort her? Did you cry for her? Did you cry for yourself, severed from your one loving link to home in this strange land? Dear Perce.

And poor Aunt Margaret. Two misfortunes to burden a grim heart and delicate mind—Arnaud's illness and Perce's death.

Margaret was on the landing, looking down at her. "I suppose it couldn't be helped," she said softly.

"You mean Perce?"

"That dress," Margaret said, her face full of sorrow. "The skirt is woefully short."

God's breath, a bath. A hot bath.

Devon could barely contain her agitation. She fidgeted in her spoon-backed chair as two black women made repeated trips carrying full wooden buckets. Another woman entered bearing two tin buckets with steam obscuring the bails.

Devon leaned back in her chair, exhausted. She longed to stretch out on the high four-poster bed with its white mousseline spread and dainty powder-blue dust ruffle. But she was too grimy to think of approaching it—yet.

Her skin had not itched nor her corset chafed so maddeningly during the whole trip as it did while she sat listening to the silky slosh of water being poured.

Finally, the servants left and did not return. A statuesque black woman in a plain white day dress and bibbed apron entered with toweling, soap, and clothes.

Unlike the other slaves who bustled efficiently or moved silent as shadows, this young woman had a haunting grace and self-absorbed poise. She was beautiful with a long oval face. The vertical plane was balanced by a strong slash of brow, a sensuous ridge of full lips, and cheekbones that rose broad and proud.

She had velvet black skin, her heritage uncompromised. And she maneuvered the room with a secret knowledge apparent to artists: Black is the color that eclipses light, not the color that lacks it.

"I am Portia," the slave said.

Devon stood.

Portia slipped buttons from their loops, then pulled the blue twill dress over Devon's head. Next went the flounced petticoat, then the cotton one underneath. Portia began to unhook the hip-length corset, and as each bone stay loosened its hold beneath her bust, Devon felt her physical weariness lighten.

She sat, and Portia unbuttoned her dirt-streaked shoes. Up again, and Devon's knee-length drawers slipped to the floor. Sitting once more, her garters and stockings were pulled away. Finally, Devon was free except for a knee-length cotton chemise. The garment was simple and loose, with a low-slung neck that barely hid the light pink nipples of her breasts. Devon impatiently pushed its straps down over her shoulders, stepped out, and eased cautiously into the warm tub.

She slid down until only her neck and knees were above the water and sighed loudly, a groaning plea for relief that seemed to resound in the metal enclave of the tub. "I never want to move," she murmured as she felt her joints and muscles grow lax in the soothing warmth.

"But I must wash your hair now, so that it will dry by dinnertime," Portia said.

Portia spoke more grammatically than other slaves, Devon mused, with long-drawn vowels and an articulate cadence. She was educated. Was she favored by her mistress or simply by circumstance?

"Must I go to dinner?" Devon asked. "All I'd like is bread and butter sent up to my room. Then I'll visit my uncle again. Would that be acceptable?" She looked at Portia.

"I am not the judge of etiquette in this house." Portia smiled stiffly as she ladled warm water atop Devon's long blond hair.

"Mmmm, that's wonderful," Devon said as Portia's fingers massaged a solution of citrus and soap into her scalp. "Can't you tell me anything about Jasmine's Reach? I'm not at all familiar with the history of the house, or of the Brants, for that matter."

Portia did not move, but Devon sensed her drawing back, taking social trust with her. The ladle continued its rhythmic dip and pour. Portia did not answer.

"Was it such an impertinent question?" Devon asked with an apologetic shake of her head.

"I understand. You are curious," Portia said. "But in this house we can be punished for talking. I do not gossip."

Lemon-scented lather rinsed across Devon's shoulders, fresh and clean, and Devon settled into a safe silence, like Portia's. She would not coax Portia to talk about the people and policies of Jasmine's Reach. This house would succor its secrets like all ancestral manors.

In the corridors of Jasmine's Reach, dusty damask swagged below iron-bracketed lanterns, and Devon had caught a scent that stirred childhood fears. A whiff of crusted, hidden decay, the stale foment of a house that cocooned its secrets in the mustiness of halls, where the words and spent breath of generations collected in common passages.

She had encountered that dank stillness long ago in the dim-lit hallways of Langley Place, when she and her sister, Bertrice, had arrived as orphans. Uncle Arnaud had followed the penny-pinching preachings of his forefathers. Eschewing security for thrift, he rigidly rationed the kerosene whenever he was home from sea assignments, walking the halls like a general inspector, the wood floors creaking obei-

sance to his weight and pecuniary indignation. Thus, the
hallways held pockets of blackness that swallowed the form
of a person and expelled a ghostly materialization a few
steps later. The sight had often petrified Devon as a child,
and she had found herself driven to scrupulously work
shadow and shading in her drawings, taking command of
the dark.

In truth, she had no control of the shadows. Her uncle lay
ensnared in them now, in a high-ceilinged bedchamber that
reeked of the sour outpour of his stomach, the bloody refuse
in the chamber pot, and the acrid ash of his Spanish cigarillos.

Even though his illness would allow barely a crust of
bread to rest in his stomach, Arnaud Picard consumed the
slim, tobacco-wrapped cigarettes with fierce gusto. It had
been his habit since a boyhood sojourn in the Pyrenees, and
Margaret had disapproved vehemently throughout thirty-
seven years of marriage and Arnaud's honored military career.

"Your hair is done." Portia's rich voice interrupted Devon's reverie.

She crooked her neck down as Portia pinned the water-
darkened mass high on her head. Then Devon sank languidly into the water, relaxing her back into the welcoming
curve of the tub.

As Portia sponged her arms and neck, Devon returned
her thoughts to the sickroom at the far end of the hall, and
her visit with her uncle.

When she and Aunt Margaret had entered the room, her
uncle Arnaud was propped on a mound of pillows. His chin
had imperiously raised as Devon approached.

He was still angered by the scandal with Roger, she'd
thought, still angered that he'd been forced to raise the
daughters of a ne'er-do-well brother instead of fine sons of
his own.

But Arnaud's mouth had curved slightly in a small gri-
mace of greeting, and Devon sensed that her uncle's hard
gaze stemmed from his physical condition, not his moral
judgment of her.

Even without the ravage of illness, she could see that age
had called with a vengeance on her robust uncle. His thinning hair was wiry and gray. The wrinkled flesh of his

cheeks sagged off the edge of his jaw with a pasty softness. Sharp, pinched grooves radiated above his dry lips, forming natural troughs for the beads of sweat formed there.

The room was hot and rank. With only two table lanterns for light, it appeared small, its ceiling foreshortened by the haze of smoke hovering above.

Arnaud's right hand trailed weakly over the edge of the bed, yet the dark cigarillo between his fingers seemed firmly pinched. The tip, like the smoke, showed gray-white in the dim light.

"Devon's here. You mustn't smoke," Margaret said, walking to one side of the bed and nervously patting Arnaud's left hand, which lay inert across his stomach.

Devon moved nearer his side. "Forgive my appearance, Uncle," she said.

"Of course, if you will forgive my indisposition . . . and lack of niceties," he said hoarsely. "The messages? They are safe?" He struggled to sit straighter.

A tall black man emerged suddenly from a shadowed corner to help him. The slave's hair was close-cropped and neat, exposing a twisted knob of flesh where one ear should have been. He had broad shoulders and long arms that ended in massive hands. He grasped the frail Arnaud gently by the shoulders and positioned him higher among the nest of white pillows. The slave wore the day coat of a high-ranking attendant, Devon noticed, yet he had been relegated to the sickroom like a maid-of-all-work.

"Victor is Miles's valet, and mine," Arnaud said. "We must share, because the Confederacy demands the services of too many slaves. And," he added stiffly, "because we are too hard-pressed to recapture fugitives who betray their masters and flee to the hypocrisy of the North."

Victor gave no notice he had heard. When Arnaud was comfortably propped, he faded back into the shadows.

Devon drew the folded papers from her dress. "They are a bit tattered—"

"As you are. But unharmed, my child?" Arnaud asked gently, watching her as he drew in on the dark cigarillo between his lips.

"Unharmed," she whispered.

Arnaud's eyes closed, and he nodded as he exhaled a

gray-white stream of smoke. "Thank God. And this soldier, Morgan. He just happened to be on his way here?"

Devon nodded, uneasy. "He had escaped from a prison camp. I don't know how or when he came aboard the train."

"Margaret says he may have some knowledge of the alliance." In Arnaud's tone, the statement was a baited question.

"You must speak with him yourself. I don't know what he knows," Devon said, and handed her uncle the alliance communiqués.

"Ambiguity is the mark of a good agent. Let's hope he's one of ours." Arnaud took a last deep draw on the cigarillow, then discarded the stub in a glass dish on the littered stand by his bed. His hands shaking slightly, he unfolded the large piece of foolscap first and scanned the coded contents. "I need the books on my desk."

Devon knew which two books he required: *Tottel's Miscellany,* a slim volume of sixteenth-century Renaissance poetry; and a popular travelogue, *Travels in North America in the Years 1841–1842.* The numbers on the foolscap corresponded to pages in the books, but neither she nor Margaret were privy to the key.

Devon watched Arnaud read the shorter message, the warning note from his old friend "Bivey," Earl of Grayshire.

Arnaud lay his head back on the pillows. *"Salaud!"* he whispered.

"Arnaud? What is it?" Margaret leaned worriedly over him.

"A traitor," Devon said softly.

Arnaud's head snapped forward. "Quiet!" His voice rang with authority. "Both of you. You are guessing at matters you know nothing about! I must work! Victor! Go! In an hour bring me bread and warm milk. Nothing else."

The black man bowed and silently crossed the room.

When Victor closed the door behind him, Arnaud seemed to shrink smaller into the pillows, his breath uneven. Devon suddenly realized how much dwindling strength he had expended during this visit.

"Arnaud, dear." Margaret hovered over him with a cool cloth, bathing his forehead.

Devon remembered that the note had three pendulum-like insignias representing the monkey fist, the sailor's knot that had been adopted by alliance organizers as a passkey and symbol of their conspiracy. "If Lord Grayshire's sign is three monkey fists, what sign is yours?" she asked her uncle.

"I was fourth to take the alliance oath," Arnaud said weakly. "First was Khaled the Egyptian, managing partner. Then Count Beaumond, second. Fifth and sixth were the patriotic ship contractors, Tad and Clarence Quincy. Good, solid men."

"And the seventh?" Devon asked.

"Only once did we all agree to convey the sign on a conspirator outside the founding circle of six."

"On whom? Please tell us the name of the person Lord Grayshire suspects."

"Devon," he wearily admonished her.

"I am sorry," she said, aware that she asked too many questions. "I was wrong to read the note."

"Oui, but I was wrong to involve you, both of you." He grasped his wife's hand. "Leave now," he said to Devon. "We must talk later. Tonight. I grow weak."

"You've been ill five days. What does the doctor say is the matter?" Devon asked.

"An irritation of the bowels, *à la gomme, ce mec!*"

"What do you think it is?"

He shook his head impatiently and reached for a fresh cigarillo.

"You should go now," Margaret told Devon, and walked around the bed to usher her out.

Devon paused. "It would be better if you warned me of the traitor's identity," she said to her uncle.

"It would be best if the alliance left its work to soldiers and fighters and freed its women of complicity, *non*?" Arnaud tried to smile.

Devon left the room with a heavy fear in her heart. There were too many secrets in the house, and her uncle Arnaud was the victim of one.

FOURTEEN

Khaled al-Sayed Dexter and Count Valerie Beaumond held top hats firmly in hand as they strolled the foredeck of the *Sentient,* an aging sloop whose sails arched in a stiff midday wind.

"Over there"—Khaled pointed west across the ocean with his cane—"is Wilmington, two days as the crow flies. The good admiral, Arnaud Picard, is no longer so far from us."

"Tomorrow we dock in Nassau, *non*?" the count said.

"Correct." Khaled leaned across the shiny brass deckrail and watched the bow cut a froth across the rolling waves. "Admiral Picard will join us there within the week."

"You are sure the cipher reached him safely?"

"Yes. But I arranged to verify it. A blockade-runner from Nassau carries confirmation details to the admiral and Colonel Brant."

"And will Colonel Brant be joining our celebration in Nassau?" the count asked with a skeptical smile.

"I gave instructions for Brant to stay in Wilmington and confirm transport service to the front."

"Politic of you, considering Lord Grayshire's sensitivity to the mere mention of the man's name. Truthfully, though, Brant was too clever to damage our accounts severely, *non*?"

Khaled shrugged. "He diverted a large payment for ship's stores in Mayaguana, holding fees for tender ships in Cárdenas, commissions to ships' carpenters in the Leewards . . ."

"*Pffftt!*" the count said dismissively, running a hand through his thinning salt-and-pepper hair. "Brant took a cup of relish off a giant banquet table. Did he touch vouchers for munitions, gun mounts, artillery, iron plates, coal reserves, engineers' or officers' stipends? Did he leave even one of our lascars without a hammock? No. Brant is a brilliant scavenger."

"Quite the barracuda," Khaled murmured.

"Now, now," Count Beaumond admonished. "At least he marauds with his brains, unlike that boorish pup of Grayshire's."

"The earl knows young Roger has no head for business or politics."

"I thank God the young rakehell is not privy to his father's affairs, else he would be with us now, preparing to imbibe and copulate to his full prurient potential at the Royal Victoria." The count flourished his lace handkerchief to daub beads of perspiration at his temples. "By the way, is that shipment of Bordeaux I ordered on its way to our hotel?"

Khaled turned away to look at the low-hanging clouds on the horizon—and to hide the disapproval on his face. "Yes," he said tightly. "I think four hundred bottles a trifle excessive. You realize our operating funds are sorely depleted by the expenses of this expedition."

"My boy! We must entertain. We celebrate the culmination of an arduous eighteen months. But I understand your concern with lodging and supplies. With Bivey on board, we will need food for a thousand, *non*?" Beaumond grinned.

Khaled's grip on the brass deckrail tightened. "It would be more helpful to us all if you ignored Bivey's personality and concentrated instead on the immense amount of money he has generated."

"Hah! By the sheer law of physics anything that man does is immense."

Khaled paused. "You dismiss him at your peril. He's one of the most powerful nobles on the Isle."

"You think I do not know that, *m'sieur*?" The count's voice hardened, the derisive dandy gone. "I have sat across the bargaining table with this excessive Englishman. He bulges with money, with royal connections, with mercantile contacts around the world."

"Indeed," Khaled said, "we must pray that Allah makes him big enough for our two great rulers to hide behind."

The count gave a cold smile. "Come, Khaled. Your spendthrift Pasha needs more than prayers. The national debt of Egypt is the size of a mountain."

Khaled turned away to watch clouds billow like high white mountains on the horizon. On his finger, the scarab ring shifted with the uneasy anger of its wearer.

A warm breeze fluttered the curtains of the second-story bedchamber at Jasmine's Reach. Devon stepped reluctantly out of the tub, thoroughly, pleasantly fatigued. Portia toweled her dry and slipped a fresh, rose-scented chemise over her head.

Crossing to the tall mahogany armoire, Portia pulled out a collapsed circle of crinoline, then laid it on a chair beside Devon.

Devon caught the scent of old cedar in the lace yarn that connected the watch-spring steel hoops, a homey fragrance that beckoned comfortably of bedroom and sleep.

"I want to rest before I dress," she said.

Portia nodded and left, taking with her the effortless poise that made her subservient conduct seem strangely out of character. Perhaps paradox was the only weapon a slave could brandish in this house, Devon thought.

She lay back heavily on the bed, but she was unable to sleep. Portia haunted her conscience. The young woman was not property to be bought, bred, and worked. Yet Devon's activity on behalf of the alliance might already have advanced the cause of the Confederacy and Portia's life sentence in servitude.

There would soon come a day to take sides publicly, Devon thought. On that day, Arnaud and Margaret Picard would decry the evidence that Frederic's blood coursed through her veins.

How easy it had been to accompany Damien James to money-raising soirees for American abolitionists. The trips were kept secret from her aunt, satisfying little episodes of adolescent rebellion. Afterward at Langley Place, Devon would unlock a musty dower trunk and hide copies of *The Liberator,* a crusading newspaper that demanded freedom for American slaves.

What a selfish and cowardly demonstration of ideals, she thought now. Real reform called for commitment, even when actions were misguided, like those of her father.

And what of Gentry? she wondered. Were his actions in service to the alliance misguided? Was he—

"Ma'am?"

Portia's voice at the door startled her.

She had spent an hour wrestling with her conscience and still felt no firm grip on her feelings.

Devon hurried to dress for dinner.

Portia led her down a wide staircase laid with moss-green Wilton carpet. Devon walked with arched-back grace, retracting the blue-velvet hem of her gown as she descended. The white silk skirt hissed richly as it slid against the undercage that lifted it fashionably high and round.

At the bottom of the stairs, scrolled posts were topped incongruously by rearing brass griffins. Devon grasped a fierce eagle's beak to brace her pivot toward the main corridor.

Portia was far ahead down a hallway sconced with oil lanterns. Devon moved more quickly to catch up. Just as she passed a set of double doors, one side opened and a uniformed officer backed out of the door calling to someone inside, "Courier that immediately to Gener—"

Devon could not avoid the collision. She was thrown sideways toward the wall, but the gentleman turned quickly and wrapped his arm around her waist, drawing her unsteadily upright against him.

"My pardon, dear lady." Miles Brant smiled as the lithe creature slid out of his grasp and regained her balance.

She raised her proud, lovely face to his, and Miles felt his smile grow genuinely warm with pleasure, for there were the eyes of the beauty he had shot at. Deep black-brown, a color unexpected in her fair blond nature. Most assuredly, he would find other surprising attributes. Thank God's merciful irony that she had not been assassinated according to orders, for she was a superbly interesting piece.

He stepped back and allowed the brace on his leg full view. "You must be Devon, my dear cousin so disastrously delayed. You arrive safely, only to be accosted by my clumsiness!"

"It is I who should be asking pardon," she said apologetically.

Her glance took in the rigid black frame that encased his

left calf. She steadied the set of her crinoline and straightened her shoulders.

"Miles Brant. At your service." He bowed elegantly, knowing that his full-dress uniform enhanced the courtliness of the gesture; knowing, too, that the narrow confines of the hallway created an intimate sphere for greeting a beautiful woman.

"Colonel Brant." She nodded and offered her hand.

She seemed shy, he mused. How charming for one who had trolloped off to bed with her fiancé. Miles pressed his lips lightly, warmly to the back of her gloved hand.

He did not release her. "You faced beastly travail for a cause dear to my soul. Your courage and dedication deserve another kiss, but that would be improper."

"Quite," Devon murmured, withdrawing her hand.

"Shall we join the others then?"

His smooth baritone voice made the long Southern syllables quite pleasant, Devon thought, and she was uncertain if his compliment had been heartfelt or provocative.

He extended his arm, and she crooked hers lightly in his. They walked the hall slowly, Devon keeping pace with the strangely dancelike rhythm of his limp.

Miles chatted inconsequentially about the war and its imposition on social life and how his poor wife was so glad to have notables to entertain.

Devon judged Miles to be much older than she, older than Gentry too. Though nearly Gentry's height, Miles's build was more slender. Still she felt a coiled strength in the rhythm Miles was forced to keep. He was handsome, with well-proportioned features. His eyes met hers often with a glancing warmth, compensating for their chilly color, the gray of a winter storm.

His uniform dress coat was fine cut, tailored expertly in length and breadth. The coat was double-breasted and resplendent with braid, gold buttons, and ribboned medals. From his shoulders, shimmering lengths of braided bullion fell from circles of gold epaulets.

He seemed supremely at home in the ornament of his station, she thought as they passed through a tall swagged archway into the drawing room.

And thoroughly familiar with squiring a newly met woman to dinner.

A gilt-framed mirror hung above the Carrara-marble mantelpiece in the drawing room, reflecting the back of a magnificent ormolu clock. To either side rose classic urns in blue john, and processions of bronze statuettes and Copenhagen figures.

War had not ravaged this home as it had Magda Selliger's, Devon thought.

Regina and Aunt Margaret waited in the large room. Regina had arranged herself in the center of the settee, her teal-blue skirt spilling over the cushions. She nodded a cool greeting and unfurled a French fan.

With some embarrassment, Devon disengaged her arm from Miles's and greeted her aunt.

Margaret Picard sat self-absorbed on one side of a chintz sociable. The high, curved back of the chair rose well above her shoulders, and she looked like a sickly wren in her sedate brown silk.

For years, Margaret had made a place in her life for her phantom husband, Devon thought. And for years Margaret had waited in the shadows of empty chairs. Arnaud had never remained in London more than a few months before requesting another assignment that would allow him to serve his mother country.

Now they were reunited, but Margaret was still without a dinner companion.

"Is Uncle Arnaud feeling any better?" Devon asked, placing a hand on Margaret's small, thin arm.

Margaret shook her head. "At least he is no worse," she said, her pinched voice convincing no one.

"You are as strong a patriot as Arnaud," Miles said. "Your ordeal with the mercenaries was an unconscionable violation of Confederate propriety, and I assure you it would not have happened with a cadre of loyal Southern soldiers."

"I'm sure not," Margaret said, looking up at him with a strange nervousness.

Could she know? Miles wondered. He continued to radiate a warm, sympathetic smile as his thoughts returned to the kidnapping seven days ago. The night of Margaret's interrogation at Landry's camp, Miles had been careful to stay masked and out of view as he directed Reg Landry's questioning and intimidation of the two elderly women.

The maid had immediately fainted. Plucky Margaret,

though, had endured a bout of rough handling before succumbing to threats, admitting she didn't have the alliance messages.

"Of course you ruffians don't have them either!" she had said. "Devon's made of stern stuff. She'll succeed, you know."

The disheveled old woman had spoken with so much conviction, Miles had barely suppressed his laughter. Now, of course, he knew better. Devon had indeed prevailed, and Gentry had shown up with his forelock securely attached to his skull.

On whose orders had Gentry been sent to protect the alliance courier? And did Arnaud now have knowledge of the missing vouchers and the funds Miles had withdrawn from alliance accounts?

For safety, the admiral must fall a bit more under the weather, Miles decided. But not before deciphering the long, coded letter Victor had glimpsed.

"I hope Gentry joins us soon so that we may dine," Regina said.

"I'm sure he'll be right along, my darling," said Miles, leaning down and grasping his wife's hand in both of his.

It was a gesture of fondness, and Regina's cool exterior faltered for a moment in surprise. He let her hand go and she fluttered her fan.

"I just hope he has a dress uniform," she complained lightly. "You know how he is about formal affairs."

"You may know how he was, my dear, but it's been years since you've seen him. He may have changed."

Miles took an aperitif from a tray, then turned to Devon with a devilish smile. "Tell us now, truthfully, Devon. Was our Gentry a well-mannered escort?"

FIFTEEN

Devon saw Regina and Margaret look attentively at her, eyes trained to detect a telltale blush.

She gazed directly at Miles. "I found him a man of integrity, if that's what you're asking. If you're asking whether he tied his cravat for tea, the answer is no."

Miles smiled as he sipped.

"I, for one, am very grateful to the young man," Margaret said, satisfied. "All I could think of was how safe we'd be once we all reached Arnaud. And then I find my dearest one bedridden, with barely the strength to squeeze my hand! How unfair," she whispered.

She suddenly bent forward, choking back a sob. Devon sank to the floor beside her aunt, consoling her.

Gentry Morgan passed silently through the damask-draped archway, survival instincts on edge as if he had entered an enemy camp. He noted the positions of Miles and Regina, then allowed his gaze to settle on the beautiful young woman who nestled low in a billow of white silk.

He barely recognized the tattered creature with whom he had traveled. Her golden hair was rolled at her neck, long satin ribbons trailing at each side. Her shoulders were bare, the delicate skin in the hollow of her throat pale and translucent. Her breasts swelled above the neckline of her gown with a tantalizing, natural fullness.

Had he truly embraced this woman once? Without finery or pretension, only a glistening sheath of water between his skin and hers?

"Gentry! Welcome!" Miles hailed him and made his way slowly around a bent-wood rocking chair.

Gentry's face became a guarded mask as Miles approached. He had known that his brother-in-law had been injured in the Charleston bombardment the year before, but not that he had been left crippled.

He ignored Miles and observed the set of Devon's shoulders as she drew away from her aunt. She rose slowly, her body speaking to him with a stiff, silent reserve, like a tethered animal warning another still free.

Miles stopped a handshake away from Gentry, archly smiling and waiting.

When the silence threatened to grow awkward, Gentry raised an angled hand in salute.

Miles, still smiling, did not return the gesture. "No need for that in family quarters. We are all equal here." He signaled the slave to bring the tray of aperitifs.

Gentry's uniform belied the pronouncement. His coat was clean but thread-worn and bare of regalia, with only two rows of shiny buttons running from high collar to waist. He wore the three-bar chevron of first sergeant on his sleeve. His soft woolen trousers held no crease.

In deference to neatness, he'd brushed his hair back and tied it at his nape with a rawhide thong. The style only accentuated the exotic cast of his features and gave him more the look of a seventeenth-century courtier than a modestly dressed enlisted man.

"I take it there were no dress coats in regimental supply?" Regina asked.

"There is no supply, Regina," Gentry said, refusing an offer of sherry from the tray. "Everything's in the field. I'm lucky to have borrowed a clean uniform for the occasion."

"I wish you had borrowed a pair of shears as well," she said.

"I wish the infantry had half the food we will consume tonight."

"Nobly, but impudently, put." Miles raised his glass in an airy mock salute.

But Devon saw the tension in Miles's handsome face, and she sensed that Gentry had too quickly drawn a line of contention between them.

With a sharp snap, Regina collapsed her fan. "I think we're all growing a little ravenous, Miles. Perhaps we should lead the way to dinner."

The group sat down at a long table that prevented any pretense of family intimacy. Regina and Miles reigned at each end, while Devon and Margaret sat across the table from Gentry.

Regina kept up cheery commentary as the soup tureen went around. She was obviously delighted to be entertaining.

"I've been quite busy making fancy goods for the end of the war," she said, taking a sip of julienne soup. "We'll have great fairs for the charities and summer fetes again, once the war is over."

"It's kind of you to let your artistry benefit others," Devon said.

"A lady of gentle birth never parades her talent, you know." Regina looked at Devon. "Why did you?"

The busy click of utensils on porcelain stopped.

"I draw because it pleases me," Devon said. "I suppose I published because it pleased me."

Margaret coughed indelicately into her napkin. "Self-gratification does not make for ideal behavior, Devon," she murmured.

"Ah, but honesty makes for an ideal answer, doesn't it?" Miles said.

From across the table, Gentry studied Devon intently.

Miles took a leisurely draft of wine, then returned the conversation to folk art and its proliferation before the war.

Devon turned her attention to the next courses, giving noncommittal nods to Regina's prattle and full attention to the fillet of beef in burgundy. After a week of trail jerky, dry biscuits, and beans, the aromatic meat was mesmerizing.

The chicken course had an unfamiliar spicy bouquet.

"It's chicken with Hungarian paprika, made from sweet red peppers," Regina said. "Very mild." She held up her hand, and a slave in white apron refilled her wineglass. "Highly recommended for dyspepsia and torpid livers."

"Do you think it would be beneficial for Arnaud?" Margaret asked. "Perhaps we should send him a portion."

"I'm afraid he couldn't tolerate such a dish," Regina said. "Doctor's orders."

"Frankly, Uncle Arnaud doesn't care for his doctor," Devon said. "Is there another physician we can send for?"

Miles straightened and smiled. "My dear, Doc Hiller is

my very own surgeon. He saved my leg. I'm sure he can save your uncle's digestive tract."

Devon did not smile. "My uncle's illness is quite serious. He needs a physician in whom he has confidence."

"The medical corps is stretched thin at Wilmington infirmary. But I'll see what I can do," Miles said stiffly.

"Perhaps Sergeant Morgan should be seen there," Devon said with a concerned glance at Gentry.

"Treated? For what?" Miles was instantly attentive.

Devon knew she had misstepped and looked away from Gentry. "Sergeant Morgan was wounded after we escaped the bandits on the train."

"They hired two snipers," Gentry said. "One got me before I got him."

"All in one fateful day, you escaped a kidnapping and an ambush by snipers?" Miles asked, sympathetic concern in his voice.

Devon paused. "Yes."

She was lying, Miles thought with amusement. He had not sent Bloxie Taft after them until the day after they eluded Landry's raiders. Miles covered his smile in a sip of wine. Devon and Gentry had had that first night together, alone.

"You should have told me you were wounded, Gentry," Miles said. "I wouldn't have assigned you to that reconnaissance run tomorrow."

"I can ride," Gentry said.

"Well, you both were fortunate, taking shelter with that farm lady before linking up with the infantry corps. Are there any more stirring episodes in your journey we should know about?" Miles asked nonchalantly.

Gentry met his gaze. "No."

"Well, then, Gentry, I was just wondering where you would be headed after your leave is up. You have your troop assignment?"

"I'll go back to Jeb's regiment until I'm told different."

"I salute you then. The field's a treacherous place to be. Frankly, I'm surprised you lasted three years out there. But to die fighting is the way of the Indian, isn't it?"

Gentry's expression was guarded. "To die in battle is noble. But there's little honor in this. A mad scream of artillery and men die. Thunder and butchery. One soldier on the hill swabbing hot cannons with water is more important than a whole patrol fighting hand to hand in the valley."

Regina laughed, then drained her wineglass. "How nearly eloquent, Gentry," she said, her cheeks flushed with the heat of wine. "Teague loved that, you know. He used to coax it out of you, make you angry just so you'd talk to him. You never talked enough to suit him."

"I did nothing enough to suit him," Gentry said.

"You sprung from his loins, and that appeared to be sufficient."

"Dearest," Miles said sternly. "It's poor taste to expose internecine conflicts to guests." His tone was an obvious warning for her to curb her wine consumption and her tongue.

She ignored him and spoke to Devon. "You see, Gentry is Teague's natural-born son. He wasn't adopted, like me. I've often thought Teague took me on as a charity case. My daddy and mama were killed off by some bloodthirsty Sioux, you know."

Gentry placed his napkin on the table and scooted his chair back.

"Leaving, Gentry?" Regina asked. "Just because of one little reminder about the savages you married into?"

"My wife's tribe is Lakota, Teton Sioux," he said mechanically as if he'd said it too often before. "You were attacked by a band of Santee."

"Now how am I supposed to know one stinking heathen from another?" she asked.

"You don't. You don't know at all." Gentry stood. "I apologize," he said to his sister. "It's obvious my presence is a provocation—that it incites pain—"

Regina rapped her fist on the table. "You are not excused, Gentry Morgan. This is my table and you are not—"

"Regina!" It was Miles's voice, clear in its command.

"Wait, Mr. Morgan!" Margaret exclaimed. "Arnaud said he must see you tonight." She nervously pushed her chair backward. "Miles, I'm sure you understand Arnaud's delicate state. Please excuse us to attend him."

"Of course." Miles spoke automatically, his eyes on the tall soldier and the tiny woman who had quickly taken his arm.

Miles watched them make their way up the stairs to the man who had the trust—and cash vouchers—of the alliance.

How much did Gentry know? he wondered. And how much would Arnaud trust him? Surely Arnaud was lucid enough to see there was too much coincidence in Gentry's presence aboard the train. Surely Arnaud could reason skeptically now that Miles had reduced the dosage.

Gentry. Gentry. The bane of his existence.

Miles sat lost in thought. A partnership between Arnaud and the venturesome half-breed would be quite intolerable. He needed to drive a wedge between them, and quickly.

Miles looked at Devon. Devon. He smiled.

The dinner table had grown ghostly quiet, the only sounds the clink of dishware and the starched rustle of the slaves' white skirts.

"You must forgive our little family broadsides, Devon," Miles said. "Gentry's wife was—"

"Gentry's *pregnant* wife," Regina interrupted morosely.

"—was killed quite some time ago and Gentry hasn't been the same."

"Gentry's the same godless troublemaker he's always been," Regina said, gesturing for more wine. "We're the ones who've changed. We are."

Miles frowned harshly.

Regina made a moue at him and began a disjointed monologue on the paucity of cooking wine for Cook's good sauces, Cook's famous honey corn bread, and the problems of the house staff.

"Don't even have a governess for my Grace. Every capable young woman is stitching shirts and rolling bandages. We just have Portia."

"Portia's quite quick-witted and knowledgeable," Devon said. "I'm sure she's an asset."

"She's an uppity pain is what she is. A misguided preacher taught her daddy to read, then Victor taught Portia. Then my dear husband gave her permission to use our library. Talk about putting on airs. She's not disciplined enough. I think my dear husband has a blind spot when it comes to smart darkies." Regina's chill gaze rested on Miles.

"We're all fatigued, Regina," Miles said, his voice low and ominous. "We must leave after-dinner conversation for a less trying time."

"But I wanted to call Grace to play piano for Devon in the—"

"Go on up and retire, dear." Miles stood. "I'm going to show Devon where I've put her easel and chalks and paints."

He held Regina's chair. Suddenly quiet, she rose quickly and virtually fled from the room.

Devon was wide eyed. Miles came to hold her chair, acting as if nothing out of the ordinary had transpired.

"I have a modest collection of contemporary folk art. I would appreciate your expert opinion on some of the pieces."

Devon gave uneasy assent, and he escorted her deep into the main hallway to a high arched alcove with Italian cupids painted on a canvas ceiling. It was the obvious juncture of a wing that had been added to the manor.

Miles turned and led her through a narrow corridor that ballooned abruptly into an indoor solarium tower. On the balcony walkway above them, glass tables gathered dust and tall pottery urns were empty of plants. One lonely palm tree raised ragged fronds toward the domed glass ceiling. The windows were cranked closed, and the cavernous space was uncomfortably humid.

"Sad, isn't it?" Miles looked upward. "I have no time for my nursery, no slaves to tend it. One cannot harvest unless one sows."

She felt his hand clasp her arm to urge her forward. The touch was warm and personal, subtly exploratory.

"It's late," she said, uncomfortable. "Perhaps we could see your collection tomorrow."

"Nonsense. I have learned to assure my pleasures at the moment they occur to me. You may learn to do the same as you grow older. This way." He smiled as he released her and lifted an oil lantern from its sconce.

Devon followed the metal jangle of his brace.

He stopped in front of double doors. The lantern glow reflected in the deep, even grain of Honduran mahogany.

"Does the sound of my brace trouble you?" he asked suddenly, turning to face her.

"Of course not," she said, taken aback.

"It's silly, but I worry that it makes me seem a mechanical sort of man. And I'm really quite emotional in my decisions. Instinctual actually."

He opened the doors and held the lantern high so she could pass.

SIXTEEN

The room was dank and stagnant. Nothing was visible beyond the wavering shadow cast by his lantern.

Miles hovered behind her, pressing his leg close enough to upset the balance of her crinoline.

"Shall I help you light the lamps?" she asked.

He heard the breathy beginning of anxiety in her voice and withdrew the pressure, stepping past her. "I can manage. Here are your things." He pointed to a large woven bag that sat amid dusty china candelabra on a drop-leaf table.

As Devon eagerly unbuckled the battered satchel, Miles lit a candle and left the lantern on the table. He knew she was checking the state of her pencils, inks, pads, and watercolors. They were intact. He had already looked.

He kept up a low-toned monologue as he lit bracketed lamps in the room, knowing she needed the comfort of a friendly voice amid the ghostly sheet-draped chairs of the gallery. As he spoke, he watched her closely. She pulled out tiny jars of ink and tightened lids. She ran her fingers across the soft tips of paintbrushes. She flipped critically through the pages of her sketchbook, reestablishing contact.

He remembered some of the drawings. Quite good. A baby crawling toward a window; her nephew—Cyril, no doubt. And a chubby little girl in a smock: Sarah. A lake and summer house; an orchid blooming beneath the panes of a glasshouse with a nice mirrored effect.

My, how excited she looked. And how very, very beautiful. She had an oval face and even features, a creamy, smooth complexion. Then one noticed the inviting, deep velvet softness of her eyes, the sensual ebb in the bow of her upper lip where it met the swelling fullness below. And there was no shy, shrinking English chin. Her jawline rounded firmly, decisively underscoring the cast of her lips.

She would be headstrong, he thought, ruled by emotions as all stubborn people were. He would have to maneuver carefully. She had intelligence enough to second-guess the instincts he aroused, and possibly, courage enough to throw truth in his face.

"I thought this would be a good room for you," he said, approaching her. "It takes the morning sun."

"It would be quite nice for painting, but for the most part I will be sketching outdoors, thank you." She packed away her supplies, leaving sketchpad, pencils, and charcoals on the table.

"Allow me to show you some of the more quaint pieces here." He extended his hand to her.

Her hands stayed delicately on the rise of her skirt. "May we begin with this intense young man right here?" She turned to the wall near the table.

"My pleasure." He walked closer, taking his time. "Most of my collection comes from New England. This is a John Brewster portrait of an anonymous young gentleman, barely at an age to shave, I'd say."

The painting was puritanically dark, with only a white stock at his neck and light-complexioned face to draw the eye. Wispy hair and light sideburns framed an even-featured face with precise, finely focused eyes.

"The artist is a well-known deaf mute from Connecticut," Miles said.

"That explains the serious intensity in the eyes," Devon said. "Like deep wells of words, unsaid."

"I prefer to think of one's eyes as maps of hidden treasure." He looked intently into hers. "Delve deeply and you come away with delightful surprises."

Devon did not reply.

He smiled as she concentrated on another picture. Like all the paintings in his collection, it was the work of an itinerant artist. It lacked dimension and proportion. Soft lighting played on the trusting face of a young child, little more than an infant, in a peach-colored dress. A gray kitten swatted at a ball of twine near the baby's feet.

"It has a quaint charm," Devon said tersely.

"The artist is Joseph Whiting Stock, a man known for anatomical illustrations as well as portraits. He was paralyzed from the waist down in an accident."

"Do you buy the works only of artists who are impaired?"

"Of course not. It's just that too often I find the artist more interesting than the work produced. This oil is by James Bard. One of the most popular marine artists in America. This is his latest. A steamship called the *Milton Martin.* I have an old family friend in Washington, D.C., who interceded on my behalf. She's a Frith, one of the lesser-known Richmond Friths, but Lilly does know how to wield her influence."

"Congratulations on the coup," Devon said, gazing politely at the poorly colored mechanical rendering.

"Your satire acquires a sweet but nasty bite when you're fatigued. But a critique is what I requested, after all. I do hope to add one of your works to my collection someday."

"I am more adept at illustrating than painting."

"Then I hope you will consider doing a rendering of Jasmine's Reach. I would be happy to commission it."

She shook her head. "I cannot accept your money, nor the commission. I have no idea how long we'll be staying. My uncle is—"

"—in for a long recuperation, I'm sure. I am quite frankly doubtful that he can continue his work here."

"Then I assume he will shift his concerns to you."

"I don't know." Miles smiled ruefully. "He is an irascible man, not known for temperate decisions, especially in his current state. He has refused to see me until he has decoded the message you brought."

He moved into the glow of the table lantern and picked up her sketchpad. He began to flip through the pages.

"Please. Those are quite personal efforts," Devon said, walking toward him.

"How apt." He closed the book and held it out to her. "I consider *you* a very personal project."

"What do you mean?" She grasped the sketches, but Miles held tight to them.

"Quite simply, I'm captivated." His fingers began a gentle, knowing glide along her arm.

"On the contrary, you're trespassing," Devon said hotly,

stiffening as his hand reached her shoulder and swept up to her neck.

She dropped the sketchbook and arched away from him, only to find his other arm suddenly around her waist, holding her close.

He smiled. "There is no trespass when another has trod the path before me."

She froze.

"Rest assured I do not think you a woman of easy virtue," he added. "You are simply a woman of high standards. Because you refuse to wed your fiancé after bedding him, I assume you found Roger wanting in some respect."

Her palm met his cheek with a loud crack and a velocity neither of them had expected.

Fighting to keep his anger in check, Miles grabbed her wrist and twisted. His face remained frighteningly calm as the sting reddened his cheek in the lamp's yellow glow.

"You have much to learn about controlling a man," he said softly. "Physical sensation only begets a hunger for more."

She stopped struggling. "You are mad," she whispered.

He shook his head. "Simply honest, my sweet. I would apologize for being so boorishly physical, but war leaves little time for niceties. And I did want to make my position clear."

His fingers raked slowly through the mass of hair coiled at her neck. He dislodged pins, and long strands fell free.

She struggled anew and pushed herself away from him.

Miles allowed her to stumble backward. The rage in her eyes was so gratifying. He felt a rush of uncontrollable warmth in his loins.

"I advise you to hear me out before you flee and run the hall with such fetchingly loose hair. You may meet a servant, or even Regina, and you should understand how your report of this meeting would be received. You are known in this family for a prior indiscretion. Another one would be in keeping with your independent nature. I, on the other hand, am a devoted husband. Regina will uphold that. Obviously the entire household is mine to command whatever story I wish revealed to public or family. And I am, of course, a man of limited ability to pursue."

He extended his leg and twisted his ankle slowly so that

the brace creaked as a leather buckle tautened. "Credibility will lie in my court."

"Truth rests in mine," she said.

"Only in bed does one lie down with truth, Devon. Did Roger not teach you that?" he asked gently.

"You know nothing of truth! Nor of me!" she cried, her voice resounding in the corners of the neglected room.

"Only that you are a marvelously engaging woman to fight with, my dear. In my experience, that makes a woman extremely invigorating to love. Though it may seem as if I hold all the cards in our private little game, you hold the ace. You see, I will not take you by force. I give you my word—"

"And from which fork of your tongue comes this promise?"

He smiled, unruffled. "You will surrender to me, on my terms."

"I have only to talk to my aunt or my uncle to reveal your despicable nature."

"Your aunt is addled and your uncle deathly ill. Both are preoccupied and intensely sensitive about the whole Roger Bivens affair. Arnaud has expressed private doubts about you. He does not believe Roger used undue pressure to force you to submit." Miles told the lie easily. "I, on the other hand, am quite honest in my desire to have you, even honest in announcing the deceits I will use. I thought you would appreciate the lack of pretense in my pursuit."

Devon stood motionless, watching him, harboring a quiet intensity that made him anxious.

"What I appreciate, 'cousin,' " she said slowly, "is the complete lack of passion in this farce. Why? Why are you doing this?"

She had seen the illogic in his sudden desire, he realized, and she was demanding an intellectual base for it. He smiled.

"I told you I make instinctual decisions. You are one of them. I am a respected man, but a lonely one, with a good wife, but an unlovable one. I am sorely in need of your wit, and the sense of wonder your youth would bring to love. These gifts are not so easily had these days."

"You are a married man, for God's sake."

"You are a tarnished woman. Whom did you expect to love you?"

She was shocked into silence. She walked closer and stooped woodenly to pick up her sketchbook. Then she turned and left.

He waited until her footsteps echoed faintly from the far end of the corridor. He needed to give her time. Time to think about how tawdry she must be to receive such a crude and bold proposition. Time to realize how few people she could depend on to help her elude his unwanted pursuit. Time to seek solace and protection from the only other outcast she knew—Gentry.

It was there Miles wanted to catch her, in Gentry's arms or in his bed. He was out to tempt Gentry, and quickly. Once Gentry succumbed and was denounced for taking advantage of a proper young lady, Arnaud would reject the half-breed as a trustworthy agent for the alliance.

It was just a matter of evening the odds. Gentry guilty of seduction would make Miles's greedy embezzlement a much easier fault for Arnaud to digest.

Death would surely claim the self-righteous old admiral in a few days, and it was crucial Arnaud pass battle strategy and payment vouchers to him.

Miles picked up his lantern and pulled the gallery doors closed with a loud and energetic slam.

SEVENTEEN

Devon reached the entrance hall and ran furiously up the stairs. She stopped on the landing, out of breath.

Because of her night with Roger she was already receiving insulting propositions unworthy of a lady. What could she tell Aunt Margaret? Public disgrace had been Margaret's greatest fear—and the reason she had paid servants handsomely to keep their peace about Devon's appearance at Roger Bivens's expansive apartment on Trelawny.

Devon leaned weakly against the banister. Had it truly been so wrong? She had learned she could never love the man betrothed to her. In the end, the great wrong had not been that she had fallen into his bed. She had rejected him, the prestigious prize Margaret had arranged—an earl's son, entrance to the aristocracy, compensation for the blight Devon's iconoclastic father had bred on the family.

Even though Devon had explained how Roger had pressed her persistently, drunkenly, Margaret knew it was Devon who had said yes, Devon who had succumbed to curiosity, Devon whose character had been compromised in the eyes of both families.

Though appalled at Devon's refusal to marry Roger, Margaret had acted with stoic devotion and delicacy in smoothing the Bivenses' ruffled feathers. "Has a mother any choice?" she had asked, the question barbed with added guilt for Devon. The childless Margaret had long sought to supplant the memory of Devon's long-dead mother. For just as long, Devon had fought to keep her daughterly feelings in an empty shrine, calling to a ghost she did not know, desperate to keep ties to her past and her identity.

With a soft hiss of silk, Devon began to sink to the step. A gentle hand under her arm stopped the decline.

"He must not see you bend so easily," Portia whispered. "Come. Quickly."

The muted jangle of Miles's brace sounded from deep in the corridor.

Devon nodded and negotiated the groaning wood steps as · fast as she could. At the top of the stairs Portia led her down the hall past Arnaud's room to her bedchamber.

Once inside, Devon dropped her sketchbook and gasped for breath, her arms clasped around herself in an effort to control her racing heart. "Lock the door," she whispered.

"He would not risk coming to your room," Portia said.

"Lock it!"

She heard the swift clank of the key setting the lock and turned to Portia. "How did you know?"

Portia didn't answer at first. She walked over to the washstand and poured water into a china basin. "It's easy for one woman to see another entering hell, especially in this house," she said at last.

Portia lay a folded washcloth onto the water and pressed it downward with slender black fingers. "He likes smart women."

She wrung the cloth out, then drew it, wet and cool, across Devon's cheek.

Portia's face had relaxed its mask. Devon saw a vulnerable and very young woman, younger perhaps than she. She took the cloth from Portia, and the black woman turned to the chifforobe, rummaging in a drawer to find a lace shawl.

"Your uncle asks that you attend him and Sergeant Morgan in the sickroom," she said.

Devon drew the cloth along her neck and shoulders, where Miles's hand had explored with unhurried intimacy. She could still feel the warmth of his fingers. Her eyes closed for a moment. "You said he must not see me bend. Why?"

Portia paused at the door, avoiding her eyes. "Weakness makes him angry." She opened the door. "You must come. Quickly."

Portia rushed Devon through the door and out into the dimly lit hallway.

Two doors away, Devon stopped outside Arnaud's room,

trying to clear her mind of Miles's threat in order to entertain a different one.

Had Arnaud discovered Gentry was a spy, or a man pressed suddenly into a mission he knew little about? Gentry had been too persistent about seeing the alliance letters for Devon to believe his was the involvement of an ignorant soldier. She was sure he had copied the communiqués at the Selliger farm, though he claimed he had written a report to President Davis. Gentry had not dispatched his "report" through military couriers. He had mailed it when their escorts from Henderson's corps had stopped for rations in a small town.

Devon knew she should answer honestly when her uncle questioned her about Gentry's conduct. But would that not give Gentry leave to answer truthfully about her own actions? Could he not say that she had willingly handed him the coded letter? And more? That she had bathed boldly in his presence and innocently shared his bed, gathered to him like a child needing comfort? That she had accepted the depth of his kiss and returned it willingly, her body alive?

He would never reveal those things. Nor would she. They were intimacies, locked safely in the hearts of two people, remembered each time they would meet. As now, when her stomach dropped weightless with anticipation, vanishing past a strange and tangled knot.

The lantern sconce by her uncle's door gave a sickly glow. Portia draped the pink lace shawl across her bare shoulders, opened the door wide to accommodate the span of Devon's gown, then backed away and closed the door.

The room was fouled by sour bedclothes and the smoke of Arnaud's thin black cigars.

Arnaud sat shrunken and frail against the pillows. One hand lay limp at the edge of the bed, a smoldering cigarillo trapped between thumb and forefinger. "Ah, Devon." His voice was surprisingly firm. "Perhaps you can help us. Sergeant Morgan here has been able to answer distressingly few of my questions."

Gentry acknowledged her briefly with a dismissive glance. It did not matter. She felt his awareness of her, sensing her movement, her placement in the room. She was instantly conscious of the space between them, as if distance held the key to their decorum.

She walked close to the foot of her uncle's bed.

Gentry stood to one side, his body at ease, virile and alive in a room filled with the pall of decay.

The lantern beside the bed burned high and bright, casting Arnaud's wasting body into garish relief. He was no longer pale. His face was colorless ash. But his eyes held a fierce brightness. He was clinging desperately to his ability to concentrate.

"I've already explained to the admiral," Gentry said. "A soldier is offered no answers, only assignments."

"So obedience covers all contingencies?" Arnaud said. "Not in matters of espionage, Sergeant Morgan. In that case, we need the sign, the password assuring us that you are one of us. Devon, did Sergeant Morgan ever indicate he knew the alliance signal?"

"He said it was never passed to him," Devon said.

"Humor me once again, Sergeant Morgan." Arnaud's smile was weak. "You escaped prison, made your way to high command in Richmond, and were appropriated for this mission by whom?"

"An assistant to the secretary of the Navy," Gentry lied, repeating the cover story Pinkney Dobbs had created for him. "I was told that President Davis signed the order temporarily placing me on this special duty."

"But you carry no such order?"

"After three years as a Confederate scout, you learn not to be caught with papers of any kind. They're always the wrong ones."

Arnaud smiled again. "True. Scouts are interchangeable with spies—and just as apt to be hanged by the enemy."

"My only mission was to protect and escort the alliance courier. Now that she is safely here"—he nodded at Devon —"I have no further interest in your plans. I'm sorry I cannot be of more help to you." He turned to go.

"And you do understand I need help, don't you?" Arnaud's words were soft and calm as he brought his hand to his lips. He inhaled weakly on the small cigar. It was the only movement he had made since Devon had entered the room.

Gentry swung back, looking directly at Arnaud. "You have a determined enemy."

"And how can I be sure it is not you?" Arnaud asked.

"You can't be sure. I have no password to offer. But I wager you have more to fear from those you trust."

Humor briefly lit Arnaud's eyes. "So I should be wary of comrades who know the code phrase, eh? A good twist."

Gentry walked to the door.

"Wait," Arnaud said as Gentry's hand reached for the knob. "Before you go, I would entertain more of your thoughts on this predicament."

Gentry turned. "I know one thing: Poison is the weapon of a coward."

Poison? Devon circled around the foot of the bed, close to her uncle's side.

Arnaud's hand lifted mechanically to his mouth. This time he drew in deeply. The ash of the burning tip showed a girdle of gray. "I suspect you come from a race that treats its enemies with a little more respect."

"We make a habit of openly confronting our enemies," Gentry said. "It is the honorable way."

Arnaud gestured weakly at the pans and pitchers beside the bed. "I agree. This is a messy, degrading way to go."

"Uncle!" Devon said, astonished at the accepting, self-defeating tone Arnaud used.

Glancing at her, Arnaud spoke slowly. "You must understand that truthful men talk openly of such matters." He looked back at Gentry. "Perhaps that means you are an honest soldier and not a spy. Perhaps I am a dying man who has no choice but to trust you. What do you think, Sergeant Morgan?"

"I think your enemy doesn't want you dead yet. Or maybe you consume the poison in very small amounts. Is someone tasting your food?"

"Margaret does."

"God in heaven! How could you—" Devon began.

"She is my wife!" Arnaud explained impatiently. "But I eat only bread and broth. And she has not become sick."

"And you do not drink spirits?"

"Not since I was first taken ill."

"Most poisons are bitter, best disguised in liquor, especially a sweet one," Gentry said.

Arnaud smiled grimly. "I shared a particularly robust glass of port with Miles the night before I was stricken. Do you suspect a certain poison?"

Gentry shrugged. "It's everywhere. Foxglove on the hills, daphne and nightshade in the woods."

"I keep nothing in my stomach or my bowels. And sometimes my heart wants to leap from my chest."

Gentry paused a moment. "Maybe foxglove," he said.

"How do you know?" Devon asked.

"I don't. But the shamans give foxglove bitters for a jumping heart."

"Do you know an antidote?" she asked.

He shook his head. "Other than to stop ingesting it." He gave Arnaud a questioning look.

"No, my friend. I cannot afford to have my executioner killed . . . yet."

"It is Miles then?" Devon asked. "He is a traitor to the alliance?"

"He is a nothing but a clever thief," her uncle said. "Still he is very important to the success of the conspiracy. More important than I, if truth be told. He has personal control of transportation and supplies to back up the attack on—" He halted, as if suddenly awakened.

"But I grow addled," he went on, "prattling things you have no need to know, my friend." He frowned at Gentry. "Know only that if I have him killed, I endanger months of planning, a fortune in money, and the lives of many brave men. If I do not have him killed, I die. A very difficult situation, eh?" He smiled wryly and brought up his hand to take a last puff from the small, dark stub.

Devon suddenly grasped his thin arm, interrupting the cigarillo's journey. "If you cannot eat, your stomach does not hold the poison. Perhaps it enters another way."

She looked to Gentry, questioning. He moved closer.

"Maybe you inhale the poison," she said to Arnaud.

"Impossible. I would taste it," Arnaud said.

"After thirty years of swallowing char? It's doubtful you know whether this is good Spanish tobacco or rolled sheep chips." She took the butt from his fingers and tossed it into an enameled plate that held a dozen more.

"There is no need to disparage a manly habit. My cigars are imported, handmade in Europe. They cannot be poison."

"All the same, we should inspect them. Where are they kept?" Gentry asked, drawing his knife.

"Victor keeps them in the right-hand drawer of—" Arnaud stopped.

Gentry had spun suddenly toward the door.

Devon heard the noise then: a tiny creak of the floor outside. A footstep.

Gentry silently approached the door, turned the knob, then yanked the door wide. The hallway was dark. Someone had doused the lantern by the door.

Gentry disappeared into the corridor.

Devon stayed with her uncle. Who had overhead the talk of poison?

A jumble of footsteps and uneven scuffles preceded Gentry's reappearance. He pushed a black man before him, his knifepoint pressed to the slave's side.

"Victor?" Arnaud whispered. "Ah, Victor." He shook his head. "Now that you're here, you can show Sergeant Morgan where you keep my little cigars."

Gentry withdrew the knife.

The tall black man straightened and tugged the lapel of his jacket to correct the fit. Then he crossed the room to a mahogany chest.

Gentry took a last look in the hallway and closed the bedroom door.

Victor pulled open the top right drawer of the chest and retrieved a wooden box. Walking to the bed, he set the box on the covers. He moved without apology or furtiveness, showing the same erect poise as Portia. Quite unlike an eavesdropper who had been caught, Devon thought.

"Get the lamp. Hold it close," Gentry said to her. He opened the box, and the lantern cast its glow inside. Picking up one of the thin black cigarillos, he held it close to the lantern globe. He turned the cigarette carefully, searching for any irregularity in the outside leaf that wrapped the cut tobacco inside. Then he turned each end to the light.

"I'll show you," Victor said quietly. He took the thin cigar from Gentry and held the tip to the light. His fingernail raked a tiny edge of leaf free from the tip. "A hole reamed small and filled with a tiny quill."

"Show us the powder." Gentry handed the knife to Victor.

"Morgan!" Arnaud exclaimed. "You give him a weapon?"

"In the hallway he could have easily escaped," Gentry

said. "He had the advantage of the dark, his size, and knowledge of the house." He looked at Victor. "You wanted to be caught. Why?"

With sudden vehemence Victor ground the cigarillo between his hands. "Because I am not a murderer!"

He firmly closed the cigar box. "It does no good to open them. The grains are few and they take on the color of tobacco."

"Foxglove?" Gentry asked.

Victor nodded.

"Tedious work. Who does it?"

"I did, at first. Then Marse Miles made Portia do it. She's careful. She loses less. I told her to dilute it with cornstarch. But sometimes she can't. He watches."

"Dear God, what kind of monster is he?" Devon asked.

"There is a better question," Arnaud said. "What kind of man acquiesces to such atrocity?" His voice trembled with as much rage as he could muster.

"Perhaps a man whose job it is to acquiesce," Victor said with a strange intensity.

"*Mon Dieu,* are you some mindless creature?"

Victor's brown eyes glistened with outrage. He turned away to the window and eased the point of Gentry's knife into the wood of the sill. The wood gave a wrenching plea and a large splinter tore upward.

"I would prefer having no mind," Victor said. "Then I could not think and reason why I bend to a vile man, why I am born with a will, forbidden to use it."

Arnaud grew alarmed. "Seize him!" he cried.

"Victor is the reason you linger among the living," Gentry said.

"I must thank him for this?" Arnaud said, bringing his hand to his sunken chest. "A weakened heart and shrunken body!"

"We could have saved you more anguish had you smoked less," Victor said.

"Ludicrous," Arnaud whispered. "My killer chides me."

"Miles is your enemy, not Victor," Devon said hurriedly. "We must decide what to do."

"Do you want Miles arrested?" Gentry asked her skeptically.

"He mustn't know what I've told you," Victor said, coming close. "He would—" He stopped.

"He would hurt Portia," Devon finished softly.

"All of you, out!" Arnaud said. "I trust no one. No one but my niece." He rubbed his brow with one bony hand. "I am such an imbecile. I am powerless here. No friends. No allies. Isolated from Wilmington command. Miles takes care of everything. I am his touchstone for the alliance and its monies. That is all. He knows I cannot risk exposing the secret of the fleet to the general commander here. If this port shows undue activity, it would invite scrutiny by the Federals—"

"I must go," Victor interrupted, looking warily at the door. "He expects me soon." He looked down at the knife in his hand, then extended it, handle first, toward Gentry.

"Keep it. You may have use of it," Gentry said.

"Morgan," Arnaud protested weakly.

"I'm afraid you've been too long from the battlefront, Admiral. You don't recognize your own personal guard. Good luck," he said to Victor, following him to the door.

The tall Ashanti took the half-breed's hand and laid it palm to palm with his.

"All blood runs red," Gentry murmured.

The quiet phrase hit Devon solidly, in memory from an abolitionist meeting a year ago. "All blood runs red, all hearts beat free." It was a rallying call to those battling slavery.

The certainty stopped her breath. Gentry Morgan was a Federal spy.

She turned to her uncle to avoid Gentry's gaze after Victor left.

"You must smoke no more," she said.

"Mon Dieu. Je suis mort," he muttered.

"You will not die," she said firmly.

"I am so tired," he whispered. "But there is so much to tell you. Leave us, Sergeant Morgan. Leave us now."

Gentry looked at Devon. She summoned the courage to meet his gaze.

You are the chosen one, his gaze said. *He will pass on the knowledge. And you will be the courier once again.*

EIGHTEEN

Gentry stopped at the top of the stairs, breathing with relief. Arnaud Picard's room had reeked of the spoor of the death spirit that had lingered in the huts of the resettlement camp.

Unbidden, a medicine blessing slipped soundlessly from his lips.

Quickly you have drawn near to hearken, Blue Sparrow-Hawk. Sweep down upon the intruder. Let relief come. Brown Rabbit-Hawk at rest there above. Quickly scatter— scatter the . . .

The words? Where were the words of his beloved uncle? Too wispy to grasp, dusty with neglect. Arnaud's dry, poisoned body too readily reminded Gentry of another wasting sickness. Cholera had taken his uncle, Waits the Deer, in Gentry's ninth winter.

The displaced Cherokees had called the sickness "too swift to stone." Although there were many symptoms— retching, diarrhea, icy skin, hoarse and feeble speech—the trait that most impressed the shamans was how rapidly a body stiffened after death. Rigor mortis set in early, and muscles often contracted in bizarre gestures. They read omens in the death postures. Waits the Deer turned to stone with one elbow pulled high, two fingers outstretched, splayed against his cheek as if his hand had released a bow-string. It was a good omen. Waits the Deer would have good hunting in the spirit land.

Gentry had not often thought of his uncle. Memories of his boyhood in the settlement served only to summon other more painful memories.

He abruptly unbuttoned his jacket and the high collar of

his shirt. It was too hot for uniforms. But it was not the clothes that discomforted him. He was more deeply warm; somewhere beneath skin, in a sheltered visceral awareness, a fire had been fed. He had gained fresh evidence of the immoral heart inside the master of Jasmine's Reach.

If Miles could poison an old man and force slaves to criminal acts, couldn't he easily have committed murder eleven years ago? High on a windy hill, while gunfire and raiders occupied townspeople down the slope, could Miles have taken aim at the Indian woman who was to give birth to a Morgan heir? Could he then have lifted her dress and—

Dear God. Ancient One. The dress had been calico, soft and blue. Gentry had traded dearly in buffalo skin for it. Could the bastard have lifted the dress and taken a knife to—

Kai-ee-nah! His fist hammered the banister thrice, each time harder than before, and the wood rail absorbed the impact with a wretched cracking of joints. Kai-ee-nah . . .

Miles's drawl projected loudly up the stairs. "Glad to see I'm not the only one maddened by that old man's eccentricities."

Gentry's anguished reverie turned to chilling awareness of the shadows at the bottom of the staircase. Miles emerged, looking up as he came around the stairpost.

Gentry waited, on guard. Why hadn't he heard the warning jangle of the brace that marked Miles's movements? He could hear it now as Miles approached the bottom step.

He carried his jacket over his arm, the gold bullion of the shoulders dangling upside down. He had loosened his starched white collar, and it lay open in a disheveled V.

Gentry gathered caution around him like a cloak. Nothing in his manner must hint at his hatred, nothing must reach Miles's predatory senses.

Miles began his ascent. "I've been working in the study. I take it your meeting with the admiral was less than productive."

Gentry didn't answer.

"I myself have succumbed to frustrated displays after butting heads with Arnaud's peculiar brand of reason." Miles took each step with a measured rhythm.

Most people, Miles had noticed, averted their gaze politely after a while. But the half-breed at the top of the stairs never wavered in his watch. No sympathy there, Miles thought, only the emotionless scrutiny he remembered from those first days with Gentry at Teague Morgan's estate. It was more than a decade ago, and Gentry had been quite Sioux then, resplendent in a fringed and beaded buckskin tunic his pretty wife had made for him. Now, looming at the lip of the stairs, he was no longer recognizable as Sioux, nor as Cherokee or white. Free and unattached, he belonged to no one. Hard to compromise such a man. Hard, but not impossible.

Miles reached the halfway point and stopped on the landing. "How is Arnaud feeling tonight?" he asked.

"His mind and his mouth appear strong," Gentry said after a brief hesitation.

"Ah, yes." Miles smiled. "But it is his body that is our concern. I trust you found him better?"

Gentry shrugged. "This is the first I have met the man. He's very ill. Still, he smokes."

Miles gave a tsk and shook his head knowingly. "Nasty habit. Shortens the breath." He raised his stiff leg to the next step and began to ascend. "But then, life is full of debilitating little tendencies. We all have them. I don't know that you are personally disposed to self-defeating traits, but for a brother-in-law, you do have one annoying habit." He stopped three steps below Gentry and smiled up at him. "You're too damn quiet."

Gentry didn't smile and didn't move.

"Fortunately, I talk enough for both of us," Miles said easily, but he was anxious. What was Gentry waiting for? He took another step upward. Then another. He had passed into the glow of the torchère mounted on the banister post. Gentry remained in front of him, one step higher.

Blocked, Miles leaned tensely against the railing, both hands gripping the banister.

Gentry stared down at the pale, fine-boned fingers and the smooth skin on the back of Miles's hands.

In the awkward silence, Miles slowly realized what Gentry was looking for. He suppressed a smile of relief and relaxed his tight grip. "It was really quite a surprise to hear you'd come for a visit. How long's it been? Eleven years?"

Gentry could not control the stiltedness in his voice. "In September," he said. "Eleven years in September."

"Well, no one would say we're close as families go, would they?" Miles thoughtfully massaged his jaw with the thumb and forefinger of his right hand.

Gentry's eyes followed the gesture, as Miles had known they would, making note of the faint indentation and shadowy lines in the meaty fold connecting Miles's thumb and forefinger.

He extended his hand, spreading the fingers, and rotated it before Gentry. "We all carry scars of that tragic day," he said pensively. "Luckily, mine healed after a year. The stitches hurt like hell, though. Your father's cook sewed me up. The doctor was too busy, you know, tending a bunch of your dad's damned abolitionists. But you weren't there for the aftermath, were you? You left too soon. You didn't see how your family mourned the tragedy."

"My 'family' grieved an event. I mourned my wife."

"Now, Gentry. It was a time of terrible sadness for all of us. You had only to look at your daddy to understand that, plowing through the house like a gut-shot bear."

"He got drunk."

"Your information's not quite exact: Teague *tried* to get drunk. Finished off a quart of corn liquor and was madder 'n' hell because he still wasn't numb. As I recall, he broke two chairs, four glasses, and a Bible stand before he passed out. Never saw such black madness in a man, not even in my own daddy. All we could do was stay out of his way. Personally, I think he should've gone out and shot himself a couple of John Brown's nigger-lovers. Would've made us all feel better. But he never did believe one of those fanatics killed Ka-nee—Kay-na—" Miles frowned, struggling with the pronunciation.

"Kai-ee-nah," Gentry whispered.

"Of course. Teague said it was one of the border raiders, not one of his precious abolitionists. But who could tell? Both sides fighting over a little one-horse town half-slave, half-free. Teague just about hounded that federal marshal to death. Cobb, wasn't it? No. Dobbs. Marshal Dobbs. He nosed round your daddy's house a little bit, looking for suspects. Made me glad I had an alibi." Miles clenched, then opened his hand.

Gentry's eyes fixed on the hand. "You were cut."

"As you know, I wasn't about to fight men of my own

political sympathy, no matter what my future father-in-law thought. So I started assembling the wounded behind the feedstore. But one of the guerrillas didn't stop to ask my vote on the slave question. Stupid bastard jumped me. We fought hand to hand. And he cut me. Nicked the muscle right here." Miles traced the scar with his index finger. "Turned me into a diligent student of the anatomical sciences, that's a fact. I was amazed what a man couldn't do with his opposing thumb out of commission. I couldn't fire a gun for months."

Gentry was quiet a long time. The silence grew edgy.

"You really do doubt me," Miles said with a faint smile. "I probably would, too, if I were in your shoes. I'd be hoping against hope that I could reach out and get my hands around the neck of the right son of a bitch."

Gentry breathed high in his throat, like a hunter too close to his prey.

"I didn't kill your wife, Gentry."

The prey looked dead-on into the blind.

No fear or guilt darkened Miles's face. He held himself calmly, assured. Where was the wariness that shadowed the eyes of a guilty man? Gentry wondered. Or the false pitch that escaped the throat of a liar?

Gentry felt numb inside. He moved to the other side of the staircase, allowing Miles to mount the final step.

"Are you here to find a murderer, Gentry?" he asked.

"The killing's done. I have killed enough."

Miles frowned. "Then why'd you come here?"

"To guard the alliance courier."

"She arrived safe. I guess you consider your mission accomplished."

"That's what Admiral Picard and I were discussing."

"I see. When will you be leaving?"

"That's up to Admiral Picard."

"But he's not your ranking officer in this enterprise."

"He's just a man with answers."

"Who's your commanding officer?" Miles asked.

Gentry didn't answer.

Miles tried to keep his voice low. "Flagrant disregard for procedure is not characteristic of the alliance I've worked with for twelve months!"

Gentry looked directly at him. "They're no strangers to rule-breaking. Someone's already shown them the way."

Miles swallowed, then slowly turned his head to look down the hall. "Is Devon still with the admiral? Imagine he's got lots of details and whatnot to get off his chest."

Gentry felt the hair at the base of his neck rise.

"Ah, well." Miles glanced back at Gentry. "What an edifying conversation. The only time we've traded anything but distant animosity. I'm sure we'll grow closer, as this little enterprise requires. Secrets always do that, you know. Bring people close whether they want to be or not."

Gentry started down the stairs.

"One more thing," Miles said.

Gentry halted.

"I want to offer my commendations on your conduct on that challenging journey. Devon said you were quite the man of integrity. I admire your restraint. Especially given the fact that she's a compromised woman." He paused, waiting.

Gentry took one more step down.

"Perhaps you don't understand," Miles continued. "She was the object of some gossip in London before she left. She spent the night with her fiancé, then refused to wed him. Obviously a woman of exacting standards, don't you think? An earl's son, I believe. Titled and monied, but somehow inadequately endowed."

Miles smiled. "I'm sure the scoundrel unfairly pressed Devon into a compromising position. Still, I appreciate your gentlemanly behavior. Virginity is such an arbitrary measure of a young woman's virtue, don't you think? And by the way, forget about that recon run tomorrow. I'll assign another sergeant."

"Why?" Gentry asked. "I'm fit."

"I see that. But you should have a chance to rest. Besides, I can't give you orders. I'm not your ranking officer, am I? Good night, Gentry."

The brace jangled in diminishing counterpoint to the clomp of his boot as Miles disappeared down the hallway.

Gentry listened until a door closed and the rhythm stopped. Then he descended the remaining steps slowly, puzzled.

Miles had offered the vile gossip about Devon like a gift,

then grandly cleared the way for Gentry to seek time with
her tomorrow. He had baited a trap and spread its jaws. A
smart animal would deny hunger.

But Gentry knew this prize, how she looked, how she felt
in his arms. In the farmhouse she had trembled against him,
accepting the depth of his kiss with the trust of the untried.
She had stood dripping and bare, the light of the night glistening on the mounds of her breasts. He had pressed the
coolness of her body against him for a fevered timeless moment, and then she was lost to him, until he embraced her
innocently in their bed, with no passion, only a tired tenderness he had not felt since he lay as husband to Kai-ee-nah.

Kai-ee-nah had been inexperienced, but not innocent, the
first time she shared his blanket. Who took a woman first
was unimportant. Fidelity was the measure of a woman's
virtue, for it took time and many couplings for a woman's
spirit to entwine solely with one man's. How many suns
must rise on robes marked with the scent of seed before a
man's soul could remain with his beloved, and hers with
him, so that they touched each other, even in the longest of
journeys or the smallest duties of the day.

Gentry's uncle, Waits the Deer, had once revealed the
secrets of a virtuous woman. She must be bold in courage,
strong in judgment, healthy in stature, he'd said. And she
must be honest in her song, for a woman's song is powerful.
It surrounds the man. Woman sings to suckle the baby warrior, to scrape the skins that protect great hunters in winter,
to mourn the death of kin, to assuage the spirits of the earth.

When Gentry had chosen Kai-ee-nah, he'd known he possessed a virtuous woman. Her song could sweeten the air,
high and light, as if a lark tendered words from atop a
strong oak. She sang of her warrior, his kills and his coups,
his bravery and cunning, the pride of their nights—

Gentry stopped suddenly on the bottom step. It was so
long ago. The memory provoked only a sad sweetness.
Where was the pain that maddened him, the sorrow that
fueled him?

Upstairs, a door closed softly. He heard the rasp of her
silk.

He waited.

Soon she walked into the yellowish glow of the torchère.
She saw him below and stopped, turning to face the stairs.

Gentry looked at her. She was a woman bold and strong and healthy. But her song was not yet honest. She was burdened by duties of family and pressed to acts of falsehood, sedition, and war.

He could see that her beautiful face had grown dark with the secrets Arnaud had passed. She looked wearied and haunted by precious knowledge, as if she sensed greedy spirits hovering around her.

She needed someone to protect her, but he could not. His own instincts burned with an avarice he no longer wanted to fight. One of her shoulders was bared by the lace shawl, one breast lifted high by corset and crowned by a bursting fullness, creating a shadowy crevice between swells of warm flesh, where his lips could seek sweetness, where his breath could bathe a cleaved path with one gentle whisper.

She cast her eyes down and slowly pulled the shawl around to cover her chest.

"You are well?" he asked.

She nodded.

"You are telling the truth?"

She shook her head.

"You are kind to let me know when you lie."

"I hope someday you'll show me the same courtesy," she said. Her tone was formal, as if she thought someone were listening.

"A man can't always be kind," he said. "And a woman, not always strong."

She turned her head away, shadowing herself. Gentry realized how much he did not know about this woman, and how dearly he wished to know.

She was the key to so many chambers. Behind one door waited Pinkney Dobbs, desperate for a message conveying the alliance launch date and targets. Behind another lay a dying village in Lakota territory, where the wind blew chill in September and where Kai-ee-nah's family needed white man's medicines to fight the white man's pox. In a third chamber was the stern Washington courtroom where Pinkney Dobbs would present evidence to convict Kai-ee-nah's murderer. He would show that Miles had been seen leaving his position at the height of the border raiders' attack, and that Miles had returned with blood-soaked trousers. Even with the injured hand, Miles had a shaky alibi.

He'd murdered her. Or else he knew who had.

Vengeance was close. Gentry felt it, warm and glowing like a heated rock beneath his ribs.

The warmth seeped lower, encompassing his awareness of the yellow-hair. She was the key to burying what was past. She was the path to his future. He could not avoid her.

So the trap must spring around them, and he would find a way to free them together.

"Sleep well," he said.

The promise must have carried in the timbre of his voice, for her dark eyes fixed on him until he was lost in the shadows below the stairs.

NINETEEN

Devon hugged her shawl tighter, wanting to call Gentry back to the light, to take him to a secret place where they could talk without being overheard.

She wanted to tell him she had no choice but to be strong. Clutched in her hand was the small brass key Arnaud had given her. The key would unlock a bronze box that held Arnaud's reports. She was to be his personal courier and emissary to a meeting of the alliance founders.

In two days, she and the stout box of payment vouchers and correspondence would be aboard a ship bound for the island of New Providence in the Bahamas.

Arnaud had told her what to do. He had not asked nor commanded her. He'd simply assumed her loyalty and trapped her in a cause not her own.

How could she refuse him? He was gravely ill. Yet how could she let him play her as a pawn in a game to help the slaveholders?

If Gentry was a Federal spy, he would need to know about the gathering of the monkey fists in Nassau.

The Federals hadn't even been able to discover the alliance password, she mused. How little they must know about the conspiracy's plan and potential.

They desperately needed a sympathizer within the alliance network. They needed a conduit for information. They needed her.

Could she do it, sink deeper into the conspiracy in order to topple it? What would she need, beyond the courage of her convictions?

Him.

"Gentry." She whispered his name. She needed to know what he thought, how he felt, what he would do when next they kissed. For they would kiss again. And embrace again. She would press her parched soul to the blood-warmth of his, accepting the depth and troubled nature of his spirit, if he would accept hers. Her fantasy had gone far beyond the wish to run her hand along the expanse of his skin; her palm sweep free and low along the solid ribbed flesh that tightened his belly; her hand inch into the warm, secret corridor where desire swelled in a form she had never seen, only sensed in strained outline, a live force held in its trap, awaiting a freedom within her power to grant.

It was she who wished to be freed, to feel the pulse in her groin, the beat that mimicked her heart but fed only her senses, rushing blood tight against her skin, holding her prisoner to what she could see, smell, and hear in the air around him, prey to the deep timbre of words, to the taste of his tongue, the touch of hands hardened with work, delicate with knowing.

These were not the girlish senses Roger Bivens had teased to giddy life. These were not the feelings destroyed that night, nor the feelings Miles Brant threatened with his twisted, selfish game.

These were her hopes and fears for oneness with a man whose heart and mind were unknown to her. She knew only that he called to her, though he tried not to; and that each time she answered, though she tried not to.

When next he called, could she reply with the depth of honesty he required of her?

Ahead in the hallway, a door opened. She tensed.

Victor stepped out carrying a tray of emptied crystal and silverware.

She was about to hail him as he neared, but the stiffness of his body and the hard set of his face warned away her greeting. He passed by her quickly, giving only a correct nod, servant to mistress.

A musical clank behind him sounded the reason for his reserve. Miles stepped from the bedroom door.

Devon's heart stilled. He'd promised. He'd promised not to force her into his bed.

She walked forward cautiously, her white skirt rustling against the dark wainscot on the wall opposite him. "Up late, Cousin?" he said, smiling pleasantly. He ambled into her path. "Could I inquire about your uncle?"

Devon had to halt. His tone was careful, as if the walls hid the ear of an eavesdropper. "He's not at all well," she said. Thanks to you and your cowardly poisons. She kept the words from her tongue, but she could not hide the hatred glistening in her eyes.

"I know he is important to you, Devon," Miles said with sympathy in his voice, "but he is also important to a cause. He has work that—"

"Is finished," she interrupted, impatient to leave. "The letter is translated."

"And did he mention no message for me?" Miles asked, his voice lowering.

"I will pen the instructions for you tomorrow. May I pass?"

He did not move. "So you have been anointed his new lieutenant? Congratulations. It will be a pleasure to work closely with you. Of course, you look a bit burdened by the honor," he said thoughtfully. "But still beautiful." His voice warmed. "Ever beautiful."

The change in his tone caught her off guard. It signaled a shift in his intent. The air around her seemed to entrap her as his gaze fixed and isolated her.

His smile faded and his face grew serious, its distinctness blurring as she became more aware of his loosened shirt and the gracefully disheveled form he presented. She watched his gray eyes grow bold with a carnal wish, an ageless salute to woman's role that needed no words.

Her cheeks flushed pink. She felt small and endangered, like a moth riding the hot air current above an uneven flame.

Such a pretty and foolish maid, Miles thought, unnerved by the intensity of the moment. Sensitive and intelligent, she would be fascinated by the process of seduction, but too inexperienced to appreciate it. Unfortunately he, too, was at a disadvantage. He had grown too practiced at the game for his own pleasure.

But why then did he feel strangely fervent as he studied her? And why so touched by the sweet color in her cheeks? She looked engagingly innocent, terribly susceptible. His only goal was to scare and confuse her. But the lady poised before him was an elegant fixture, an immature work of gold

awaiting the knowing hands of an artisan. And God knew
he was gifted in the art.

He reached slowly to take her hand.

"Master?"

The word struck him keenly from behind.

Portia.

He lowered his arm without touching Devon and looked
at her, her soft lips parted, phrasing no words, only high and
shallow breaths.

"Has Portia come to save you?" he murmured.

Devon was silent.

He reluctantly stepped aside. "Dream sweetly, dear
cousin. I promise to do the same."

Devon felt the pressure in the air ebb, as if a door had
opened. Devoid of energy, she could not move quickly. She
pressed her hands to the bell of her skirt, controlling the
crinoline's sway as she passed Miles. She was sure her gait
conveyed a sedateness she did not feel.

Devon did not know what to say to Portia as she approached the slim black woman standing in half-shadow.

Portia didn't move, nor did she acknowledge Devon. She
waited, her eyes cast low.

Miles's voice carried evenly. "Portia, see me after you
attend to Miz Devon."

In Devon's bedroom, neither woman spoke as Portia
helped Devon undress.

"Light the lantern," Devon said harshly, her throat tight
with unreleased tears.

She sat at a small writing table and hurriedly scratched
Arnaud's instructions for Miles:

> *Fleet rendezvous Aug. 20. Using your battle plan.*
> *Notify Richmond to fortify ground support, begin*
> *movement of troops. Stand by in Wilmington to super-*
> *vise transit of goods.*

"Here." She hastily folded the stiff note in uneven quarters and affixed a small paste wafer of lilac. She stood and
thrust the letter at Portia. "Perhaps he will be more concerned with this than with you."

Portia hesitated, then took the paper and clasped her
hands in front of her white, starched skirt. Noble, unread-

able, she shook her head, her expression making Devon feel hopelessly young.

She turned and walked silently to the door.

"Portia! I don't know how to help you!" Devon cried, desperate.

Portia opened the door and did not look back. "Free me," she said softly.

Midnight had long passed. Gentry walked the sloping grounds below the manor house, a saddled horse beside him.

The horse tugged impatiently on the reins, and Gentry gave the animal slack to graze. He had been too restless to stay in the plank-board cabin where he had chosen to bunk with the three infantrymen from Henderson's Fifth.

The young soldiers who had served as escorts were gone, their wagon loaded with precious dry goods and salt pork. They would rendevous with the regiment outside Augusta. Sherman's Federals were snapping off railroad lines to Atlanta like spokes in a wheel. The Macon & Western was next. If Confederate forces didn't rally to protect it, Atlanta would fall hard and soon.

Gentry was not sure where he would ride. He knew only that the night was peaceful while his heart was not. The summer sky loomed above like a mountain without a peak, smoky and velvet, hazy with starlight.

The night was too warm for clothes. He stripped off his shirt, then repositioned black suspenders across his bare chest.

From a distant pond bullfrogs harrumphed a gravelly chant. In a nearby elm, a barn owl whorled a hollow beware.

"Be warned," Gentry whispered, uneasy. His mind drifted even as his eyes sought the lantern-lit window that he knew was hers.

> I arise from dreams of thee
> In the first sweet sleep of night . . .
> And a spirit in my feet
> Hath led me—who knows how?
> To thy chamber window, Sweet . . .

The lines of Shelley numbed his mind like smooth whiskey. Foolish romantic, Shelley. Foolish Gentry for remembering the words of long ago. He had read "The Indian Serenade," expecting it to evoke a song of his people. But on this earth Indians were everywhere, halfway across the world and back. Each of the world's peoples, white or dark, separated by nation, tribe, or band, each thinking itself the Chosen Ones.

"Why are we, the Real People, chosen for this defeat?" Gentry had asked his mother one day. They were walking the dust-clouded path from the Cherokee camp to the house of the reservation agent, a sour man who gave out gray flour, dried corn, and wizened squash.

"We do not know the plans of the great spirits," his mother had answered, even though the chill of the fever was on her and she walked with a blanket across her shoulders in the sunrise.

"The spirits did not follow us," Gentry had said with the skepticism befitting a nine-year-old. "Selu grows no corn. Kanati sends no deer. Anisgaya Tsunsdi holds the rain. This is a land of night-cry birds and witches."

"Is Nunda not here to light each day?" Calla Summer Sky asked.

"We need more than sun to live. When will the white man with coal-black hair come to help us?"

"Soon, I hope," his mother said.

"You hope too much," he said angrily.

"Perhaps because our children have forgotten how."

She was always so calm and wise, but much too stubborn. Each week in duty and prayer she beseeched the spirits to send Gentry's father to help the tribe survive the wasteland.

She knew Teague Morgan was somewhere in the territories of the West. He had sent her a letter once. She had carried it for eight years, reading it even though the paper grew delicate and pliable as baby skin.

With single-minded discipline, Calla Summer Sky had taught Gentry to read his father's writing, just as she had forced him to attend the reservation school so that he could bring back books for both of them.

And each passing of the moon she sat and told him the story of his father, so that Gentry would know him.

Teague Morgan was a strong man, she said, with the chest

of a bear. He had eyes blue and bright as forget-me-not. She called him Come Glistened With Coal, for the tall Irishman's unruly dark hair covered his brow with shining strands. She'd thought when they met they would only be lovers, but he wanted her as his wife. He was of poor family in his homeland, though, and had crossed the Big Water to work the land of his cousins, rich people who grew corn and tobacco and housed many slaves.

His family said he could not have Calla Summer Sky to their house as kin. Teague Morgan told them Calla was growing big with his child. They told him to leave. So Teague Morgan wrote a letter, delivered to Calla Summer Sky by a white servant in black coat and tall hat, as if she were a great lady. Teague said he was moving west, away from the constraint and disapproval of his family. He had taken the money he had earned and would return for her and the child when he prospered.

Soon Calla Summer Sky bore a strong son with azure eyes, as her grandmother had before her. She gave the child a name that would reflect his place in the white man's tribe when Teague returned for them. He would be Gentry. She waited, but received no letters, and never again caressed the dark brow of Come Glistened With Coal.

After the next summer's passing, President Jackson's soldiers arrived to herd the Hiwassee Cherokee with Indians of many nations, like cows of many colors, and drive them from their homelands.

Calla Summer Sky nursed her two-year-old son so he would not starve like so many children buried along the Trail of Tears. She saw the barren reservation in the plains, without forest for wood or stream for water, but she did not give up hope that Teague would come for her.

She believed, even as the members of her tribe died around her, victims of cholera, cold winters, and idleness. Finally, in Gentry's ninth summer, she, too, lay shrunken and bedridden, dying from cholera.

"Your father will come for you," she whispered hoarsely to Gentry. The death rattle was deep and urgent in her chest. "Follow him. Honor him."

Gentry did not acknowledge his mother's request.

"Give me your word," she whispered.

He sat silent, anger for his absent father swelling his throat.

Slowly, with a strength surely no woman but his mother could summon, Calla Summer Sky raised herself upward, long hair, lank and lusterless, draping her shoulder. She grasped his arm with fingers tensile and thin as a claw. Frightened, he pulled away from her.

She fell back limp onto the quilt and skins that were her deathbed.

He scrambled atop her, cradling her face in his hands. "Mother!" he cried. "Do not leave."

"Your . . . father . . . will come." He could hardly hear her words. "Promise . . ."

His tears shamed him. "I promise."

He never knew whether she heard.

When her body stiffened, her head drew forward and down toward her chest. Her knees bent and her arms reached outward. The tribe's medicine chief, already sick himself, pronounced the omen neither good nor bad. But Gentry knew the meaning. She had supplicated herself before the memory of his white father, and it was toward Teague Morgan that she reached, even as she began the journey to the Land of Many Lodges.

So long ago, Calla Summer Sky. Sad, wise woman of the Cherokee. What would she say of the yellow-hair coveted by her son?

Gentry smiled sadly. She would say, "Does the yellow-hair desire my son in return?"

He tore his gaze from Devon's window where lamplight still glowed in the dead of night. He mounted his horse.

At her window, a shadow suddenly filled the glass, draped full like the robe of an angel. He paused.

Could she see him?

The light in her room dimmed, died.

She would sleep at last, he thought. But he would not.

He pulled the grazing horse to attention, ready to leave, when he noticed a faint movement in the house. An image faded, then reappeared. A gray rise of light moved past a ground-floor window.

The shadow grew lighter, whiter, approaching French doors that led to the veranda. He saw a lantern. Then a woman stepped through the door, her hair braided at one shoulder like thick rope.

How softly she closed the door. He heard nothing but the steady chorus of the frogs.

She walked with the stealth of the conjured, a hovering image slowly crossing the veranda to the steps. The night breeze snaked the gown to the curves of her body like the molding hand of a lover.

Gentry heeled the horse forward, up the gentle slope, to the flat lawn that met the veranda steps.

Devon waited, the lantern glowing beside her on the step.

The breeze cooled the bare skin of his chest, but his heart beat fast, feeding his warmth.

He drew the horse to a halt alongside her. She descended one stair so that they matched evenly in height.

Her face had an ethereal calm, her full lips pressed decisively tight. Her eyes, unflinching, told him nothing. Her gown gaped deep between her breasts.

They did not speak for a long moment.

"What is it you seek?" he asked.

"Someone who will help me."

"Willing hands wait inside." He nodded at the house.

She slowly shook her head and looked away.

"My hands?" he asked softly.

She did not answer.

"Why?" he asked, and reached toward her.

"Reason is not part of this," she whispered, turning her face into the warm cup of his palm.

His hand slid behind her head and down her back, then he leaned low to encircle her waist and draw her up onto the saddle.

She placed one hand at his shoulder and the other on his chest, and he felt her chill against his skin. She was so frightened.

He kissed her temple, her lashes, her lips, and her mouth responded warmly, tenderly, with a willingness to give that made his hunger surge.

Her eyes sought his, and he could not interpret the deep sheen there. Without speaking, he righted her and held her to him. The horse ambled slowly across the lawn, hooves crushing high grass.

From the corner window on the second floor, Miles laid

his cheek against the window edging. Craning uncomfortably, he could just discern the figure of the shirtless half-breed riding away. Billowing white fabric draped the side of his horse.

A bit dramatic, he thought, pulling away from the window. Now where would they be headed? Gentry had no domain at Jasmine's Reach, only the old slave cabin in which he had bunked with the escort soldiers.

Miles frowned and pursed his lips disapprovingly. What a crude trysting place for such a lovely lady. It was quite bare and rustic, though there was an old frame bed. Probably a straw-ticked mattress. No slaves would have it, even though the sturdy log cabin stood secluded on the property.

It was the conjurer's place. Slaves respected a dead conjurer as much as a live one. Conjurers were too powerful. They cast spells, avenged wrongs, interpreted dreams, and used plants for medicine, poison, or magic.

Miles had been truly sorry when One-Eye Poe crossed over Jordan—if that was indeed the direction death took him. One-Eye had been a mean and ugly rascal, a mulatto with yellow-brown hair and a nose for making money. He had been Miles's best informant when slaves were planning runaways. When One-Eye died, a bevy of slave women cleaned his house till it squeaked, clearing away every last powder, potion, squirrel tooth, and snakeskin, so that One-Eye Poe couldn't mix up anything and come back as a haunt.

Miles took a last look out the window. Gentry's horse was nowhere in sight. Exposing Gentry and Devon that night would be gauche and bad strategy, he thought. There was much more potential in allowing the bond to develop.

That assumed, of course, that Gentry had feelings for the girl. He should at least have pride of possession, Miles mused. For a man who had lost one beautiful woman, it would be devastating to lose another.

It was with Devon that Miles had to exert real caution. With Arnaud's confidences, she had gained unknown stature within the alliance—and a sudden hold over cash vouchers.

Damn the timing. He was only one small down-payment away from acquiring a major parcel along the Missouri. He might have to raise the money by running more black-market items than usual. In a few days his blockade-running friend Beque Trouvier would ride the morning tide to safe harbor with salable merchandise. Hat frames from Le Havre, a cache of whiskey from the Isles, woolens from Aberdeen, and most importantly, rifle cartridges being secreted to the Confederates by sympathizers in Baltimore.

The cartridges were an undercover transaction in which Miles's childhood friend Lilly Frith had had a hand—and most likely, more salacious parts of her anatomy too. Sometimes Lilly sent intelligence reports with contraband goods, and the reports were always profitable. The last one had earned Miles his colonel's commission.

Business. Always business. Yet Miles would really have it no other way. It made his time for pleasures all that more intense.

He glanced at his bed near the fireplace. Portia was pretending sleep, a ruse the brave young woman had never stooped to before.

He had succeeded in ruffling her regal composure that night.

He smiled. His victories were only beginning.

TWENTY

The land dipped gradually to a stand of elm. The horse and its riders drew around the trees to a clearing. A dark pine cabin huddled under tall boughs twenty yards away.

Gentry halted the horse and dismounted.

Above them, leaves riffled and rasped in the wind.

Not a word had passed between them on the short journey.

Devon didn't move. Her bare leg held its tuck snug against the warm hide of the horse. She felt the massive ripple of muscle as the horse lowered his head, patiently awaiting an empty saddle.

She looked down at the man whose presence she felt even when he was gone from her, when his face hovered in her mind's eye and his words echoed in her thoughts. His body, though, could not materialize in the beat of her heart or a flick of memory. His body was solid and real, something she must touch to know. She reached out to him, aware of her risk, aware that the vibrant fear in her heart foreshadowed deep knowledge.

His hands encircled her midriff and lifted as she fell forward. He turned her in midair.

She faced him, dressing gown loose and flowing. She felt the prickle of soft grass along her ankles. A naked tingling of awareness rose with the current of air beneath her gown.

His arm swept close, and his fingers tugged at her braid, walking each link higher, loosening and freeing her hair. Finally his hand rested in the mass at the back of her head, enclosing a fistful of hair.

His other hand curled in the neckline of her gown and

pulled it aside, allowing her breast to emerge naked to the night, to him.

She felt her nipple burn and harden.

His hand clenched tighter at her nape, and he pulled down forcefully, arching her head back, extending her bosom. His mouth captured the stiffening bud.

She cried out as he sucked.

The startled frogs in the pond beyond the trees lost their song. All was still, except for the rustle of the wind and the uneven moan of the woman.

As his mouth left her breast, his hands slipped the gown over her shoulders. The garment billowed empty to the ground.

Gentry impatiently slid suspenders off his shoulders and unbuttoned his trousers. The dark pants slid past narrow hips, allowing him to rise freely.

Devon looked away.

For a moment Gentry thought she would run from him. Had she not seen the first man with whom she had lain?

He slowly stepped away from the woolen at his feet. She stood deathly still, a porcelain mold bathed in dim, otherworldly light.

Gentry circled her, not touching, taking in the cascade of golden hair that licked the small of her back, the dark line where firm buttocks met in hidden joining, the sweet belly that would wax hard and soft against him.

He felt seed swell in its sac, eager for freedom, and he could no longer distract himself from the need to take her. He swept her into his arms, fitting the curve of her waist against his side. Her breast pressed young and silken and warm against his chest.

He descended with her to lie on the soft gown and felt her body tense as he gathered her close.

"Daloni-ka." *Yellow-hair.* He whispered her name and let his lips travel the soft crease in her neck to the hollow of her throat. He cupped and smoothed her breast until he felt the nipple rise against his palm.

He kissed her urgently, insisting her tongue join his. She arched away from him, but he rode the motion, demanding her response. Her tongue thrust sweet and slick to the base of his, tasting his hunger, roaming the softness of his cheek.

But Gentry was impatient for a different thrust. He lay

hot and rigid, branding the hollow above her groin with a
need too long ignored. Soon a drop of seed would seep free,
and he knew he could wait no longer.

He pressed himself to the crown of light hair that hid the
furrowed swell. But her legs did not part for him.

He slid his finger gently, quickly, into the warmth he
craved, and though she gasped and stiffened, he found the
path moist, yielding.

He wedged his thigh solidly between hers and opened her
legs wide as he positioned himself above her.

He sensed her hesitancy. She did not raise herself to greet
him. But he could not be gentle, not this time.

Gentry rode the first thrust deep and hard.

Her sharp cry astonished him, for he heard surprise and
fright and pain.

He held himself deep inside her but didn't move.

Her head was turned to her shoulder, away from him, and
she breathed quick and light, as if she would cry.

He bent his own head, holding fast to her, inwardly cursing the impatience that had blinded him to the signs. But the
curse was light, because the hunger for her burned so fierce.

"I am first?" he whispered.

Her eyes closed in a silent "yes."

He breathed a kiss in her hair and shifted gently atop her,
letting her feel the ease with which he moved in the place
she had made for him.

"See me, Devon."

She slowly turned her head, but could not meet his eyes.

"We are joined now," he said. "We move together, until
the pleasure comes."

He began a slow and shallow rhythm, so that she would
feel his fullness without pain.

Her eyes closed, and he knew the motion had sent her
thoughts low in her body. She would hear her own slick
readiness, would feel the measured push and pull, and begin
to welcome the homing of each thrust.

An exhilaration quickened his rhythm. He was first. Of all
men, he claimed her first. Inexplicably, it drove him deeper
with need.

She writhed beneath him, to respond or to escape he
didn't know, for his seed sensed the lick of the fire and

surged upward. He rode the madness with a violent tremor, hugging her close.

Soft strands of her hair fell across his cheek and shielded him as the night wind rose above, roiling leaves in noisy waves.

Slowly he grew aware of how evenly she breathed, how patiently she lay. He slid his hand under her and cupped her buttocks tight against him. Then he rolled gently onto his back, holding her on top of him.

"Do not move, or I will die," he said, hiding a smile.

"You face this death with great content."

"Not always," he whispered. "Not always." He ran his hand across her back, soothing, exploring. "We lie well together."

"Men and women do, quite commonly." Her soft voice held stirrings of guilt and remorse.

He could not expect her to know how rare it was to lie fulfilled, without impatience to leave, without the need to disguise how cursory the joining and medicinal the release.

They did not speak for a while. Then Devon eased herself from him. She gasped as he left her.

Reaching for her gown, she slipped it over her head. Gentry rose and donned his trousers.

She stood carefully distant from him. Her gown whipped her legs, stirred by the wind. She looked up the slope toward the house, grateful for the barrier of the trees. She should return now, in the dead wake of night, as quickly as she had left, returning changed but unchanged, filled but emptied, touched inside by a man, giving space to him and drawing his strength, an act so intense and so brief that contentment lay warm around her yet strangely beyond her grasp. The yearning with which she had begun her journey had only burrowed deeper, grown stronger. Nothing had ended with the yielding of the delicate wall inside her. His knowledge of her, her knowing of him, had only begun.

She was unable to move toward the house, away from him.

"We must talk," he said, and took her hand with a gentle tug, as if to awaken her.

She followed him along the woodland border, skirting the herbs and low shrubs, raising her gown clear of the high grass and flowers.

She crossed the threshold of a cabin into loamy dark. She could hear Gentry moving in a far corner. The glass flue of a lantern screeched free of its metal prongs. The air carried the pungent tar of oilcloth, then the acrid waft of sulfur when he struck the match.

The light enveloped him suddenly, showing a tall, dark figure bent forward, long hair skirting the set of his jaw, hiding his face.

So much of him was hidden from her. But the thought did not deter her, for what she knew was profound.

He was not cruel nor crude nor inherently manipulative. He had had a wife. He had loved her, and she him, Devon knew, because Gentry's touch was warm with the caring of one whose love has been buoyed and returned.

She wished with all her heart to have her love held and named and nurtured with such care. She had long been alone in a world too rich in ornament and poor in spirit, alone with friends and suitors of narrow mind and pinched heart.

That night she'd lain with a man whose heart was wide and secret as a sea. Though his life was fragmented by pain and loss, he walked as one with the world around him. She would learn from him, as long as she could.

Her life and her future compressed into the small space of the cabin, into the narrow breadth of the night's wee hours, and she dared not breathe too deeply for fear of hastening the unsaid between them.

He straightened, lamplight golden on his chest.

She remained in the shadows at the edge of the lantern's reach, aware of the vague and tender ache surrounding her womb, and the warm pool of his seed gathering inside her thigh.

"You didn't tell me you were untried," he said.

"You didn't ask."

"I believed the story of a liar."

"Did you want to believe?"

He paused. "Perhaps."

"You needn't have worried. I wouldn't hold you responsible."

"I don't fear responsibility," he said. "I fear women who don't know what they want."

She turned from him, her slim neck bent beneath the

weight of the hair he had loosed. "Do I seem so uncertain to you?"

He was quiet a moment, then shook his head. "No. Just afraid. What are you afraid of, Devon?"

She walked deeper into shadow. "The path," she said softly. She sat on the edge of a straw-ticked bunk. "Always the path is laid for me, and I follow, as I've been taught. But once the path crooked and led to my fiancé's bed. . . ."

"You have nothing to explain," Gentry said.

She shook her head. "The story you heard was not a lie. Just a family's assumption in the midst of damaging circumstances."

"You did not submit. You would have nothing to explain if you did."

Devon was silent. She had nothing to explain?

"Devon," Gentry began.

Her throat was dry. "You do not care?"

"You should have asked that earlier tonight, and I would have known to be kind."

She looked away. "I did not find you unkind."

He walked closer to her. "Why find me at all?"

He stood so near she could touch him, if only she did not have to push him away with her answer. "I decided you are a man of significant virtues—even though you are a liar."

"Liar?"

"You are not sent by President Davis, nor the alliance. You're an agent for the Federals."

He waited.

"And you're an ally to the slaves," she continued quietly. " 'All blood runs red, all hearts beat free.' It's a call to brotherhood a Confederate would never invoke in the presence of a black man."

"It is also," he said after a moment, "a credo from closed rooms where English ladies digest more than tea and biscuits. Where did you learn it?"

"In London. Last spring. At a meeting to raise money for fugitive slaves."

An abolitionist, he thought, raising an eyebrow. How often she surprised him. "Monied abolitionists like to walk the shore and gather the pious. You're surfacing in deep water here."

"If I don't get word to the Federals, the South may rally

enough to prolong—or win—its war. And women like Portia will never live free."

"You would do this for Portia and other women?"

"For myself. For my conscience. For a people who have endured enough."

He took a deep breath and sank to the floor to rest on one knee before her. "My motives are not so noble."

"Money?"

He shook his head.

She knew he would not tell her more. She took a deep breath. "You realize my uncle will disown me if he finds out I work against his cause."

"Arnaud Picard will not live long enough to lay judgment on anyone. The death spirit waits with him."

"I don't believe in spirits."

"It has nothing to do with belief. Spirits are there to be felt, like wind or rain or the brightness of sun."

"And what spirit guides the touch of my hand?" she asked, reaching out to him.

He placed his palm flat against hers. "Hige-ya Tsune-ga, the spirit in Yu-we-hi, the sphere of living humanity."

"We walk different spheres, Gentry," she said sadly.

His hard, calloused skin pressed the soft ridges in her hand. "I walk alone," he said. "I belong to many people, and so to none."

Her hands lighted on his shoulders. She slid thumb and forefinger down the tight span of suspenders to the deep mottled scars that sat high on his chest, then she pulled the straps aside, letting the bands retract down his arm, exposing both scars. "How did you get hurt?"

"I was eighteen," he said. "The Sun Dance is sacred, a ritual of commitment."

"A rite of pain," she said.

Her hands returned to his chest, but gave wide berth to the numb ridges where the tissue had lain open to heal twisted and flayed as rope.

How could he describe it to her? he wondered. The comforting madness of the chant, the sweet blindness born of searing pain. How he had welcomed the sharp pierce of the skewers in the tender skin above his breasts. He had danced longer than any other warrior, stepping and swaying around the sacred pole with drums drowning his heartbeat, a rawhide thong tied to each skewer and to the pole, so that he could pull and tense and twist and fall until skin and muscle screamed like a thousand hawks feeding at his heart. Then he soared free of the pain, free of all thought, free of the face of his beloved, placed lonely on the tall bier he had framed with her face to the great Sun. Kai-ee-nah. Gone. Forever.

Gentry looked at the face of the yellow-hair whose fingers danced on his skin now like droplets on a hot rock. He no longer remembered the touch of his wife. He knew only her touch now, the tentative question in the slim hand that traced the knotted hollow below his stomach, a hand so white that his skin seemed smoldering shadow against her sunlight.

"I wish no commitment nor pain on either of us," she said, breaking the long silence.

"Then you must take care."

"I doubt there's time. In two days, I board a ship for Nassau. There's a meeting of alliance partners."

"And you will attend in your uncle's stead?"

She nodded.

"The launch of the ships?"

"I don't know. My uncle said the ships rendezvous in a fortnight."

"How many ships and where will they attack?"

"He wouldn't say. The naval assault will be supported with ground troops. The battle plan is one of Miles's devising. And Miles is ordered to stay here when the alliance meets."

Gentry thought a moment. It would take at least a week to get a message through to Dobbs, via his agent in Wilmington. And how long to increase ocean-going patrols and fortify the South Atlantic Squadron?

They had so little time. Yet he had no wish to talk of duty. At the moment he ached to listen to nothing but the sweet whisper of her gown as he leaned his head to her bosom; to explore the length of her legs with his restless hands, roving high to the crease at the top of her thigh that led inward to the soft darkness still wet with his leaving. "Daloni-ka," he murmured, impatient. He pulled off her gown so there would be no clothes between them.

Then he stood and shed his pants so that she could see the

mark of her innocence on him, not yet dry. "Is it a gift of shame?" he asked.

Devon felt frozen by the moment, by the boldness that came so naturally to Gentry. Her "gift" to him was a barrier that everyone assumed she had already broken, a chastity that had become too heavy a burden and too light a care in the short time she had known him.

Slowly, her hand reached across a great distance to touch him, to feel the vestige of herself he offered. The smear of blood lay warm on him, small and slick under a blanket of seed.

His tight, sculpted hood had emerged swollen and seeking. She held it lightly, cautiously. He tensed, rigid, as her fingers traced an undulating line that circled his breadth, then swept long down the hovering bow to hair black and surprisingly soft.

With the heels of his hands pressing gently at her temples, he tilted her face upward. She could not read his dark eyes, except to guess that he would take her with gentleness. He guided her to the bed.

He pressed forward, and she lay back onto the mattress, feeling the hard plane of his abdomen settle on the thin giving pad of hers.

He kissed her, and his hunger forced her mouth wide. She felt his hand roam her back, her buttocks, her thighs, testing firmness and curve, pressing each part of her to muscled flesh, as if he could mold her smooth, soft form to his body's memory.

Her pink nipples rose small and tender against him, and she lifted her pelvis to receive him. He entered slowly, and she felt his fullness tunnel deep inside her to a place beyond pain or pleasure, a place where feeling knew no words, only movement. The motion held her breathless at first, then she arched against him, feeling breath stop when he sounded the depth of her. Then came a cry she could no longer hold. Small and high like a trapped child's, or a dove's mourning keen, the sound was torn from a part of her she did not know.

He did not stop, nor allow the madness to take him, when he heard her pleasure cry begin. He fed it with the heat of his thrusts and the pounding of his heart, until her small cry turned urgent, resonant with beginnings primitive and deep, close to the womb of their joining.

Her scream was sudden, her hand clenching his skin.

Then his own shudder overtook him.

A long stillness lay over them, until he felt her shy, tender lips against his cheek.

The lantern light flickered as the oil burned low and shadows danced on the walls.

They lay unwilling to move, enclosing so much warmth between them that Devon grew sleepy. Her head lolled in its untidy nest of golden hair and came to rest against Gentry's forearm.

There is no time for sleep, Daloni-ka, he told her silently. Dawning comes soon. We have little dark left to hide us.

He might have whispered, stirred her gently, but he felt a strange, mute fear. Her trust frightened him. How did she know he would not steal away and leave her there to be found like a harlot? How did she know he would feel such grave responsibility for the welfare of a woman foreign to his land and pale enemy to his race? How did she know he had not looked on such faith and trust since he had taken a woman to his lodge long, so long, ago?

The lantern failed, and the shuttered cabin turned black. Faint starglow spilled weakly through the mud-chinked logs.

Gentry grew uneasy. This place was a conjurer's domain. In the dark it seemed spirited and hungry.

But in his arms lay a stronger spirit, one whose presence did battle with much that was dark in his life. He must not grow to depend on her, or he would be crippled in the fights to come.

Slowly he withdrew from her.

She moaned, so honest a protest that he breathed a kiss in her hair and let her sleep a minute more, for he, too, understood the solemn ache of emptiness.

TWENTY-ONE

They walked to a tract of wild laurel that sprawled in gangly patches between the trees and the cleared, sloping ground below the house. The sky showed an urgent fringe of pink on the horizon.

Gentry had taken a dark wool blanket from the bedroll on his saddle and wrapped it around Devon to ward off the morning chill. But her feet were bare, and she could feel the cool quickening of dew on the soft grass.

They stopped within cover of the trees and looked up toward the house.

"I don't expect to meet Regina so early. She imbibed quite a bit," Devon said, thinking aloud. "And Aunt Margaret will be tending my uncle. And Miles—" She stopped and tucked the blanket ends tighter under her chin. "Miles . . ." She shook her head.

"He wanted us to be together."

"What happened is our doing, not his," she said quietly.

"He baits a trap. Just beware."

She turned her head to let the breeze brush her cheek free of a tangle of hair. "You report for duty and leave soon?" she asked, wishing his arms would close around her. But to touch him now would make their parting even more difficult. Already her head felt light and her feelings raw.

"Miles rescinded the patrol orders. But I have business in town. And you?"

"Uncle Arnaud may need me. But I'd planned to sketch this afternoon."

He looked at her. "On our way to Jasmine's Reach, we passed a rise of land west of the iron gate. At the top you can follow the rock bed of an old creek to a place that's high and quiet. The view is good there."

"I'll find it." She backed away, holding fast to the hope that she would see him later that day.

He mounted his horse. Taking his hat by the crown, he seated it firmly and drew the lanyard slip tight under his chin.

Neither said good-bye.

He wheeled the horse sharply and headed down the slope.

She walked uphill, across the hollow where he had appeared in the night, to the veranda steps where he had come for her on horseback, to the French doors, still unlatched.

She made her way through the halls without haste. When she set foot on the main staircase, a thin black woman appeared in the foyer.

Devon recognized her. It was the housekeeper, Evaleen. Her dark eyes held no censure, only curiosity.

"Is Portia awake yet?" Devon asked.

"Portia in her cabin, ma'am," Evaleen said hesitantly.

Devon turned to face her. "Is she all right?"

Evaleen paused. "Marse Miles say I be your maid awhile."

Dear God. What had Miles done to her? Devon clung to the banister. "I see," she whispered.

She went to her room and slept fitfully. She awoke when the sun was high and her room hot. She dressed in a riding skirt, billow-sleeved blouse, and waist jacket. Evaleen helped her pack sketchpad, pencils, and apron in a saddlebag. Devon showed the housekeeper which dresses and accessories to begin packing for the trip to Nassau.

On her way out, she stopped to see her uncle. He slept, and Margaret barely acknowledged her presence. On the bedstand, no dark butts littered the glass dish.

"He doesn't smoke," Margaret said. "That's a bad sign. See how his chest barely rises when he breathes?" She sat by his side in a wrinkled skirt, hands clasped between her knees, gray hair wisping loose from her chignon. Her gaze was fixed on her husband. "This is not good."

"No," Devon said softly. On impulse, she took her aunt's hand. "I'm so sorry for hurting you," she said, aware that her words had the sadness of a warning—and a farewell.

Margaret did not notice. She began to rock, forward and

back, as if she were listening to music no one else could hear. "Not good, Arnaud."

Devon kissed her aunt on the cheek with an affection that lingered beyond the perfunctory gesture Margaret had always shown.

Margaret rocked absently and said nothing until Devon opened the door to leave. "White gloves, Devon. Don't forget white gloves for riding."

Devon looked down at her bare hands. "Yes," she whispered. "I'll remember."

She ordered lunch for Margaret, then left. She put on her hat as she crossed the front porch. Under the white-columned portico a boy held her horse, a gentle-natured bay wearing an English saddle. He had brought a stool to help her mount.

Evaleen came around the house from the kitchen with a linen bag. "Corn bread and fresh-fried side meat," she said.

"Thank you." Devon hung it on her pommel.

"Where you be goin'?" Evaleen asked." Miz Regina wants to know."

"East of the manor where the land's flat," Devon lied. "It's an easier ride for me."

"She say don't go far. I'll tell her you be home before dinner." Evaleen paused. "Marse Miles staying at the fort tonight. Victor took him clothes."

Devon smiled faintly. "Thank you, Evaleen. Please give Portia my regards."

The thin woman backed away nervously at the mention of Portia's name.

"Is Portia all right?" Devon asked.

"She gonna be soon, I 'spect." Evaleen's voice was soft. "You best be off, ma'am."

Devon nodded a stiff greeting to the guard who opened the iron gate at the edge of the estate. Then she cantered out of sight around the bend and found a diagonal path that led up the hill. She quickly located the dry streambed and followed its winding swath to the rise that Gentry had described.

The hill was not high enough to offer a vast view, but pockets of rolling land converged and descended in pleasing lines. She took off her hat, put on her white apron, and chose the ground beside a shady maple as her seat.

An abandoned mill rose beside the streambed like the misplaced turret of a stone castle. Its paddles hung useless below the steps of a dry fall where a trickle of water found its way to the bed below, meandering between stones like mercury in a maze.

Devon eagerly opened the lunch bag Evaleen had sent. The meat and corn bread were wrapped in separate towels. The thin fried pork was still warm, and the corn bread was distinctly honey-flavored and cakelike. The taste and texture nagged at her memory. She had eaten a similarly sweet bread, dry and crumbled, only a week ago, that first night she and Gentry made camp. The provisions were in the saddlebag of the masked bandit, whose horse Gentry had stolen.

Had the masked man and his corn bread come from Jasmine's Reach? Devon searched her memory for clues to the bandit's appearance. Though he had Miles's slim build, he had not been crippled. She remembered the elegant gait that marked him out of place in the woods.

She brushed the crumbs from her apron and wrapped the major portion of the meal for Gentry, then gathered her supplies. It felt good to hold a pencil again.

Devon studied the land before her and smiled. She hated landscapes. Her fingers bent immediately to the task of shaping a face on the page, a face half in profile. She positioned the eyes and straight nose in light, unfinished strokes, then the mouth and chin, so that she could find the jawline and mark the length of his hair, the cord of his neck. It was an empty face, and she could do no more than shade for depth until she had a chance to study her lover.

Lover. Did one night together a lover make?

"Yes," she whispered, her body remembering the force of the thrusts that drove him closer, ever closer to her, freeing the savage cry that lived clenched beneath propriety's sigh.

Devon hugged herself, eyes closed with the memory. Yet her own arms did not embrace as tenderly as Gentry's in the moments after they loved. He could be so gentle—and so rugged. Savage and schooled, calm and tempest-tossed. All the contradictions she could voice were vented in his nature.

Perhaps that was why she could not draw his face. Perhaps he could never be known to her.

She turned the page and began a somber scene, her uncle

in his sickroom, a man made small by the surrounding darkness. He seemed to shrink under her pencil, as if she viewed him from far away.

She realized as her pencil worked that she would not return to London with Margaret no matter what happened in Nassau. But she had little money to support her. Perhaps Damien could advance payment for another book project, or for newsmagazine illustrations of alliance ships.

She sketched as she thought, visualizing herself alone in a city, seeking assignments, living frugally. Or she could see herself in a ridiculously grand abode riding a wave of recognition for skillful etchings.

But she could not see herself beside Gentry. She did not know where they belonged in the world. Their lives converged in a perverse twist of politics and personal mission. She was afraid to hope, afraid she could not bear the disappointment.

Her pencil stopped. She had lost track of time. Five of her tablet pages fluttered in the wind, five sketches outlined and set, awaiting detail. None of the pictures were commercial or reportorial, none worthy of Damien's editorial attention. What a poor correspondent she made.

She put her pad aside and laid her head on her knees. Silence broke suddenly with the harsh snap and parting of underbrush nearby. Devon's heart beat fast, confused. Gentry walked with stealth and sureness. It was not he.

She retrieved her pad and pencils and stood, uncertain whether to flee the open space of the knoll. But then a hat appeared above the curve of the slope, a blue felt crown with tinted netting trailing the brim.

Regina appeared, pulling the reins of her horse.

"The guard said you took this trail," she said, "but I didn't believe him until I rode the east field. Couldn't find a trace of you. No wonder."

"Sorry," Devon said, keeping her voice calm. "This setting seemed much better."

"I'm sure," Regina said, lashing her reins to a sapling. "I haven't been up here in years. I'm not fond of hills."

"Vertigo?" Devon asked.

"Do I look like a vaporous twit? I'm just partial to level ground."

Regina walked past the maple, beyond its shade to the

sunlit grass at the lip of the hill. She stood there a moment looking across rolling meadows grown yellow with hay grasses that would not be scythed and stacked that year.

"Shame we can't spare any slave stock to cut the fields," she said, pulling the fingertips of her gloves one by one. "I'll let Miles explain that to the livestock this winter. I hope you don't mind my joining you. But I so seldom have an excuse to get my riding clothes out of the chest anymore."

"The war makes it difficult to live any semblance of a normal life, I'd imagine," Devon said.

"War is hell for a woman," Regina said bluntly, peeling off a glove. "It changes everything. Turns refined women into nursemaids, but it makes every man a hero. Though heroes come home crippled, don't they?"

"I'm sorry," Devon murmured.

"Oh, don't be sorry for Miles, nor for me. Miles is still the same dashing gentleman I married, talented, hardworking, genteel, and kind. It's been nearly a year, but he's still not over it, you know. He's so self-conscious. When he came home from the hospital, he wouldn't let me tend him. He just knew my sensibilities would reel at the sight of it. Dear God, it must be horrible."

"You've never seen his leg?"

"Of course not! I'm his wife, not a bath attendant. He took a separate room and absolved me from wifely duties. He was afraid I'd be repelled by the disfigurement. I thank God each day for such a caring, noble man. Wouldn't you?"

Devon held her breath, unbelieving.

Regina didn't wait for an answer. "Now, I didn't ride all this way just to stimulate my digestion. I wanted to warn you about Gentry."

"I see no cause to be fearful."

"Then you're not very perceptive for a young woman who's had firsthand experience with man's baser nature."

"My experience has been with the base instincts of people who assume guilt on the mere appearance of impropriety," Devon said tightly. "Your brother is not—"

"He's my brother in circumstance, not in sentiment," Regina interrupted. "His family lineage is savage. And it bloodied the roots of mine."

It was useless to argue. Devon took a deep breath. "Understand that I, too, was orphaned. I know how it feels to be

thrust into a relative's household without choice, carrying
your indebtedness like a lead weight in your heart."

Regina laughed. "You don't understand at all. I'm not
indebted to Teague Morgan. He owes me. I managed his
house from the time I was fourteen, a whole year before his
detectives finally found Gentry in Oklahoma and Teague
went down to pull him kicking and screaming from that
resettlement camp. I was there first. Don't you understand?"

"Isn't Gentry his son?"

"No. Gentry's his bastard." Regina turned and again
gazed out over the crisscross of neglected fields and wild
pine woods. "Teague Morgan never married that squaw. But
he got a lawyer to draw up a piece of paper that made
Gentry legal. And you know the really galling part? Gentry
never wanted that. He never wanted to live with Teague and
me. Never wanted to be a farmer or a horse breeder. Never
wanted to go to West Point and get called all kinds of names.
All that's what Teague wanted. Gentry just wanted to go
back to living like an animal. And he did for a while. But he
came back. Teague knew he would. Teague knew Gentry'd
never forsake his inheritance, 'cause he made it impossible
to deny. Teague named his property for Gentry's mother.
It's called Summer Sky." Regina slapped the limp gloves
against the side of her skirt. "Calla Summer Sky. Lord God
Almighty, how Teague used to talk about her when he was
sloshing in his cups. And how many evenings I had to listen
to that sorry drivel. In this whole wide world, there's no
more romantic fool than a drunk Irishman."

"Perhaps he really loved her," Devon said quietly.

"God yes, he loved her! Because he lost her. Let her slip
through his fingers and she got put out on the prairie with
thousands of others like her. You know, one year he spent
four hundred dollars on hired detectives. Four hundred dollars! I was so mad I could spit. Here I was, managing things
better than any wife or housekeeper, and he throws money
out the window at a ghost. You realize that with just one
hundred dollars of that, I could've made the downstairs parlor breathtaking?"

"Regina . . ." Devon tried to find words to break the
frenetic recollections.

"Well, Miss Calla Summer Sky never got to visit her
namesake. But her daughter-in-law did." Regina's words

slowed, as if of their own accord. "Just all of a sudden, one day Gentry and his wife showed up. Pretty little thing. Dark though. Darker than Gentry. But she made ole Teague's eyes light up. You would have thought a queen had come to Summer Sky. She was in the family way, you know. So right there in front of Teague was Morgan history in the making. He treated that little savage like royalty." She paused. " 'Course I wasn't even married yet. Miles and I were just engaged."

"I'm sure it was a difficult situation," Devon said, moving closer, about to take Regina's hand and lead her away from the lip of the hill.

Regina suddenly turned to her, and Devon could smell the liquor on her breath.

"I didn't mean to hurt her, you know."

Devon held herself very still. "Of course not."

"Sometimes I—" She stopped suddenly and looked at Devon as if frightened. Then Regina's look turned critical. "Sometimes I talk too much."

"We all do."

Regina shook her head, her eyes never leaving Devon's face. "Not you. You don't talk much at all. Lots of things happen to you and you don't explain, 'cause people would start asking questions. Am I right?"

"What is it you want to talk about, Regina?" Devon asked calmly.

"Your fiancé, for one." Regina's voice turned saucy, and Devon could hear the liquor-born recklessness in her. "Wasn't he man enough for you?"

"Regina—"

" 'Parently not, or you wouldn't have tried to take mine."

Chills rushed through Devon, as when Miles's slim finger had first begun its deft marking of territory.

"I'm referring, of course, to your amorous display in the gallery last night. Miles told me all about it this morning. He's a gentleman through and through, much to your dismay, I expect."

"He told you lies."

"Shame!" Regina cried, gesturing wildly. "He never called you a name once. Given the nasty talk about your marriageability, he was quite understanding of your forward behavior. He ascribed it to the confused condition of your nerves right now. Gracious, gracious man, and a truer husband you won't find."

Devon seethed. "I wasn't looking!"

"Now don't get mad. 'Cause I'm not. I understand, Devon. You made a mistake. It's so easy to make the wrong move. Just when you think you've got every little thought under control and all those bad feelings locked up tight, then boom!" She giggled, a short teetering laugh, high and false. "They go off, like that!" She snapped her fingers.

"Regina."

Gentry! Devon turned. He was close to her, close enough to have heard the entire exchange. He was watching Regina.

"What are you doing here?" Regina nearly screamed the words.

"The guard said you two were up here. I came to check," Gentry lied. He had come for Devon. Instead, he had found Kai-ee-nah's killer.

He walked toward Regina, his chest hollow, like a fire gone to ashes.

"Get away from me!" She backed up, edging toward the loose-dirt rim of the hill.

He stopped. "Take care, Regina," he warned softly.

"I'm always careful!" she cried. "Always!"

"But the memories come anyway, don't they?"

Regina clasped her hands together to control their trembling. She cupped them against her corseted abdomen and held herself silent. The angry flush in her cheeks drained pale, but the wild brightness in her eyes remained.

"I have nothing whatsoever to say to you," she said in an uneven voice.

"You would have told Devon," he said.

"She's safe! She's had to live with what she did wrong. She knows what it is to make a mistake, a horrible mistake. But you . . . You're an arrogant man, Gentry. You never make mistakes. You never look back and worry 'bout, well, I should've done this and not that. I should've stayed here and not gone over there."

"You should've stayed at the house, Regina," he said.

"I told her that! I said, 'Keena, we can't go out there. It's too dangerous.' But she said she had to see you fight and she went right on out the door. I ran to Teague's library and got the revolver from his desk drawer 'cause I knew she didn't have a gun."

"She had a knife," Gentry said, barely audible, for he could not reach too deeply for breath. "My knife."

"It's so funny. We walked together up that hill and she was as calm as if we were gonna meet you and Miles for a picnic. She talked about Indian things—what a great warrior you were, how much meat you brought to her family's lodge, how big a buffalo you were gonna kill when you two got back to the village for the hunt. And then she waited, like she was giving me time to talk about my 'warrior.'

"I said that my people don't brag about their men. It's unseemly, I said. 'Then how do people know that you honor your husband?' she asked in that respectful voice I knew was false.

" 'I honor him with my actions and my decorum,' I said.

" 'To speak well of your man is a telling action,' she said. And she smiled, like she knew she was smarter than me. And I began to see that she was just as arrogant as you. In her sweet little ways she was false. False with Teague and everybody else. But I held my tongue, 'cause we were at the top of Sugar Bluff and we could hear the gunshots coming from the edge of town. Sounded like a raggedy ole string of firecrackers that never stopped popping, and I got nervous, 'cause the shots got louder, like the fighting was movin' our way. I looked way down the hill toward Plain Shade and I couldn't see Miles anymore. He'd been ducked down behind the water trough at the feedstore. I knew him by that clean white shirt and blue vest. K'eenah'd picked you out, too, way down the street behind the livery stable, the only man with a feather hanging in his hair, picking off border raiders with a muzzle-loader. And I'd be willing to bet it was Teague there beside you, wasn't it?"

"He was with me," Gentry said tersely. The yesterday lay fragmented before him now, its images hazy but its sounds thunderous with the cross fire of thirty guns, and its taste like lotus root—raw, unwashed. Each low, frantic movement scattered dry dirt, so that each panting breath left grit to swallow. Teague was there, loading as fast as he could to keep up with his son, who had pinned down the enemy, the proslavers. They had fought on the same side that afternoon. One day, one time.

But Regina's voice, the nasal manic drawl, rang louder, clearer than any ghost of gunfire.

"I told K'eenah we needed to go back, but she stood up on the bluff, straight and tall, like the wind wasn't blowing cold as pump water, her apron flapping back so you could see her tummy sticking out. She was proud of that. I could tell.

" 'Course Miles and I hadn't even had our first night together, 'cause we weren't married yet. But I knew, even if I came back to Summer Sky swollen as a cow the next year, Teague wouldn't care. He only cared about K'eenah. And you, of course. Always you, Gentry.

"That's when she turned to me all of a sudden and said she wished she hadn't come here. She missed her family, especially her father, I guess. She said an Indian name. Then I realized I never did know your heathen name. And I asked her. She told me some strange nonsense, then she was gonna tell me what it meant, but we heard two gunshots real close by and I was scared, so I started pulling out Teague's gun and yelling for her to get down. And I heard the gunshot."

Regina paused. "I didn't even feel the gun go off, it was that fast. But I heard it, that explosion, and I nearly jumped out of my skin. Then I looked over at her. And she was lying on the ground.

"My heart froze. My knees froze." Regina's voice was quieter, slower. "All of me froze. I don't remember moving or thinking until I saw Miles's white shirt come up over the rise. He looked at me with such astonishment, as if he couldn't believe I was so careless. I hid my eyes I was so ashamed, and so scared. And when I looked, he was kneeling beside her.

" 'Free the child,' she said. Dear God, Gentry, she said, 'Free the child.' Miles looked at me, kind of helpless. And then he picked up that long knife. 'We have to grant her last wish,' he said. And I ran. Never, never have I run so fast. I thought God would strike me dead in the teasel burrs on the side of the hill. So I picked up my skirts and ran faster, all the way to the chicken coop, and I slammed the door behind me and the hens cackled and flew around beating me with their wings till I thought I was going to smother. But I hung there with my fingers in the chicken wire and my face pressed so hard to get air that my lips had little diamond creases. And they hurt. They hurt. That's where they found me, scared out of my mind, when the raid was over. And someone told me one of the border ruffians had shot Gentry's wife up on Sugar Bluff. And right then I knew Miles and I would get married sooner than we thought. 'Cause we had a bond."

Gentry turned from her, his fists clenched tight.

Regina shook her head once, then tilted it thoughtfully. "You took K'eenah's body away, but you didn't take it, poor little thing. The baby was just too little, too little to live. So I buried it in the tiniest little box, way out beyond the fence by the corn patch. And I said a prayer and planted flowers, lots of pretty daisies and blue periwinkle. And then I put a ring of purple saffron around it so the animals wouldn't graze it. And I cried for that poor little thing. And I cried for me. I think I cried too much, 'cause I'm so dry inside now. So dry."

Gentry was silent.

Devon saw Regina bend her head and shield her eyes with her hand, a posture of prayer. Devon waited. They all waited in the lengthening shadows that cooled day's end. But no tears crossed the tight, grimacing line at the corner of Regina's mouth.

"Take her to the house," Gentry said finally with a hoarseness that fought the anger he felt. He spoke to Devon without looking at her. It was not Regina he raged against. It was Fortune and her spin of the wheel. Last night he had dared ride to the top, knowing it would make the long descent all the more painful.

He had found his wife's killer. There would be no prosecution, no vindication, only a bitterness and hatred he would never overcome for the child Teague Morgan named as Gentry's sister.

Devon watched as Gentry gathered her saddlebag and sketchpad, not seeing the empty face of the man on the page. He took the reins of her horse and led it to Regina's old sorrel. Then he waited. He would not go to Regina.

Devon approached her slowly and placed a hand on her arm. "Come now," she said.

Regina obeyed, stumbling like a child, not taking her hand from her eyes, purposely, safely blind.

Devon took the reins from Gentry. She offered no solace, no entreaties, for she knew he would not follow them.

He would stay there, with the cold abandoned mill and the stream gone dry, with the memory of the woman he had loved.

TWENTY-TWO

God damn him for being an old, vain fool.

Clammy rain soaked his overcoat, but Pinkney Dobbs trudged on, lumbering like a bear on the scent. He scattered puddles on Quincy and dodged a pothole and a hansom on Trowville.

He should have seen it coming. If he had only added it up. Every week for a month Lilly had excuses.

"Oh, this awful catarrh, Pink," she had said with a drawl gone nasal and her eyes watery red.

Then there was a touch of pleurisy. "Runs in the family, Pink. My aunt Aggie took a spell and died at Christmas dinner, I swear."

And the curse, of course, was good for a full week.

All that time and he never thought to connect her excuses with the night shift of a clerk at the bureau, a clubfooted young man so quiet and shy and diligent, he was entrusted with filing Dobbs's paperwork.

For a month, the office clerk had found himself the object of Lilly's bodacious libido. And Dobbs had found things missing from the stack on his desktop.

Wise woman. She took only a few things from the bottom of the pile. Fortunately, the clerk didn't have keys to Dobbs's desk drawers. They were trip-wired anyway. Still, there were enough sensitive papers in the routine correspondence on his desk to make the Confederate secretary of state beam for a month.

Dobbs swallowed his panic and let the sour acid in his stomach gnaw on it. Shrugging the collar of his overcoat higher against the cold, drizzling rain, he winced when the movement caught like a needle in one shoulder. Rheumatism too. Christ.

By the time he turned onto Maple and approached Lilly's flat, he was stiff, uncomfortable, and mad as hell. He stopped at the steps, one hand on the iron rail, to rally some composure. Checking across the street, he saw one detective huddled under an awning. Another would be in the alley outside the kitchen. He didn't think she would run. But he hadn't thought she would patty-cake someone on his own staff right under his nose, either.

He knocked, and Lilly's maid let him in and took his soggy coat. He waited by the fire in the parlor, rolling his cigar across his tongue as he thought.

He knew that Lilly's superiors had had great hopes when she'd landed him in the sack. But he made sure that the leads she passed on were contradictory or inaccurate. She wasn't a professional, so she never tried to verify information. She was a simple conduit, and some of the things she took didn't matter. Better Reb agents than she had already passed on memos about Sheridan's regrouping in the Shenandoah. And anything mentioning the England-based alliance was locked up in his wall safe or communicated directly to the President.

But there were a few little things she'd picked up that could hurt. That month-old roster of Reb prisoners in Delaware, for one.

Dobbs stood with his back to the door, but he knew she was coming. Her jasmine scent rounded the corner before she did. It was one of the reasons she would never be mistaken for a lady. She overdid everything.

Behind him, the crisp, businesslike scratch of starched cotton got louder. It whisked to a standstill, and he turned around.

"Pink! You're so early! I haven't even made myself ravishing yet!"

"Sorry," he mumbled, cigar fixed in the corner of his mouth.

"You mush-mouthed ole thing! You're supposed to say I'm ravishing already!" she said, eyes sly and teasing.

"I guess I take it for granted you know what I'm thinking. We been together a long time." He took the edge off the words by pursing his lips around the cigar and drawing short puffs. Turning from her abruptly, he tossed the cigar into the grate and walked through the smoky cloud to an armchair.

Lilly's smile froze for a moment, that wary pause that stops a cat when her whiskers are tingling.

If only she were on the right side of this war, Dobbs thought. All he had to do was train her. Her instincts rang pure as crystal.

She sashayed across the room toward him. "If I always knew what a man was thinking, I'd be bored as a frog on a log. Prob'ly woulda hightailed it to a convent long ago."

"Sure would've devastated the male population of Washington," he said, a little too seriously.

She stopped in front of his chair, playfulness gone. "You got an itch in your pants you're dying to scratch? If you want to call me a whore, Pink, do it and get out."

"You're no whore, Lilly." He slouched down comfortably in the chair and folded his hands over his gut. "You're a thief."

"And you're wearin' an ugly streak a mile wide!" She stomped her foot, and her dark brown ringlets bobbed like cushion springs.

She turned, holding her spine tense all the way down to the first ruffled tier of her skirt.

He rose, and the chair announced his leaving with a soft *whomph*. "Nervous, Lilly?"

"Nervous? Just because you've got a tiger paw ready to swat my head?"

"I'm not sure I'm mad enough to hit you. Yet."

"Well, just remember that bloody meat draws more flies."

"You think I'm worried 'bout some little Confederate flies, Lilly? I'm more worried 'bout how to keep rope burn off your pretty little neck."

She whirled around. "They don't hang women and you know it!"

"I know one thing. A pretty little spy screwed her way into a breach of security. And she stole some important papers along the way."

"'Important' my fanny. Anything noticeable and you would've plucked my tail two weeks ago."

Two weeks. That was when she would have sent the memos to her contacts. Two weeks was more than long enough to reach Richmond by mail. About long enough to send a packet by coastal cruiser to ports north of Savannah. Damn.

"You could argue with me, Lilly. Just try and convince me not to lock you up till your hair turns gray."

"Arguing makes you mad. And I'm not sure what you'd do when you're crazy boiling mad at me."

"Nothing I'd regret," he said softly. "Not for a long time."

She seemed to shrink, yet she didn't move. "I hurt you that bad?" she asked, her voice frightened and breathy.

"No," he lied. "I just need to send a darn clear message to Richmond."

She turned and hurried to the bell rope to summon the coffee tray. "For God's sake, Pink, restrain yourself. Where's your code of honor?" She laughed nervously.

He grabbed her by the shoulders and spun her around. "I got none, Lilly. And neither do you." He placed a rough hand on her breast and thrust her backward into a chair.

She landed in a sprawl, and her chest began to heave. A scared mew escaped her throat, but she didn't cry.

He raised his fist, but waited a long moment, containing his anger so that it would build along with the terror he saw in her eyes.

It wouldn't take much to scare her. He remembered one night when he had played real rough in bed to see how experienced she really was. She had scrambled away, legs kicking like a baby rabbit's, backed against the door out of his reach, eyes wide and shiny, just as they were now.

"Pink, wait," she whispered. "I can tell you. I can tell you what I took."

He said nothing, but he allowed his fist to relax.

"You're such a smart man, Pink, 'cause you don't keep much on your desk." She inched herself upright in the chair as she talked. "I remember most of it. Some transport notices for artillery. And an old letter from a man named J. B. Moody."

The notices to shift arms to Culpepper were old and the orders canceled. They actually made a good red herring. J. B. Moody, though, was the *nom de guerre* of a double agent in Hanover Junction. They had his address now. He was as good as hung.

"And there was a prisoner list," she said, sounding more calm, in control. She smoothed her skirt with reassuring strokes.

It was a list that had Gentry's name underlined. Dobbs cursed his own stupidity.

"And a little ole note about Fort Ridgely and a case of quinine, I think," she added, tucking a fallen strand of brown into the curls gathered over her left shoulder.

The supplies he had promised Gentry he would send to the Lakota Sioux.

Dobbs's stomach clenched. He was botching his part of the bargain, but Gentry was sure keeping his. That morning Dobbs had received a cipher on the back of the crumpled map he had given Gentry four weeks earlier. And there were a few lines about a "monkey fist." He'd sent the letter on to code experts at army headquarters, but preliminary reports were bad. They couldn't do much unless the agent sent some information about the book that was key to the code. They said a monkey fist was a sailing knot and probably the symbol used to recognize trusted contacts. Gentry could make use of that password, but Dobbs had no way of relaying it. If he could just reach his agents in Nassau and Fort Fisher—

"Coffee, ma'am."

Lilly's maid appeared in the doorway with a tray.

Dobbs heard Lilly's sigh of relief. "Right here!" she said brightly, pointing to the rosewood table by the sofa.

"Leave us," Dobbs told the girl. "Miss Lilly'll serve."

"Of course," Lilly said with a pinched smile. "Sit down, Pink. The least you can do is offer me a civilized tête-à-tête before you call your men to cart me off."

She lifted the urn and ungracefully splashed coffee into the two dainty cups. "I guess you'll want to take back the key to your office door. I only had one made."

One? Little liar. "I'd like that," he said evenly, the hair on his neck beginning to rise. She was offering too much.

"Over there in that box on the mantel," she said.

Dobbs rose, keeping her peripherally in sight. She made no moves other than to heap two spoonfuls of sugar into his cup and to turn hers to caramel brown with a deluge of cream. She stirred noisily, the spoons ringing in their porcelain bells.

As she stirred, he carefully and quickly opened the box

and retrieved the key. He was about to close the lid when he heard a tiny, discreet click behind him. He turned. Lilly was reaching over the table to set his cup nearer his chair. Saucer met table with an unladylike clatter.

"Your mother never imparted many social graces, did she?" he said, sitting opposite her.

"Don't be snippy. She tried, bless her heart. I just could never put my mind to teacups and stitching circles," Lilly said, her eyes down as she reached for her cup.

He stopped her and grabbed her hand. It was cold as ice. "Take mine, Lilly."

"Whatever do you mean?" she asked, uneasy.

"Drink my coffee."

"Pink, you know I don't take sugar in mine!" She yanked her hand from his.

"Drink, dammit! Before I ram it cup and all down your sneaky little throat."

"Pink—" she began, but he had shoved the saucer and cup into her lap. "You're going to spill on my dress!" she cried, steadying the cup with two fingers.

His hand clasped her forearm like a claw and pushed upward. The cup in her fingers rose quickly, so close to her mouth that Lilly shut her eyes.

He pushed the cup against her lips so that she could feel the thin rim slide inward, pressing like a bit.

Then he suddenly thrust the cup away. Shards scattered against the hearth.

"Pink . . ." she whispered. "Pink, I'm so sorry."

He took her left hand. "Let's see how sorry." He pulled roughly at the large garnet ring on her middle finger. The filigree setting sprung open, revealing a small cavity and a powdery residue.

"I'm a pretty big man. Weren't you worried that wouldn't be enough?" he asked, tightening his grip on her hand.

"You were going to hurt me, Pink! I know you were! I just wanted to put you to sleep. Just for a while." She sobbed, tears cleaning a streak across the rouge and talcum mask on her cheeks.

She was misery uncapped, and he let her bawl it out. Dobbs was a man untouched by a woman's tears. But there were times when he found himself wishing he had the same cathartic option.

"I know I ain't never been much," she mumbled, sniffling as she began to settle down. "but I am a patriot, a true patriot. Don't you understand, Pink?"

"You broke the law, Lilly!" He was still holding her hand, but gently now. "You broke it," he said more softly.

"Don't tell me what I did! You never felt nothin' for me! You used me." She jerked her hand away. "A body gets what they give. You gave me lies, and that's what you got."

Dobbs reached into his vest pocket. He felt the weight of an old man's unsaid words piling up on his tongue. He knew better than to speak.

"What is it you want from me, Pink?" she asked as he pulled out a fresh cigar.

To turn back the clock, he thought. But he would settle for cleaning up his mess as best he could.

"Tell me the name of your contacts," he said. "Where did you send the papers?"

"Not to Richmond. Those popinjays don't care about me anymore. I sent the papers to a smart man. A dear old family friend. A highly decorated colonel too. Miles Brant."

Dobbs was holding a match to the end of his cigar, but he couldn't seem to breathe in.

"Suck in or shake out your match, Pink," Lilly said. "You wanna get burned?"

Devon saw Regina to her room at the far end of the upstairs hall. The corridor was dark. Dusk had fallen on Jasmine's Reach, and the two women walked toward the yellowish glow that hovered beyond the chintz in Regina's suite.

"My head's about to split in two," Regina said, pressing fingertips to temples. She sank down on her bed, eyes closed. "Be a sweet thing and get me a drink."

"I think it would be better for you to undress and take a cool bath," Devon said.

"I think it'd be better for me to get it myself, and for you to get down off your high horse! Great God Almighty." Regina took the decanter from a silver tray and picked up a glass with amber pooled in the bottom. " 'Course, you can afford to be a little self-righteous, not having sinned quite as mortally as I have.

"Would you look at that?" she went on with disgust, setting the decanter back on the table. "A fly died in my glass!

You'd think, 'tween Tulie and Evaleen, somebody could get me a clean glass." She rapped the glass on the edge of the tray, and the fly tumbled out onto the silver."We're just too shorthanded for niceties anymore. I am so sick and tired of this. I want to go home."

She poured the glass half full. "Miles is buying us land out Missouri way, right next to Teague's place. Lots of land. As soon as this war's over, I'm gonna take my daughter and go home."

"Get some rest," Devon said, her hand on the doorknob, ready to leave.

"It was an accident," Regina shouted as Devon left, firmly shutting the door.

In Arnaud's bedchamber, three lanterns glowed near the bedside. Her aunt sat on the edge of her chair so she could hold Arnaud's limp hand. A small man in a nondescript vest bent over the pale form in the bed. He pulled aside the fever-soured nightshirt and placed his ear to Arnaud's heart.

Devon turned away. The skin on her uncle's chest hung dry and slack; the bones protruded in skeletal rows. How long could a heart beat when the body around it hung so frail and thin?

"He's not through yet," the doctor said as he rose. "But his ole ticker's racin' like it can't wait to jump the fence."

"Arnaud can be so stubborn," Margaret said absently. "But you know he doesn't smoke anymore? He always smoked . . ."

"A man in his condition can stop doing anything he wants," the doctor said impatiently, packing his instruments.

Devon introduced herself. "You're Miles's physician?" she asked.

"Doc Hiller. Pleased to meet you," the doctor said, putting on his hat.

"Miles had high praise for your care of his injury," she said.

"Miles is prone to exaggeration, I'm sure," the doctor said with a peculiar smile. "If you'll excuse me, I have many needy men to attend."

"Of course."

"Miles did ask me to relay a message. A ghost's been sighted eight miles out."

"A what?"

"Blockade-running steamship. They're painted gray, hidin' in the fog and all that. Your ship will be here on the morning tide."

"My ship?"

"Miles said you would be leaving on the next outbound trip. He's sending a wagon for your things tomorrow noon. You'll board at the customhouse down by the waterfront."

"Thank you," she said, and saw the doctor to the door.

This was what it meant to be a spy, she thought as she smiled good-bye. To project the mask of the mundane and hide the lies.

The coming journey frightened her. She had to find a hiding place for the small wooden chest that held Arnaud's papers. And she had to get word to Gentry. She went quickly down the servants' staircase and emerged below the ground floor in the cool, flagstoned kitchen.

Across the room, Evaleen talked with a black woman in linsey-woolsey who worked at the pastry board.

"I need someone to take a message to Sergeant Morgan, immediately," Devon said. "I leave tomorrow. I need to speak with Portia. Is she here?"

The pastry cook kept her eyes low.

Evaleen clasped her thin hands together and shook her head. "She's not here, Miz Devon."

"Then take me to her."

Evaleen's eyes grew wide. "Can't do that. She's too sick."

"Good God, if she's ill, we must get the doctor for her! Take me at once!" Devon said urgently, and moved toward the door.

Evaleen ran to her and placed a hand on her arm. "Wait," she pleaded in a whisper. "Wait. Please don't bring no 'tention to her."

"Then you must tell me the truth," Devon said. "Where is she?"

"She's gone, Miz Devon."

The words left her cold. "What do you mean?"

"She run away."

Dear God. "Does she know where to go? Does she have friends who'll hide her?"

"Portia, she's smart. She'll get through," Evaleen said fervently.

"Are they hunting her yet?"

Evaleen shook her head. "Miz Regina thinks she sick."

"What happens if she's caught out there?"

Evaleen didn't answer.

"What happens if she's caught and brought back?" Devon persisted.

Evaleen squeezed her arm and gave a reassuring smile that made Devon feel like a child. "She took her a knife. She gonna be free. One way or another."

Disheartened, she returned to her room. She undressed slowly, her fear for Portia prompting worries about her own safety at the coming enclave of the alliance.

Behind her, she heard the door open and close softly. She waited. A servant would soon speak, but a lover would be quiet.

The silence brought him nearer. When he stood still, she made no move to close the distance. The space was filled by another woman, her tragic death, the hard, painful years of grief that tethered her ghost to his heart.

Slowly he reached out to her. The back of his hand caressed her cheek, spreading the wetness so it would dry.

"Do not cry for me," he said softly. "My wife is dead."

Arms heavy with sadness closed around Devon, and she leaned against his chest, embracing Gentry with youth and hope, knowing that this was not enough to counter the weight of such a loss, knowing, too, that he desperately wanted her to try.

TWENTY-THREE

Devon rose on tiptoe to seek him, and his mouth fell to hers
with a lingering tenderness that slowly heightened. He
tasted the drying salt of her tears, and his hand moved
gently, possessively, to her breast mounded high in a jacket
of long coralline stays. Her nipple and its pink shadow were
hidden by the soft yoke of her chemise.

His fingers slid into the moist warmth between her
breasts. He gripped each side of the corset and pressed inward. One hook released. The curve of her bosom descended
against his hand. He loosed another hook, then another,
working slowly downward to her abdomen, until six hooks
lay open and the sateen-trimmed corset fell empty to the
floor. He grasped the short, gathered sleeves of her chemise
and pulled downward, unclothing her bosom and waist.

Already her nipples had hardened, as he had. He passed
his thumb across each tight, swollen tip, his palms cradling
the silken weight of her breasts.

Then he splayed both hands in the curve above her hip
and let his thumbs stroke the small soft pad around her
navel, the holding place for a child someday. Pray God it
would not be his.

Tonight, the simplest want overwhelmed him. To be with
her, to be wanted by her. The desire enticed and infuriated,
for before him, in the luminous cast of her eyes, lay the most
innocent snare of all.

He pulled her against him so roughly, she gasped. "Love
is no gift, unless it's returned," he said, his voice strangled
and harsh. Never could he return the love she offered. His

gift would die, exposed, unable to cross the distance between their worlds.

"Gentry, I leave tomorrow," she whispered.

He released her, pushing her away. Already? Already must he practice making a dream of last night, when he could still feel the shyness in her first touch of him?

Already he must bid her safe mission when both knew the venture held only threat.

Must he face an unwanted journey again and risk the loss of one who shared his blanket and his path? Maker of Breath, not again in one lifetime.

He backed away, then walked to the door.

"Will you not say good-bye?" she asked, her voice shaky.

He was silent a moment. "No." He shook his head and turned the brass key in the plate beneath the knob. He would say be wary, be warned, be ready to die in the small places in your heart, Daloni-ka. But he would not say good-bye.

Devon watched him cross the room to the green velvet armchair in front of the hearth. Silently, he removed his soft, scarred boots.

He would stay. She drew a trembling breath. Her heart had stilled at the sight of his hand on the door. Now, with a caution befitting the threat, her heart pumped slowly. Now, time would march past them, ignorant of its loss, for as soon as he'd sat to tug the heel of his boot free, they were safe, behind a door time could not open. With this freedom she felt responsibility to collect their moments like keepsakes. Their intimacy had no home, only desperate, hallowed campsites.

She pulled the chemise high to cover her breasts, then turned to the bedside stand where the lantern glowed golden. She turned the wick higher, casting an aura of brightness to the hearth. The artist in her wanted to see his body clearly. The woman in her wanted to be able to remember him, the private motions and dressing-room ritual; to project him as now, tugging on a coat sleeve behind his back and shrugging the coat off one shoulder, then the other. To watch his hard and calloused hands work nimbly at buttons on his linen shirt. To see the wave of muscle cross his shoulder as he rolled his arm backward, suspenders riding down his arm, leaving sleeve and shirt empty and his dark bronze chest bare. To know that he watched her as he loosened the buttons of his pants and let the suspenders' weight drop his trousers to the floor. To hear the soft woolen hiss as the cloth slid past tight buttocks and smooth, hard flanks, giving her open view of his desire, tumescent, unashamed, stretching away from the heavy, rounded sack, low hung and shadow soft. She was amazed to find a part of him so delicate, so vulnerable.

He waited patiently, honoring her right to see him, even as his desire pulsed harder.

"What do you see?" he asked softly.

She averted her eyes. "A man cast in bronze."

"So cold a metal?"

"Gold, then," she said. Burnished, malleable, a metal hard to the touch, but yielding.

"A man is only clay," he said.

"Then what am I?"

"A woman not yet bare."

She walked toward him, casting off the chemise, aware of the warmth that flooded her face, her chest, her loins, as she neared him, fearing that his patience and gentleness would be consumed by such a heat.

Her hands reached down to untie the waiststring that held her pantalettes, but his were there before her. He jerked once, hard, to break the knot, then sat down in the chair as the garment fell. He leaned forward and gripped a buttock in each hand. Tugging her toward him, he pressed his cheek to the soft nest of curls, stirring the quiescent woman scent, breathing her readiness, aching to taste.

Unsure what he intended, Devon writhed from his grasp, but his arm trapped her, encircling her waist. He pulled her over the arm of the chair and onto his lap. Holding her against him, he demanded nothing except contact of her skin with his, her silken curve and flow against the muscled cord of his chest, smooth, rounded cheeks fitting firmly, yielding softly, in the crook of his groin.

She trailed soft kisses along his chest, up to his neck, raking a handhold in his long hair to pull his lips to hers. Her tongue was not timid, and it inspired his hands to a bold and deliberate search. They roamed the length and breadth of her, fingers spread wide to touch every curve of milky

skin, stroking reverently when he could, but pressing hard
on the crown of tight curls that hid his resting place.

He abruptly broke their kiss.

She nuzzled her face to the warm darkness along his neck,
waiting.

His hand probed lower, gently cupping gold-furred lips.
He parted them so that one finger could reach a straining,
succulent prize.

She gasped and stiffened and tried to pull away, but his
finger retained its firm, gentle hold, and he kissed her hair,
her temple, the hollow of her ear, to let her know he would
not hurt her, that he would never treat harshly a part of her
that swelled to bursting with a longing as mindless as his
own.

But Devon did not relax, did not know that she need only
let him rest there, that the weight of his finger, its ridges and
roughness, were enough to bring pleasure, that his trespass
was an invitation to glide against him and heighten the ache
and the joy.

He released her, suddenly impatient. Each of their nights
was beginning and end. There would be no other time.

He kissed her with a desperate hunger, holding her mouth
to his, delving for sustenance as he righted her on his lap.
Then he guided her to sit astride him. He entered her slowly
as she leaned against his chest, allowing her to control the
depth of his journey. He kissed the crown of her head and
guided her in the motion that would pleasure them, its
rhythm an ageless dance, its drumskin ancient and raw,
toned to the pounding of hearts.

He led the pace, rising with her, arriving with hot, maddened spasm that left him blind but sharpened his hearing so
he could know the long and sonorous moan she muffled in
the tufted back of the chair.

They rested, clasped together, the light from the bedstand
lantern near the chair striking their skin, red-bronze against
cream, in bright definition.

Gentry gathered Devon in his arms and carried her to the
bed. He lay beside her on the white linen spread, aware of a
sweetness in the air. Lavender. The bed linens were sprinkled with lavender water.

The bed was comfortable, and he pulled her close, nuzzling her buttocks in the bend of his body. So close that his

cheek lay in the cascade of hair down her back. He could sleep there. A long long time. But it would soften him, make him unprepared for the next spin of fortune's wheel and heedless of the sting in Lady Fortune's fickle hand.

"Tell me about her," Devon said softly.

He smiled. Lady Fortune lay next to him. And she struck wisely, when he was pliant and lulled by her lovemaking. But strangely he felt strong of voice.

"Will you be jealous?" he asked.

"How can I be? I'm not a wife, or a mistress who has claim to you.

"You are worse than either. You're a lover offering hope— for a price."

She turned in his embrace to face him. "I made it clear. I demand nothing from you."

"Such nobility incurs the highest debt of all," he said, smiling.

"Then you shall be charged derelict in your dues." She laughed. "And I sentence you to my prison!" She trapped his neck in a fierce hug.

She had laughed. A small sound of joy he had not heard before. A void began to open in him and his heart raced. He rolled onto his back, wrestling her atop him to disguise the silent yaw, holding her more tightly than she clung to him.

In her laughter was the sweet-remembered balm of a woman's companionship, the times his wife had gentled his spirit, offering a constancy and loyalty created only for him. She had moved to his rhythms, and he to hers, in speech and work and love.

Now he waited, silent, hoping Devon would find words to break the balm before he came to crave it. He felt her relax and stretch out full-length, her toes playing against his calves. She lay her cheek in the curve of his shoulder, and with one question began the gentle unraveling of the knot in his chest.

"What does her name mean?" she asked.

He closed his eyes, in order to begin. "Kai-ee-nah. You would say Many Reeds Singing. She was born in a summer camp, high in the mountains where reeds grow tall beside the lakes." The story spoke itself, as if he had not pulled it out from a rusty, hidden place.

"Her father was a great hunter and a flutemaker. Though

she was only a girl, Kai-ee-nah took the reeds and made flutes for her friends. She watched her father when he cut the wand of birch or cherry and stripped and dried it and reamed its pith. She made a wooden flute, one that fell on the air like a mockingbird's call. And her father knew the bird's spirit lived in her flutes and they would have great power."

Devon lay with her hand in the center of his chest, afraid to stir lest she break the tenuous thread with which she was weaving a picture of his life.

Under her hand, imprisoned and tight, his voice rose and fell with the telling, until gradually she felt a resonance begin, rich and deep like a purr, something freed.

She learned that they had married in Gentry's sixteenth winter, after he had run away from Teague Morgan's home for the last time. He had stolen two Mandan ponies on his way to high country at the headwaters of the Missouri. When he approached a band of Sioux tepees camped in a circle in buffalo grass, he was ignorant of the Lakota tongue and spoke with signs of his hands. He tethered himself to a stake in the ground and said he would cede one pony to the man who could draw his blood.

Kai-ee-nah's brother took the challenge, drew Gentry's blood, but ended the fight limping, with the trail of Gentry's knife streaking his chest and leg.

Though young, Gentry was claimed by one of the war leaders and joined a soldier clan. He was stealthy in raids and bold in attempting coups, but he survived and grew in stature in the village.

"And everyone rejoiced when Ton-weya came," he said.

"Who was that?" she asked.

"A great chief," he lied. "His presence was a great omen. He blessed our marriage." Not even the yellow-hair, with her sweet and giving spirit, could know Ton-weya.

"My lips are worn," he said. "It is time for you to tell a story."

"My life is just beginning. It's too short a story. You're so much older, you need more time."

"A tongue that stings like a wife's? Where's the gentle lover I carried to bed?"

"Attached to the tongue that stings." She kissed him, her full lips playing at his mouth, pursing and probing.

He smiled and pulled away. "Wise and wicked wasp. Here I lie willingly, nettled to death. But if I go, I survive." His voice was soft.

He saw tension set her jaw. "So soon?" she asked.

"They will come to take you to the ship long before dawn."

"Cruel words. Leave me better ones to remember."

He lay the palm of his hand to her heart, caressing her breast. "There are no beautiful words for good-bye."

"I need some!" She thrust away his hand and rolled off the warm pallet of his body. "I need something!"

"You need sleep and surcease and a servant to bring you tea." He got up.

"Don't condescend to me, Gentry! Don't belittle what I feel!" Her voice rose. "Don't—"

His hand clamped her mouth. "Don't," he said softly, sadly.

She stopped. She closed her eyes and reached up to grasp his wrist. He smelled of leather, faintly of lavender, unmistakably of her. After a long while, she nodded and he let his hand slip away.

Devon felt stiff inside, as if something soft had dried and hardened in light of the bargain she had struck. She would honor her word. No attachment, no obligation for him to stay with her beyond the boundaries of this room.

Time had returned in a choking cloud, but she did not let it tear her eyes, not even when she saw him draw trousers over his nakedness.

She busied herself pulling a pale blue dressing gown from the bureau in the far corner of the room. "Will you return to Washington?" she asked raggedly, struggling for conversation, bits of detail that would fix his whereabouts in her mind.

He shrugged, not telling her that he had already left the rendezvous information with a double agent from Fort Fisher, a Confederate hospital steward named Atkin. Hospital supplies were always given priority transit. The information would be on its way to an agent in a Richmond infirmary by the next morning.

Devon tied the white satin drawstring at her throat. "Did you know Portia has run away? I'm afraid for her. But I think she'll get through. She's very wise."

He slipped his suspenders over his shoulders, not acknowledging the hope in her voice. He had heard the dogs. From his post high on the hill, where Regina's words had torn his spirit and laid its pieces to rest, he had seen in the swale two men trailing four hounds on long, taut ropes.

Find the spirit of the eagle and beat long, strong wings, he had prayed for the unlucky, hunted one.

He stood and set his heel more firmly in his shoe.

Devon nervously buttoned her gown. "I'm not sure I'll know what to do in Nassau. I've never been a spy."

"I've never been to Nassau."

He walked close to her and let the silence speak privately to both of them, stripping away her fear. "Tell your uncle you want me to be your escort," he said.

She stood before him, her body still with gladness, in a gown pale as dawn's sky, hair light as the tasseled gold of wheat. A beautiful woman, a virtuous woman.

One who, incredibly, sang only for him.

In that moment he heard the voice of the ancient ones, whispering the song that binds the love of one woman to one man. The words were faint, for he had heard the sacred formula long ago, as a boy tending the fire in the *asi* of the elders, when color had symbolic power. Red was success, triumph; blue, defeat and trouble; black, death; and white . . . White was peace, The White Woman the spirit of happiness.

Gentry felt his soul whisper in beginning: There in Elahiya you are at rest, O White Woman. No one is ever lonely when with you. You are most beautiful—

He stopped, afraid of the power of the words, afraid of the longing in his soul.

"You are most beautiful," he said softly to Devon.

Only this, Daloni-ka.

For now only this.

General Farwell's quarters at Fort Fisher were cramped and makeshift—a spare, pine-log room with a table, a chair, and a cot. The general's pacing only made the room smaller.

"You must understand my position, Miles." General Farwell frowned, and his right hand worriedly pinched his sideburns as he walked.

Miles produced a reassuring smile, protective and warm. "Of course, sir."

"I'm not authorized to let you board a privateer ship to negotiate arms shipments on foreign soil," Farwell said.

"I remind the general we're not talking about blunderbusses. We're talking about a thousand Sharp's rifles, ammo included," Miles said. "Do you know what General Lee could do with a thousand Sharp's?"

"Blow a knothole in Grant's backside," Farwell said wistfully.

"Captain Trouvier's information is always reliable." At least that much was true, Miles thought. "He says there's a French trader in Nassau who has the rifles stowed on one of the out islands. The trader's just waiting for the right offer, and his sympathies are with us, not the Federals."

"I have no authority to—"

"Perhaps a simple leave will alleviate the problem," Miles interjected. "The voyage takes two days there, three days to conduct negotiations, and two days return. A week. No more."

"Still, to undertake such a clandestine meeting—"

"I'd like to request a week's leave, General. It's as simple as that. Any negotiations will be done by a patriot on behalf of the Confederate States. You need not be involved, except to allow a veritable treasure in arms to be shipped to your garrison for distribution."

General Farwell stopped pulling at his sideburns. "You're sure this blockade-runner of yours is trustworthy?"

"Certain. Captain Trouvier is a sound friend of the Confederacy."

"Then emergency leave it is, with my blessing."

"I'll be gone on the tide aboard Trouvier's steamer," Miles said, saluting perfunctorily. He turned to the door before disdain could twist his parting smile.

Miles crossed the yard to the carriage that awaited him. Victor stood beside it, impassive in dark coat and string tie, proper in attire and demeanor. Victor would accompany him to Nassau, even though there was a risk. He might try to run away, invoking the Federals' Emancipation Proclamation.

But at that point Miles could invoke the service of any

number of bounty hunters. And there would be no problem.
Miles had a friend or two in Nassau.

Besides, Victor was a model slave, Miles thought. Had
been from the time Tom Creel sliced off his ear.

What would it be like to wake up without an ear, he
wondered, blood blocking all sound so that the scratch and
thump and crackle of life drowned in the muffled flow inside
your head?

He felt Victor's hand on his elbow, helping him up the
step into the carriage. Miles stretched out his leg on the
cracked leather seat and reached down to release the lever
that held his heel and ankle stiff. Then he flexed and extended his heel, relaxing and tightening the calf muscles
boxed inside the brace.

The lever was a simple solution hidden inside an orna-
mental contraption. Miles had known he could never create
a consistent limp unless he had a real physical restraint. He
had also known his leg muscles would atrophy while he
awaited the right time to announce a miraculous healing,
one that would occur when he was securely ensconced in a
commission far from the hazards of field warfare.

So he had devised the small, painless clamp that re-
strained his foot and ankle when the lever was locked. The
rest of the brace, with its long iron rods and short leather
straps, was for show. His leg remained free inside the clanking cavity. The brace was heavy, but he had purposely refused a lighter design. His thigh had grown hard and dense
with muscle from wielding the weight.

Unfortunately, he had not had much time to exercise in
the past two days. No feinting and fencing with Victor, no
fisticuffs, no weighted pulleys to strengthen both legs. He
could make up for it during the crossing and spend most of
the time in his cabin, conditioning his leg.

His absence on deck would make it so much easier on
poor Devon. She would be disconcerted enough just knowing he was joining her in the pilgrimage to the alliance leaders.

The carriage rolled through the inner gate of Fort Fisher,
then through the outer yard and onto the high road that
paralleled the sea.

Miles craved his rightful taste of the celebration before the
Confederacy's secret little navy trained two hundred rifled

cannon on the South Atlantic Squadron's defensive line outside Charleston Harbor.

Alliance ships would be well armed, their holds packed with goods vital to the troops under Hood's command outside Atlanta—arms and ammunition, shoes and camp gear, cheese and bacon.

Charleston was on a direct railroad link to Atlanta. Any alliance ship grounding beyond the Federal batteries on Morris Island could be unloaded by waiting shore parties of Confederate reserves. It could be the biggest single military-transport effort of the war: 75,000 Enfield rifles, 3 million ball cartridges, 5 million percussion caps, 10,000 revolvers, and 10 four-and-a-half-inch rifle guns with shot and shell.

Alliance steamers would have to evade Federal frigates, survive bombardment from iron-clad coastal monitors, and sail deep enough past the mouth of the harbor to bask in artillery protection from Forts Sumter and Moultrie.

If Hood's Army of the Tennessee received even half the alliance shipment, the Confederates could beat back Sherman, hold Atlanta, embarrass President Lincoln, and demoralize the American public. And on November eighth —Federal election day—there would be a changing of the guard in Washington, D.C.

Lincoln's Democratic opponent, General George B. McClellan, had fervently promised peace and an end to the fighting. The cost to end the bloodshed would be a separate, sovereign nation of slaveholding states.

If all went well. A huge if. It wouldn't be wise to choose a suit for the victory celebration just yet, Miles thought. The carriage crossed a sandy spit to the mouth of the inlet where Trouvier's lay at anchor.

Everything depended on how many armed ships massed on August twentieth. And on how long the Federals could be kept in the dark.

A long time indeed. Miles sighed and smoothed the lapels of his unbuttoned jacket. Inside his breast pocket, a packet of papers crackled obediently.

Dear thoughtful Lilly. Such a sense of timing for one so unschooled in the political arts. She had sent assorted papers from the desk of a very important personage in Lincoln's administration. And Gentry Morgan's name was on one of those papers.

Fortunately, he had received Lilly's gift early enough that morning to act on it. Gentry's whereabouts in Wilmington had been monitored from the moment he'd set foot in town. He had been hard to follow, but Miles's network of "correspondents" was vast. Gentry had finally ended up at the hospital, requesting a healing salve.

Miles had a list of "regulars" in the hospital, discreet personnel who ferried and fronted black-market goods. He offered a hefty sum to anyone who sniffed out a Federal sympathizer in their midst. A hospital steward named Atkin was delivered to him. Eventually, Atkin was persuaded to lead Miles to a letter addressed to Lincoln's secret service chief.

No longer would he have to apologize for a piffling diversion of funds. It was recompense he rightly deserved after months of discreetly preparing routes for blockade shipments.

The self-righteous old gadflies of the alliance would be aching to punish him, but how could they decry his small crime if he presented evidence of a bigger one? Evidence of a Yankee spy in their midst.

Gentry would be hanged, a traitor.

Miles would be cheered, a hero.

Regina would become heir to the Morgan estate.

Dear God, what could be better? Miles sighed, content, then his eyes crinkled in a thoughtful frown.

The air was heavy with misted salt. Snow-white herons tucked wings tight against the winds as they dredged the sandy mud for crustaceans.

A blond mistress would be nice. A woman-child just broken in, her mind supple and sensitive as her body, to challenge and invigorate him.

A strumpet with breeding.

Quite nice.

TWENTY-FOUR

Clutching her sketchbook to her chest, Devon leaned into the wind and forged her way astern. Dodging hawsers and crates, barrels and turnpoles, and towers of canvas-wrapped bales of cotton. She made her way to the windbreak she had discovered next to the *Cyrus Tern*'s giant side-wheel. The paddle wheel dipped and rose with a gushing wash that rained sheets of salty froth. Her traveling dress, a pale gray satin with moiré stripes, had been mottled and ruined by the invisible spray. But she had donned the dress again today, her second day at sea, because she had been allowed only two trunks—two day dresses and an evening gown—to last the entire stay in Nassau. Only God knew how long a sojourn it would be.

"Bonjour, M'em'selle Picard!"

Captain Trouvier ducked the boom of the main mast and smiled at her. He was an infectiously gregarious man, tall and gaunt with a face of promontories—an overhanging brow, sunken eyes, and high-ridged cheeks. Homely traits made affable and disarming by his grin.

"Land!" he exclaimed. "Can you smell it?" His chest rose with a deep breath and he lifted his large nose to the wind.

Devon gave a mock-serious smile. "Since embarking, I have only caught the scent of damp wood, fish bait, and men who missed their yearly bath."

"How can you chastise your host?" the Frenchman said, pretending hurt.

"How could you refuse my belongings?" she asked. "For the sake of four more bales of cotton, you left two of my trunks on the beach."

"This is war, m'em'selle."

"This is greed, *monsieur le capitaine.*"

Trouvier smiled. "They are entirely complementary vices, *non*?"

"I suppose I should be grateful simply to be aboard," she said, smiling stiffly. "Isn't a woman bad luck to a ship?"

"A woman is only bad luck to a man. One man. At a time, that is. You boarded the ship accompanied by two. I am still speculating who is the luckless soul—my friend Miles, or the stern-faced fellow who spends his days wishing for earth beneath his feet." Trouvier nodded toward the other end of the ship where Gentry leaned against a tall coil of rope.

Devon allowed herself a long glance at the tense figure at the bow. She and Gentry had carefully avoided each other since boarding the ship. Like the force of magnets bearing the same poles, they pushed each other away by look and gesture, unable to touch.

Without acknowledging her, Gentry continued to whittle with his pocketknife.

Devon looked quickly away to the bright blue water, still holding Gentry in the periphery of her vision. The wind played at the open neck of his shirt, billowing one side, holding it open so that the twisted scar below his shoulder darkened in the sun.

She turned back to Trouvier. "One man is my cousin, the other a guard appointed by my uncle. I'm no threat to either."

Trouvier tilted his head playfully, and his mouth twisted upward in a one-sided grin. "Ah, but a beautiful woman is always *dangereuse.* A smart one, lethal. I would be leery of you myself if I were not married already to the sea."

Behind Devon, a tight metallic jangle punctuated the thump and clatter of deckhands at work. It was a sound to which everyone had grown sensitive in the small galleyways of the vessel, a noise that pinched the heart, a warning of something shackled.

She turned as Miles approached. He was impeccably dressed in coat and cravat, his chin raised elegantly above a starched collar. He carried his tall felt hat in his hand, letting the high wind ruffle his light hair, his pale gray gaze on Devon.

Unconsciously, she clasped her sketchpad tighter against her chest.

"Your quartermaster went below deck looking for you," he said to Trouvier.

"It's time to signal the coastal pilot," Trouvier said. "The reefs come up quickly here." He raised craggy brows and took his leave with a tug on the lip of his cap.

Miles took a deep breath and lifted his face to the sky. "Trouvier is worried, I think. He says the wind is changing. I can't tell, can you?"

Devon did not answer. Her hatred of him burned, consuming any feint of politeness.

"We are out of our element here," he went on, his drawl clipped, businesslike. "All three of us, but Gentry most of all. He's done nothing but carve. Quiet as a cat, leaning up against the front rail just waiting for a glimpse of Mother Earth. Are you as scared of the water, Devon?"

"People scare me, 'Cousin,'" she said softly. "They frighten me to death." She turned to go.

His hand clamped firmly on her arm. "You don't look afraid to me. Angry, maybe. But not frightened. Not yet."

She glared at his offending hand.

His hand closed harder. Then he smiled and lifted his warm fingers off one by one.

"I'll be with you when you report to the alliance," he said.

"You think they want to hear a thief? I know I don't."

"Money's like water. It returns to the source."

"Repaying funds you stole can't buy their forgiveness."

"Perhaps, perhaps not," he said easily. "I'm willing to try, for the good of the cause."

"For your own good, Miles. Everything for your own good."

"At least I'm honest about it. Some skulk around pretending they're noble when they're really as two-faced as a totem pole."

Devon felt a tingling chill begin at the base of her spine.

"Those are the people who have to be careful," Miles said softly. "Not me."

He left her.

Devon did not move from her safe haven in the windbreak until she sighted land in the distance.

She watched a small boat set out from the sickle-shaped

island and approach the *Cyrus Tern*. The vessel brought a
local navigator to pilot the sleek steamer past the northwest
tip of Eleuthra.

As the ship neared the island of New Providence, the sun
sank lower on the western horizon, pulling sky-blue from
the water, leaving dark and steely depths.

Anchorage was crowded. Dozens of small sloops and
schooners tugged at their moorings between sail-rigged
steamers and merchant craft.

The *Cyrus Tern* sloughed in at slow speed, threading its
way past the stern lines of anchored ships. Finally, the side-
wheeler edged to a berth alongside four other identical vessels, slate-gray steamers in various stages of unloading cargo
on the wharf.

Everywhere Devon looked, bales of cotton with gunny-
sack girdles were stacked by the dozens on the dock and
beyond, lining alleyways of narrow wooden porches
and storage sheds. The din from the docks was exhilarating
and exotic, strangely homey, too, for Devon heard Cockney
and long English vowels in the marketplace mix of com-
mands and shouts, grunts and laughter. Black islanders and
white crewmen passed small bales of cotton down a fireline
of hands to the deck of a tall-masted clipper. Tufts of dirty-
white fiber fell loose in a stream like errant snow.

Clerks with sweaty coats and loosened ties barked tally
counts and marked ownership vouchers. Devon saw Captain
Trouvier tower over a jut-jawed little clerk with a roster.
Trouvier gestured, cajoling; the clerk looked at his pocket
watch, unsmiling.

Weary with waiting, Devon decided she would leave the
ship. "Abby!" she called.

The slight young girl came running, a carpetbag and a
hatbox in one hand, artist's satchel in the other. Abby, only
twelve, had hurriedly been named Devon's maid in the absence of Portia. Abby was shy and clumsy and had no training as a dresser. She tended animals at Jasmine's Reach
while her mother worked the cotton and indigo fields.

Abby was the lightest-colored Negro Devon had ever encountered, with creamed-coffee skin and rust-gold streaks
that made her soft hair an unnatural brown. She never spoke
much and was of little help, but Devon couldn't scold the

girl. Abby was homesick and frightened. Last night she had cried herself to sleep in Devon's arms.

Devon wouldn't have minded leave to do the same. Though Gentry was on board, Miles's presence was always between them, a living barrier to any feeling of safety.

Gentry approached her on the gangway.

Abby was safely distant, waiting.

Gentry removed his hat and smiled, signaling polite, negligible discourse to everyone but Devon. "Where will the monkey fists gather?" he asked.

"Captain Trouvier says there's only one good accommodation in Nassau. A nearly finished hotel, the Royal Victoria."

"Miles won't want me there."

"How can he keep you away?"

He shook his head impatiently, preoccupied. "Just remember not to be alone with him. He wants more than alliance favors."

"Consider me forewarned."

"And armed?" he asked.

"No."

"We're in a city of bargainers, thieves, and spies. Surely I can find a revolver and get it to you tonight."

A jangled clank and footstep sounded caution. Devon stiffened.

"Gentry, could I trouble you?" Miles asked, coming up behind him. "We will have to see to our own baggage, I'm afraid. Victor needs help with Devon's trunks. Would you mind?"

Gentry nodded to Devon, then put on his hat as he left.

Miles looked at her. "Shall we go?" he asked, and extended his arm.

His elbow remained outstretched a long moment. Finally, he lowered his arm to his side. "Devon," he said with mild exasperation. "Whatever my crime, I am still the seventh monkey fist, and I am duly accorded the privileges of this select group of visionaries."

"But they have never met you," she said.

"Both you and I will be meeting these gentlemen for the first time, I representing myself, you representing the much-loved Arnaud Picard. Charm them. Castigate me. Do what you must. Now." He tapped his cane playfully on the walkway ahead of him. "We must leave before that filthy drunken sailor and his harlot over there claim our carriage."

He was so confident. What buoyed his spirits?

Devon ignored her feeling of dread. "Come, Abby," she said, not waiting for Miles. She walked down the wide plank and threaded her way among pinewood crates. When they passed piles of yellow bananas and mangoes darkening in a cloud of fruit flies, Abby looked longingly at the fruit. The sickly sweet aroma spurred Devon's hunger too. "We'll get dinner soon," she promised, and pulled Abby along.

They reached the dirt street, but Devon couldn't see a carriage in the crush of freight wagons and wheelbarrow carts. She held tight to Abby and they climbed rickety steps onto a long, narrow porch that connected a row of one-story buildings. Bulging burlap sacks and boxes of cargo lined the porch. In the coolness of sunset, dozens of men slept on cotton bales or sat propped against the walls. They stared openly at Devon. She slowed and stopped. This was not a street for ladies after dark.

"Look. Marse Miles is right over there," Abby said hopefully, pointing to the street where a horse-drawn carriage was passing.

Devon saw Miles tap his cane on the shoulder of the driver. The carriage halted.

Miles tipped his hat politely, then looked down the line of curious dockhands and laughing sailors waiting for Devon to pass. He raised his brows in a silent question.

She stepped off the porch, a flush of defeat in her cheeks. "Come, Abby," she said.

The driver helped Devon into the seat beside Miles. Abby climbed up on the driver's perch and the carriage rolled forward.

Miles kept one gloved hand on the silver grip of his cane, the other on the knee that was next to Devon. She appeared quite nervous, stealing glances at his hand to make sure it didn't move.

"We need not talk, you know," he said finally.

"We aren't," she said.

"Ah." He remained silent for several minutes. At last he said, "Petulant silence is the way children handle disagreements. I had hoped you were a bit more sophisticated."

She did not answer.

"You must not have appreciated my embellishment of our gallery tryst. I'm sure Regina told you. She glories in gossip that maligns anyone but her."

In profile he saw Devon's eyes close and her jaw tighten.

"But wasn't I honest in some regard? I warned you I would make you the culprit. You must learn to believe me, Devon," he said quietly, watching her hands. She had intertwined her gloved fingers so tightly, they trembled. How she ached to strike him.

And she had correctly surmised that he would be more bothered by silence than by any words she uttered. This was actually an endearing challenge, if she didn't take it too far.

"Nassau has such a distinct colonial air," he went on in a chatty tone. "You English must feel right at home here."

They passed pastel-colored shops and an imposing building atop a terrace of cut coral steps. "Home of the governor, if I'm not mistaken," Miles said. "Temperate fellow. I met him in Savannah."

The carriage slowed, then swerved left, following a larger carriage and a cab into a wide dirt driveway. The vehicles circled to a portico with unpainted columns and temporary wooden steps that led to high double doors with classical moldings and French panes.

Despite the unfinished facade and incomplete trim, the Royal Victoria Hotel showed no signs of vacancy. Doormen in brass-buttoned jackets helped guests up and down the sagging steps.

Miles rose and used his cane to brace his descent to the running board. With more haste than grace, Devon exited the carriage on the other side.

She hurried up the makeshift steps of the hotel. After two days in cramped quarters and difficult company, she had a crying need for privacy.

But a room was hard to find. Finally, the registry clerk emerged from a far hallway, brushing at a startling white smear of plaster on the sleeve of his black jacket. He announced that the dry goods broker from Philadelphia had agreed to share a room with the munitions manufacturer from Bergensdorf, thus freeing a room for Devon.

"Do understand we're a bit Spartan right now," the clerk said as he bent over his book, changing names in the registry.

"Is Lord Grayshire a guest here?" she asked.

"Yes, ma'am. All the yachtsmen of the Savannah Sound Men's Society arrived yesterday. They are planning a grand soiree tomorrow to celebrate."

She asked for pen and paper to write a note to the Earl of Grayshire, Harcourt Bivens. Arnaud had instructed her to give his box of reports directly to Lord Grayshire, his loyal friend. The meeting would be uncomfortable for Devon. The earl, Roger's father, had been quite embarrassed by her sudden refusal to marry his son.

She signed her name to the note and added four carefully rendered hieroglyphs: the monkey fist. "Why did you open the hotel before it was finished?" she asked offhandedly, blowing softly to dry the ink.

"The visiting populace was desperate, of course," the clerk said, peering at her over his round English spectacles. "There was no place of distinction for gentlemen to lodge. As you may have noticed, Nassau has entered a prosperous era."

"And when the Americans end their civil war?" she asked, looking up as she sealed the note.

"Not too soon, I hope," said the clerk, annoyed by the question.

TWENTY-FIVE

Devon's room was at the end of a wing on the third floor. The smell of whitewash was pungent and fresh. Furnishings were adequate and reasonably clean, once Abby disposed of the brass spittoon that showed a fresh black dripping of snuff at its mouth. The dry goods salesman had not been a complete gentleman about the inconvenience.

Devon had a light dinner sent up as she and Abby unpacked and prepared for bed. The room was hot. Devon followed Abby's example and stripped off all but a cotton petticoat. She took the coverlet from the small bed and spread it on the floor. Abby settled there and neatly folded her linsey-woolsey shift for a pillow. Exhausted, she nestled on her side and was soon asleep.

Devon sat by the window and braided her hair. She was tired but too apprehensive to sleep. How would she find out how many ships the alliance had commissioned and where they would strike?

She had already read through Arnaud's reports. They were mainly expense records, charting payments for ships stores, and for repairs for three screwsteamers in Cárdenas and two schooners in the Caymans.

Surely the alliance had more than five ships. Arnaud had said the Arab, Khaled al-Sayed Dexter, was the organizational mastermind. How could she wrest the information from him without appearing overly curious?

She sighed, wishing she had Gentry's chameleon instincts. How easily he played the roles of Southern patriot and Federal spy. After three years of scouting troop movements for the Confederate cavalry, he was used to appearing committed to whichever faction he was confronting.

Devon, though, felt drained by the lies and pretense of allegiance. She knew missteps awaited. And Miles.

The thought of confronting Miles within the alliance circle gave her a rush of fear. Miles was incredibly confident. He did not act like a man about to face the judgment of powerful peers.

She lay back on her pillow and crooked an arm behind her neck.

Would Gentry come? Was he safe? Could they love?

Devon could not explain the feelings he engendered when they made love. She felt as if he anchored her, yet let her soar; as if he smothered her, yet gave her breath; as if he knew her body, but was discovering each part, celebrating her separateness, uniting it with his.

She laid her arm across her eyes. How close she had come to accepting less. What Gentry honored in her, Roger Bivens had tried to demean.

She had come to Gentry harboring a hazy vision of what it meant to give herself. He was teaching her, each time they lay together, that the gift was to herself, that the power came from her, not from him.

The night was lonely without him.

The next morning when she stopped at the registration desk, she found a note requesting her company in a second-floor salon. Lord Grayshire had not signed it, but a hastily sketched monkey fist ended the message.

Devon let Abby carry the brass-hinged box that held Arnaud's reports. They climbed the main staircase, newly carpeted with an Aubusson runner that sent dark green English ivy up the length of the stairs. Except for occasional bowls of citrus and pineapple in the lobby, the hotel bore no evidence of the bright tropical environs outside. Inside, the Royal Victoria was English colonial in ambience, decor, and expectation.

The door to the second-floor salon was opened by a servant with coal-black eyes and chestnut skin, not African, but Turkish or Arabic, Devon decided.

The boy motioned her to a seat, then stood beside flame-stitched draperies that blocked passage through an archway.

She settled on a low ottoman that could accommodate her skirts. Abby stood in the corner, stealing glimpses of the dark-skinned man with perfectly straight hair.

From behind the curtain Devon heard the low voices of three men. One was very English, but he spoke with a tone too even to fit the blustery temperament of Lord Grayshire. The second man spoke with languid rhythms, and once he laughed softly. The third man was French, with a voice too intense to be discreet. His words often carried through the thick draperies.

". . . twenty-four ships? That is all? . . . Why only four traversing carriages? . . . Barbados for coal . . . Ten thousand rifles? Did I not tell you the Mexicans could work fast with French supervi—Drat it, Dexter. Why do you try to shush me?" There were low-toned mumblings. "Then meet with her!" the Frenchman said suddenly. "We will talk again after the gala tonight, no?"

She heard chair legs scrape across the wooden floor, then one set of footsteps.

The servant parted the curtains and a self-possessed young Arab emergd. He was impeccably dressed and handsome, but dark circles under his eyes were evidence of lack of sleep.

"Miss Picard?" he asked.

She nodded.

"Khaled al-Sayed Dexter."

"A pleasure, Mr. Dexter, but I requested a meeting with Lord Grayshire," Devon said, smiling politely. She rose and shepherded her skirts away from the ottoman.

"I'm afraid the earl is indisposed after the long voyage," Khaled said. He eyed the brass-edged box that Abby held.

"My uncle's instructions were distinct regarding who should receive his report. Please relay my sympathies to the earl and tell him I will see him when he recovers." Devon gestured to Abby, ready to leave.

"Miss Picard," Khaled said quickly. "I assure you I can speak with you in his stead." He glanced back, giving an imploring look to someone in the meeting room.

A familiar jangle sounded, and Devon felt her knees grow wobbly. The clank of the brace grew louder with each step toward the arch.

"Good morning, Cousin," Miles said with a smile. "I believe Mr. Dexter here is sorely afraid you're going to leave without relinquishing the documents Arnaud sent. You wouldn't withhold alliance property, now, I'm sure."

"Have you explained why the reports are being delivered by a novice like me instead of a 'trusted' colleague like yourself?" she asked.

His eyes narrowed a little, like a hawk's assessing which way the rabbit will run. But he said nothing and looked at Khaled.

The young Egyptian cleared his throat. "Colonel Brant has explained the delicate situation that caused a rift between him and Admiral Picard."

"And that is?" Devon asked.

There was an uncomfortable silence. Khaled cleared his throat again. "The alliance committee favors Colonel Brant's battle plan over Admiral Picard's. I fear we have an unfortunate conflict of professional pride."

"My uncle lies in sickbed with death aching to attend him, Mr. Dexter. You think he has strength to waste on petty jealousy?"

"My apologies," Khaled said heavily. "Even if Lord Grayshire were here to meet you, he would immediately turn the admiral's correspondence to me. I am secretary. I must cross-reference the payment schedules and equipment invoices Admiral Picard kept."

"I must fulfill my obligation to the admiral," Devon insisted. "I'm sure you understand—" She stopped, appalled, as Miles purposefully approached Abby.

Without a word he held out his hand.

Abby immediately relinquished the box to her master.

"Was that all the admiral wanted you to deliver?" he asked Devon.

His tone challenged her. She met the cold gray of his eyes, but caution stilled the retort on her tongue. He was fishing to find out what else she knew.

Victor's life depended on her silence. If she accused Miles of poisoning her uncle, Miles would brand Victor the perpetrator, then would punish the slave for revealing the crime.

"Uncle Arnaud wanted me to relay two things," she said quietly. "His best wishes for success of the battle fleet, and his dismay that a man of high talent harbors the instincts of a pickpocket."

" 'Pickpocket'?" The word was repeated derisively from behind the curtain, then the Frenchman stepped into view. He was a balding man, grandly turned out with embroidered ascot and ivory buttons on his coat. Four rings on his fingers flashed intricate settings as he stroked his goatee. "Your cousin does tend to cut one down to size, eh, Miles?"

Miles, unruffled, smiled companionably at the Frenchman.

"May I introduce Count Valerie Beaumond?" Khaled said hurriedly to cover the count's rude entrance.

Beaumond nodded at her. "Before you regale us about the atrocious crime of theft, ma'm'selle, let me assure you that Colonel Brant has made amends!" He sliced the air with papers folded in his hand.

It was obvious Miles had made allies of those he had wronged. What gift had he offered for their forgiveness? she wondered, her discomfort growing. She was the outsider there, and Miles, the candid embezzler, was solidly ensconced at the alliance table.

"I have no interest in my cousin's plan for reparation," she said. "I am a reluctant volunteer, here at my uncle's request. He had questions about the area of fleet readiness, and I pledged to meet with you and relay the particulars upon my return."

She could see the consternation in the count's face. Khaled was trying to hide his shock.

"This is no activity for a woman," he said.

"I was pressed into courier service on my journey from England, and I've endured my share of misadventure. You think it is more ladylike for me to play the mule than to sit aboard the wagon?"

"The issue is proper procedure, not gender," Count Beaumond said archly.

Devon walked close to him. "The issue is loyalty to a cause and who has shown it. My uncle deserves representation in the final hours of a project that has sapped his strength. Miles Brant cannot speak for Arnaud Picard. I can. I assume this is a matter for more than a minority of the monkey fists to decide?" she asked pointedly.

"Ma'm'selle!" The count's soft exclamation was a rebuke.

"I think, dear cousin," Miles said, "what the count is trying to explain is that this isn't some parliamentary committee where someone gets appointed to replace someone else. If the admiral's not here, he's not here."

Color rose to her cheeks, and she knew Miles was thoroughly enjoying her confusion.

She drew all of her courage around her. "Then you will be pleased to hear me deliver my last message for the alliance," she said, "from my uncle to Lord Grayshire. My uncle says, 'Do not sit at a table with a thief. What he steals will not be apparent until you stand and feel the draft.' "

The insult left its mark. Two blotches of red appeared on the count's prominent cheekbones. The quiet Egyptian, hands sedately clasped, began to finger nervously the ruby scarab on his ring.

"I, for one," Miles said, his eyes bright, "am just grateful that your fine nerve and high good humor are on our side, Cousin."

She held her breath, as if a hole had just opened in the floor in front of her.

"We do expect to see you at the soiree tonight," he continued. "I even sent word to Gentry to join our celebration. I've told the count and Khaled here how helpful he's been, getting you safely to Jasmine's Reach and all." His smile was too familiar to be respectful. "As a matter of fact, I got a report Gentry is already sitting in a barber's chair in a little place on Bay Street. I'm sure he doesn't want to look the savage tonight."

"You are sure of entirely too much," Devon said.

"Tends to be disconcerting, doesn't it?" His smile turned annoyingly sympathetic.

Devon turned abruptly to the door, and Abby scurried to open it for her. She closed it behind them with a timid click.

"My word, Miles!" The count strode across the salon and grabbed the neck of a decanter. "You warned us that she was bold, but not that she has a scythe for a tongue. One *sphhtt!* and you are sorely nicked."

Miles didn't move. "What is it you French say? Formidable? Just goddamned formidable, isn't she?" He stared longingly at the door.

TWENTY-SIX

The ballroom of the Royal Victoria was intact, but unfinished. The most glaring omission in the room were arched paned doors that led outside to a garden walk. Folds of gauzy mosquito netting hung slack in empty doorframes.

Devon shifted a small cambric handkerchief from one gloved palm to the other. Her hands were damp with perspiration. Miles had said Gentry would come tonight. Somehow, she had to speak with him alone and relay what she had overheard in the anteroom of the salon.

The musicians behind her tuned their instruments, and she saw two young men approach her, dandified gentlemen whose smiles indicated they assumed she was a woman of ease.

She quickly turned her back and walked past the orchestra. She had made a mistake, coming early and alone. The room held only sparse cliques of partygoers. Lifting the hem of her skirt so that she would not stumble, Devon crossed the room as quickly as decorum allowed, steadying the bounce of watch-spring steel hoops in the crinoline. She wore a dark emerald gown with a skirt in three tiers, each silken layer trimmed with lace frill. The last tier ended well above her petticoat, showing an amber underskirt beribboned and festooned for display.

Cream-colored Maltese lace edged the yoke of her gown, which dipped to accentuate her bare shoulders and slim neck. The lace was scratchy and stiff; Abby had used so much starch, she'd had to steam the shelf-stiff folds into an elegant drape at the last minute. The humid steam had tightened the natural wave in Devon's hair, causing tiny curls to escape the severe chignon.

Dressing Devon's hair had been a long and arduous ordeal for Abby, and she had been heartsick at the thought of repeating it. Then her teary sadness became homesickness, and she'd bemoaned the indignities of white men who pinched her openly in the hotel halls, and she'd disdained the black islanders belowstairs who pledged to help her run away and court her. All were entranced by the peach undertone of her skin. Abby wanted only to go home.

"But the island boys say big storm's comin'," Abby had cried. "Ships blow 'way. Houses blow 'way. We be stuck here."

"When, Abby?" Devon had asked, frowning. "When do they say a storm is coming?"

Abby had shrugged. "Storm suck away the wind an' the air hold still. Then it be comin'."

Devon, pressed for time, had downplayed the threat. Neither she nor Abby had wanted to redo the hairpins and reposition the sprigs of silk jasmine that framed the chignon, so Devon was left with a frame of soft ringlets around her face, vaguely Grecian, quite unfashionable.

She ignored several disapproving stares as she crossed the marble floor of the ballroom to the garden doors. She nodded to a servant, who quickly brushed aside the mosquito netting like a stage curtain. Outside, she stepped into a coral-rock courtyard. Its centerpiece was a fountain that curled moatlike around a statue of one the Crown's eighteenth-century emissaries. She walked past the fountain, toward the garden steps. Then she stopped, aware of hushed voices nearby, aware, too, of how loudly her skirts rustled in the sudden silence.

A short, well-dressed man emerged from one of the trellised alcoves along the building wall. He nonchalantly tapped the ash off his cigar and gave a small bow. Behind him rang the familiar chime of Miles's brace.

"Seeking surcease in the garden, Cousin?" Miles asked. His voice was buoyant, untroubled that he had been caught in a conspiratorial stance. "So were we." He walked closer. "I'd like to introduce one of the dignitaries attending our little soiree tonight. Evan Kenilworth, Queen's governor for these fair isles."

"Honored," Devon murmured, and curtsied.

"Sir Evan and I were just reminiscing about the promising crop of tobacco I was nurturing along before the war. Better than Havana's latest, I wager." Miles smiled at the other man.

Sir Evan dismissed the claim with a wriggle of the cigar between his fingers. "Still prone to inflate conversation as well as your price, Colonel Brant?" He shook his head and smiled.

"Exaggeration is the soul of emphasis," Miles said grandly, his gaze on Devon.

"I've found exaggeration the soul of the Southerner," she replied.

Sir Evan laughed and Miles saluted her.

"If you'll excuse me," she said, and began to back away.

Miles placed his gloved hand lightly on her wrist. "It seems your escort has vanished, Cousin."

"He was called away suddenly," she lied. Miles had sent a note to her room requesting the honor of accompanying her. She had quickly invented a phantom acquaintance as escort.

"Insensitive fellow. I fear things could get quite boisterous tonight."

"Quite," Sir Evan said dryly.

"Luckily I'm free to squire you," Miles added, placing her hand atop his arm. He gave her hand a paternal pat.

Devon controlled the impulse to jerk away and stood stiffly until Sir Evan had taken his leave.

"The governor's very kind," Miles said, locking Devon's arm in the crook of his and walking toward the ballroom. "He's agreed to help the alliance in a very sensitive matter."

"The governor's virtue is in question if he's a friend of yours," she said, trying unobtrusively to withdraw her arm.

"Release me before I embarrass us both with a scene," she warned Miles.

"In a moment. First, look at me, Devon." The dandyish drawl was gone. In its place was a soothing coil, something intimate sprung between them.

"You will need me tonight," he said.

His assurance shot a tingling wave of apprehension through her. "One requires the services of a vulture only when dead," she said. "Do you have a death planned for me, Miles?"

He shook his head. "A small dying, perhaps, easily survived."

"Is this a warning?"

"No. A promise. I will help you tonight, if you ask."

"I would never seek your consort! Your soul is black with lecher's rot."

"Ah, Devon," he said, amused. "So adolescent in epithet, so wise in instinct. I don't know quite what we're going to do with you," he whispered.

Her breath stopped in her throat. That phrase. That whisper. The masked bandit who'd held her at gunpoint in the woods. Everything hidden but his voice. And his walk. Her gaze slipped involuntarily to his left leg, the black boot gleaming in its heavy metal cage.

"I sometimes worry that you are repulsed by my impediment," he said. "I wish to assure you, I can be a whole man for you, Devon."

She was stunned. Was his limp a ruse? Her admonition was weak: "Without morals, a man is never whole."

He smiled indulgently. "Morality is defined by cicumstance, not catechism. In fact, you've allowed events—and certain base responses—to shape your own code of ethics. The one you practice with Gentry, for example."

She was silent.

"I know that you're quite swept away by him. And I'm going to save you from that."

Dear God. "Tonight?" she whispered, afraid for Gentry.

"For always, my sweet. Always." He released her hand and bowed. "I do expect a dance soon. Just remember to take two steps to one of mine. It creates a certain poignancy of movement. Very touching."

He ushered her through the netting and smoothly left her side to greet formally clad guests entering from the hotel's promenade.

Devon drifted through the growing throng, pretending to have a destination, hoping she did not look as anxious as she felt. She was certain it was Miles who had shot at her in the woods when she was running from Landry's men. He who had walked toward her with a peculiarly elegant gait, surefooted, free of handicap. When had his leg healed? Why did he continue the ruse? What kind of man would suffer such torturous adornment? Perhaps Victor would know. Gentry must be warned.

As she neared an oasis of bushy oleander and date palm, she saw the Egyptian Khaled Dexter standing nearby. He met her eyes cautiously and lifted his glass in greeting. Beside him was a gargantuan expanse of good wool broadcloth. Lord Grayshire! With luck, an ally to Devon in her effort to discredit Miles.

She took a deep breath to compose herself, then joined the group. Count Beaumond accepted her presence with a barely gracious kiss of her hand. Lord Grayshire greeted her with a chill cordiality, obviously still piqued over the private scandal she had wrought with his son. Even so, the earl seemed anxious for news of his old friend Arnaud.

"He is grievously ill," she said. "And he sent private salutations to you. Perhaps I could share them as you walk with me? The buffet looks quite inviting."

Lord Grayshire swung his bulk to the right and glanced at the feast set up in a sideroom. Mounds of pâtés and jellied pastries sat amid platters of cold fillets and shellfish cocktails.

Khaled Dexter casually placed a restraining hand on the earl's shoulder.

"We still have much to discuss, milord," Count Beaumond added carefully.

The earl looked stone faced at the count. "Admiral Picard should be here to lend his opinion to our discussions. I want to hear what my good friend has to say through the auspices of his capable niece." He downed the remainder of his brandy.

Khaled stepped close to face the earl. He was silent a moment, giving import to the words that followed. "But here and now? Surely you could give Miss Picard more attentive audience tomorrow?"

Lord Grayshire paused, staring at Khaled. Then he turned to Devon. "Dexter here is persistent. But he's unfailingly correct about this sort of thing. I hope it will be possible for us to meet tomorrow."

"Of course," Devon said stiffly. None of the group wanted her to bend Bivey's ear. "I will leave you gentlemen to your discourse, the foremost concern of which, I'm sure, is the weather."

"What do you mean?" Lord Grayshire asked.

"The natives anticipate a major blow. I assume that means all ships will be battening their hatches and pointing prows to port or somesuch."

"Dexter?" Lord Grayshire said. In the one word was a host of critical questions.

"We cannot shift plans on the speculation of a few islanders. You know how superstitious they are." Count Beaumond's clipped voice preempted Khaled Dexter.

"What about our review of the *Banshee*?" Lord Grayshire demanded in a low voice. "Still two days hence? Is Hyde Cay the safest anchorage? And I don't like the idea of staying overnight, no matter how loyal this indigo grower you know. Plantations are flat! We'll be exposed to the elements! Will we be protected, man? Will the fleet?" His voice was rising, his neck growing more flushed.

Uncomfortable, Khaled began a low-toned explanation. Devon knew her presence was unwanted. Count Beaumond quickly drew her aside and started an inconsequential conversation about Paris fashion.

Devon kept her ear turned to the anxious words Khaled was using to soothe Lord Grayshire. The Egyptian stroked the ruby eyes of his scarab ring as he talked. Soon, he turned Lord Grayshire toward the buffet room. The earl bumped testily through the crowd like a tethered balloon.

Count Beaumond hurriedly took his leave of Devon.

Relieved to be rid of the alliance members, Devon climbed the stairs to the top of the promenade so she would be high enough to survey the crowd. She found her quarry on her second sweep of the room.

Gentry materialized from the shadows near the musicians' stand. She watched as he wended past crooked elbows and full-belled skirts with trailing hems. He did not push. He moved when gowns swayed or conversation turned, when pockets opened and closed, eyeing the rhythm of the crowd. He advanced without seeking attention, but he was noticed by men and women alike.

It was more than the burnished cast of his face or the astonishing blue of his eyes. With his hair newly trimmed, his jaw joined his chin in a bold, defined curve. And his brow gathered black and threatening over eyes set deep and Irish. Clean-shaven, he wore no beard to deflect the broad expanse of cheekbone or the strong nose. His face was too singular to be handsome, too proud to be dismissed.

He carried himself lithely, and he cut a superb figure in black coat and vest, white linen shirt, black silk cravat, and creased trousers.

Devon found herself staring as he approached. She had never thought he would camouflage so well in gentleman's clothes. Would he always surprise her?

They stood alone on the steps.

"It has been a long time," he said.

Her breath stilled. She carefully interlaced her fingers, else her hands would seek the warmth of his body, then her arms would follow and enfold him without shame.

"You have not danced," he added.

"And you?" she asked.

"I may have forgotten how."

"There is memory in motion."

"Then help me remember."

Devon extended her gloved hand. He held it correctly in his, his thumb bridging her inner hand, pressing where flesh yields willingly. Unhurried, they descended the wide steps to the ivory floor, locked in a decorum as warm as their desire for each other. For encased in the smoothness of his white gloves were fingers that had scaled the tender rise of her nipple, aching and slow.

Each casual movement of body and garb unsettled the air between them, and the warm wave of his hunger reached her, tingling as a touch.

"We must stop," she said, halting abruptly.

"We've not begun," he said, and gently pulled her forward.

To everyone in the room, their closeness was obvious, and enviable perhaps, for the pair first drew attention from resplendent ladies. Pleated fans rose, rippling like a warning flight of birds, as women stole glances from behind the delicate silk screens.

Then several gentlemen cleared gin-dry throats, aware of the mismatched couple approaching the columns of the dance square—the man so dark and work-strong; the woman fair as porcelain, a lady bred. Incredibly, the two advanced without awkwardness, without acknowledging the error that joined their hands.

The melody of a Mozart divertissement ended with energy, to no applause. Chitchat and merriment had grown subdued around the dance arena. Gentlemen called quietly for more gin or the sweet succor of port to accompany the small spectacle unfolding.

Devon and Gentry faced each other. He placed one hand at the small of her back and offered the palm of his left.

Her hand found the crest of his shoulder, and she hooked the gold chain at her right wrist to the skirt pull on her gown. Her skirt fanned to a discreet semicircle as she placed her hand in his, the tension restraining the bob of crinoline, holding its erratic sway in line.

Poised, Devon looked expectantly at the orchestra. The room had quieted. A sudden wind billowed the mosquito netting. The gauze rose in undulant folds.

"I fear for you tonight," she murmured to Gentry.

"I fear Miles will cut short our dance, given half a chance. We must talk. Can you dance without music?" He stiffly shifted forward.

She stumbled.

He caught her tightly against him. "I know only the waltz," he whispered.

She felt the kiss of his breath in her hair. She lingered against him, not wanting the circle of his arm to loose its hold.

When it did, she took her stance. "Begin slowly. I will follow."

He swept her backward on the count of one and hesitated the change step on two-three. But her skirt hid the tentativeness of his steps. On the second set he whirled her more boldly. On the third she was nearly giddy, and he wrenched a soft laugh from her as he pretended a flourish.

A great volley of strings and brass blustered the introduction to Strauss, loudly as if to reprimand the insensitive couple who danced to a private strain.

Gentry swept her grandly up to tempo. A few adventurous couples joined them on the dance floor.

"You learn quickly. Were you always a good student?" Devon asked, breathless.

"A rebellious one. The only tutor to best me was a three-hundred-pound Jesuit staying the winter at my father's. He had a very un-Christian uppercut."

Folds of her skirt whirled crisply as Gentry turned her suddenly in a new direction. She saw that Miles had emerged on the edge of the crowd. He watched with a cryptic smile.

The waltz entered the allegro.

Some instinct tightened Devon's stomach.

As if he knew, Gentry pressed her closer to him. "Did you learn the location of the assault?"

"No, but there are twenty-four ships." She related all that she had overheard.

Gentry slowed so she could catch her breath. "—and they plan to review one of the ships in two days. A place called Hyde Cay."

"Devon." The word held a strange, regretful sigh. "Remember this name: Red Jack Bettes. He's a smuggler who drinks at Sudder's Block. He and I have the same boss. Go to him with information."

"Why not to you?"

"I am going away."

"You cannot." Her feet grew leaden. She could not move.

He stopped. "I must go now, Devon. Now!" His voice was urgent.

She backed away, puzzled. "Why did you come if you knew the danger?" she whispered.

"I'd rather have blue-blooded witnesses than be lynched alone in a tree. Besides, I could hardly disappoint Miles."

"Don't joke, Gentry." She shook her head, frightened, so frightened.

"Don't hope, Daloni-ka," he said, his voice hardening. Then he grabbed her roughly by the arm.

Her fear was genuine. She was afraid for him, for what Miles could do.

He thrust her away and she nearly fell.

It was then that she had a clear view of the red plumes interspersed above the crowd. The governor's militia. The cadre of white-uniformed soldiers marched forward as Gentry stalked off the floor.

He swerved suddenly and dived shoulder first through the thickest part of the crowd.

Screams erupted and spread woman to woman. The crowd convulsed like a concertina, women fleeing one way to escape Gentry and his posse, indignant men leaning in-

ward to grab at anyone who struggled guiltily. Most of the
soldiers made little headway in the pandemonium. But ones
stationed near the walls drew their guns because they spotted their quarry. Gentry ran for the garden doors. One mili-
tiaman drew a bead with his pistol.

"Hold your fire!" screeched Sir Evan. "You'll shoot a civilian!"

Gentry ran through the curtained doorway to the courtyard.

A dozen soldiers converged on the netting and pulled it
down. They ran out, sticks drawn.

Devon could hardly see. She was surrounded by ladies
who called for air or moaned about the tear in their taffeta.
What she could see was how brightly their eyes burned with
excitement, for in the outrage, their boorish escorts had
transformed into solicitous, vibrant partners.

"Interesting how spectacle always feeds the shallow,"
Miles remarked calmly over her shoulder. "They never digest life, they just consume, always hungry."

She glanced back. He hovered behind her like a shark.

"Stay away from me," she demanded, but her voice was
weak as a plea. She suddenly felt unsteady. She wavered.

Miles clasped her about the arms and held her up. "So
glad he didn't hurt you." He spoke close to her ear. "Spies
are desperate men sometimes. But then they can also be
desperate ladies, too, can't they?"

"Stop it!" Her anguished scream reverberated in the hall.
But she had no strength to push away from Miles, no
strength to cry. She lolled, near faint, the back of her head
against Miles's chest. God make her small, she prayed, so
small that she could slip away from all of them, so small
that she could not hold the hurt. Run, Gentry. Run.

"Quiet!" Sir Evan's yell carried above the busy bantering
crowd. "We've got him!"

Devon closed her eyes, but she could still hear. The rough
scuffles, the sharp admonition of the captain of the guard,
the snap of heeled boots on the cold marble floor.

And Miles. "Hmmm. Four soldiers clamped onto him.
His hands are tied. He must have put up quite a fight. But
we knew he would. I insisted Evan have a cadre stationed
outside. My, that's a nasty gash over his eye."

His vitriol crept over her like an icy wind. Devon felt herself grow cold and solid.

"That's it. Wake up," Miles said, constituting his voice like a tonic. "Be a strong girl, now. Face him for me."

What a puppet she must be, to be propped and prodded about, Devon thought. Yet she had no will to leave the farce Miles had planned. She twisted slowly, sadly, against him, trying to pull herself free.

He released her with a condescending gentleness.

Trancelike and yet with eerie dignity, she walked toward the cocky red plumes she saw at the edge of the crowd. Rustling taffetas and bright watered silks parted before her in voluminous waves, their wearers casting furtive glances as if Devon cast too bright a light.

She saw Gentry at the end of the walk. He was surrounded by uniformed men with high-bowled hats and shiny brass buttons. Miles had lied about the gash. A small cut at Gentry's temple bled insignificantly, but his clothing was torn and disassembled. With his hair mussed he looked wild and unpredictable, but Devon sensed a tiredness in him. He had partaken of civility that night, postured correctly in his clothes and his dance, and been dealt with savagely. No matter how much he may have expected it, the irony was draining.

Her heart ached as she approached him.

"Miss Picard," Sir Evan admonished her, "I must caution you—"

He stopped when Miles raised a reassuring hand. "This is important, Evan. We must clear Miss Picard's good name."

Devon heard the prompting in Miles's voice. She looked into Gentry's eyes. He had heard it too.

She shook her head. She did not want to be saved if Gentry were lost.

Gentry looked beyond her, to Miles. "What is the charge?" he shouted.

"Spying for the enemy and treasonous conduct," Miles said.

"Your proof," Gentry demanded.

Miles pulled a letter from inside his coat. He flourished it close enough so that Gentry could see the handwriting as his own.

"Confiscated from a Federal sympathizer two days after

your meeting with Admiral Picard," Miles said. "And here are the extradition papers that allow us to take you home to court-martial." He whisked documents from another pocket, but he did not unfold them for inspection.

Gentry took a long look at Devon, then exploded with rage. His struggle caught his captors by surprise, and they hurried to subdue him.

"Damn you!" he shouted at Devon. "You tricked me!"

She shook her head, confused.

Women in the crowd gasped at the vulgar language.

"Saying I should confide in you, depend on you," he raged on. "You told them about the letter, didn't you?"

Devon remained silent.

She heard Miles's brace draw close to her. He placed a hand on her shoulder, to the outward eye consoling her. But when he leaned close, his words were patronizing. "For God's sake, say something to support his story. He's trying to save you from consort with the enemy."

She shrugged his hand away and took a step closer to Gentry.

"There is no trick. I love you," she said, even toned, not loud. But onlookers carried her response through the crowd like a recurring echo.

Gentry froze, horrified that she did not take the lie he offered. But a terrible pride and possession erupted alongside his concern. She chose him. In public, in her world, she was his.

He glanced at Miles.

Miles's face had hardened. Gentry could not tell whether Miles wanted Devon badly enough to save her now.

"What are you saying, dear girl?" Sir Evan asked point-blank but kindly.

Devon did not speak.

"She's revealing the depth of subterfuge this Federal spy employed on her sensitive nerves," Miles said. "Though he used her cruelly, she had enough presence of mind to tell me about the message he was sending to his superiors. I think her delicate constitution has endured enough battering from this man. Take him away."

The soldiers pushed Gentry forward.

Devon watched numbly.

The crowd drifted away on a tide of murmuring voices.

Gentry looked back only once, his dark visage a deadly promise to Miles.

Miles took Devon's arm as Gentry watched. "They will put him in irons, you know." He paused, to make sure the image of Gentry in chains was implanted. "I can intercede though."

"At what price?" she asked.

"One night with you. This night." He wanted her. Simply, irrationally, on the night she had declared her love for the half-breed, Miles wanted to mark her with the spume of his manhood.

"That is the difference between you," she said, turning to face him.

He was disturbed at her high tone. Her name and reputation sullied before a hundred people, and she dared speak like a teacher to a dunce?

"Gentry would never risk my dishonor. You demand it. A fool could tell which man is the savage."

She walked away from him then, up the steps to the promenade, her skirt swaying gracefully, her breeding evident, her shoulders straight and her bearing as self-possessed as a bust of Aphrodite, her hair singularly done with Grecian curls. And that face, the face that scorned him, the face that would not surrender even when her lover's dignity lay on the chopping block.

Very well, Miss Picard, Miles thought, still smarting from the chill archness of her tone. Let's put something less optional on the block.

Gentry's life.

TWENTY-SEVEN

Devon raced up the stairs and to her room, locking the door behind her.

"Abby," she called into the darkness, trying to keep her voice calm.

"Yes'm?"

She heard a sleep-slowed rustling from the pallet across the room.

"Light the lamp. Quickly." Devon hugged herself, arms gripped tightly, trying to close the void that yawned like an icy pond inside her.

"I need your help, Abby." She leaned her forehead against the wall near the door. The lye in the whitewash stung her nostrils, pungent as salts.

Abby twirled the lantern wick higher and the glow reached Devon. "You all right, Miz Devon?"

Devon swallowed hard. She was careful to speak slowly. "Go immediately to Colonel Brant's room. Tell Victor I must see him tonight. Let him set the meeting place. It must be soon, before Colonel Brant returns from the ballroom."

"You hurt?" Abby asked, afraid.

Devon bit her lip, shaking her head.

"You got doctor pains?"

"No," Devon whispered. "Go."

"Man pain?"

"Abby!"

"My mam say a conjure lady the only way to stop a man pain."

"For goodness' sake, Abby, scoot!" Devon nearly cried.

Was her maudlin panic so obvious a twelve-year-old could diagnose it?

Devon had never felt this kind of dread. Fear for Gentry held her prisoner against the wall, and fear for herself. Tonight's trespass would be publicly criminal, not something her family could hide in a private circle of friends.

She was going to help Gentry escape. If she was caught, there was not money in the world to save her from the attention of the London tabloids. Her escapade would play heartily against the democratic and alcoholic decrepitude her father had modeled. And the dance-hall legacy of her mother would add the right touch of salaciousness to Devon's defense of her lover.

With unsteady hands, she pawed through her trunk for her evening cape, floor-length and black. From a beaded whatnot box she retrieved the money she had requested for incidentals. She wrapped the coins securely in a handkerchief so they wouldn't jangle, then placed them in her reticule.

From a drawer she took two garters and slipped both onto her thigh. She opened the barrel of the revolver Gentry had sent and emptied six bullets into her hand. The gun she strapped to her thigh; the bullets she put in a special pouch in her cape.

Then she waited, but not long. Abby returned, out of breath.

"Victor say take a carriage to the big church. He meet you there."

Devon gave hurried instructions. "If anyone asks you where I've gone, say that I was upset and left to take some air. Don't say where. And don't say I'm with Victor. It would make trouble for him."

"You comin' back?" Abby asked, looking down. She nervously twisted a chipped button on her shift.

Devon paused. "I hope so." She dug five silver dollars from the reticule. "Keep these. You may need them to get home. Or to buy your mam a present."

She hugged Abby, then left the room, tucking her blond hair into the hood of the cloak and pulling the black broadcloth close around her face.

At the hotel entrance the doorman summoned one of

three open carriages lined up outside the portico. A driver with a high top hat and an infectious grin pulled up.

"Trinity Church," Devon told the driver.

"A beautiful cathedral, that it is," the driver said. " 'Course, I don't know that you'll be seeing much of the grand stained glass and all tonight. Dark, you see."

"Isn't church always a place of light for the soul?" she asked, feeling hypocritical.

"O' course, o' course it is," the driver hurriedly agreed. "Just that it's dark this time o' night, you understand."

Devon said nothing. The driver seemed nondescript in feature beneath his tall hat. As the carriage lantern swung wildly on its post, she caught a glimpse of gray-flecked beard and threadbare collar.

"Quite a commotion at the hotel, I hear," he prompted.

Devon didn't answer.

"They caught a Federal spy, is what they say," he said, a little huffy that she wasn't helping with the story. " 'Course, that's ridiculous. Everyone here's a spy for one thing or the other. Spying's just pirating of a different stripe, you see. Here, we're always depending on pirates and smugglers and wharf rats for money changing, if you know what I mean."

"This spy you're talking about. Is he dangerous?" she asked, trying to direct the driver's rambling tongue.

"I saw 'em escortin' him out at a right smart pace there. A big strappin' man. Wouldn't want to tangle with him myself, not at my age, now. Rheumatism, you know. I got a joint swelling on every limb. Hurts whichever way I turn. Effie—that's my lady friend, you know—she says her grandma dosed herself up with skunk-cabbage powders and could hunker down to pull turnips till she was seventy-three. Hard to believe, now, hard to believe."

Devon bit the inside of her cheek to keep from screaming. "I assume prisoners are locked somewhere secure. I wonder where would they hold a spy?"

"Now that's the funny part. Usually they'd take him to Fort Fincastle. It's that triangle-sort of building southeast of the hotel, you know. Built to look like a ship's prow. Looks like an old lizard head to me. They've got a little stockade there for holding foreigners."

"They didn't take him there?"

"Took him straight to the city prison. It's that rock build-

ing with eight sides to it, see? Just on the next block now."
The driver pointed. "That's where they took him. A man
gets outta there, they walk'im to a tree and tie'im his last
cravat."

"You can't be serious," Devon said quickly.

"Well, ma'am, sad as 'tis, it's only before God that all men
stand equal. The law hasn't got the peering power of the
Almighty, but they sure pretend, now, don't they? Here we
are, ma'am. Whoa there, T'eobald." He reined the horse and
set the brake.

"Will you be wantin' me to stay and wait?" the driver
asked as he jumped down. He landed with an "oof." "Be
glad to do it even though this is a bit of a short run for me
and all. But I wouldn't mind a'tall."

"I would appreciate it if you could wait, Mr . . . ?"

"Dawkins, ma'am. Harley Dawkins at your service, and a
pleasure it'd be to see you back safe after your Christian
duty is complete. Yes, ma'am."

"Thank you," Devon said. She turned and walked toward
the high mahogany doors, shining in the glow of two ornate
sconces. Above the lintel a gabled roof rose to a spire.
Higher yet was a large wheel window, its stained-glass garden of color lost in the shadow of night.

She pressed the wrought-iron latch, and the door swung
toward her with a trembling moan at the hinge.

She entered the narthex, its high, angled rafters hovering
formless in the dark passageway. A lantern burned atop a
small table. Above it, the looped rope of the tower bell hung
on a peg in the wall.

Taking a candle from a small basket, she fitted it to a
holder and lit the wick. Slowly she proceeded down the nave
of the deserted cathedral, raising her candle as she passed
each pew, waiting for a glimpse of Victor's tall figure.

Her wavering candle found him seated far to the left of
the chancel in the front of the church. Like her, he was
cloaked in black, and he was bent forward in prayer. A
worthy activity given the enormity of their task that night,
Devon thought.

She entered the row, her skirt hissing against the bench
seat.

Victor appeared not to hear.

She stopped, uneasy, and raised her candle higher. "Victor?" she whispered softly, hopefully.

"No. Not Victor."

The brace gave a muffled clank and Miles stood.

Devon turned to run, but her wide crinoline caught on the kneeling rail. Miles lunged and caught her easily, grabbing the wrist of the hand that held the burning candle. He drew her toward him.

The light cast a garish yellow on his cheeks. His gray eyes lightened like a cat's.

"Mind the wax, Devon," he said with an eerie calm.

She glanced down and saw the candle holder was tilted precariously.

He twisted her wrist and righted the dripping candle. A line of tallow droplets streamed across her white glove.

"You must be careful," he said softly, loosening her finger from the ring in the candle dish. "Fire and crinoline are a disastrous combination."

He set the candle on the pew in front of them. Then he pulled a lantern from under the bench and heightened its glow.

Slowly he slipped the hood from her hair. "Have you any idea how annoyed I am with you?" he asked as he straightened folds at her shoulder and around her neck.

His fingers brushed her chin and she shivered.

"You went to Victor. That's forbidden, Devon. He's mine. No one meddles with my slaves. First, Portia. Now you're trying to lay hold of Victor. Why?"

She swallowed hard. He was so close. He would sense a lie. "I just wanted someone to help me," she said.

"You really don't know what to do, do you? Not one of the monkey fists will trust you now, even though I keep telling them you were duped. I'm trying to save your neck, Devon. I hope you appreciate it."

"I ask nothing of you!"

"Ask, no. But you would steal something quite special. Victor's a superb specimen. Ashanti. A great fighting race. And I already walk a delicate line with him. I've put so much training into him. Fencing. Wrestling. Gentleman's sport. I'd hate to have to shoot him because you compromised his loyalty."

Her eyes, hot with outrage, met his. "You have no right to murder."

He abruptly grabbed her shoulders. "The strong thrive and the weak only survive! If you commiserate with slaves, you'll be weak like they are. Don't you see?"

"Yes, I see!" She struggled to break his hold. "I see a gutless imposter who steals sympathy because he hasn't the dignity to earn it!"

In fury, she kicked his leg. The brace gave a startled clank. The ping echoed in the dark vault above.

Devon stopped struggling. She could not read the expression on Miles's face.

Surprisingly, he laughed. "Irreverent little witch!" He shook his head and released her. "What nerve. To kick a cripple."

"Only your backbone needs bracing."

"My, how vicious. There's something a little ruthless in you. Do you feel it? The will to succeed at any cost? You're just about the perfect complement to a man's vices. And virtues, too, of course. The question that remains"—his voice turned soft—"is whether you're too virtuous for me. Sit down."

She did, for her knees were beginning to weaken. In God's house. What could he do here? Would she have the chance to get the gun, and the courage to shoot it?

He sat down beside her.

She clasped her cold hands tight in her lap. Underneath, the gun pressed solidly against her thigh.

Miles bent to attend the straps on his brace.

He was going to free himself!

She scrambled for the aisle, but he sprang from his seat while she was still within arm's reach. He grabbed a handful of her hair.

Her cry rang in the black emptiness of the cathedral. He pulled her back down beside him, the fistful of hair as leverage.

"Now, then." He turned her head to face him. "I don't intend to hurt you. And I don't practice carnal rites in the house of God. That would be impolite at best, and most impolitic. All I want, my dear . . ."

He fell suddenly still.

Devon closed her eyes, for his gaze was roaming her face,

absorbing her features, flicking hungrily where the light shone brightest, feeding a desire that glistened strange and cold in the orbed well of his soul.

"All I want is a dance," he said finally, softly.

He splayed his hand in her hair and raked gently to loosen the strands. "Will you agree?" he asked absently, intent on the pins in her chignon.

The heavy coil of her hair tumbled free.

She held a cry in her throat as Miles's fingers worked there, nimbly slipping a bone button from its loop. Her cape swagged down off her shoulders. He draped it neatly over the seat behind her.

Her bared shoulders felt the touch of a cavernous coolness in the room. Air coursed over the swell of her breasts above the lace neck of the gown.

Miles paused.

"Don't," she whispered.

"Don't what?" He smiled and pulled gently on the lace ruffle, loosening it. Her breasts adjusted, settling in the small giving space he had made. He tugged delicately on the other side, with a grooming detachment, pulling the neck of her gown lower, forcing her breasts higher.

She felt nothing but his breath on her skin, yet the deliberateness of his action, his intense attention to the yield and fold of her flesh, was terrifying.

"I'm a connoisseur, Devon. Unlike anyone you'll ever know."

She felt herself growing physically weak, unable to turn away from the caress of his hand along her cheek.

"One dance?" he whispered. His finger traced the full curve of her lower lip.

She closed her eyes. "Yes." Let him stop. "Yes."

"Good." He released her, with some reluctance, then bent to the task of unbuckling his brace.

"I thought you would like to compare us," he said. "Gentry and me, I mean." The tongue of one buckle jingled and a leather strap flapped free. "I must admit my chagrin at having a half-breed as a rival. I guess we're all drawn to the ungodly in one way or another. Is that why you chose a heathen for your lover, Devon?"

"I chose a noble man," she said softly. If only she had not unloaded the gun Gentry had given her.

"You chose a mercenary spy." Miles's tone was dismissive. "I still don't know exactly why he's so quick to help the Yankees. He doesn't care about money. Flicks a finger at his father's fortune. Teague Morgan's sitting on a real estate gold mine. A man content to walk away from that isn't noble. He's stupid. Too stupid for you, believe me."

She heard the soft scrape of leather on the buckle. "Isn't it funny how I know things about you?" he went on. "Just a little sixth sense after you left the ballroom made me think, 'I better check Victor.' And it's a shame I have to get back to that paltry affair. The count and I have a strategy meeting soon. He's acting directly for the French emperor in this, you know, no matter what he says about 'sympathetic aristos.'"

The heavy iron brace opened its harmless jaw, and Miles swung his leg free, sighing with relief. He tapped his heel, then stood and walked a few steps away from her, turned and walked back. "Victor usually massages the muscles, takes the stiffness out.

"I bet it was Victor who chose this meeting place, wasn't it? Africans are very spiritual. Victor, especially. He has rituals for everything. Been trying to get his gods to drop me dead for years. But heathen gods aren't worth diddly in the grand scheme of things. And that's where I've always put my faith, Devon. In the grand scheme."

He extended his hand.

She stood reluctantly.

He was quiet a moment, looking down at her darkly, privately. "You are lovely," he said, almost in a whisper.

She looked away, conscious in a shamed and terrible way of her breasts.

"Amazing," he said. "My mother would turn her head, just like that, when my father looked hungrily at her. Of course, Big Josey was a drunk and a lout, not worth the spit to shine her shoes. With me he was a mean son of a bitch. I have no idea how Mother Nature does that, grows a creature of intellect from the seed of a moron, but she did. I'm completely my mother's child. She taught me to dance, you know. Shall we?"

Devon was chilled by his strange deportment. With a formal grace he guided her to the center of the aisle in front of the altar. He walked slowly, placing elegant emphasis on the leg freed of the brace.

The only sound was the swish and bristling of her gown. Without the metal collar, his steps were as silent as a cat's.

He smiled and took his stance.

Devon stepped back, faltering, unable to place herself in his arms.

"You must keep your word." His hand slid around her waist to the small of her back.

She weakly took a fold of skirt in her hand and was still.

"Your hand, my dear," he said, his own poised. "How else am I to guide you?"

"I cannot follow you."

"Have confidence, my love," he said softly. He held her intimately against him, eerily patient, until she placed her right hand in his palm.

She felt a terrible moment of darkness, as if in completing the stance she acquiesced to something far beyond physical demand.

An abnormal satisfaction glowed in his eyes. He held her, not moving, so long content with the pose that she stiffened and tried to pull her arm down.

His grip closed on her hand, and he began an infinitesimal sway, his hand at her back moving side to side, slowly, gently, massaging her rigidity. Patiently he rocked her to an unheard rhythm, and she felt her tensed body ease into lithe, guarded motion. As he tendered her body, he meant to tender her will. Knowing that, she still could not anticipate his move.

He pressed her backward suddenly and firmly, before she could protest, and pulled her around in a turn, beginning a series of exuberant whirls, so that she could not stop for fear of falling. He held himself hard to her, an anchor in a forceful tide.

In intricate eights he danced, advancing then retracing their path. The small aisle of the church became a long hall down which she could not discern their progress until she felt him slow the pace.

Suddenly they were at the end of the aisle, at the back of the church with its one flickering lantern. He swung gracefully to a stop. Her skirt rushed gaily around his leg, taken with the dance, taken by him.

Devon stood still, like a doll in his arms, a doll with burning eyes, afraid to incite response.

He looked down at her.

Only her chest moved, constricting, fighting sound like the fluttering of a voiceless dove.

He bent tentatively, then lowered his face to hers. He slid his cheek across her wet one, his mouth roaming the slick heat.

"Fierce tears, angry tears," he murmured, close to her ear. "But any step away from hate is progress. I can be patient, for a while. As long as I know you will dance."

His arms slid away.

She felt his presence retract like an opening door, lost in the shadows along the aisle. Then she heard the buckles flap against the frame of the brace as he hoisted it. In the front, near the sanctuary, a door creak closed.

Gone. But he had made sure his presence would be felt long after he left, bestowing outrage with the forced melding of his body to hers, revulsion with the vulgar play of his lips on her cheek, shame with a last appraising glance of her bosom.

After a long while, Devon walked down the aisle toward the uncertain glow of the candle she had lit. Her chest had quieted with swallowed cries. Her eyes were raw and dry.

She retrieved her cape and the diminishing candle, its tiny flame flickering in a puddle of wax. "Don't die," she whispered. "Don't die."

The flame surged weakly, then spent itself in a spiral of smoke.

She walked the aisle in the dark.

She was alone in this. Victor could not help her. And Miles had made sure she was the cripple, breaking her confidence and self-respect with each step of his dance. How strong was she?

God in heaven, how strong?

She shut the tall mahogany door of the cathedral and approached the carriage.

As she neared, she heard a droning vibration that grew to nose-rattling thunder. Nothing moved, except the horse's ear, which twitched maniacally each time Harley Dawkins heaved a snoring breath. He was stretched lengthwise on the driver's perch.

Devon shook the carriage. "Mr. Dawkins?" she called.

Dawkins raised his head with a final phlegmatic snarl. "Good gosh Almighty, ma'am, here you are, finished already? Resting my eyes just a minute." He rubbed his elastic face, like a cook kneading dough.

Devon didn't wait for him to help her into the carriage.

"I have a proposition, Mr. Dawkins. A simple errand." Her voice felt wooden, not cordial.

Dawkins cleared his throat and turned to peer at her. His brows lowered over wary eyes. "This here errand, it takes into account my age and my rheumatism, wouldn't it?"

"Yes. And your garrulous sociability as well." She mechanically smoothed her skirts.

"O' course, o' course," Dawkins said doubtfully.

"I need to get a message to a friend of a friend of mine. A man named Red Jack Bettes. I believe his tavern of choice is Sudder's Block?"

"It is, ma'am," Dawkins said. "When he's in port. Got his own spot worn on the bar rail, if you know what I mean. Big fella. And you're surely right not to go there yourself, no place for a lady, no place at all. Now, I was wonderin', just how much . . . er, what you was proposin' to . . ."

"One guinea, free and clear. A shilling for your transport and a shilling for a draft of beer. You'll want to be sociable while you're telling Mr. Bettes how important it is that I see him immediately. Tell him I'm a protégé of Mr. Morgan."

"O' course, o' course," Dawkins said, eyes wide. He hoisted the reins and clicked his tongue. "Haw there, T'eobald," he called energetically. "Now where will I drop you off while I go to fetch Red Jack?"

"I was hoping you'd have a suggestion," she said carefully.

"I see. Uh-huh. Don't want to go back to the hotel?"

"No."

"Need a kind of a . . . what you'd call, outta-the-way place?"

"Exactly. I'm prepared, of course, to offer recompense for the discretion and hospitality I receive."

"O' course, o' course."

Dawkins paused, pretending to think. "The best outta-the-way place I know is my Effie's. Conch chowder's good. And there's usually a room free this time o' week if you care

to freshen up. Not elegant surroundin's, you understand."
He swung around to look at her, one brow arched in a question.

"I understand completely," Devon said quietly."Do your best to hurry, Mr. Dawkins."

TWENTY-EIGHT

It didn't take Harley Dawkins long to get to the bayfront and head east to the intersection of Sweeting. Not far down Sweeting Street he turned into a two-rut road. The carriage jostled through a jungle of breadfruit trees and elephant-eared philodendron.

In front of a brightly lit house, the horse snorted and stopped. Small lanterns were knotted along a rope on the porch. Two torchlights burned on high posts beside the steps.

"Here 'tis," Dawkins said proudly. "Me Bonnie Bay."

Me Bonnie Bay was a two-story clapboard boardinghouse with worm-rotted gingerbread trim. The front windows were covered with sagging shutters, some weathered and black, tilting outward like tightrope walkers fighting a fall.

Inside, the house was alive with rum-fed laughter and well-fed men. A sailor traversed the front hallway with shirttail flapping and hat askew, one hand clasped to a tankard, the other groping for purchase on a good-natured tart.

To the right was a parlor with a plump horsehair sofa worn to the nap in the middle. To the left was a dining room set with table and benches and a slow-stewing pot on the hearth. There, Harley Dawkins huddled a moment with a matronly woman who wore a neat ruffled cap and a saintly smile. A light pink apron crossed her stout bosom tight as a jib bracing a wind.

"I'm Miss Effie, ma'am," the large matron said, greeting Devon. "Proprietess here." Her voice was dainty and bright. "You kin have the second room to the right o' the top o' the stairs. I'll bring you some hot food directly. There's clean toweling in the rooms at all times. Anything else you'll be needin'?"

"Pen, paper, and inkwell, if possible," Devon said.

"O' course, ma'am, by and by. I must get back to the kitchen, and Harley here will be off to gettin' your gentleman friend." Miss Effie smiled sweetly.

Devon wielded her wide crinoline up the narrow stairwell. She hesitated at the second door and prayed the room was empty. It was, and already lit. The washstand was meticulously supplied. Wash linens were pressed and clean. The tepid water in the pitcher was fresh. She squeezed a cut lemon into the basin. The citrus scent sliced acridly through the thick yeastiness hovering around the bed.

Devon freshened up, then took the gun from her garter and loaded it.

Writing supplies were brought up by a young cook's helper who smelled of fish. Devon wrote as quickly as she could, filling two pages with a summary of her knowledge of the alliance and its plans.

Then she sat in a chair beside the window to rest. She lost track of how long she waited; once she caught herself nodding in sleep. She did not hear the door until it shut firmly and latched.

She stood and found herself facing a barrel-chested man whose size made the furniture seem doll-like. He had a fiery-red beard that grew up around his ears and ringed the bottom half of his scalp. The top of his head was bare and freckled brown.

"Mr. Bettes?" she asked quickly, hopefully.

"Aye, duck. Don't tell me someone remembered me birthday." Two bottom teeth were gone. The sodden ferment of rum bathed each syllable.

As he walked closer, Devon raised the revolver. "Birthdays are for children, Mr. Bettes."

"Well, I ain't in a playful mood, being dragged away from me game," Red Jack said. "An' I don't discuss business wtih a gun in me gut."

"And I don't give you salable information in fear for my virtue."

"Virtue ain't worth spit in one of these rooms, duck."

Devon controlled her temper with difficulty. Time was wasting. "I am not your ration of poultry, Mr. Bettes! And if you're not prepared to help me, I'd just as soon see you stretched out in eternally peaceful repose!"

She deliberately cocked the revolver. Her hand was trembling.

"Whoa, now, fer Christ sakes, whoa! Keep hold o' that hammer and get a grip on yourself." His guttural growl was gone. "You made your point. Ease it back now. I just wanted to test your backbone."

"And how's my backbone, 'duck'?"

"Middlin' firm," he said tersely.

She slowly reset the hammer. Red Jack didn't blink until the head settled softly against the plate.

"Do you know where Genty Morgan is?" she asked.

"This burg's so small the governor can't break wind without everyone catching a little sniff," Red Jack said. "You want me to get word to Morgan?"

"I want you to get him out."

"Impossible."

"You're lying. Or else you're very unimaginative."

"Now don't go high-nose on me! I'll walk right outta here and back to the cock ring where I have a chance of winning!"

She knew he meant it. "I'm sorry. I'm a bit on edge. And I sorely need your help."

"What's my stake in this?"

"Whatever it takes to free Gentry and get word to a Federal ship. A Confederate fleet of falsely registered and illegally commissioned ships will attack soon."

"What's my take?" he asked.

She swallowed hard. "Whatever the U.S. government will pay for this information." She held out the papers that held names, dates, and details of the alliance conspiracy.

"Read it to me," he said.

When she was halfway through, he interrupted. "That's enough."

"It's valuable merchandise."

"Facts ain't worth no more'n bananas. All perishables. Gotta reach their destination before ripe runs to rot."

"I agree," she said. "The Federals need this immediately in order to prepare. Can you do it?"

He tugged his beard as he thought. "Smart people here

are beginning to batten down their hatches in case of storm. You wantin' me to sail out like a fool?"

"No! I want you to navigate like the brilliant seaman you're reputed to be!"

"You're blowin' my horn, but I don't feel puffed up, no siree!" Red Jack shouted. "What stake's an English lady got in all this anyway?"

"I'm just an abolitionist, recently shamed into service as an agent against this conspiracy."

"Takin' a lot o' risk on account of shame. Safer to confess to a good bartender any day."

"I have no bartender. Only a conscience. And you wouldn't have left a lucrative game unless either your conscience or your moneybag was itching." She angrily snapped the papers in her hand. "This will take care of your coin purse. I have nothing to scratch your soul."

He was silent a moment. "A little young for this kind of work, ain't ya?"

A lump rose in her throat at his softened tone. "I'm aging as fast as I can, Mr. Bettes," she whispered.

Red Jack looked down a moment, then gave his boot a resigned stomp. "How much money ya got?"

"An eagle, ten gold pieces."

"Not good. But not too bad. Helluva sight more'n I send the captain of the guard every month."

"You bribe him?"

"Ya bribe everybody here. They need the money most. A gold piece each might do."

He turned to go.

"Wait!" Devon said. "I'm going with you."

"C'mon! A little shank o' trimmed mutton like you?" Red Jack said derisively.

"Get me some clothes. I'll change."

"Naw. I need me a boy for what I have in mind."

"For God's sake, Mr. Bettes, couldn't you make it a bit easier on me?"

"Easier, she says. Easier? You're askin' me to put me buns on the block for a man I never drank with till yesterday? Then I'm gonna have to lay low for months, and ya know what that does to a man in a delicate business?" He paced like a lecturing professor, punctuating with his hands. "It hands his territory to a greedy bastard like Poppy Lopez—

squinty-eyed little garlic-eater—on a flippin' gold plate! So if I don't put a little pinch on ole Poppy tonight, I'm shootin' meself in the foot, ain't I? An' no matter how much your Federal friends pay for those words there, I ain't fond of limpin'!"

Devon closed her eyes. "Then why even contemplate helping me?" she asked, exasperated.

Red Jack was quiet, thumbing his beard. "Ya want the truth, missy? Ya ever smelled misery? Real misery? I mean a stench that slams yer gut and makes yer head swell, yer eyes water, and ya say, 'Gawd Almighty, how could there rise such an air, and how can people breathe in it, bleed in it, eat in it, hope in it, pray in it'?

"I got press-ganged to crew a slave ship when I was a boy. An' I got that misery smell on my clothes. Ain't been shed of it since. And that's a fact."

Devon paused, then laid her gun on the table. She folded her letter and handed it to Red Jack.

"I can be a boy," she said. "Just find some clothes."

His red beard bristled upward as he pursed his lips. "Stubborn little duck." He assessed her. "Might work," he said without conviction, the fight gone from his voice. He shook his head as he left the room.

Devon was relieved when he returned ten minutes later.

He threw a bundle on the bed. "Don't mind tellin' ya it's gettin' God-bloomin' late. I sent a runner to get the steward to ready my ship. Might even sail tonight. Depends on the wind and how many authorities I've got up my arse." He turned to leave.

"Where are you going?" she asked.

"To wet my whistle while ya change."

She didn't want him any more drunk. "We've wasted enough time. Just turn your back." She was already tearing at her buttons.

"You trust me, 'duck'?"

"Of course not. But if you peek, I'll leave word with Miss Effie that for a man of your size and promise, I saw you exhibit a shockingly tiny capability tonight."

Red Jack angrily hooked his thumb in the band of his trousers and hiked the pants protectively. "Blast you, you wouldn't!" he shouted. "Not a woman here who'd believe you."

"Mr. Bettes," Devon said slowly, intently. "I have graphic powers of description."

"Ya wouldn't—" he began, but his voice choked. Abruptly, Red Jack turned. He didn't look at her again until she said, "Ready."

He shook his head.

Black leggings hugged slim calves until they met the loosely fitting knee breeches. The white linen shirt hung loose, but not loose enough.

"Fer pity sakes, here," he said, wrenching off his snug vest.

The flaps met nearly twice around her torso, effectively covering her bosom.

"What about yer hair?" he asked impatiently.

She tried to pin it up in the dockboy's cap he had brought, but her hair was too long and thick. As she headed for the door the cap fell off and her hair tumbled out.

They could lose no more time. "Do you have a knife?" she asked.

"Aye."

"Cut it," she said, miserable.

"I don't think—"

"Cut it, or I will!"

He scratched his bare pate. "You're sure?" He approached her reluctantly, knife in hand.

"Do it," she whispered.

"Paul's balls," he swore. But with surpassing gentleness, he hacked one long strand.

"Hurry!" she cried, teeth together, eyes closed.

She felt each swatch part from her neck. With every length that fell, she grew more naked, and more resolved. She was marked. There was no turning back.

"Is it the Union or the half-breed you love?" Red Jack asked.

She kept her head bowed and didn't answer.

"Son of a lucky bitch," he whispered reverently.

The wagon rattled over knobs of coral on its way across the cleared plot in the center of the city.

Red Jack had complained the entire ride from Me Bonnie Bay. He had had to purchase outright two of Harley Dawkins's horses.

"Now whatever I say, don't talk," he instructed Devon, tapping a bamboo whip on the rump of the slow-moving mule. "And if I grab ya, shut yer trap. None o' those little girlie screams. And for God's sake, part the waters a hair, would ya? You sit with your knees together like that and they'll know you're hiding family jewels o' one set or 'nother."

He stopped the wagon in front of the Nassau jail. The octagonal building had only one entrance.

"Ho, there! Ho, there!" Red Jack jubilantly hailed the guard who stood outside the door.

"You sound drunk as hell," the guard said, walking close to the wagon. He smiled, toothless.

Red Jack climbed down. "I could be. Then I could be just tickled to be leavin' this rock. Get underway in a day or two. Have me some business inside first." He nodded at the jail.

"Who's this?" The guard indicated Devon.

She kept a sullen profile.

"Me new mess boy," Red Jack said as he thumped and jangled paraphernalia in the back of the wagon. "Ah, here 'tis!" He held up a tall black medicine bottle.

The guard walked over to him.

Red Jack smiled and took a sip from the bottle. *"Oooo.* Nothin' better'n Jamaican, eh?"

The toothless guard flicked his tongue across his bottom lip. "Where you taking those horses?" he asked, gesturing at the two horses tied to the back of the wagon.

"On board me ship, the *Sirius*! Gonna dock at Havana and add'em to my farm stock. I got a little place outside of Cárdenas I'm building up. War can't last forever and the Rebs gonna run outta money 'fore the Federals run outta navy. Gotta plan for me lean years." Red Jack burped heartily. The guard said nothing, eyeing the bottle.

"Heard you boys were sore pressed at the hotel there tonight," Red Jack went on."What was it? Thirty to one?"

The guard looked sheepish. "The governor's idea."

"An' the rest of the boys over at The Clam House drinkin' away their shame, eh?"

"Not all of us." The guard shrugged, loosening up. "Who says hurricane's a'comin'?"

"Waterspouts off the Caicos, I heard. An' something's

suckin' up the wind. Ain't been breeze enough to float a good piss since Wednesday. Storm comin', mark my word."

The guard dug one heel in the sandy soil. "What are you here for?"

"Need to see your rankin' officer," Red Jack said seriously, and took a slow pull on the medicine bottle.

The guard grew uncomfortable. "Sergeant Mead? What for?"

Red Jack turned and stared at Devon, something shifty and offensive in his eyes. She grew edgy and looked away.

"Have some 'cough surp' while we talk?" Red Jack asked confidentially, leading the guard behind the wagon.

Devon climbed quickly from the wagon while the guard wasn't looking and crept close to the building.

"Miz Devon!"

The man's whisper was only loud enough for her to hear. Victor. It was Victor's voice.

She stole around the side of the building while Red Jack continued talking with the guard.

She could hardly discern Victor pressed against the wall in the blackness.

"I come to help Marse Gentry," he whispered.

"But how did you get away? Where's Miles?" Devon asked.

Victor held up Gentry's long knife. "He tied me up when I was coming to meet you. I cut free." His voice was hoarse, pained. "I took my bag. Stole some meat. I'm not going back. Seventeen years and he hog-ties me, ready for butchering. I lie for him, fetch his poisons, stand aside while he shames my Portia. No more. He can't make me take no more!"

She could see his hand shaking in the shadow.

"Boy!" Red Jack's irritated voice was close.

Victor froze.

"It's me he calls," Devon whispered. "Wait here for us."

She pulled her cap low on her face and strode around the corner of the building. She hiked her pants at the waist, as if adjusting them after answering nature's call.

Red Jack harrumphed, hiding a laugh, she suspected. "I explained the situation," he told her. "We can go on in."

The guard, medicine bottle in hand, opened the heavy planked door for them.

The inner corridor was long and dimly lit, but there was enough light to trouble Devon. She still wore traces of lip rouge.

"We have a friend outside," she whispered.

"I don't need no help," Red Jack said, anxious. "Just remember to keep yer trap shut, no matter what I say."

The corridor ended in a small room that was the hub for several doors. In the center of the room was a desk littered with papers. Through one of the open doors, Devon heard men laughing, the scuff of chairs, the plink of coins. They were playing cards, or gaming.

Red Jack stuck his head in the door. "Ho, there!" he called.

The gaming stopped. "Red Jack, ya slippery eel!" a jovial bass voice replied. "Never thought I'd see you in here."

"I ain't been arrested, Tyler, ya turtle-head! I came to pay my respects to the sergeant." Red Jack put on a drunken leer. "Got 'im a nice surprise. Somethin' ole Poppy Lopez said to be on the lookout for."

Devon heard chair legs scratch the floor as the guards rose. Three faces appeared at the door behind Red Jack. "Here 'tis!" He gestured at her with a flourish. "The prettiest boy on the wharf. Fresh as a daisy." Red Jack gave the guards an exaggerated wink. "Ole Poppy said Sergeant Mead is partial to'em that way."

Devon looked down to hide her flaming cheeks.

There was silence among the guards for a full minute.

"You sure Poppy said Sergeant Mead was a—er, wanted . . ." The guard's deep voice trailed off with a choked sound.

"Slim lads, Tyler. Just like he likes." Red Jack grinned.

"Maybe Poppy was pullin' your leg," another of the guards said hopefully.

"No, sir. Poppy's been on the sergeant's good side for years. I'd like the same consideration," he added with drunken seriousness.

"Holy horse manure." One of the guards whistled and went back to his game. Another joined him. There was sniggering.

The third guard, Tyler, was clearly uncomfortable. "Take the boy in that room over there and wait," he said finally. "Sergeant Mead is patrolling the prisoners. I'll go get him."

Red Jack shoved Devon into the room opposite the guards. "Stay here!" he rasped.

Then he fell into step beside the stocky Tyler. "Takes all kinds o' grass to make hay, don't it," he said.

Devon watched them from the doorway. The two approached a barred door. It was unlocked. Red Jack and the guard Tyler went through and left it open. She heard their footsteps grow faint as they turned a corner in the hallway.

Apprehensive at being left alone, she sat down and pulled her cap low. She settled her knees apart and slouched in the chair, arms across her chest, terribly uncomfortable.

Across the hall, there was little noise from the two guards. The silences grew longer, like something alive and searching, and her heart began to pound.

A chair scraped.

Devon sat bolt upright. She couldn't let them catch her as an imposter before Red Jack had time to free Gentry.

She kept her face averted from the door as both guards sauntered across the hall to her room. One man was young and cocky, his thumb hooked in his suspender. The other guard had salt-and-pepper hair and a grizzled mustache.

"I ain't even had a girl as pretty as him," the younger guard joked.

His companion didn't smile.

"I'm going on back to see how the sergeant's takin' the news of his 'present,' " the young guard added, and left.

The older man stepped into the room and closed the door.

Devon would not look at him.

"Mead's a decrepit old boor, ya know."

The guard walked nearer, head bent while he straightened his shirt collar.

"Cryin' gout half the time, hollerin' for bilious powders the rest. Sure you were sent here for him?"

Devon didn't answer.

The guard tipped her jaw upward.

She jerked away. *"Cochon,"* she swore, low and fearful.

"We'll get along well. My French comes from the gutter. Just like you." His slap caught her by surprise and she barely choked her cry.

"Got no *couilles* at all?" he chided. He grabbed the waistband of her pants and pulled her upright.

She struggled, trying to reach the gun strapped to her leg,

but the guard's hand viciously encircled her throat. He shook her until she was still. "You fight like a bitch." He smiled, his eyes rheumy. "Get on your knees like one."

Suddenly he turned his head to the door.

Devon heard it too. A metallic shake, rhythmic, growing louder.

Dear God, she thought. Not Miles. Not here.

The guard frowned. Drawing his gun, he cautiously opened the door to the hallway.

Silence.

He inched forward into the doorway, then leaned out quickly in order to see.

Jangling iron cuffs landed like a hammer on the guard's wrist. The gun fired aimlessly, and Gentry swung his chained hand once more, catching the guard square on the jaw. There was a sickening crack of bone, and the guard fell to the floor, his gun clattering across the tile.

"Gentry!" Devon ran to him. In the same second, hinges on the front door creaked a warning.

Gentry instantly fell against her in a blanketing hug, diving to the floor as a musket ball stung the doorframe where she'd stood. He quickly jerked her up again, ready to run, but they heard a crash of glass.

Gentry looked back toward the front door, at the guard from outside who had fired on them.

Victor stood inside the open door, the neck and shard of the black medicine bottle in his hand, the guard sprawled on the floor at his feet.

"Quick now!" shouted Red Jack, running up the corridor from the jail cells in the back, three pistols in hand. "I got'em all locked up back there."

"The key!" Gentry said, shaking the long, heavy chain shackled to his wrists. "Who has the key?"

"The captain!" Red Jack said, rushing to the door. "He's drinkin' with his boys at The Clam House. But if you prefer to wait, I'm sure he's gonna be right here when word of the gunshots gets around."

Gentry pushed Devon ahead of him, scooping up a revolver from the floor on his way out.

Victor already had the horses untied.

Red Jack climbed into the wagon. "Best head out to the

beach and let the sea eat your tracks, then strike out west across the bush."

"The runaway towns, where are they?" Victor called as he mounted.

"Head southwest after you clear the pine barrens. Anybody can get you out, they can." Red Jack tapped the mule's rump with the bamboo pole. "Smoke them hoofs or I'll smoke yer lazy hide!" The mule lurched forward indignantly.

Gentry mounted and pulled Devon up behind him.

"Godspeed!" she called to Red Jack.

"Won't help! Devil's got me head wind." His voice shook as the wagon lumbered across the lot.

TWENTY-NINE

Victor took the lead. They raced the horses until they reached the secluded, moonlit beach. There, they held to the edge of the surf.

The air was heavy, weighted with the sound of rushing water, thick with the taste of salt.

The horses soon lagged. They were drawing stock, not fast mounts.

Devon clung to Gentry. His body was tense. With each lope of the horse the chains rang, solemn markers of slow progress.

The riders approached a sparse settlement of weathered houses and thatched huts. Inland they could see a range of low-lying hills. They urged the tired horses across the dunes. Victor scouted until he found a wagon rut that ambled around dense thickets of sea grape and saw-toothed sprays of palmetto.

Finally, they reached an abandoned field of sugarcane, and Gentry demanded speed from the stubborn horses. Tiny tree frogs trilled their night song and pithy cane stalks broke crisply under the horses' hooves.

Short trees began to appear, acacia and lignum vitae. Finally, a tall, scarred mahogany rose on the outskirts of pine woods that marked higher ground.

Devon swayed wearily with the rock of the horse. Though she could not see his face, she knew Gentry was drawn and tired. The manacles shackled his spirit as well as his hands. But they could ill afford the noise of the bullet that would break the lock. Wide iron bracelets hid the cuffs of his shirt. His silk cravat had been lost somewhere in the melee of arrest or escape. His coat sleeve was ripped, and his vest buttons were gone. The neck of his shirt gaped open, bloused and cool.

Victor, too, was dressed in good broadcloth, befitting his valet rank. But he was no longer a servant, Devon knew. The severe set of his face showed him an angry man, but he had acquired a strange calm since striking the guard at the jail. He seemed lighter somehow, riding without weight on his shoulders, as if he had shrugged off the need to lower his head and hide his size. He rode with confidence, unconsciously lifting his head to feel the freedom of the wind. The torn and desperate slave had become a fugitive, and the decision to be hunted sat well with him.

For Devon, exhaustion lay on her like a heavy blanket, bending her forward. She rested her forehead on Gentry's back, just for a moment, but she felt his cool hand cover one of hers, a warning to stay alert.

He whistled softly.

Ahead, Victor halted.

"Rest," Gentry called quietly. He turned in the saddle and steadied Devon's slide down the horse's flank.

"How far to the runaway village you spoke of?" he asked Victor.

Victor shrugged as he untied his knapsack from the saddle. "A man told me once, go to the edge of the woods until I see three palms."

"But there are palm trees everywhere!" Devon said.

Victor was quiet a moment. "This man say the loas will guide."

She frowned. " 'Loas'?"

"The gods," Gentry said harshly, jerking the chain taut between his wrists.

"And these island spirits, will they provide a key to free your hands?" she asked bleakly, her back against a tree.

"Loas don't make keys," Gentry said. "They give us misfortune so we learn to make our own."

Victor didn't smile.

"How much ammunition can we waste on this?" Gentry hefted the chain in his hands.

"All that we have is in the guns," Victor said.

"How many guns?"

"Two revolvers. And the big musket I took from the jail guard."

"Did you get his cartridge pouch? Or a powder flask?"

Victor shook his head. "I don't know much about guns, Marse Gen—"

"Just Gentry."

"Nobody teaches a slave to shoot."

"Get ready to learn. I want you to blow a hole in each of these." Gentry indicated the padlocks that locked the thick iron bracelets to his wrists.

As Gentry showed Victor how to handle cartridges and the revolver, Devon ran her hand over her breeches. The gun was still there, strapped to her thigh with black garters.

Victor's escape would probably not be discovered until morning, she thought. Miles had an important meeting scheduled with Count Beaumond after the soiree.

Over the months, Victor had probably overheard dozens of small details that might be helpful in trying to sabotage the alliance. "Victor—" she began.

Gentry shushed her suddenly. He stood motionless, listening.

Devon strained to hear.

Far in the distance, a faint bark.

"Dogs," Victor said, glancing around anxiously. "Dogs are comin'."

"It's hounds, not a platoon of grenadiers!" Gentry said. "Get out your knife, quick." He jerked his coat up and over his shoulders. "Cut it off!" Victor hacked and slit the sleeves of the coat as fast as he could until the garment fell off.

"Cut it up. All of it."

Victor slit and tore pieces from the coat.

Gentry mounted his horse and pulled Devon up behind him. Victor handed him an armful of coat scraps.

"Scatter them over hell's half acre," Gentry said. "We'll separate, east and west. Then head back to the edge of the woods. We'll meet at the three palms."

Gentry backtracked half a mile to the abandoned field, then headed east along a wagon trail. Devon tossed pieces of the ripped coat to either side.

Shifting direction, Gentry cut across the field and headed back toward the tall mahogany. He held the horse to a cautious gallop as he skirted the woods in a wide arc, pressing across a shallow valley in the limestone plateau.

In the distance he heard the excited bark of the hounds. They had found a piece of the coat, and they would zigzag their handlers until they had located each piece. In the confusion, Gentry hoped the dogs would be forced to backtrack to pick up the original scent of horses and riders.

In the bright glow of the moon, he scanned the terrain for three lone palms. He saw only the dark, lofty fronds crowning hundreds of tall trees.

Suddenly, he reined in beside grassy underbrush. Off the trail in a patch of high grass grew three young coconut palms no higher than a horse. At the apex of the triangle their fronds had been trimmed, leaving one long frilled leaf pointing like a finger at the woods.

Hooves pounded loudly behind them. Gentry pivoted the horse, gun raised.

It was Victor.

"Leave the horses," Gentry said, dismounting and helping Devon down. He quickly stripped the saddle of its supply bags and swatted the horse.

Victor sneezed as he pulled the musket from its saddle strap. "Damn!" he said, stanching his nose against his sleeve.

Gentry looked at him curiously.

"I seasoned the bait," Victor said, sniffling. He patted the heavy knapsack he had thrown across one shoulder. "Red pepper."

"What else do you have in there?" Gentry asked.

Victor shrugged off the question. "Medicine. Powders."

Gentry didn't press. He quickly ducked beneath a bower of sweet-smelling bougainvillea.

Once inside, the path was easy to find. It sloped slightly down, snake-twisting. It had been trod by many, and recently, Gentry thought. He was uneasy as he followed beaten grass and broken brush deeper into the forest.

He held the chain taut between the shackles to stop the rattle. They had bought a little time by creating a detour for the dogs, but they didn't have a good lead on the hunters. The posse must have formed immediately upon hearing reports of gunfire at the jail. Given Miles's friendliness with the governor, Gentry was sure the captain of the guard had dutifully sent word to the hotel about the escape. And Gentry was just as sure that Miles was somewhere on the hunt, riding in a gentlemanly fashion at the rear, waiting for the foxes to be flushed.

It was the red fox Miles wanted, Gentry knew. In the ballroom, when he was being dragged away by the governor's militia, he had seen the look of triumph on Miles's face. It lay in his eyes, ecstatic and warm.

Gentry paused on the path and breathed deeply, aware of the sudden race his heart ran. If Ton-weya lived, Miles could not win.

Ton-weya was the weapon. Ton-weya was Gentry's triumph.

Victory lived only as long as the young Teton Sioux, though. Gentry remembered how Ton-weya shook with the fever of malaria each summer. In a weakened village of smallpox and disease, Ton-weya would be a target for the death spirit, no matter how strong he had grown in the eleven years since Gentry had left.

The medicines Pinkney Dobbs had promised to send were crucial. If Dobbs was true to his word, they should already have been delivered to the winter village of the Sioux.

Gentry started forward again. His fear for Ton-weya lived inside him, blunt and patient, like an old friend. His fear for the woman who trod the path behind him now, silently, willingly . . . that feeling was raw and sharp.

He had tried to offer her a way to save herself when he was arrested, yet she had refused to decry him in the ballroom. She had consciously set herself apart from the arch, assembled poseurs whose breeding she shared. In trade, she had made herself a fugitive in boy's breeches, a woman whose courage burned bright as any man's.

He glanced back at her. He could not make out her face, only a pale softness under the dockboy's cap. Slipping from the edge of the cap were the hacked ends of her hair.

She had sacrificed to play her part in freeing him. She could not easily return to a comfortable room and mannered amenities.

For the moment, she was more dependent on him for survival than for love. He found that mortal responsibility the easier one to bear.

Gentry wiped beads of sweat from his upper lip. The air

was moist in the foliage, and warm, always warm. Even though the land was strange to him, he felt at home, seeing, smelling, and hearing it.

Less than a mile in, he heard the drums begin, the pounding even, moderate, drummers testing the cant of their sticks, the tension of the skins.

Without a word, Gentry slowed and let Victor pass before him. If there was a ceremony to be interrupted, Victor would make peace with the worshipers.

The tall black man stepped cautiously around knobby boulders studded with thick tongues of bromeliad. There was torchlight dead ahead.

Victor entered the clearing first.

The drums died.

All eyes were on the three strangers.

Victor faced the gathering. He kept his eyes low, reverent. "I am Victor Batu, long lost from my homeland. Lost from my loa. Am I welcome?"

No one spoke. Even the brown rooster tethered to a stake stopped flailing its wings, cocking its head with a one-eyed stare.

A white-robed man stepped forward, past tall torches that glowed above the circle of sacred symbols traced in the dirt. He was short, sinewy, with a self-possessed stride. He was unhurried, and unhappy. The talismans around his neck swung and collided as he walked, a sound of disharmony.

The priest stared at Victor, but Gentry felt the chill dismissal of the *uga*'s words.

"On this island, the lost seek the obeah man." The *uga* spoke slowly, as to an idiot.

"I have been to the obeah man," Victor said, uncowed. He reached into his knapsack. "He gave me a powder." He pulled out a tiny rabbit-skin sack on a thong and swung it forward. It landed in the circle of sacred symbols.

Around the circle, the worshipers stirred.

"He gave me a chant from the powerful book." Victor withdrew a book with a worn leather cover.

The priest's eyes widened. Victor walked forward and placed the Bible gently at the *uga*'s feet.

"But I am Ashanti, of a great tribe, too far away," Victor said softly. "My loss is too great for the obeah man to conjure."

The *uga* interlaced long, ringed fingers and regarded Victor fiercely.

"Believers have come for the visiting," the *uga* said in a deep, rolling voice, "to ask Ogoun to raise his hand against ill winds and push them far from our homes. We do not come to hide criminals."

His flock looked in unison at the white strangers, the man whose hands were chained, the woman whose pale hair had been cruelly lopped, as in punishment.

"Cannot the hunted be the wronged, the hunters the offenders?" Victor asked.

A gust blew into the clearing, rustling the thatched leaves on the hut beyond the circle. The strong scent of burning camphor mixed with the acid sweetness of cut oranges. A distant sound rode the air. The bark of a hound. The rooster flapped wildly and hopped around the stake.

"You dare bring such trouble to the vodun?" the *uga* whispered harshly.

"I am guided here, where only the loas can protect us," Victor said. "I cannot refuse. Can the *uga* say no when Ogoun chooses to speak through his body?"

The priest didn't answer.

"I, too, am given no other choice." From the bottom of his knapsack, Victor pulled a limp bundle wrapped in clean white linen. He held the bundle outstretched in his hands and moved closer to the sacred circle, closer to the *poto mita,* the offering bowl.

He knelt at the edge of the circle and slowly peeled back each corner of the linen until the spotted kid was revealed. The goat was not yet dead, but its limbs were stiff and stilled. Only its eyes moved, restless, and its racing heart, waiting the grip of the snake poison Victor had laid on its tongue.

Gentry heard Devon's sympathetic gasp. He gave her hand a warning jerk.

Victor remained kneeling beside the offering.

The *uga*'s talismans clattered nearer.

Victor rose to face him.

The *uga* did not speak. He raised his hand in summons, and a slender, teak-brown woman stepped from the covey of worshipers.

She was a *mabo,* priestess, with bracelets of brass and a

necklace of pink, polished shell. In the torchlight her turban swirled with creamy rouges, violet, scarlet, and white. Small parrot feathers of brilliant green and yellow trimmed the bottom of the headdress, banding her forehead with regal color.

Victor looked once, boldly, into her eyes. They were large and luminous.

The *uga* spoke to the priestess in a patois Victor did not understand.

The *mabo* slowly walked around Victor, her head tilted far back to scrutinize his tall frame. "We cannot refuse an Ashanti brother who believes," she said finally.

"The intruders do not believe, Marcelle," the *uga* said.

"Then this is a test, no? Ogoun's great test." Marcelle had a sonorous, honeyed voice that paced her words like a song. "We make the hunters miss this prey and Ogoun make the hurricane miss this island."

"Already the vodun are too few on this island," the *uga* said. "If we trick the white hunters, we will have to leave, or hide."

Marcelle smiled. "The vodun already hide. And we are not small. We are just the right size to honor Ogoun and call his magic to fight the mischief of the wind. Power must rest in the hands of the few, for the many will waste it, eh, Be'nard?" she said, using the *uga*'s given name.

Bernard signaled the drummers, and the deep, hollow beat began. "We do not fear," the *uga* intoned. "We honor Ogoun, and our devotion is fierce. It is the hunters who fear. They honor a loa no one can touch. They worship like slugs in the sea, sitting, grazing on small words that pass. They must beware of those who the gods move!"

Marcelle had grabbed a torch as Bernard spoke. She glanced at Gentry.

"Let's go," Gentry said to Devon.

"Without Victor?" she asked.

"He can hide in his skin here. You can't. And it's my skin that's drawing the dogs."

They followed the barefoot Marcelle into the bush, tunneling through philodendron and pepper trees to the bottom of a rocky embankment. A footpath led upward on a diagonal line, back toward the clearing.

Marcelle's nimble feet hurried up across rough rocks.

They could hear the *uga*'s voice below as they climbed higher and higher.

"This is a powerful night! Ogoun is at work!" The *uga* paced around the sacred circle of the *veves,* anointing the dark fetish shapes he had molded from the earth.

As the climb turned steeper and rockier, Gentry felt better protected from the tracking hounds. The camphor smudge pots burning in the clearing would help confuse the scent.

Finally Marcelle stopped at the mouth of a small cave. They were no more than a hundred feet above the vodun in the sunken clearing.

Marcelle was anxious to return to the ceremony. "Stay close to the front of the cave," she warned hurriedly. "Not far in is the guano."

"The what?" Devon whispered as Marcelle climbed quickly down.

"Never mind," Gentry said, ignoring the dank scent of the cave. He hid his unease by pulling at a clump of fern.

The plant's shallow roots gave way instantly, bringing up a plot of dirt. "Lie on your stomach and scoot back inside the cave," he said, scanning the gray sky for signs of dawn.

"There is plenty of room for us to sit," Devon said.

"Lie down," he commanded, and slid in, boots first, on his stomach.

Devon followed suit.

Gentry held the fern in front of them. They could easily see through the feathered fronds. Below, the chant had become singing, and the believers were swaying and jumping with the need to dance.

Gentry spotted Victor in the outer circle. He had donned a robe and an angry half-mask that left only his mouth visible. He moved as those around him moved. But Gentry knew he was not yet touched by the spirits. There was no abandon in his body, not like Marcelle, who bent and spun and reached for the sky, the fiber of her spirit on fire, kindling the believers around her.

When the fervor of the *uga*'s chant waned, the vodun drew closer to one another, crowding around the sacred circle of the *veves.* Strong voices repeated the invocations of their priest.

Gentry and Devon could not see the circle of symbols, but

they could hear the raucous squawking of the fowl as it was brought to the center of the vodun. Gentry knew the time of bloodletting was near—as were the dogs.

From his vantage point he could see the shaking of the brush. How many men followed the dogs? Frenzied invocations rose from parched throats and blended in crescendo. The fowl was silenced. The gods were summoned by twenty fervent souls.

One thundering blast of a shotgun silenced the worshipers.

Slowly they backed away from the sacred circle and focused dazedly at the intruders. A dozen men in uniforms spread themselves along the rim of the clearing. Four dogs strained their leather reins, noses sniffing, quivering.

From his post above, Gentry could see Victor in the back of the assembly. The masked slave slid a hand into the left sleeve of his robe, gripping a revolver.

From the bush behind the intruders came Miles Brant, his face hidden behind a ghostly mask of white netting.

He tucked his walking cane under his arm, removed his canvas helmet, and methodically tucked the net inside the hat brim. Then he made his way to a soldier wearing gold braid.

The eyes of the vodun were on Miles's metal brace. A drum began, a soft, slow throb.

Miles turned to the vodun, looking at each one. "Not a redskin among them, Captain," he said finally. "But I know he's here. He's Cherokee. Partial to the woods."

"The dogs seem stymied, Colonel Brant," the captain of the guard said firmly.

"Understandable, after all that cayenne. Their tracking ability's about as solid as pudding right now."

"I'll have the men search the immediate area, and then we should go, sir," the captain said.

"We cannot just leave," Miles demanded.

The captain drew himself up with a deep breath. "Sir, I am quite tired. My men are tired. We will pick up their trail later in the morning and be much more effective with a bigger squad."

"But Captain, I'm sure they're hiding something," Miles said, his steel-tipped cane pointing at the quiet vodun.

Marcelle tilted her head and began to hum, a soft, nervous

singsong that carried high, all the way to the cave, a song to guard against the anger of a man whose leg was in a cage and whose eyes burned cruel as a *gangan*'s cat.

Miles stared at her.

Marcelle's song grew breathless, then silent.

"You have grossly impudent coloreds here," Miles told the captain.

"They're not mine. Or yours. Slavery was abolished in '33."

"It's a mistake, you know, to let them pray together. Then they can plot together." Miles's gaze rested on the brown woman who was not afraid of him, then he turned back to the captain. "Run the dogs around this whole area."

The vodun remained silent as the dogs scouted the clearing, nose to ground. One dog dashed through the brush and discovered the footpath toward the high rocks.

Gentry and Devon watched from above, still as stone.

Then, as naturally as a breeze rising, Marcelle began a song.

The dog barked frantically as it picked up the scent on the steep trail beside the rocks. Devon laid her forehead on her hands. Gentry felt her hopelessness as keenly as if it were his own.

But others of the vodun had taken up Marcelle's gentle song and made it stronger, even as the dog impatiently pawed the hillside trail, hauling the laggard human on the other end of the chain.

With each second the sky lightened with the coming of dawn. Gentry let his breath flow in cadence to the chant of the people below, allowed his spirit freedom to feel the ancient power of those who sang one song.

The dog neared the flat boulder at the mouth of the cave, so close Gentry could hear its excited pant.

It was then that the bats returned.

Their undulating black column appeared in the sky at the crest of the hill. Though tight-knit in flight, they slapped with discord at the air, thousands of diaphanous wings beating.

Devon heard them and turned a frightened face to Gentry. He instantly clamped his hand over her mouth, apology lingering in his eyes for he could not warn her, he could only shield her under him and muffle the terror in her throat.

Her scream began when the first of the winged rodents soared unerringly into the cave, swerving upward to bypass her body.

Her shrill cry fought Gentry's hand for release, but he pressed harder and gathered her closer. The homecoming had only begun. Hundreds more followed the leader's precise line, casting their flight upward over the warm human hurdles. They passed as one, claws poised in a delicate curl, shriveled faces intent on ending the call of the night, their feeding done.

Devon struggled and kicked, but Gentry could not allow her to escape the cave. He lowered his head, protecting hers against the wafting of wings and the scent of their musk, and he waited, heart racing, for the assault to die.

Countless creatures streamed past, thick and black, choking the air.

Devon fell limp beneath him.

Outside, the hound dog shied instinctively at the ferocity of the bats' looping descent. Farther down the hill, the dog's master pulled an insistent retreat on the chain. The dog whined useless pleas as he was jerked back down the trail.

In the cave, time seemed to stop. Gentry did not hear the hunting party leave, even though the flapping about his head had ceased. Restless scratching and rustling echoed from the depths of the cave, the sounds of a colony roosting, becalmed.

In his arms Devon rested, still in faint. With difficulty he groped and pulled himself upright to sit against the wall in the cramped space. He gathered her to him, grateful that she slept, no matter how cruelly.

He brushed small pebbles from her hair and held her tenderly. His chest swelled tight, and he had to gasp to relieve the pressure.

Once before he held a beloved limp in his arms.

He lowered his head until he felt movement in the hand he held so tightly.

THIRTY

The small donkey cart plodded for miles across palmetto flats, past gumbo-limbo and a wild grove of mango. Devon jostled comfortably on a pallet of palm leaves. Cluttered around her in the bed of the cart were the possessions of the vodun priestess—torch poles, teak masks, wood bowls, fetish bottles, and one sheathed knife with a shiny brass hilt.

The sun was directly overhead. They had been traveling since dawn southeast toward the sea. There, Marcelle had said, they would find camps made by runaway slaves, now abandoned and used by sojourners, the needy, and the criminal.

Marcelle walked on one side of the donkey, Victor on the other. They maintained a cautious silence. Gentry held rear guard. Devon noticed how often he massaged his left wrist, encircling it with thumb and forefinger to break the phantom weight of the chains.

He had broken the shackles hurriedly, before the vodun drums left the worship ground. With a stick he had dug a space in the sandy soil for the padlock. He'd fitted the nose of his revolver against the keyhole and waited while Victor mounded dirt over the lock and the length of gun barrel.

The drummers began pounding, strong and even strokes.

Gentry fired with the sticks on the downbeat. The recoil kicked the nose of the gun upward, heaving the dirt. The bullet rammed cleanly through the lock. He quickly repeated the silencing technique with the right cuff.

"I will take them," Marcelle said as he removed the shackles, and she placed the broken chains in the cart with her talismans and vestments.

The rattling iron was indistinguishable from the worka-day creaks of the cart's many loose parts, and Devon wel-comed the noise. It drowned the wallop of leather wings, a sound too vivid to leave her memory. She sat numb, huddled against the side rail.

Marcelle stopped the donkey in the shade of a ficus tree. Root filaments dangled like blackened rope, twisted and thick, and Devon swept them aside to get out of the cart.

"We can rest here," Marcelle said. She rummaged in the cart and withdrew a wooden cask.

Victor dodged the hanging roots and followed Marcelle deeper into shaded foliage.

"Where are they going?" Devon asked.

"To find food, water," Gentry said. "Perhaps a place to lie down."

"They have just met."

"Victor has just escaped a great demon. It is reason enough to celebrate." Gentry leaned against the trunk of the tree. The sun dappled his hair and shoulder.

"And us? Have we escaped?" Devon asked. She stood in front of him.

Gentry was quiet, sad. He reached out and pulled the cap from her head.

Her cropped, tousled hair fell to just below her ears.

He slid two fingers along a strand of her hair, the short, ragged distance from temple to jaw.

Her eyes searched his, questioning.

His fingers gently grasped her hair. "If beauty were arti-cles of dress, I would have only to close my eyes and you would be gone. But you are behind my eyes. So bright that sometimes I cannot see where I go."

His hand rested at her nape, and he pulled her forward. "And that's not good. Not good," he whispered.

She laid her head against his chest, as exhausted as he, feeling the warmth of his skin against her cheek.

He sank to the ground with his arms around her, settling in a trough of gnarled roots. He pulled the revolver from his waistband. "We rest," he said.

For the first time since they had begun the voyage, he held her as a lover, with their bodies stretched long to extend the solace of touching. His arm was her pillow, but she did not relax. His other hand lay atop his chest, pistol snug and ready.

Victor brought back fresh water. Marcelle had folded up the hem of her skirt to gather fruit—tiny finger bananas, sweet, juicy mangoes, and soft litchi nuts inside hard, crusty hulls. They talked as they ate.

"Why aren't the men in white interrupting our fine lunch?" Gentry asked Marcelle. "They should be right on our tail."

Marcelle smiled. "Why should policemen be out in this terrible heat? You ruined their dogs. You kept them out all night. Let them rest." She peeled and sliced a mango in a blackened teak bowl. "This is a small island. No one escapes without a boat. The first thing they do is alert the harbors and look for informers. The last thing they do is ride out like highway bandits in the dead of night. The limping man has much power to force such uncivilized behavior, eh? Do not worry. They will find you when they want to."

"An enemy ship will stop at a place called Hyde Cay. Is that far?" Gentry asked.

She shrugged. "Not far. Not far from the hut where I take you. You have a boat?"

"No. Won't a ship anchor close to shore? Worried about the storm?"

"Half this island believes the hurricane comes, the other half believes no. But we ask Ogoun to spare us, no matter which half are fools."

"What good will it do to attack one ship?" Devon asked Gentry.

"The commotion may draw the attention of a Federal ship."

"You can't sink a ship without mortars or cannons."

"I could sink it with fire."

"And you don't want even a little boat?" Marcelle teased. "Will you walk on the water with torches in your hand?"

Gentry shook his head and smiled. "What I need are weapons, not rowboats."

"Look in the old fort. There are very old things there, my people say. Too old even for the governor's men."

Devon rose and helped Marcelle hide the refuse of the meal under moist leaves in a thicket of jasmine.

"Why do you help us, Marcelle?" she asked.

"It is the job of a priestess to guide the faithful. Especially I want to guide that man." Her neck cricked once in Victor's direction.

"Victor is good," Devon agreed.

"Victor has power, here!" Marcelle tapped her fist lightly against her heart. "And here!" She tapped her head. "He knows reading, and powders and plants. He can teach me much. And I will teach him. But first I must help him with this thing of the ship. And then he can hide until the war passes. He will be free of the bounty hunters then."

"But what of his family in America?"

Marcelle shrugged. "He has only women there, no wife."

"What about his daughter?"

"He say his daughter die on the way to freedom land."

"How does he know she's dead?" Devon asked harshly.

"He say the dogs hunt her."

"Maybe she fooled the dogs like we did! Maybe she found people to help her hide like we did! Maybe she's safe across the border now!" Her voice had gone strident.

"Miz Devon?" Victor said from behind her.

She turned.

In his face, an ageless certainty spoke to her, an intuition born in persecution and fed by its indignity each day.

"Couldn't she wait?" Devon whispered. "We work to free her."

"She free, Miz Devon. She free herself."

Devon felt a hollow well open inside her from which she could draw no tears, only a sad and angry burning in eyes that remembered the face of a young and beautiful girl, a being whose mind held such promise, whose heart held no hope. Miles had enslaved even that.

By dusk the tired troupe walked a path between tall clumps of sea oats and crepe myrtle and came to a thatched hut. As the sun set red fire to the horizon, Marcelle drew maps in the sand, tutoring Gentry in the scape of her land, in the subtle landmarks of the bush, so that he would know how to find the old fort beyond the tall trees to the north; how much white sand lay between him and Hyde Cay, a spit of land two miles to the south.

Marcelle shared their meager supplies, and Devon placed the fruit atop a dilapidated trunk in one corner of the hut. As Marcelle and Victor prepared to leave, Gentry took Marcelle aside, walking her to the water's edge to speak privately. When they returned, Marcelle gave Devon a strangely sympathetic glance.

As Marcelle's donkey cart crackled brush on its way across the dune, Devon and Gentry walked toward the hut. The shelter had a slatted floor and three sturdy, plankwood walls. The fourth side was open, facing the beach. A wide thatched overhang extended the roof on all sides. The air inside was cool with the smell of reed mats and dried palm.

Devon turned to Gentry. "What did you say to her?" she asked.

"I told her to spread gossip like wildfire in Nassau. To rumor that the Confederates have a privateer navy ready to break the blockade. That the Yankees are in trouble because Britain and France have bought many guns for the ships."

"Lord, what a diplomatic hornet's nest that will raise."

"Exactly."

"Honesty is a powerful weapon."

"But it shows how poor we are in firepower." He smiled. "A man hurls truth in last resort."

"What else did you tell Marcelle?"

He looked away. "I told her you would be returning to Nassau tomorrow, that you will need someone to take you there."

"Then you lied! I'm not leaving. My work is not finished. Neither is yours."

"There is nothing for you here," he said quietly.

Nothing? Fear swelled a sickening wave in her stomach. "Gentry . . ." she whispered.

His fingertips pressed against her lips with a gentleness that stopped her words and her breath. "Let me speak tonight," he said. "Then you will understand."

He bent to her and she rose on tiptoe, desperate to kiss him, to stop the feeling of finality that chilled her. She kissed as if she were afraid not to, with small cries that choked her questions.

She felt Gentry's lips on her cheek, her neck, her throat. He affirmed her body with outspread hands that encompassed her back, sliding low to the dip above her buttocks, then plunging beneath the waistband of the trousers to grasp firm bare cheeks and pull her tight against him. But the revolver at his waist lay between them. He loosed her reluctantly and shed the gun and his shirt.

The sun was sinking. The rays sent a half-light of hazy color across Gentry's face and chest, darkening him, warming him. Devon moved near.

He tugged impatiently at her shirt, raising it over her head.

Her breasts emerged softly, shy sentinels of intimacy, creamy and free, shifting subtly with each move against him. He pressed his hand to one and captured the warmth in his palm, her nipple in the crease of two fingers, the tip alert and erect, tender as baby skin. The bud tilted to his touch with delicate tenacity, strangely moist.

He bent and licked the pale areola, drawing it into his mouth and tasting. He sucked gently, evenly, not stopping when she gasped, not stopping when she tried to push his head away.

His hands slid her pants low, past the soft hair of her mound, and his fingers grazed hidden lips, seeking the fullness of their curve, then testing the ease of their parting, gliding gently to open the island to his touch. He pressed the swell of wanting. He heard her sensual sigh. He deepened the yield of her path, passing moist ridges, seeking the place of beginning.

She shook her head and pushed away to sit on the pallet and undress.

He was quicker at disrobing, less self-conscious than she, and he knelt nude before her and yanked impatiently at the boy's stockings and loose knickers.

He cradled her head as they fell back on the pallet. He entered her without warning and she cried his name, She embraced him tightly, with the desperation of the lost, her naked need a warm and glistening bond.

Raw desire allowed him no peace to lie atop her, no time to revel in the fluid mold of her body. He thrust hard, blindly and primitively, aware that no thought held sway now, no amount of reason could mark the triumph of escape and the chasm that awaited them.

Devon arched to him, caught in a dark torrent of feeling, her thoughts an unformed stream that obeyed the incessant push and pull, the parting in order to join. She rose to a faraway peak. Her body shuddered, breathless with the long journey back.

They remained still in the silence for a long time, shaken by the brutal need they had fed, mourning its brevity, unable to ignore the thorough fatigue that followed.

Devon slept close to him, entwining limbs and curves with innocent abandon like a kitten in a box, fearful of separateness.

She awòke suddenly, with a strange feeling tingling her senses. The wind. The wind was rising. She could hear the rush and bristling of thousands of fronds.

Quietly she left the pallet and walked to the edge of the thatched overhang so she could see the night sky. Black and starry, the roof on the world seemed benign. The wind was present, but not cruel or threatening. The cool air found her nakedness and skimmed the undercurve of her breasts, the pad of her belly, chilled the moist semen that lay inside her thigh.

How quickly he had taught her not to be ashamed of her body, nor of his, and how slowly and painstakingly her heart would die if this was their last time together.

Clouds the color of uncleaned cotton shifted in pods across the darkening sky. Dear God, where could they run?

Devon felt drawn to the water. Starlight bounced on its dark, dimpled surface. Her feet met the velvet tickle of the surf. She kicked the froth. Each slap and sparkle of the water made her feel kin to the sea's secrets, for she, too, could be home to life. If their lovemaking begat a child, to whom could she turn?

She walked farther into the cool surf, the sand under her feet shifting, as if she were walking on water. She could not leave footprints; they were immediately whirled away.

A strange light-headedness made her stop. Only two months ago, she had been a sheltered Londoner of strait-laced family, her hours spent with her sketchbook or on outings with family. Now she was sheltered by nothing from her past, except one demanding ideal of social justice.

Devon crouched low, the sea at her waist, its waves buffeting and prodding her, the salty current washing her.

She did not hear Gentry approach, but she felt the warmth as he shielded her from the wind.

He knelt in the shallow surf behind her, placing his hands

on her shoulders and pulling her back to sit against him. She did not realize how chill she was until her shoulders rested against his warm chest. His arms enclosed her. She sat facing the sea, feeling him without seeing him. The water washed and receded in endless motion around them.

"The sea always searches," he said, speaking as if to himself. "Groping the shore to find what it lost."

"It loses only what nature discards," she said. "Empty shells, grains of sand, dying weed."

"Sometimes wonderful things are lost."

She was quiet a moment. "How long must you search, Gentry?"

The question was too forward. She felt his arms tense around her.

"When a man has important things to say, a woman must let him dance around truth before he partners it."

"Actually, you tell stories better than you dance," she said.

He relaxed. Perhaps he smiled. "Then I offer a story. It begins with a boy. He was called Red Wolf Running."

And Gentry spoke softly into the night breeze, telling her of his mother and the promise he had made to her on her deathbed.

"The boy went to his father's house, a place with many rooms and fine food, many books and many workers. The boy held his anger in silence, and his secret madness grew black like the earth floor on which his mother had lain to die.

"The white father gave the boy many things, many horses to ride, many tutors to hear, many manners to learn. All this is yours, his father said proudly. But always between them was the white father's failure to honor his pledge to Calla Summer Sky. If he had married her, she would have journeyed with him and known many of the white man's pleasures, for she loved these things, the books and cleanliness and prettiness of life in a wood house.

"And the boy would have had stature in two worlds. Instead, he had to leave the uncles who'd taught him the ways of the Ani Yunwiya, and he had to be outcast among his father's people and bear the jealousy of a girl child adopted into his father's house.

"Regina took care of Teague Morgan's house. Regina

wanted his house. She did not want the boy to find peace there. She taunted him, kept him angry, told him his father was shamed by him. The boy, caused much trouble and embarrassment for his father in the town.

"It was Regina who taught the boy to dance in white man's clothes, Regina who made Red Wolf stumble. Red Wolf left his father's house and pledged never to return.

"The Sioux rode free in the north, a proud people, a fighting people. The boy wanted to be with them. He rode many raids on the Chippewa and stole many ponies. And after one season's buffalo hunt, he had enough wealth to make a lodge and claim a wife. She was young and beautiful, a strong and virtuous woman. And she wanted Red Wolf to visit his father."

The steadiness of Gentry's voice broke. He closed his arms more tightly around Devon.

"Kai-ee-nah was killed," he said finally, "and her womb torn to free the boy child nōt ready to be born. And Red Wolf left his father's land with greater anger and shame and great need for revenge.

"But he left with a secret. Kai-ee-nah's womb carried his second child. His son, Ton-weya, was safe with other babes in the lodge of his wife's sister."

A son, Devon thought. Gentry had an heir. Regina and Miles would never inherit the land they coveted.

"Red Wolf fed his madness many years, seeking white men who were there the day his soul died, killing men who fought his accusation, never satisfied. He joined a war of the whites on the side his father hated so that he could kill more. But the killing never filled him.

"Then one day he stopped in his homeland, at the river Hiwassee, and he was captured in the land of the ancient ones. They took pity on Red Wolf's anger and his not-knowing. They sent him to prison where there was a guard, a range rider from his father's land. This man knew that Miles Brant told lies about the day Kai-ee-nah's blood ran into the earth.

"But the spirits were also wicked. They begat a woman who troubled Red Wolf's plans. This woman touched his heart and turned his mind like no other. And in her presence, the smiling eyes of his wife, Kai-ee-nah, grew dim in his memory, and he was frightened. So frightened, for this woman made him live in the now, feel in the now. And he saw that his now had no future."

Gentry's voice, so close to her ear, faded as if he had lost strength. Only the ocean spoke then, its slap and slather unintelligible, unsoothing.

"Is there no more?" she whispered.

He did not answer. He picked her up out of the water and held her against him.

She clasped her arms around his neck and laid her cheek to his shoulder. He placed her gently on the sand beyond the water's reach.

"The story is sad, without an end," she said.

"There is always an end, Daloni-ka." His fingers caressed the curve of her cheek, as if tracing it to memory.

"This woman shared much with Red Wolf, her courage, her virtue, her hunger for freedom. And Red Wolf saw that his fight had been a small one, a selfish one, and he felt shame for the years he had wasted, the men who had died. And he knew that his penance would be great."

"No," she whispered. She shook her head. "No. We can run away, find a boat—"

He pressed his fingers to her lips. "Red Wolf was destined to fight alone, to keep his pledge to the white lawman. And his beloved must be returned to her world."

"It is not my world! It's not my choice!" Devon cried.

"His beloved must survive—"

"I would rather die with you!" Holding Gentry's face in her hands, she searched his eyes. "You know that!"

"*Sge,*" he soothed. "Listen. The story is not ended. Red Wolf had a great request of this woman. He asked her to travel far and see his son. Make sure he is well. Tell Tonweya of Red Wolf's fight. And the greatest request of all, to take Ton-weya to meet his grandfather.

"For this woman was the only one who knew that Red Wolf made peace with what had passed, that he wanted Tonweya to know his white grandfather."

Gentry paused.

"And this woman, did she agree?" Devon whispered.

"Red Wolf never knew," he said softly, "for his beloved grew silent and saddened to leave him. And he had to touch her to let her know that he would always be with her, for he had been her first, and he had not meant to love her, and he had fought the fire in his heart as long as he could, but he had been so long without a wife, without so virtuous a woman. And so he told her that if she wished, she could tell Ton-weya that she had been wife to his father, a wife honored and worthy, who must share Red Wolf's property in the village of the Sioux and on the estate of Summer Sky."

Gently, his arms enclosed her.

"For if Red Wolf lived after his battles, and he was not maimed or imprisoned, he would want to live with this woman in his world, he would want to feel her heart next to his each night, for it would make his world complete."

THIRTY-ONE

The wind died away by sunrise, and an uneasy quiet woke Gentry and Devon.

His hands swept over her like wordless whispers, clearing away the solemnness of the night, giving her solace with light and knowing touches.

She pulled away from him and dressed, then began to ready the fruit Marcelle had left. They ate on the open deck of the hut, watching a lone brown pelican dive for his breakfast on the ebb tide.

Victor arrived to help Gentry hunt for weapons. They would scavenge the ruins of a fort long abandoned by English colonizers.

With Victor was a boy and a donkey.

Gentry walked Devon to the hut. "Marcelle sent these," he said, handing her a brightly colored shift, skirt, and scarf.

She laid them on the reed mat where she had slept so fitfully, keeping her distance from Gentry. Sadness, as deep as an abyss, encircled him.

"How do you know you'll be killed?" she asked.

"I don't know for certain."

"It's me you're unsure of, isn't it? You think I'm an ingenue seeking a fine lark, and I can run back to a safe little parlor and live in prosperous, predictable comfort the rest of my miserable days!"

"Those are your fears, not my thoughts."

"Then tell me what you think," she pleaded.

"I think it's foolish for one soldier to attack a big ship, but a soldier is trained to fight against the odds. I think it's foolish for a marked man to ask a well-bred woman to wife, but a marked man must also fight great odds."

"Who asks her to wife?" Her voice was strained. "Gentry or Red Wolf Running?"

He smiled faintly. "That's why my request is so unfair. You would be woman to both of them, and I husband to one. Only one," he whispered.

She turned her back, her head bowed. "You must go," she said with difficulty.

"But you leave with me."

"And I with you," she whispered as the floorboards groaned with the weight of his footsteps. Then silence.

Devon stood by herself. She donned the berry-red skirt and blouse Marcelle had sent. She felt a chill. The wind again, so fitful, unsure whether to be calm or stormy.

Gentry had told her she must leave the island immediately, seek help from Harley Dawkins at Me Bonnie Bay and book passage on the next ship out.

She had nodded agreement, avoiding his eyes, because she did not want him to see that she had no intention of obeying him. There was one small way she could help him in his mission. By returning to Nassau and the alliance lair, she could plant false information to keep the alliance off Gentry's trail and unaware of the trouble planned for the ship anchored at Hyde Cay.

Of all the obstacles she would have to face, she prayed God omit only one: Miles. She loaded the revolver and hurried across the dune to the boy who would guide her to Nassau.

She walked in silence, careful to feel only the things outside herself—the sting of the sun's heat on her cheeks, the swish of the donkey's tail when she ventured too close, the sudden buffeting of wind that molded her skirt to her legs.

They stopped in the shade when the sun was high. The boy offered her papaw and akee. The fleshy fruits were filling, and Devon devoured them.

By sundown they were on Blake Road nearing Nassau, and they weren't alone. Rickety wagons and three-wheeled carts rumbled along the dirt road. Coconuts rattled in the bins of huge wheelbarrows. The air was filled with the scents of nutmeg, ginger, and spices, the grassy aroma of woven

straw baskets and hats, the sugary ferment of bruised bananas and cane.

Black islanders drove the wagons. Women and children
walked behind the donkey carts, prodding the beasts with
palm stems.

The boy told Devon the next day was market day. Not
even talk of a hurricane could threaten market day. It was
the time of news and gossip.

The melodious chitchat of the islanders faded when
Devon joined the caravan. She walked beside a wagon
loaded with large round breadfruit. She did not explain her
strange, sunburned presence and the islanders did not ask.
The breadfruit driver offered her a seat on the highboard of
his wagon, and she accepted gratefully.

It was long past dark when he let her off at the gardens of
the Royal Victoria Hotel. Exhausted, abashed about her appearance, she had no wish to encounter one of the debonair
alliance principals while dressed as a subordinate.

With the help of the driver and an amused scullery maid,
she sneaked through the kitchen and servants' quarters, by-
passing the grand lobby. A servants' stairwell led to the
second floor, a heavily trafficked hall of smoking rooms and
game salons.

There Devon brushed the road dust from her skirt, tugged
the shift higher on her bosom, and smoothed her tousled
hair. Having done her best, she crossed the hall to the main
staircase. She passed three astonished Dutchmen in the hall
and barely escaped a pinch from a tipsy English soldier on
the stairs. Good Lord, she thought. What a tawdry sight she
must be to rouse the oats of a knock-toothed, flush-faced
tommy.

As she approached her room, she remembered she had no
key. She prayed Abby would be there.

When she tried the knob, the door was unlocked. She
entered the darkened room. "Abby?" she called softly.

The door shut behind her.

She turned in an instant and reached for the knob, but a
warm hand firmly grasped hers.

"The servant girl is not here, ma'am."

The man's voice was young and respectful, with a foreign
accent. He did not release her hand.

He spoke quickly to someone else in the room in a language she did not recognize.

The lamp near the table began to glow, brightening the dark, clean-shaven face of Khaled al-Sayed Dexter, standing on the far side of the room.

He shook his head and smiled at her. "A blond English-woman riding to straw market with the hawkers? Amazing how word travels on the street here. The servants' quarters are better than a telegraph office." He nodded to his servant. "Thank you, Ahmed. You may leave us now."

The man released Devon and left. He locked the door from the outside.

She faced Khaled. "Would you care to explain this intrusion?" she asked.

"No. Would you care to explain your whereabouts the past two days?"

She was silent.

"There, then, we eliminate unnecessary exposition, no?" He smiled.

"I am quite fatigued," Devon said.

"Of course you are. I, too, have spent sleepless nights since arriving here. Things have not gone smoothly. It is not my fault, you understand. I did not vote for nor against granting Colonel Brant a monkey fist and authority in our group. I did not vote for nor against the arrest of the enterprising Mr. Morgan. I merely stood in the background, facilitating the discussions."

"You cannot be 'mere,' Mr. Dexter. You have coordinated the chaos, dispersed hundreds of thousands in British sterling, and hidden an entire private navy in a house of paper—if my uncle's assessment of you is accurate."

"Thank you, m'emoiselle. It is good to be appreciated, even by a spy."

"Spy? You return compliment with accusation, Mr. Dexter. Is that palace etiquette in Cairo?"

"No, my dear. It's fatigue and degenerating circumstance taking its toll on my manners. Come sit down." Khaled indicated an armchair near the bedside.

She sat on the edge of the chair, aware of her bare, sunburned shoulders. She clasped dusty hands in her lap.

Khaled perched one hip on the windowsill, his leg swinging free.

"Did you know a pretty boy helped Morgan escape?"

The question was comment and she did not answer.

"Young people are so adventurous. Marvelously inventive. I admire that. Truly." He paused. "Did you know a smuggler named Red Jack was captured this morning?"

Devon was silent.

"In light of your indelicate position, I would like to get straight to the point. Where is Gentry Morgan?"

"I don't know," she said.

Khaled sighed as if greatly burdened. "You were Morgan's 'dupe,' I believe Colonel Brant termed it. So you know what Morgan plans for us."

"Colonel Brant is a habitual, though selective liar."

"Colonel Brant is protecting you and the reputation you have shredded to nothing."

Devon fixed a fierce gaze on Khaled. "I want no favors from a murderous thief. You do not know him, Mr. Dexter, else you wouldn't count his lecherous nature and petty deceits as assets to your cause."

"Colonel Brant runs a shipping and distribution network central to the success of an expensive military venture," Khaled said. "I need not admire a man to accept his talent. This is business, m'emoiselle. Serious business. And I advise you to search your memory for clues as to Mr. Morgan's whereabouts."

Devon was quiet a long moment, then she shook her head. "He is gone," she said softly.

"Left the island?" Khaled asked. "From which harbor?"

"You think me stupid? Should I add sight to a murderer's gun?"

"I protest, m'emoiselle!" Khaled took out a lace-edged handkerchief and blotted the perspiration above his lip. "I am no murderer."

"You have been made to look like a blind lackey to one. I would take care, before your reputation takes on tatters like mine."

Khaled smiled, but nervously. He was immaculately dressed for evening, a daring red cravat around his neck, two tiers of gold chain draped across his black vest to the watch tucked in his pocket.

"Warm tonight, but there is a nice breeze, thank Allah," he said stiffly.

"There has been no lack of hot air here since the arrival of Count Beaumond and Lord Grayshire."

Khaled laughed unexpectedly. He looked quite young at that moment.

"Are you fishing, m'emoiselle?" he asked. "Searching for signs of ill feeling toward my overbearing colleagues? A clue to my weariness in working for pompous peaçocks? Oh, you will find no complaints, m'emoiselle. I am used to the challenge."

"Are you a diplomat, Mr. Dexter?"

"I am but a poor and trusted servant of the Pasha, born in Alexandria, raised in London, educated in Paris."

"Your worth in this venture must be priceless."

"What is priceless is the future of my country. Our export of cotton has quadrupled since the Civil War cut off American supplies. The price has quadrupled also," Khaled said with pride.

"Then Egypt would not mind if the Civil War lingered long and bloody."

"Neither would a country like France," he added pointedly.

"What does France gain from helping the Confederates?"

"Diversion. Napoleon the Third wants Lincoln's long nose to the grindstone of civil strife so he won't worry about the buildup of the Mexican Army along the Rio Grande. The longer the South fights, the better chance Napoleon's puppet Maximilian can retake land in Texas."

"And what of England?" Devon asked. "I know the textile barons wish to support a good cheap source of cotton, but why have Lord Grayshire and the landed gentry gambled so much on this alliance assault?"

"They are men of stubborn vision. To save the South is to demonstrate once and for all that democracy is intolerably flawed."

"They must also yearn for something more definite. A sympathetic Confederacy as the shipping hub of colonial business in the Caribbean, perhaps? Come now, Mr. Dexter, surely there is a more immediate, concrete goal."

"I think you are asking, Where will the alliance fleet strike?" Khaled said softly. He smiled at her.

Devon looked away.

"That is the major bit of information you lack, isn't it? That means your friend Mr. Morgan lacks it too."

She abruptly left the chair.

"Do not chide yourself, Miss Picard. You were not clumsy. You simply had to take the chance, eh?"

Slowly she smoothed the peasant skirt, trying to control her apprehension, sensing finality in the interview.

"Ah, m'emoiselle." Khaled sighed deeply and rubbed his temple with one finger. "I wish you were still on our side."

"There are many sides to this affair," she said.

"Yours is about to be silenced. You will be shipped back to Wilmington under guard tomorrow morning," he said briskly. "The United States consul is looking for you."

That night, Gentry and Victor worked silently in the light of a fire outside the hut.

Around them were the supplies Marcelle had gathered for them: a lantern with oil, a few phosphorous matches, a coil of hemp rope, a small flask of gunpowder, a bullet mold.

They had found few items of use at the old fort that morning. A small cylinder of lead and three rusty grenades.

Gentry had to resign himself to a short-range assault with the ball grenades. If the ship was anchored far out, that meant commandeering a boat and little chance of survival.

He examined the grenades. They were orange with rust, but not corroded. The fuses were rotted. He replaced them with new hemp, then checked the charge holes to make sure they were clear.

The small flask of gunpowder was enough to charge three grenades, with a scant supply left over for the flintlock musket Victor had taken from the jail guard.

Earlier, Gentry had sent Victor hunting in a swampy lowland. The Ashanti had nabbed a young, long-necked turtle. Now the turtle meat was roasting on a stick across the fire. The skin from the turtle's neck, cut in a thin spiral, was drying, twisted, on the sand nearby. It would be the string for a short-bow.

After the turtle meat had cooked, Gentry began to smelt the cylinder of lead atop the embers in the fire. Then he and Victor sat back to eat their fill of the tender meat.

Making the bow was more an exercise in comfort than strategy, Gentry knew. He had scraped and bowed a sapling, but the wood would be too green to be trusted. And he had no chipping tools and no time to make arrowheads. The bow would show a wavering velocity and very little accuracy.

Still, he had spent the afternoon scouting the bush for the straightest tree shoots he could find.

Victor had waded barefoot across a sandbar, his toes seeking out mussels and shellfish, while Gentry rigged a deadfall trap with a big flat rock near the ocean's edge. He baited it with the opened shellfish.

Soon, two white egrets landed warily, bending their heads low as they approached the trap. One slipped its beak quickly under the rock and pecked the open mussel. At the same time, the bird dislodged the sliver of wood holding the rock above its head.

The arrows would have fine white feathers.

Gentry sucked the last juicy meat from the knobby bones of the turtle and tossed the remains into the shallows. Then he picked up his knife and began peeling the tree shoots he had gathered.

"Tell me what to do," Victor said, stoking the embers with the tip of the roasting stick.

"Watch the lead. We'll make bullets when it melts. And tear these clothes to strips. I'll weight the arrows." He tossed Victor the boy's shirt and knickers Devon had worn.

After plucking medium-long feathers from the dead egret, Gentry split each feather lengthwise and scraped the pith away. He examined each shoot, setting six aside, then began unwinding a length of hemp rope to make a thin string to bind the feathers to the arrow shafts.

"Why do you make only six?" Victor asked.

He shrugged. "This is a weapon of hope, not skill. It's unreliable. And I have too much to carry as it is."

"But I will help you carry," Victor said.

Gentry shook his head. "I'm going alone."

"I am reliable."

"I know. And you've already saved my skin twice."

"Skin isn't a problem between us. I am worthy to go with you."

Gentry was silent as he whittled a sharp point on the first arrow. "But you are free now."

"Until Miles Brant sends the bounty hunter, yes, I am free. Free to choose my way, and my battles."

"Marcelle will call terrible demons on me if you're killed."

"She knows you have too many demons already." Victor smiled. "She will not waste more on a tormented man."

"Brave man, taking up with a woman who knows too much," Gentry said. His knife blade shaved with clean and rhythmic strokes. With each *thwick,* a chip fell to the sand.

"Portia was too young a woman to know so much," Victor said quietly. "Marse Miles taught her."

Thwick.

"Finally, Portia didn't want to know any more."

Thwick.

"I didn't kill him. All those years I didn't kill him. Portia'd say, 'No, Daddy. If you do, you die. And I'll be alone. I don't want to be alone with him.' "

Thwick.

"Portia's momma died a lotta years back. She's the only woman I chose. The others Marse chose for me. Her name was Ruth. She was my good friend, my good woman. And her Portia was the only child I brought up to the big house."

Thwick.

"I should've left her in the field, though." Victor spoke low, as if to himself. "But she kept saying, 'Teach me, Daddy.' I taught her to read. Taught her to speak white in the daytime, sing Ashanti at night. Then Marse Miles gave her books. And he started teaching her things."

Gentry stopped.

Victor hesitated. "Marcelle says it's hard to kill such an evil man. His blood'll stay on your hand and burn like fire. You never stop burning."

Gentry bundled the arrows together, then began to work on the turtle skin. He scraped and tugged and twisted, making hide twine for the bowstring.

"What happened to his leg?" he asked.

Victor shrugged. "Marse Miles didn't like field command. Didn't like tenting with the troops. Can't make any money that way, he'd say. Government kept taking his slaves, taking his cotton. He'd say, 'I need a situation, Victor.' Soon as he got sent to Charleston in '63, he got one.

"The Federals started shelling Morris Island. Cannons booming all day, like to make you deaf. Marse Miles's regiment was manning the batteries. Federals landed some men to take our rifle pits and there was lots of close-in fighting. One of the Yankees got so far as Marse Miles's tent. Marse Miles wounded him, just about shot his hand off.

"He yelled for me and I came runnin' in the tent. 'This is too damn close for comfort,' he said. And he shot that wounded man in the head, quick as you please. Then he took the bayonet off the Yankee's rifle and put the point down by his ankle. Then he started drawing that knife up his leg, so slow it gave me chills.

" 'I'm not going deep, just bloody,' he said, and he smiled. You know that smile? 'Lots of blood,' I told him, scared. 'I know what I'm doing,' he said. 'This is nothing. I cut open a woman once and pulled out her baby. Just like a doctor.' "

Gentry stood up suddenly.

"Leg cramp?" Victor asked.

Gentry shook his head once and pulled the leathery twine taut between his hands. "Go on," he said, barely audible.

"Marse Miles made a big bloody gash all the way to his knee, and he said, 'Victor, you're my witness. I killed this soldier hand to hand and the Yankee bastard cut me good.'

"Then I went with him to the field hospital. And I saw his work. Wasn't deep. Not deep at all. But he paid this field doctor to write a letter saying how much damage was done to his leg, saying it'd take months to get better, that he'd probably be crippled the rest of his life.

"Then Marse Miles had his brace made, heavy case, lots of buckles and levers. Looks awful. But all it does is hold his ankle straight until he flips a lever.

"So he went home a hero and he got the job he always wanted. Working contraband. And every night he wrestles with me, fences with me, moves that leg. That leg's strong, believe me."

"I believe you," Gentry said, picking up the bow. He fastened the bowstring to the bottom of the bow and used two half hitches to knot it at the top. He tested the draw. Not good. The bow was too flexible.

Holding the nock of an arrow between his first and second fingers, he slowly pulled back the string. He held the bow horizontally, chest high.

The arrow zipped across the beach and landed in the brush. Velocity wasn't bad, but distance would be a problem. He would have to be close.

"We have many weapons now," Victor said hopefully, and went to retrieve the arrow.

Gentry looked at the three rusty grenades, the musket, revolvers, and makeshift bow. A paltry lot. But he did not wish for rifled cannon or an assault troop to command.

He wished only that Miles Brant would be aboard the alliance ship when he burned it.

THIRTY-TWO

"Devon."

The voice was soft, melodic. But Devon was deep in sleep and the voice had no name.

A hand brushed hair from her forehead, then the lamp was suddenly turned high.

"Time to wake up. Our ship is waiting," Miles said.

Miles. Devon's heart pumped fast. She shielded her eyes with her forearm, trying to remember where she was.

"We sail at dawn, with our old friend Beque on the *Cyrus Tern,*" Miles said.

Devon squinted at the light as she sat up. She drew the coverlet high and quickly concentrated her thoughts. Khaled had secreted her to this room in the hotel. He had ordered her food and a bath, then left on a pressing journey.

She had dressed in a day silk. Thank God, she had dressed before she lay down and had strapped the revolver to her leg.

"You really stirred things up," Miles said. He sat in the chair beside the bed, cocking his head to one side. "You and your smuggler friend. Mr. Red Jack Bettes was arrested, you know. Seems the authorities impounded the dinghy he needed to get to his ship. So he hightailed it downtown, looking for sanctuary at the U.S. consulate. He made it to the steps. Took five men but they finally got him down. Drew a better crowd than a dancing bear. He said he was an employee of the United States government. And he yelled out your name. 'Find her and you find a friggin' Rebel navy,' he said. Indelicate fellow, your friend."

Miles paused, but Devon made no reply. She kept her gaze guarded and low. She seemed hardly to breathe.

"Fortunately, he was not able to get your letter through the mail slot." Miles reached inside his coat and drew out the alliance exposé she had written at Me Bonnie Bay. "A letter, Devon?"

Under the covers, Devon lifted the edge of her petticoat and felt for the garter around her thigh.

Gone. Dear God, the gun was gone.

"And how tragic, your beautiful hair," Miles went on in a soft drawl. He leaned forward, elbows on his knees.

She threw the covers back and scrambled off the other side of the bed. "Where is Khaled? He promised me protection to Wilmington."

"Khaled is jouncing across the countryside with the insufferable superiors he has to work with. He's nothing more than a ship's clerk, really. But he's dark. Is that why you like him, Devon?"

Silent, she looked at him. "Why does God waste breath in the body of a worm like you?"

He smiled at the disgust in her eyes.

"You have no authority to take me anywhere!" she said.

"You're a prisoner of war."

"I'm a prisoner of criminals."

He sighed and took a handkerchief from his coat pocket. "Are you always so contentious in the mornings?" He started toward her.

She turned and ran to the locked door. She had time to pound only once. Miles was upon her, grabbing her arms and wrenching them down behind her.

One hand held her wrists, and he clamped his other hand over her mouth.

"Listen carefully," he said in a low, taut voice. "The gossip is everywhere. You act like a crazed lover in the ballroom. You leave your clothes at the best brothel in town. You traipse the bush with the natives. All actions of an obviously unstable woman. I could easily tie and gag you and pronounce you mad. Or you may walk out of here on my arm in a dignified manner. What is your choice?"

She grew still, though her eyes were rebellious.

"All right, then," he said almost absently.

She knew he was growing aroused by the feel of her

against him, yet he did release her. He knocked on the door three times. It was opened by Khaled's servant.

Before Miles pushed her forward, he reached into his pocket. "I have a gun. Just wanted you to know."

"You shot at me once," she said. "You'd do it again."

"Afraid so," he said with a smile, and slowly withdrew the gun from his pants pocket.

It was her revolver.

"Wise of you to sleep with the safety on," he said softly.

She tasted the bile of nausea at the top of her throat, then a blessed numbness descended. *He touched me,* she thought. *Asleep, unknowing. He touched me.*

Miles guided her through the door and linked her arm in his. She had become quite docile, as he'd known she would.

Revulsion, when strong enough, incapacitated a woman.

He glanced down at her, one brow raised. "Lesson one," he murmured.

Two rented carriages approached Hyde Cay at sunrise. Lord Grayshire rode in one, Khaled and Count Beaumond in the other.

"Well, Khaled, what are we to do, eh?" Count Beaumond asked. He pulled off one glove, clicked open his silver snuff box, and took a pinch of tobacco.

"We have a small crisis, not an extreme emergency," Khaled said, maintaining the even tone he had affected throughout the journey.

"I see." The count sniffed delicately, his Belgian-lace handkerchief at the ready.

"Even if the spy Morgan succeeds in alerting the Federal Navy," Khaled said, "he doesn't know where the alliance ships will gather, nor where they're headed. And I think it would be healthy to have the Federals' ocean-going Atlantic Squadron strung out along three thousand miles of coastline looking for our little fleet."

The count kept a conspicuous silence.

"Seamen on our ships are East Indians, for goodness' sake," Khaled went on. "How much more exotic and merchant-minded could we appear? We sail under canvas to conserve coal, leisurely vessels. And we fly the British flag, until the rendezvous point. And then each of the captains will bring out the bill of sale showing official Confederate ownership. An easy transformation."

"And the rifled cannon on board. Exotic and merchant-minded amenities?" The count smiled.

"Wherever possible, guns will be covered. But if the Federal ships come close enough to measure the size of our cannon, we will satisfy their curiosity and fire without warning."

The count cleared his nose with a light snort. "The existence of this fleet," he said, "is a worldwide affront to Lincoln's administration. We have extraordinary firepower and financial reserves, all designed to discredit and demoralize warmongering Republicans. The Democratic candidate McClellan is willing to negotiate peace. We have only to get him elected to see the rise of an independent Confederate nation."

"Granted. Even now, Lord Grayshire has an envoy en route to meet with McClellan," Khaled said calmly.

He ignored the count and busied himself with a look at his pocket watch.

Count Beaumond dogmatically broke the quiet. "I understand that resourceful smuggler of Morgan's is talking to jail guards, the Royal Navy, and anyone in position to bargain. And the U.S. consul is in a snit, demanding that all suspicious ships be detained and searched. Just when will this 'crisis' become an 'extreme emergency,' Khaled?"

Khaled looked directly at the count. "When I am captured beyond the diplomatic reach of the Pasha, then you worry."

Count Beaumond was shocked into silence. Beaumond blotted his nose lightly, his movements cautious and contained, as if he were surrounded by something prickly. "But none of us are mentioned in your letters, correct? No one can trace us or the Pasha. You have invented businessmen and companies and addresses, sold and resold ships. You make so many knots, no one can untangle them, *non*?"

"I am the only way through the knot," Khaled said.

"Good. Good."

"And my journals the only map."

"Journals?" the count whispered.

"Do you think I could keep in my head thousands of vouchers and registries and items of correspondence?"

"Where are these journals?"

"Now? With the Pasha."

"Of course." The count snapped his teeth together. "Of course."

Count Beaumond sat in hostile silence the remainder of the journey to Hyde Cay, as Khaled had intended. He needed time to think.

The beginnings of the crisis lay with Miles Brant's flagrant arrest of Gentry Morgan. It had sparked an inflammatory breach of secrecy at a bad time.

Alliance ships were at a critical juncture. Until now, they had anchored inoffensively in ports from Cárdenas to the Antilles. They had all received arms and fittings, ship stores and crews, and had been braced for conversion to warships.

But most could not mount their guns and carriages until they had left the jurisdiction of local customs agencies.

The flagship of the fleet was at the moment the most vulnerable vessel of all, for it sat at anchor southeast of Nassau, closest of all alliance ships to the maelstrom Brant had initiated.

Both Beaumond and Grayshire had demanded to see the caliber of vessel the alliance money had bought, and Khaled had arranged for them to watch the loading of the *Banshee,* the most formidable of the three vessels he had commissioned to be built. She was a steel-plated, shallow-draft screw steamer, and she waited at a secluded dock owned by an old boarding school friend of Khaled's, an indigo grower who had cheerfully allowed a freight shipment of 13,000 rifles, 250,000 ball cartridges, 2 rifled cannon, shot, shell, and powder to be stored in his house.

Two months earlier, Khaled had thought a formal review of the *Banshee* would be a harmless deference to shareholders. Now, with gossip raging in Nassau, it seemed an unnecessary risk.

Allah be merciful. Khaled bowed his head in prayer, slipped his hand inside his vest pocket, and touched his fingertips to his heart.

The charter papers bent with the pressure. Khaled had a ship waiting in Nassau to take him to Martinique.

In case of extreme emergency.

• • •

Hyde Cay was a rocky spit of sand marked by gnarled thickets of sea grape and patches of tall sea oats. It crooked out into the channel from a shoreline hammock of pines and palms, creating a secluded cove.

Gray clouds drifted swiftly overhead. The wind was gusty.

Hidden far down the shore behind a high dune, Gentry watched a small army of seamen trod a sandy path that connected a two-story house with a dock at the end of the cay. The brush was high and he could see only heads, shoulders, and the burdens they wielded.

Sweat glistened on the sailors' dark faces and dampened their shirts as they hauled cargo to the steamer tied at the end of a long, narrow pier. The crates they carried were heavy; most required four men hauling them on canvas hammocks or with long poles stuck through wood slats.

Arms and ammunition, Gentry thought. Thousands of cases of rifles alone. He saw a man open one of the crates on the pier. Breech-loading Floberts. French rifles.

Cartons of ammunition—cartridges and percussion caps—were heaved man to man to the hold. He judged a crew of at least forty-five men.

A small floating dock doglegged off the end of the pier and ran alongside the vessel at waterline. The dock floated on metal drums roped tight in a line.

The walkway bobbed unevenly in the choppy water, tipping like a suspended bridge without handrails. Still, the seamen walked the precarious bridge casually, springing up and down, taking lighter cargo to be hauled up fore, while the heavy arms were loaded aft from the high platform of the pier.

The cargo line changed from crates to kegs as sailors walked down the ramp from the veranda shouldering one, sometimes two small barrels.

Gunpowder.

Gentry watched the men stack the kegs on the long pier, awaiting transfer to the ship.

If he could get close enough, he could land a grenade in the midst of the gunpowder and explode the dock and ship together.

If he could light a match in the wind. If the grenades were not damp inside. If the rain held off. If fate was smiling.

He looked over at Victor, three feet away on his belly behind prickly palmetto. Victor wasn't smiling. He didn't believe it would be that easy, either. The Ashanti stoically brushed sand from the crease in his neck.

Gentry gave a grim, apologetic nod. He had insisted they splash their clothes wet before approaching the cay, so the light sand would stick to their skin and dark pants and make them difficult to spot.

Gentry could see only two guards with rifles. One stood at the bottom of a ramp that led up to the veranda of the oolitic-limestone house. Another man in grimy togs was at the ramp to the pier. Surely there was a lookout somewhere.

Gentry studied the ship. High in the rigging a sailor perched close to the mast. His sight was trained seaward for signs of approaching ships. But his glance turned periodically to the shore for a long, leisurely scan.

Gentry rolled onto his side and pulled the three grenades from a burlap sack. The wind gusted stiffly across his clothes, flattening his shirt and throwing nettles of sand against his face. He paused before he opened the flask of gunpowder. He had precious little, and they were upwind of the ship. The breeze would carry sound, smell, and refuse straight to the sailors.

He edged sideways to a shallow dip behind a rise of sea oats. In the windbreak he slowly and carefully poured powder through the charge holes of the old grenades. It took all of his powder. He had already made five cartridges for the musket, rolling powder and bullet in paper and tying the paper cylinder at each end with a piece of twine.

Victor would wield the long-range musket.

Gentry strung his bow and slung it over his arm, then inched forward along the dune line close to the pines. He stayed in the shadows, ducking behind foliage. He moved as quickly as his gear would allow, pausing often to keep an eye on the sailor in the rigging, grateful for the noisy thump and scrape of loading and the harsh banter of men at work.

He stopped at the fringe of the hammock, closer to the house than to the pier. Wary of the guard by the veranda, he dashed to a tall stand of palmetto thirty feet from the pier.

He crouched, breathing hard.

All he could hear was heavy scuffling of burdened footsteps in the sand. The loading continued undisturbed.

Thirty feet was too far for an overhand lob. He would have to stand to throw the grenade, and pray the guards were poor shots at a running target.

Slowly, carefully, he laid his supplies beside him in the sand: rope, matches, rag-wrapped arrows, bow, lamp oil, and the grenades. He scooped a hole in the sand and lay the length of hemp in its windbreak.

He could not yet light the match. Men shouldering gunpowder would yell the devil's own warning if they caught a whiff of struck sulfur.

Gentry looked back along the dune to where Victor waited. He raised his fist, then splayed his fingers.

It was the signal for Victor to release his handful of spice on the next gust. He did, and the wind carried the grains of cayenne down the beach, dispersing the flecks far and wide.

A sailor suddenly clapped a hand to his eye and rubbed. Then he cursed as the small barb of red pepper began to burn.

Another man sneezed, causing his shoulder pole to tip. The canvas sling of rifles he helped carry tumbled to the ground.

"What the devil!" someone shouted.

Another man took a sneezing fit. The orderly procession of cargo halted, and the hot, tired troops put down their loads and began to grumble.

Gentry quickly dampened the rag-wrapped arrows with lamp oil. Then he struck a match and lit one end of the rope coiled in the hole. The fiber caught with a black smoky spiral. Gentry hurried, setting arrow to bow, aware of the smoke and the telltale scents.

"Ship ahoy!" The sudden shout from the lookout on the mast drew the crewmen's attention to the channel.

Holding the bow crossways, Gentry bent close to the burning rope. As soon as the rags caught, he drew the string hard to his chest and released.

The burning arrow soared onto the dock, but landed short of the pyramids of gunpowder.

A crewman hurried to the arrow and beat it out. By that time, Gentry had another in the air. But a sudden gust knocked it harmlessly into the water.

A bullet buzzed past Gentry's ear. He ducked, just as a

thunderous blast from Victor's musket sent all the sailors scattering.

Gentry rose quickly and sent another arrow toward the kegs. This one landed atop the barrels of gunpowder.

The burning arrow was too high to be reached easily, and sailors ran helter-skelter for cover, some toward the house. The men on the dock raced for the ship.

But one quick-thinking sailor poked the highest kegs in the pyramid with his carrying pole. Three kegs and the burning arrow tumbled into the water.

Victor's musket boomed again, and the sailor took off for the ship.

At the same time, the guard at the veranda drew a bead on the palmetto thicket and fired. The bullet barely missed Gentry's leg.

Gentry hunched low behind the brush and set fire to the remaining three arrows, tossing them into the dry brush ahead of him.

He knew Victor needed a minute to reload in order to cover him, but Gentry had no time. To his right, the guard near the pier rose up to fire. Gentry rolled left just as the guard's rifle cracked.

The lead grazed his shoulder.

Gentry lit the fuses of two grenades, threw the third in the hole with the burning rope, and scrambled toward the dock, a grenade in each hand. The guard by the house fired instantly. The bullet hit his thigh, its force knocking him down.

He rolled with the fall and rose up on one knee to lob the first grenade squarely at the kegs. He threw the second grenade at the end of the pier where the ship was tied.

The iron grenades landed with secure thumps on the wood planks of the dock. Gentry scrambled toward the choppy surf, dragging the leg that had a bullet lodged deep in the thigh.

Another bullet whizzed past his head, and he heard Victor's musket roar in answer.

The guard on the pier cried out and sprawled back against the kegs, jostling the topmost barrel loose. It landed with a sharp crack on the wooden steps of the pier.

One stave burst and soft gunpowder spilled black and streaming across the steps.

Gentry splashed into the water. The sandy bottom dropped sharply, and buoyancy took the pressure off his wounded leg. He dove underwater and headed up the shoreline, toward Victor. He surfaced, gasping, waiting for the sound of explosion from the grenades.

There was none. The dock was deserted. On the *Banshee,* panicked sailors were casting off lines.

Still no explosion.

"Duds!" he heard a sailor croak joyfully. "They're duds!"

Gentry trod water, craning to see the shore and his last hope.

The lamp-oil rags had burned well, igniting pine needles and dry grasses around them. A burst of wind fanned the flames to a frenzy and whipped them forward. Spark and ash floated toward the dock.

Worried crewmen jumped off the veranda, running toward the brushfire to beat it back, but a shot from Victor's musket gave them pause. Then they dove to the ground as a blast resounded across the beach.

The third grenade!

Iron shards ripped sand and shrubs. The combustion sent the brushfire rolling forward to the dock like a red tide.

Flame licked the steps of the dock. Powder from the burst keg sizzled to life. The barrel exploded in flames, the flash force igniting other kegs in a tumbling discharge of widening blasts.

The narrow pier disappeared in a mass of splintered planks. The floating dock was hurled loose. Heavy crates of munitions burst and flung lead as the powder in thousands of cartridges caught fire.

The *Banshee,* engines at full throttle, was only eight feet from the dock when the blasts rocked it. Though the hull was safe, steel-plated, flames quickly caught the rigging.

On board, sailors shouted and scrambled. Some jumped over the side, not waiting for the fire to reach a hold filled with thousands of powder-based cartridges.

As scattered raindrops began to fall, debris from the explosion fanned out with the wake. Carried far from shore by the wind-whipped current, Gentry found himself surrounded by broken slats, pieces of crating, and floating metal drums . . . and with another steamer approaching dead-on.

Choppy waves gave him little time to surface and gasp air. He made a vain effort to swim against the current, but he had only one good leg, and his right shoulder, grazed by a bullet, throbbed in complaint.

Exhausted and heaving, he grabbed at a rope that snaked by. The rope girdled a metal drum, and he quickly reeled the drum toward him, slipping his forearm through the cord that encircled it. He lashed himself securely and hung there, heaving, blinking salt droplets from his eyes with each choppy swell.

He looked toward the dock. He was almost a half mile from the *Banshee,* should she blow. But the second steamer, a paddle wheeler, moved steadily closer. The name on its prow was familiar: *Cyrus Tern.*

Sailors flailed in the white-capped waters and loudly hailed the craft, but the ship did not veer toward the refugees of the *Banshee.* It was heading straight for Gentry.

The rain grew heavy, the wind driving it like pellets. Riding the rise of a wave, Gentry saw a man on the prow of the *Cyrus Tern* with spyglass to eye. A fair-haired man, bracing himself against a forward hatch to keep his balance in the rough sea.

Miles?

On the next swell, Gentry quickly shook the water from his eyes.

Miles was lifting a rifle.

The floating drum made Gentry a sitting duck.

He immediately unhooked his arm and tried to untangle the length of rope at his wrist as he dropped beneath the water. He heard the muffled ping as Miles's shot ripped through the drum.

Gentry stayed submerged as long as he could, kicking with all his might to move out of the path of the *Cyrus Tern.*

But when he surfaced, the ship was nearly upon him. He could see the barnacles that clung to its dark gray belly and the portholes of the cabins below deck.

He gasped for air, fighting the pain that seared upward from his leg, ready to submerge once more and try to flee the paddles' swath. He filled his lungs with a deep, determined breath . . . but Miles's bullet hit before he could submerge.

Gentry's head reeled with the impact. He sank, suddenly lax.

The ship passed him, the portholes of its passenger deck salt-fogged.

Devon could see through the blurry glass. She could see the rolling swell where Gentry had surfaced, so briefly. Where his head had jerked sideways uncontrollably. Hit.

Her eyes fixed on gray-blue ripples of water. Disturbed water. Angry water.

Her hand pressed flat against the glass.

Gentry.

She pounded once.

Gentry.

She pounded again. Then again and again.

"Gentry!" she screamed.

THIRTY-THREE

Black-orange flames dipped and swerved in the rigging of the *Banshee,* but the fire soon died in the onslaught of wind and rain.

The smell of wet char blew across the beach to the limestone house, and to the two canvas-top carriages that pulled up alongside the veranda.

Khaled al-Sayed Dexter emerged from one of the carriages and ran up the work ramp to the wide, sheltered veranda.

The rain pelted the roof like a snare drum and blew in along two sides of the porch. Only the northeast corner, sheltered by a trellised wall, was free of streaming water.

Khaled stood there, shaking rain from his top hat. Water ran down his cravat to wet the brocade of his vest. He surveyed the damage, his dark face showing no emotion, only a bookkeeper's frown as he began tallying the loss.

Crates and kegs lay helter-skelter in the path to the dock, some broken with rifles protruding, all drenched. Debris lay atop prickly palms and gnarled brush. A blackened tongue of burnt ground ran to the remains of the dock. Thousands of copper-capped cartridges rolled with the waves on shore.

The *Banshee* had eased engines and lay to, waiting out the storm. Hardest hit by the explosion was her port quarter. Bulwarks were crushed and the main yard broken.

Khaled saw much activity above deck, even in the downpour. Were the plates still secure, or leaking like sieves?

The squish of soaked shoes brought his attention back to the porch. His traveling companions stomped up the ramp.

Count Beaumond was silent and grim, frowning at the

water spots wrinkling his coat. Lord Grayshire walked slowly up the ramp, only two thick legs showing under the coachman's baggage tarpaulin.

Grayshire quickly threw off the tarp as if discarding vermin, then surveyed the financial carnage. His heavy jowls shook. "Dexter! What does this mean?"

Khaled looked at him. "It means we should return to Nassau as soon as possible."

The earl began to rage, but Khaled ignored him. He leaned back against the only dry wall on the porch and fixed his gaze on the second steamer, which was, incredibly, defying the gale and cautiously entering the channel.

The *Cyrus Tern* had come to tender ship's clothing to the men aboard the *Banshee*. Now the blockade-runner was running for its life. The *Cyrus*'s captain knew that the Royal Navy, customs officials, and any U.S. warship in the area would be drawn to the cove when the rain stopped.

So Miles Brant was on his way home with a cunning captain at the helm, a lovely spy in the hold, and quite probably, Yankee gunships on his tail.

Khaled closed his eyes. He swallowed but his mouth was dry. After the storm, he, too, would be homeward bound. But much more discreetly. If the count and Lord Grayshire were wise, they would take themselves off the island and stay far from the reach of the vice-admiralty court.

Khaled thought comfortingly of the soft Moroccan rugs in his palace chamber, of bitter black tea, of the suffocating scent of hashish, and the light heart and nimble fingers of his youngest wife.

He looked longingly at the sky, but the storm showed no signs of abating.

Devon sat on the small hard bunk, holding to the handrail as she rocked with the pitch of the ship.

"Ton-weya," she whispered. She must tell Ton-weya. And she must find Teague Morgan, Gentry's father. She must find something of Gentry's and touch it, hold it, to see if his spirit was truly gone.

She bent, head to knees, folding into herself because the image would not leave. She saw Gentry, his head jerking violently, the rolling gray water swallowing him.

Suddenly she started. The latch on the door was moving.

Miles ducked his head and entered the small room, falling sideways against the wall as the ship dipped in the swale of a wave. He bent and unbuckled the leather straps of his brace. The contraption opened its jaws and he let it fall to the floor.

Devon pressed back deeper into a corner of the bunk, but the room was tiny. There was no way to create distance, a feeling of safety.

"Rough up there," he said casually. He shrugged off his wet coat, hanging it on a nail on the door, and unbuckled his belt and holster. "Beque says we're on the fringe of a southwest storm. We should be out of it soon. Doesn't look good for Cuba, though."

He hung his gunbelt atop his coat, then groped his way to a big steamer trunk along one wall, rummaging until he found a bottle of burgundy. "Ah, Beque. A man of impeccable taste. Look what he's left for us."

Miles sat at the end of the small bunk opposite Devon. He stretched out his legs and crossed them at the ankle, close to her, not touching her.

"You killed him," she said. Her words were flat, factual.

Miles slowly twisted the cork from the wine bottle, studying her. She hugged herself fiercely, close to the edge of madness, a protective madness that detached all feeling so she could function in shock, exhaustion, aggrievement.

"I killed him," he said softly, then tilted the bottle and took a long swallow.

He proffered the bottle. "I apologize"—he wiped his mouth on his sleeve—"but we have no glasses here. Would you care to join me?"

With an unearthly shriek, she swatted the bottle from his hand. The thick glass gave an ominous clank when it hit the floor, but it did not break. Burgundy glugged from the mouth in a veinal red stream.

Miles got up quickly and righted the bottle. "A childish waste. You would have hurt me less had you hit me." He smiled a small, unconcerned smile and returned to his seat.

"Now," he said after another pull at the bottle. "Are you going to tell me you have nothing to live for? That you are beyond hurt? Beyond feeling?"

"I would be a fool to tell you anything," she said.

"And of all the things you are, a fool is not among them. You're a driven young woman. Mistakes are inevitable."

Devon ignored him. She looked out the fogged port glass
at the angry sea. The ship had stopped its cradle-rocking.
Now there was only an occasional jolt from the waves.

"He was not good for you, Devon," Miles said. "He was a
man who didn't know what he wanted. He spent his whole
life searching for where in hell he belonged."

"He belonged with me," she whispered.

"*Au contraire*, my sweet." Miles smiled and took another
swallow of burgundy. "You weren't bred to live in a tent and
work a buffalo hide into britches for your man. You
wouldn't even survive in a little farmhouse with calico curtains and a Franklin stove. Isolation would kill you. You're a
talented woman. You need to be recognized. You need to
preside."

"I need to be alone!" she cried bitterly. "Leave, if you
have a shred of common decency—"

"I hold with nothing common, least of all decency," he
interrupted calmly. "Decency is ridiculously overrated. It's
a herd trait, detrimental in a leader. If I left now, I would
not get what I want."

An animal fear held her silent. She summoned a ragged
breath. She must form words, she told herself, for it was
silence she feared most with Miles. Silence was a trap. If she
fell in numb, without words enough to fight, he would consume her shell like a snake an egg, swallowing with excruci-
ating patience, collapsing her casing with one slow squeeze.

She took another trembling breath. "What is it you want,
Miles? Do you want to make me more sad or fearful? You
can't. Do you want to make yourself less repulsive? You
can't."

"You're wrong," he said, idly rubbing the toe of his boot
along her arm.

She shrank from his touch.

He smiled. "You see? Fear is a marvelous, shifting feeling.
You can't keep it all the time. It ebbs and flows, like a tide
with a mind of its own. You can't control it. I can.

"And as for revulsion, my dear, you are really too innocent to know what men do to make a woman retch. Sometimes it takes little indeed," he said thoughtfully, sipping
from the bottle. "It's an art of sorts. One has to understand
the woman first to know what she hates and what she fears.
It's quite individual. Some women need a high variety of

degradation. Others, the sensitive ones, need something simple. Portia, magnificent Portia, had such a simple fear. Hers was such a simple punishment. A significant round of sodomy, just that, and afterward she simply lay on the bed folded up as if she were shrinking, her grit and pride all gone, nothing to fight for anymore.

"I was mad when I heard she ran away. Then I was glad. I wouldn't want her around with the fight gone. And that's what I have to figure out about you, Devon. How much fight you'll show before you break."

He upended the bottle to his lips. A dark bead of burgundy escaped and he stanched his mouth on his sleeve.

He was growing sloppy, Devon thought. Dear God, what would he be like drunk?

He slowly moved closer to her.

She drew herself tighter, her head against the wall.

His body bracketed her in the corner.

"I used to ball up like that too," he said, his hand gliding down the silk sleeve of her dress. "Trying to make myself smaller so Big Josey'd have less to hit. I was small enough as it was. Then I went off to boarding school, away from Big Josey, and I got bigger. Big enough to hit back."

He smiled pensively. "Women so rarely get big enough to hit back. You have to be sneaky, lie and pretend so you can escape what's gonna hurt. I tried that too. Good, plain, reasonable lies. But they never worked on Big Josey. My daddy wasn't fond of engaging his brain. I think it was small and hard, like a little brown nuthatch egg.

"But my God, he had superb instinct. Knew exactly what a body was afraid of. He'd shut me in the cellar. A dark ole place. Cold dirt floor like a big black grave. I was seven or eight. And my mother would be screaming, 'Don't do it, Josey! He's just a baby!' An' Big Josey'd yell, 'Baby's gotta learn!'

"An' I'd huddle there at the door at the top of the stairs, all balled up just like you are, scared of what was breathing down there in the dark.

"And I would rack my brain thinking, 'What am I supposed to learn?' One day the answer came to me: You learn not to get caught.

"So I became quite the artful dodger. Don't you think?"

He stopped and ran a finger along her jaw. "Don't you think, Devon?" he repeated.

"Yes," she whispered.

"But back then I wasn't so artful," he said sadly. "I got caught a lot. I just seemed to make mischief right in Big Josey's path, and whomp, he'd find me. Found me real *indelicato* one day. Pleasuring myself, pleasure at that age being no bigger than the stub of a pencil. But he sure was enraged. I lied quick as I could. Told him Evaleen, one of the kitchen girls, had showed me what to do. He beat Evaleen till the blood ran out her ears. An' he locked me in the cellar the whole night. That was the worst. The whole damn night."

"Your father was an animal," Devon said. "You don't have to be."

"I'm no animal."

His grip tightened on her arm and he leaned close to her ear, his damp brown sideburns brushing her cheek. She felt chilly drops of rain press her cheek in cold communion, and his lips hovered in the sensitive cup of her ear.

"I'm the most formidable man you'll ever meet," he whispered.

His hand reached up to rake her short hair. "Peculiar, how pretty you are this way. I can see your face better. Beautiful face."

He pulled her to him and kissed her.

Devon did not cringe. She did not struggle. She felt the pressure of his mouth on hers, idly seeking response. Then he pressed hard, demanding acquiescence and opening.

She was detached from the thing at her lips. She could not feel, could not taste. But she smelled the sour ferment of the wine, like the queer rot of something buried inside him.

He roughly pushed her away, jarring her against the cabin wall. "How ungracious. No attempt to pretend? I demand at least that. A pretense of love."

She turned her head, sickened.

"You see how little it takes?" he said softly.

She suddenly met his eyes. "I see how little you can touch me. You, your pitiable cold lips sucking warmth, your puny posing as a man who knows women. You know nothing."

He struck her hard across the cheek. "Shut up!" He

scrambled from the bed and loomed over her, the heavy bottle in hand. "You may not scorn me! Not now!"

"You are alone," she said, holding her cheek. Her eyes were bright. "Always alone. And I will always be with him."

"Gentry's dead!" Miles shouted. He flung the bottle across the room with such force, it broke in shards against the wall. "Dead and gone. I can feel it!" He struck his chest. "Don't you think I'd know? After eleven years of waiting for the chance? Here, deep in my heart, there's a window of light now. I can see my property. I can see grass and cattle and horses and big fields of corn. Land rolling along a river, in a place where people aren't breathing down your neck to tie your hands. I've got ideas, Devon. Lots of ideas! You know what it's like trying to keep a lid on a kettle that's filled up and boiling over? I'm busting out of this heavy old pot my daddy and gran'daddy put me in. Cotton an' darkies, cotton an' darkies, all the livelong day. Till the war came. Now, when the Yankees finally march their big fat caissons into Wilmington, I'm going to be master of nothin' but a huge ole tax bill. Hundreds of acres of fields needin' plantin' and no one to work 'em!

"But I'm smarter than my daddy. As soon as Teague Morgan dies, I'm gonna be a big man. I've got an empire started."

"You've got nothing," Devon promised vehemently, hand to cheek.

The stirring conviction in her voice gave him pause.

"Why?" he asked, his eyes narrowed and sharp. He grabbed her by the shoulders and shook her roughly.

Her head slammed against the wall and she cried out.

"Why?" he shouted. He pulled her from the bunk and threw her to the floor.

She landed, and her hand brushed the jagged shard from the neck of the wine bottle. She hissed with pain and clasped one hand around her wrist. Blood began to well between her fingers.

"So help me God, you'd better tell me!" he yelled. "I've had these terrible fears, things bubbling up inside me for years. What if that heathen bastard legally married an Indian woman after his wife died? What if he was fertile as sin and already had a child by the time he came to Summer Sky? What if there's someone in my way, Devon?"

She didn't look at him. She pretended pain and bent over. At her side, she grasped the neck of the wine bottle. It had broken with a jagged edge and long pointed teeth.

"What're you trying to hide? Tell me, dammit, tell me!"

As he reached down and grabbed her, Devon made a panicked lunge, ramming the long jagged shard deep into the calf of his leg.

Miles cried out. "Goddamn!" He hobbled away from her and fell to the bunk. "Goddamn!" he whimpered, and gingerly tried to pull the huge chunk of glass out of his leg.

Devon scrambled breathless to the gunbelt he had hung on the wall. She took his revolver and aimed it, hands trembling.

Miles did not notice. He grimaced and screamed as he yanked the shard out.

"It's in there, you bitch. A big piece still in there," he said weakly. Then he saw the nose of the revolver wavering in her bloody hand. He froze. A bead of sweat rolled past the corner of his eye. "Are you a cold-blooded killer, Devon? Just what in the hell are you?"

Devon's face was flushed and hot. She reached around behind her to slide the lock bolt free of the door.

Miles slowly stood. She saw the pain contorting his face. His trouser leg was a dark mass of red.

He was so close to her. Not four feet away.

He took a step, then cried out, stumbling against the bunk, falling toward her.

It was a ruse. He grabbed for the gun.

She fired instinctively, off-balance. The bullet went wild, imbedding in the wall above the bunk.

She lurched away from him, releasing her grip on the gun so that she could scramble free.

The gun fell to the floor and Miles atop it.

In panic, Devon raked desperately at the door, trying to find the handle. Miles pulled at her skirt, and the soft silk tore at the waist.

A powerful jolt suddenly sent her sprawling backward against him. The floor gave a sharp, sickening tilt, and Miles was thrown against the planked wall. Devon lay flat to stop the rolling and get her bearings.

Hit, she thought. The ship was being attacked.

There was a tremendous moan of beams, wood straining to hold, and a boom like internal thunder on the wheel side of the ship.

She jumped up and ran for the door, then glanced back at Miles. He was not pursuing her. He sat against the wall, his hands encircling his leg, trying to stanch the bleeding. His eyes were a zealot's gray, glistening with the promise of retribution.

Devon yanked hard on the latch and stepped out, pulling the door shut behind her. She tried to restrain the cry of relief in her throat, but it escaped like a mew, weak, uncertain. She rushed through the narrow companionway, her shoulders brushing the wall as she fought for balance.

Above deck she heard the thump and scratch of panicked footsteps. In front of her was chaos. Cockney curses drowned a gargle of French epithets. Sailors squeezed together like smelly scrod in a net as they elbowed for position on the tiny stairwell that led to the aft deck.

Devon tried unsuccessfully to push her way into the crush of bodies. "Please!" she screamed, glancing fearfully behind her, where Miles was stepping across the threshold of his room.

"Move aside, ya bloody hogheads!" a short man beside her shouted. He wore a wine-red fisherman's cap. "Let a bloomin' lady through!"

A sailor in front of Devon yelped and twisted aside. Another sailor cursed, and a funneled path to the steps emerged for her.

The short man took her arm and ushered her forward with a rough push. "On with ya, now," he said.

Free of the crush, she saw why the sea of bodies had parted. The little man had a dirk in hand to prick the sailors' good manners.

Before she could ask his name, the enterprising little man disappeared on deck in a stream of crewmen hurrying to get rifles from the quartermaster.

The rain had stopped, but the wind was harsh, blowing salt spray across the gunwales.

Devon saw Captain Trouvier standing on the quarterdeck, eyeglass trained on the Federal frigate gaining ground on his starboard quarter.

The *Cyrus Tern* lurched with a sudden wave, hull groaning with the strain, and Devon fell against the bulwark. "Captain!" she called, holding the torn seam of her gown at her waist.

The tall, lanky Frenchman looked annoyed. He collapsed the glass and slid along the handrail to the main deck. "Go below, m'em'selle! This is not safe! They are holding fire, but not for long."

"The threat below is worse, Captain. You know that. You know him. I was brought aboard against my will. I want to return to Nassau."

"This is not a little ferry that can shift with your whim, eh?"

"Give me a rowboat! The Federal ship will take me aboard."

Trouvier frowned a moment, a long moment, studying the big-gunned frigate in the distance.

Then he turned to her with a humorless smile. "For you, m'em'selle, of course." He gave orders. His flagman hurried to signal civilian overboard. Two sailors readied the small skiff hanging off the captain's bridge. One of the sailors was the dirk-wielder in the dirty red fisherman's cap.

"Things so bad that you're leavin' us, Capt'n?" the little man asked as he unhitched the boat from the bridge.

"No, no, nosy Pickeral. This lady wants to leave us. And I want a diversion. Our purposes cross."

Trouvier sent word to the engine room to stand by for full speed ahead. "God willing, in this wind we can make eleven knots. That tub of Yankee lard can do no more than eight, I hope. Besides, you'll be in the cross fire. Surely they will not want to harm a lady with so many secrets, eh?"

"You are indeed a noble breed of captain," Devon said.

"I protect my crew, my ship, and my cargo, in that order. You do not want to be cargo, so . . ." He shrugged.

"Turn around," he told the men who were grappling the wooden skiff toward the deckrail. "The lady needs privacy."

"What—?" Devon began.

"How do you swim with a lead weight of cotton around your legs, eh?"

She turned around, lifted her skirt, and untied the two layers of petticoat at her waist. They fell, and she stepped over them.

Trouvier tied one end of a long rope around her waist and the other end to the oarlock socket in the rowboat. "Your lifeline, m'em'selle. I suggest you use it quickly."

Then he ordered the men to heave the rowboat over the side.

"Beque!" The shout came from behind. It was Miles.

"Hurry," Devon pleaded. "Dear God, hurry."

The small boat smacked the water, and the coil of rope attaching her to it began to unwind as the *Cyrus Tern* surged ahead.

"He will eat my ear for this one, eh?" Trouvier said. Then he lifted Devon in his arms and swung her over the side of the ship.

She hit the water with a barely noticeable splash in the rolling sea. The water hungrily soaked her silk, and she pushed up to the surface. She gasped when she reached air, feeling heavy, weighed down.

She pulled the rope hand over hand, inching her way toward the skiff fifty feet away.

She heard a splash behind her, then Trouvier's bark from the ship. *"Froussard!"* he shouted. "You liverless coward, Pickeral! They will not catch us! I spit on the eyelid of your ugly mother!"

The little sailor who had helped her had jumped ship!

Devon could not see him in the choppy sea. She concentrated her draining energy on pulling herself toward the skiff. The sea buffeted and fought her. She coughed water and held the rope taut as she rested.

Suddenly she felt herself pulled forward.

Pickeral had reached the boat and was hauling her in.

As he helped her over the side, she saw that he had lost his red cap.

"Now stay where I put ya," he said, placing her on a board seat in the bow. "I got to do some fancy rowing." He quickly set the oars in their locks, then stopped suddenly. "Here," he said, handing her a piece of canvas tarp.

She nodded gratefully, shivering wet, and draped the tarp across her shoulders.

Pickeral set a steady pace that took them slowly beyond the course of the *Cyrus Tern*.

The *Cyrus* had already steamed hard away, lengthening its lead on the frigate, which had slowed. The frigate picked up speed, but it could not overtake the sleek, shallow-draft blockade-runner in the gusty storm.

"Capt'n thinks he's so smart," Pickeral said. "Thinks he can outrun anythin'. But he can only run as fast as his coal can burn. And the Yanks have got three more ships on his tail. Look there."

Like dark nuggets on the horizon, Devon saw three shapes growing infinitesimally bigger.

"The frigate there," the little man went on. "She won't pick us up. She'll keep on course with the *Cyrus*. . . ." Pickeral talked when he stroked the oars up, was silent when he pulled water. "So's the others can keep their bearings. . . . And they'll run the *Cyrus* into gun range. . . . No more'n a day, I bet."

"Why are you helping me, Mr. Pickeral?" Devon asked.

"Beggin' yer pardon, I'm helpin' meself, mum. That's a doomed ship we were on."

"Why?"

"Money always draws fire, in my 'sperience. The *Cyrus* is carryin' one hundred thousand dollars in gold coin. To fortify the Charleston campaign, heard the colonel say to the capt'n. I'd rather sign on one of the clippers headin' for home when we get back to port."

"Will we get to port?"

"O'course. One of those frigates is bound to stop for us."

Just about then, the closest Federal ship steamed by, engines roaring. A sailor with a bullhorn stood on the bow. "Sit tight," he ordered.

"Tight as a goose's whistle, ya blowhard," Pickeral said, waving and smiling.

Devon sat still, numbness overtaking her interest in rescue. It was the cold, mostly. The cold that began in her heart; a cold that dry clothes and a warm room would not cure.

The big ship passed by with a noisy, labored wash, all hands standing by gun mounts and duty stations, petty officers and gunner's mates still as statues in blue cloth jackets, black silk neckerchiefs, and thick blue caps.

Everyone was on active alert.

Even the ship's doctor was busy in the captain's quarters

below. The captain's flattop desk doubled as the doctor's operating table.

Gentry lay there on the desk, a dirty gun rag clamped between his teeth, a messboy sitting on his leg to hold it down while the doctor's scalpel sliced deep, searching for the bullet in his leg.

THIRTY-FOUR

The United States consulate in Nassau was a gray stone building on a street shaded by tall banyans.

Devon walked up the front steps, her gown still damp under the long painted coat the Federal captain had given her. She was escorted by ten sailors from the U.S. Navy ship that had rescued her and Mr. Pickeral. The little sailor was still aboard the frigate, finagling travel money in exchange for information about the *Cyrus Tern,* her heading and her cargo.

The door of the consulate was guarded by two men in dark blue uniform. One opened the door wide. The small parquet foyer was crowded with men.

Devon stepped inside. The door was shut and bolted.

A well-dressed man with long black sideburns and an untamed mustache stepped forward. "Walter Straun, U.S. consul at your service, Miss Picard. You're safe here."

Devon said nothing. She found no acknowledgments, not one simple courtesy on her tongue. She leaned back against the door, struck suddenly by the heat from all the anxious bodies in the hallway.

"We're quite eager to talk with you, Miss Picard," Straun said worriedly.

She parted her lips as if to speak, but the silence held like a friend, far from the comforting demands of strangers.

"Walter." A woman's voice. Soft, taking charge.

As if in a prearranged dance, Straun's assistants and house staff retreated erratically, shuffling back into unseen doorways, leaving only Straun and a slim, pale woman in green faille silk.

"Miss Picard needs to freshen up first," the woman said quietly.

Devon concentrated on the woman. She had dark red hair and cheeks that were freckled and smooth.

"My wife, Peach, Miss Picard," Straun said. "She'll take care of you."

Peach Straun grasped Devon's arm and led her down the hall.

"Try to hurry, Peach," Straun said sotto voce to his departing wife. "I've got messenger craft standing by."

"Some things don't hurry, do they, Miss Picard?" Peach Straun said, holding herself to Devon's lagging pace.

"No," Devon whispered. It was all she could say. "No."

It seemed a long way to the guest room at the back of the house. As they passed the kitchen wing, Peach ordered a bath and toilette.

In the small bedchamber, she pulled light blue chambray curtains to a close across white-paned windows. "Let me help you with your coat," she said to Devon, straightening her arm so she could pull the big canvas coat over Devon's hand.

One arm fell free. The sleeve was stained dark with blood from the cut on Devon's wrist.

Peach made no notice. She talked calmly of inconsequentials, not of Devon's strange short hair, nor of the red abrasion on her cheek.

The servants entered with hip bath and hot water, and Peach ushered away all but one and helped Devon undress.

Devon passively obeyed the rhythmic flex and tug, the unfastening of buttons and ties, garment and girdle, feeling the layers shed until she stood free, safe, and attended in the private, hallowed sphere of woman among women.

She stepped into the bath, and the servant's soft sponge painted her back with panels of warm silky water that washed away the tight film of salt on her skin.

Devon closed her eyes. A soft cloth smoothed back her hair and washed her forehead, then her cheeks, daubing gently at the red mark left by Miles's hand. Devon took the rag and ran it along her jaw where Miles had touched, across her lips where Miles had kissed. Across her lips again and again, until Peach's cool hand stopped the motion.

"That's fine, honey," Peach said. "Just fine."

When Devon was dry and wrapped in a towel, Peach said, "Let's do your hair." Devon bent over the porcelain basin in the washstand. Peach dampened her hair a cupful of water at a time, patting in the wetness, refilling the cup in the basin with a syncopated clink and dunk.

Peach used lots of soap and lathered twice. Then she squeezed half a lemon in the rinse water.

The lemon drops tinkled daintily into the basin, their tangy scent rising bright and gay. Slowly, woodenly, as if awakening, Devon took over the rinsing of her hair, bending low in the basin because her hair was so short, feeling the warm water embrace the top of her head like a turban. Upside down, she twisted her head and felt the lemon water buoy her, lighten her. She cupped water in her hand and clapped it to her nape. It forked and slid clean along her jaw to the basin.

Peach toweled her hair, then told her to sit down. She combed, tugging the thick strands into a short, sleek curtain that reached just below Devon's ears. "Go get the scissors," Peach told the servant. "And bring back some foundations and underskirts for Miss Picard. And my pink lace morning dress."

As the servant left, Peach set a straight-back chair opposite Devon and sat down, her knees almost touching Devon's. She took Devon's hands in hers, careful not to brush the dark, angry line across her right wrist.

"Look at me now," Peach said. "I'm gonna even up that job on your hair and it's gonna look fine. I don't have any blond hairpieces, but I'm gonna get you some by tomorrow. A long braid maybe. And a coil for each side. Don't worry."

Devon was silent. After a long while, she looked at Peach's face. As naturally as if Peach were her mother, she leaned forward, laying her cheek in Peach's lap, on the soft gown cushioned with petticoats.

Peach rolled the heel of her hand gently across Devon's skin, pressing down in short, soothing licks like a mother cat trying to wake a damaged kitten.

"Devon, sweetie?" she whispered, pulling back the damp tendrils of hair that covered Devon's cheek.

Her hand trespassed on a flowing curtain of tears, warm as pressed silk.

• • •

All too soon, Devon was called to meet with Walter Straun and two of his assistants in the library of the consulate, a dark-paneled, masculine room.

Walter Straun lowered himself to a chair, reaching back to part his coat flaps and flip them up so that they creased cleanly. Across from him the girl sat stiffly on a striped-twill settee. In only an hour, the wet, bedraggled creature had become a pretty young woman. Even the boy's haircut had been shaped and softened to a halo of waves anchored with long silk ribbons above each ear. She looked serious, composed. Still, a wildness played strangely around her eyes.

Straun cleared his throat. "A man named Red Jack Bettes said I should talk to you," he began.

"Is Mr. Bettes still in custody?" she asked.

"Yes. But I'm working on it. The governor knew he didn't have his ducks in a row when Gentry Morgan was arrested. It was a gesture to appease that contraband-runner, Colonel Brant. The Confederacy doesn't have power to request extradition of anybody. Britain doesn't recognize the Confederate States of America, thank God. So I'm prepared to drop the protest of the wrongful arrest of a U.S. citizen if the governor will release Red Jack Bettes."

The girl was silent a long moment.

"If you don't mind, Miss Picard, I'd like to talk about this alliance business."

"I have some conditions, Mr. Straun," she said.

He bit the inside of his cheeks and counted to five. "As long as you realize time is of the essence. If there is to be an attack on U.S. ports, I'd like to send word to our troops. Quickly."

"The assault is at least a week away, if they hold to their schedule. August twentieth is the date their fleet assembles."

"Where?"

"Understand that I and others have paid a great price to get information to you. And now I realize that it is the only currency I have to protect myself and my friends. Please have your secretaries write the following in duplicate. We will each need to sign."

Straun paused at her boldness, then, agitated, gestured to his aides. Both men readied their inkwells.

Devon spoke slowly, mechanically. "First, certify that I will not be asked to testify in any court proceedings that arise as a result of the alliance conspiracy. Second. The United States will not press charges against Rear Admiral Arnaud Picard or Harcourt Bivens, Earl of Grayshire, in any aspect of the alliance conspiracy. Third. You will issue a certificate of citizenship to a former slave named Victor Batu. Fourth. I ask that you kindly lend me steamer passage to Baltimore, where I can make arrangements for my future finances. I will, of course, repay you."

Straun was so outraged, he stood up and circled his chair. "You must think I'm one powerful son of a gun!"

"You wield the seal of the United States and represent your country in delicate matters of diplomacy. I am merely trying to negotiate a fair exchange."

Straun sucked in his breath. It was a sound of compromise. "Why won't you testify?" he asked.

"I would incriminate myself, members of my family, and fellow Britons. I have no intention of doing that."

"I think Admiral Picard and Lord Grayshire are big boys. They can let the chips fall where they may."

"I cannot, Mr. Straun. They are men acting in accordance with their ideals and their integrity."

"Integrity, hell." Straun paced. "Let's sign. Time's wasting. Now where are they going to hit?"

"I'm not sure. I do know their ships are scattered right now. In Cuba. Havana and Cárdenas were mentioned. Some ports in the West Indies."

"How many ships?"

"At least twenty-four."

"Steam?"

"Yes."

"Cannon?"

"Eleven-inch rifled guns."

"Damn. They fire faster and have three times the range of eleven-inchers on our monitors. How many guns on each ship?"

"I don't know. My impression is that they're royally armed. There's a crippled steamer and a beach full of firearms at Hyde Cay that will give you an idea of the standards they were using."

Straun turned to an assistant and ordered him to address letters. To the secretary of the Navy. To the President. To the head of the detective bureau of the secret service,

Pinkney Dobbs. And a general memo to be dispersed to all Navy ships.

"Mr. Straun. Is there a 'Charleston campaign'?" Devon asked.

Straun nodded.

"Apparently the Confederates also have a Charleston objective. It's something Mr. Pickeral said, the crewman from the *Cyrus Tern.* A little man—"

"With big ears, no doubt," Straun interrupted. He immediately ordered Pickeral brought to the consulate. Then he turned back to Devon. "I think you should rest. Tomorrow we can talk about the alliance itself, who planned it, who financed it."

"I made it clear. I will not divulge information about the planners. I want to leave on the soonest passage to Baltimore."

"What's in Baltimore, Miss Picard?"

"Connections," she said quietly. Rail connections west. To Plain Shade, Missouri. To the remnants of Gentry's past.

The swinging made him logy and he could not waken. Thoughts were heavy clouds without form. Then the pain in his leg ripped the haze like lightning, and Gentry's eyes opened wide.

He swung in a shroud, sunk deep in dirt-gray netting that pulled tight across his shoulders. He tried to free his shoulder and pull himself upward, but the motion took his balance and jerked his leg. He bit back a cry and held his breath until he had made peace with the pain.

He looked around the room, careful not to twist his neck. It was swollen and sore.

He was in the crew's quarters, a low, musty hall of box bunks, rocking hammocks, and rolled pallets. Across the room, a boy slept on one of the unrolled mats. It was the kitchen helper who'd held his leg while the surgeon probed.

"Boy." Gentry's voice was hoarse.

The boy roused himself immediately, as if he'd been waiting for the summons. He scurried to Gentry's side, a long stick in hand.

"Doc says you'll need this for a while," the boy said, offering Gentry the rough-hewn walking stick.

"Where are we?" Gentry asked, sitting up.

The boy steadied the hammock. " 'Bout eight hours off the Bahama banks."

"Where are we headed?" Leaning on the stick, Gentry grimaced as he swung one leg to the floor.

"North, to join a blockade fleet off the Virginia beaches," the boy said. "We finally stopped following that blockade-runner. A lighter ship took over." He lifted Gentry's wounded leg as gently as he could and lowered it to the floor.

Gentry clamped a hand on the boy's shoulder. The swollen wound throbbed, muscle and tissue alarmed at the change of position. Gentry said nothing for a long minute, staring straight ahead, waiting for equilibrium.

"Doc sewed it shut, you know. Had to. You were losing an awful lot of blood. And walkin' ain't good for it, neither," the boy warned.

"We'll go slow," Gentry said. "I have to see the captain."

They started forward, the boy tucked under Gentry's left shoulder to give him balance, the stick supporting him on the right.

"Who pulled me out of the water?" he asked.

"Was me that spotted you," the boy said proudly. "Everyone else was looking at a big colored fellow on the beach waving a white flag. Then ever once in a while he'd point at a barrel out in the channel. I finally figured out what he was pointin' to. The barrel bobbed around and there you were lashed to it like a drowned dog. You had the rope tied up under your neck. A wonder you wasn't hung."

Gentry's thoughts went back to the stormy waters of Hyde Cay, to the giant specter of the *Cyrus Tern* approaching him, to the flaps of Miles's coat whipping in the wind as Miles took aim.

When Miles fired the first shot, Gentry had pushed away from the floating barrel, but hadn't been able to free himself of the long rope tangled around his arm.

Miles's second shot had made a long graze on Gentry's neck. Stunned, Gentry had sunk beneath the water. The floating drum had bobbed in the path of the *Cyrus Tern*'s paddle floats and was churned under, spinning like a winch, winding him toward it.

The ship passed overhead, and Gentry had surfaced with the barrel, coughing salt water. Ineptly, he'd twisted the rope around his neck and shoulder, determined to die with his head above water, away from the water spirits who danced in his burning lungs.

"Your neck's raw, like somebody tried to lynch ya," the boy said.

Gentry gingerly touched the bandage that ran under his jaw from his chin to his left ear.

"Doc didn't have no trouble with that piece o' lead," the boy went on, opening the door. "It was so close to the skin he just took a little nick and it come right out. A little deeper and you would've ripped an artery. Doc says you're one lucky Injun."

Gentry grimaced as he lifted his leg over the high threshold of the door. His uncle, Waits the Deer, had taught him that good fortune dwelt in the scars on a warrior's body.

Gentry did not feel lucky now. Merely alive. And alone.

He pressed onward to the captain's cabin to relay his knowledge. He would ask to be taken to Washington, D.C., where Pinkney Dobbs could question him, then free him from the mission.

Where would he go then?

Gentry's lust to kill Miles was keen, but not as sharp as his instinct to find and protect Ton-weya. Gentry felt mortal now, his escape from death too recent, too emptying, his need to ensure his son's survival more consuming than it had ever been.

And Devon? If Devon wished to be with him, she would go to his father's house or she would search for the village of Ton-weya.

But what if she wished to be free? Could he ever fault her for choosing her own land and people over a future he could not promise her?

He stopped and leaned heavily on the stick. He saw her face in memory the morning he left her, shorn of her beautiful hair because of him, saddened because of him.

He did not want to remember her that way. He thought instead of the night she chose him, of her beauty awaiting him on the veranda of the big house, in a gown of white, peaceful white, peaceful night, yielding her gift.

Sge! came his uncle's voice in one of the simplest, despairing chants of his people. _Gahu'sti a'giyahu'sa._ I have lost something. Now tell me where I shall find it. For is it not mine?

"Is it not mine?" Gentry whispered.

Once out of gale winds and past the Abacos, the *Cyrus Tern* took a northwestern heading, a tack that set it against the wind.

After dusk, Captain Trouvier gave the order to ease engines and rest coal-heaving crews. Irritated, he went below.

Miles was in the captain's cabin, glass in hand, an amber-colored bottle in his lap. His injured leg rested on the table. His leg was bare to his thigh, except for a large white bandage around his calf. The right half of his trousers dangled, slit open and empty like a piece of skirt.

Trouvier opened the sturdy oak doors of the cupboard. "Where's my brandy?" he asked.

Miles patted his stomach.

"Left the cheap rum for me? *Salut*, greedy bastard." Trouvier downed the drink. He made a face and poured another.

"What's our position?" Miles asked.

"Dans la merde." Trouvier tossed back the second drink.

"Surely you can be more specific?" Miles said, his tongue thick.

"We are thirty-six hours from Wilmington with a persistent Yankee frigate on our hindquarters. We are bucking a headwind and my engines eat coal like peanuts. And due to our 'slight' one-hundred-eighty-degree change in course, we didn't make our coal stop in Cárdenas. So if I don't ease engines, we'll have to run the blockade under canvas. White sails in the moonlight. Superb target practice for turret gunners, eh? *Salut encore!* Dammit." Trouvier threw his head back, Adam's apple bobbing on his long, skinny neck.

"It's the gold, isn't it?" Miles said. "The gold's putting lead in your shoes."

"We are heavier than any inbound run I've ever made." Trouvier stared blankly ahead. "But the gold is not our problem. Agreeing to tender supplies to Hyde Cay was the problem. Your petty demand to pigeon-hunt a drowning man in the midst of the chaos. Those were problems. Those cost time. And now I pay for letting you talk me into kinship with your alliance of fools." Trouvier sipped his rum thoughtfully, no longer grimacing, his taste buds numbed by the raw cut of the liquor.

"They're not fools," Miles said, barely audible, his articulation lost in drunken stupor. "They're noble men."

"When the noble lose, they lose big, my friend. That is why I have always preferred to contract the undistinguished. The margin is safer."

"Am I undistinguished?" Miles asked with sudden concern. He shifted forward in his chair, trying to focus his attention.

"You are the biggest black-market barracuda in the only port open to the South," Trouvier said with a smile. "I had to break my rule for you, my friend. Perhaps that was the beginning of my problems, eh? Your luck has changed."

"What do you mean?" Miles lifted his leg off the table and stood, drunken, threatening. He took a few shaky steps forward.

"You board my ship with your left leg clanking. Now you limp on your right. And you brought a girl to keep your bed warm. Now you sleep alone. You left Nassau with a ten-percent share of the gold that lands safely at the Wilmington docks. They did not tell you I take my fifteen percent first, so instead of ten thousand dollars you make eighty-five hundred. You see? *Pas de chance.* Hard luck for you, my friend. Perhaps for me too. I should have left in the little boat with the girl. Smart girl, eh?" Trouvier smiled.

Miles staggered toward him, then stopped. He was in no shape to fight.

"Ah, but don't worry," Trouvier continued. "I have a plan. Always a plan. I will stop engines when dark falls and drift south. The ship on our tail will keep a heading for Wilmington. We will lose a day and tack north under sail. And we will stand far out to sea and lie off until night. Then we will take our chances and run dark and silent through a swarm of Yankee ships, straight to the mouth of New Inlet and safety. Easy, *non*?"

"No," Miles said softly.

Trouvier sighed. "As I say, *la chance s'a tourné.*"

Two days later, the *Cyrus Tern* lay out to sea, waiting for full darkness.

Captain Trouvier calculated the ship's position as northwest of the New Inlet entrance to the Cape Fear River. Only a native pilot could discern landmarks on the flat, featureless Carolina coastline. The *Cyrus* would have to move in close enough to sight land before the pilot could begin to guide them to the small target—the river mouth half a mile wide.

The night was moonless, clear, and dead calm.

Trouvier looked up to the flagstaff. The quarantine flag hung limply there. He had ordered it raised to imply there was yellow fever aboard, a false message, but one that had kept a nosy U.S. screw steamer at length during the *Cyrus*'s stealthy tack up the coast.

The wheelsman steered a course due west. Engines were warm and pulsing. The paddle floats beat the water with an incessant wash.

No lights showed aboard the blockade-runner. Even the engine hatchways were covered with tarpaulin. The *Cyrus* steamed forward, its low, dark gray silhouette blending with the dappled night shadow of the water.

Trouvier took position on the bridge. He wore black. He was taking no chances. The crew was tense. They lay flat on deck, or hid behind the bulwarks, all anticipating the thunder of a Yankee gun at any moment. Miles stayed below. Trouvier was not happy having Miles spend so much time in the captain's cabin. But he suspected Miles's leg was festering. There was no doctor aboard to treat the wound.

Trouvier turned to the pilot, about to ask him whether they should cast the lead to test bottom. But a fire flash off the starboard bow made him duck instinctively just as the explosion sounded. The shot plowed water off the *Cyrus* bow.

"Hard aport!" Trouvier ordered the wheelsman.

He heard the thunder of two more guns, then a fifty-pound cannonball landed amidship, taking the flagstaff and crashing into the deck.

The crew scattered and took positions with muzzle-loaders below the gunwales.

"Fast as she goddamned goes!" Trouvier yelled down the tube to the engine room.

The *Cyrus Tern* swung about to dodge the next volley, but an exploding shell showered her port side with shrapnel. Trouvier heard a man scream. The Federals had a sure reckoning on *Cyrus*'s position, he thought. How many were there? And where were the gaps in their line?

"Steady," he said to the wheelsman as he studied the firing pattern and the flashes.

"I think we're a lot farther south than we thought," the pilot said. "Bet this is the outer squadron."

"There's no inner or outer line," Trouvier said grimly. "Just ships covering the bar thick as fleas. No way to get through now. Set your heading south. We'll make top speed for the Old Inlet."

"Better check the engine room first, Capt'n. Coal's runnin' low."

Shrapnel suddenly burst through the glass window of the pilot house. The pilot was hit and fell to the floor, holding his stomach.

Trouvier made an instant decision. "Beach her," he ordered. "Full speed ashore and ground her tight. Prepare to abandon ship."

Trouvier went quickly below.

Miles was in the cabin. He had packed a large leather bag.

"Time to run like the devil, my friend," Trouvier said, pulling a key from a pocket inside his trouser band. He unlocked the cupboard. Inside was a scrolled oak box. Trouvier quickly opened it, then he frowned and stared. He rummaged through the box's scant contents.

"Where are my papers? My commission? My license?" He looked up. "Brant, you treacherous son of a—"

"On the contrary, my mother was a saint," Miles said quietly as he pulled a pistol from inside his coat. It was an old-model Colt, .31-caliber, a long, deadly six-inch barrel. He leveled the revolver at Trouvier.

"Why?" Trouvier asked. "Why would you take my things, my registries, my—"

"—identity?" Miles finished. "It may come in handy."

"Only if I am dead." Trouvier straightened slowly.

"The ship will be run aground, or sunk where she runs. What use are you now, Captain? Aren't you supposed to go down with your ship?"

Trouvier shook his head. No—but he had no time to say the word. The bullet struck his temple, and he stumbled against the wall and fell limp to the floor.

Miles slung the bag over his shoulder and tucked the revolver back in his waistband. He made his way topside, cursing the painful limp that was now real, not feigned.

The ship lurched starboard. With a tremendous cracking of timber and wrenching of beams, the *Cyrus Tern* listed hard as she settled on the rocky bottom.

Sailors jumped into the water, still within range of the deep-draft warships. But dawn had broken, and the Confederate gunners at Fort Fisher had begun a protecting volley of shot against the Federal fleet.

Miles gasped in pain as he raised his leg over the gunwale. Damn Devon. Damn his underestimating her. He threw his bag to a sailor wading in the shallows, then dropped into the water with a dozen other men.

On board, the gravelly voice of the old wheelsman was calling above the chaos.

"Land ahoy the hard way! Capt'n to the bridge!" he yelled. "Capt'n?"

THIRTY-FIVE

The house was unbearably humid. Regina fanned herself in front of her dresser mirror. September not even half gone. Jasmine's Reach was still stifling.

Poor Miles, she thought. The weather made his recovery all the more uncomfortable.

Regina took a sip of the whiskeyed water on the dressing table. Never had she seen her strong, capable husband laid so low, so sickly and defeated, not even when he first came home with his left leg in that ugly metal monster a year ago.

Now it was his right leg, and the doctor, a new young fellow out of Richmond, said his left leg was fine.

Regina downed the entire drink. She didn't understand it and she didn't want to. After a year of having a husband with a crippled leg, now she had a husband with one leg. She just wanted to be strong, for herself and for Grace, because bad times were coming.

Atlanta was overrun and burned. Sherman was trampling Georgia with his godless horde.

Sometimes in his fever Miles mumbled strange things about Charleston's cheering the lion's feet, but Regina knew that was the fever talking.

Miles talked a lot in his delirium. Mentioned Gentry often enough. And Devon. That sneaky English tart. Miles must have said her name a dozen times, as if she were in his dreams.

Lord, what more must a good wife endure? Regina went to the window and looked out over the front grounds of the manor. Grass was dying for lack of rain. Pansies in the border beds were brown and wilted. Crepe myrtles looked sickly. No hands to work the gardens. They were all in the fields, clearing and thrashing. Victor run away. Portia dead. The little mulatto Abby gone too.

Then the Army took the plantation's best milk cow last week. That left only one.

At dinner the night before, Regina had felt as if she were going to explode. The cook had set cowpeas, a little piece of salt pork, and some stale corn bread on the table. It was the first time since the war the Brants had been served a block-ade meal like the common folk in Wilmington.

Lord. Regina tipped the glass up, but it was empty. Things had surely changed for the worse when Miles left for Nassau. That snippy lieutenant of his couldn't come up with any of the black-market necessities Jasmine's Reach was supposed to get, no cheese or salt or bolt flannel. The lieu-tenant had the temerity to tell her that a barrel of milled flour would be $1,250 in Confederate paper, just as it was in Richmond.

And the medicine Miles needed. It was breaking them. A hundred dollars an ounce for morphine. "Same for chloro-form. Everybody's hurtin'," the impudent young doctor had said when he'd come to take Miles's leg.

Well, Miles Brant wasn't everybody. Regina Brant wasn't, either.

From the herb box on her windowsill, she broke off a bushy sprig of fresh parsley. She chewed slowly, freshening her breath, then she spat the tiny cud out the open window.

Her husband was in the Trieste Room, a chamber whose bed she had never been invited to share. It was a large and hulking room, with weapons on the walls and gaming sets in the cabinets.

The room was roasting hot because Miles had taken the chills. Evaleen was with him, sitting in a chair by the win-dow.

"Don't sit there like a bump on a pickle," Regina snapped as she bustled in. "Give him a fresh rag for his head!" She turned around to close the curtains to the anteroom.

Evaleen took the cloth from Miles's forehead.

"Here, let me do it!" Regina said.

Evaleen backed quietly out of the room, a content, quies-cent expression on her face.

Regina wet the cloth in a basin and wrung it out. Then she blotted the rag gently over Miles's face.

His skin was so pasty. All bloated around his eyes. He was sweaty and fevered, his fine hair dark and matted like a plow horse's after a pull.

She had never seen Miles so unhandsome. The condition should have aroused a maternal protectiveness in her, but most of what she felt was nausea. She was married to a one-legged man. Thank God he didn't sleep with her.

"Miles? Miles, honey?" she called.

He stirred, grimaced, moaned in pain.

"It's almost time for your medicine."

"De . . ." he mumbled.

Don't. Regina squeezed her eyes closed.

"De—von," he breathed, turning his head into the pillow.

"I'm going to pretend you're trying to say 'heaven' with that longing in your voice," Regina whispered. " 'Course I'm not sure you're ever going to get there if you committed adultery. Portia's one thing," she said, soft and grim. "A white woman's another."

She freshened the cloth again and folded it across his forehead.

Miles moved fretfully. He was rousing from his sleep.

" 'Gina?" he said hoarsely.

"Miles? I'm here, honey. It's me."

Miles tried to open his eyes. He blinked and looked at his wife. "What day is it?"

"Tuesday. Five days after the operation. Four weeks since you got back from Nassau," Regina answered completely, before he asked.

"That butcher took my leg," Miles said, grimacing as he raised up.

"Gangrene was going to take the rest of you if he didn't. Let me help you." She placed pillows behind him. "Can you scoot back, honey?"

Miles hissed sharply, then held a cry in his chest as he eased himself backward.

"Where's the medicine?" he gasped.

"You have to wait. Soon. About an hour, now. Doctor said you can't take it too often."

"I'm paying for it! I'll take it when I want." He grimaced and sank back against the pillows, exhausted.

"Don't you want to check the mail first?" Regina asked hurriedly, then prattled on. "You got a letter here. Don't know from whom. Posted in St. Louis. More land business, maybe? And there's a letter here for Margaret. Arrived just in time. She's leaving tomorrow. You think she'll have some kind of fancy memorial service in London? She didn't even let us call in the neighbors. They would've brought food and everything, you know."

Miles breathed deeply. "Let me see the letters," he said.

"Here's yours." She dug in the pocket of her apron.

"Give me both of them."

"Margaret's too?" Regina frowned.

Miles held out his hand.

Regina gave him Margaret's letter.

"I'll call if I need you," he said, dismissing her, his eyes riveted on the envelope.

"I'm sure you will." She closed the curtains with a vicious jerk. The curtain rings clattered on the rod.

Devon's handwriting. Miles was sure. He ripped open the envelope.

Dearest Aunt Margaret,

I am well. I leave here soonest to fulfill a promise and seek solace after a deep and abiding loss.

I beg you to forgive the brevity of these remarks. A full explanation of events leading to my stay here in Baltimore awaits you in London, having been sent to Damien for safekeeping.

I do not know whether you will receive this letter. If you do, know that I regret any pain my actions have caused. My choices were difficult ones. Know, too, that I am grateful for all you have done, and for the life you tried to give me.

Devon

Miles frowned. Devon wasn't returning to London. Her "loss" was obviously Gentry's death. "Fulfill a promise," though? To Gentry? From whom would she "seek solace"?

He worked the letter between his fingers, then crumpled it. Only one other person would commiserate in her loss of the half-breed, the one who'd sired him.

"Teague," Miles whispered. Devon was going to see Teague Morgan. What would she tell him? That Gentry was dead? That Miles had killed him?

The threat of exposure vitalized Miles. Would Teague disinherit Regina for spite? He hadn't thought of that. Hadn't thought about Devon's seeking out Teague Morgan. Miles shook his head. He had underestimated her right and left.

Miscalculation had never cost this dearly before. He squared his shoulders and slid the letter down into the waist pocket of his wrinkled dressing gown.

Miles looked at the other letter. Postmarked St. Louis. He tensed suddenly, and the jarring motion sent a bolt of pain up the stump of his leg . . . a screaming pain . . . an unspeakable pain of remembering the teeth of the saw going through flesh, through bone to soft marrow—

Miles trembled with the effort to swallow his screams. They gargled in his throat with a monstrous fight for air. When he could breathe without shaking, he looked again at the letter in his hand. Expressionless, he opened it.

"I live."

Two words.

Unsigned.

Arrogant bastard. Arrogant *breathing* bastard.

"Regi—na!"

Miles frantically searched for a post date on the envelope. September 9. The day that vulturous shaman had dismembered his leg, Gentry Morgan had passed through St. Louis and put a triumphant message in the mail.

"Regina!" Miles screamed.

"God in heaven, what's wrong?" Regina came running to his bedside. "I'll give you your medicine. I was just trying to—"

"Go," he interrupted her. "Go to the fields. You. Personally. Pick out a big nigger. A strong one. He's going to help me up. I want to take a walk."

"Miles, you can't—"

"I can. Then I want you to send a message to town. Get a woodcarver out here. He's going to measure me a wooden leg. And last, bring me two flat pieces of kindling, a little jar of whitewash, and a paintbrush."

"Are you going mad? Take your medicine, you'll feel bet—"

"No more medicine. It fuzzes my mind. Do as I say," he ordered bitterly. "I have work to do. Regina, I'm making a pledge here and now. Inside of two months I'll be leaving for St. Louis. There's a problem with the parcels we're buying around Teague's place."

"That's crazy! You're discharged from the Army. You can finally take care of this place."

"Jasmine's Reach is dying, Regina. And I'm not going to follow suit. Now do as I say."

"But what do you need kindling and a paintbrush for?" she asked, nervous at his sudden recovery of command.

"I have to paint a sign."

"Well, I swear." Regina looked at him critically. "I'll have Evaleen bring those things right up. You rest now."

When the supplies arrived, Miles chose the smoothest side of the kindling. Trying to ignore the raw fire in his wound, he painted slowly, sweating. P-O-R-T-I-A.

Up on the north ridge, her grave lay unmarked, like the others. The slave cemetery was rocky ground, not much growing there except a big, forked sweet-gum tree. On that ridge he would look for bare, fresh-turned earth. And he would plant the little cross in Portia's resting place.

"You had to learn," he whispered. But the punishment had driven her away. He no longer had her proud body, her soft, silken warmth, to lie next to, her skin like the night, her eyes like a well, deep secreted, harboring the dark, harboring him.

"She hurt me, Portia," he whispered. A haze began to cover his eyes. "Did you know she was going to hurt me?"

Each afternoon when the weather permitted, Devon tucked her sketchbook in a satchel, put on a long wool cloak, and walked to the park across the street. She was staying with a Baltimore family, friends of Peach Straun's, in a three-story brownstone that overlooked a crescent of woods.

It was already November. She had left Nassau two full months before. Now she was almost ready to leave again.

Upon her arrival in Baltimore, she had sent a letter to Teague Morgan in Plain Shade, Missouri. The letter had been brief, difficult to write. She'd managed to tell of Gentry's courage and integrity, making broad references to his work as an agent for the Union, afraid to be too specific, concerned that the letter, like too many others, would go astray. Summoning a courage that had left her numb, she'd written of the assault that had left Gentry stranded in an angry sea, of seeing Gentry wounded by Miles, of watching terrified as he slipped beneath the water. "I fear he is gone," she had slowly written, "but I cannot yet feel it. There is so much cold here. I beg leave to visit you as soon as arrangements can be made. . . ."

She had dispatched a long missive to her mentor, Damien James. She'd written candidly of the alliance and of her precarious family situation, holding Damien to secrecy in both regards. She'd received his reply from London during the past week. Damien swiftly had transferred funds to an account in her name at a Baltimore bank. In return, she had posted to him twenty illustrations with descriptive captions attached. None dealt with the conspiracy. Most were of war life in Nassau—the fortresses of cotton stacked aboard blockade-runners, the crowded harbor, dock life, and rustic streets.

She had also sketched weary young soldiers at camp, using as models the Confederate boys who had escorted her and Gentry to Jasmine's Reach. And there was the boy Eben from Magda Selliger's farm. And Victor Batu, noble in half profile, his dark, gentle eyes fixed on the future, the great flare of his nose and breadth of his forehead commanding attention.

Devon had no pictures of Gentry. She had started bravely many times, but she could not draw him. His features blurred beneath her pencil. He was lost to her in every tangible way.

She had saved the *Harper's Weekly* that chronicled the U.S. Navy's triumph over a "mercenary fleet that assembled in stealth and diplomatic treachery." Though the article made reference to "a conspiracy against the sovereignty of these United States," no foreign nationals were charged. There was mention of "a secret organization in support of the belligerents, whose leader was called The Monkey Fist."

How quickly the consul, Walter Straun, had acted to confuse the press, Devon thought.

While at the consulate, Devon had heard Straun discuss recommendations he would make to President Lincoln. Instead of revealing that the alliance was the brainchild of high-placed international sympathizers, the U.S. would deplore the actions of Confederate agents who falsely garnered contributions from upstanding British subjects and French businessmen. In return for its sensitivity and legal largesse, the United States would negotiate high reparation fees and generous trade agreements.

The *Harper's* article was a battle story, glorifying the Federals' victory and heralding the efforts of "loyal Union agents" who relayed warning of the forthcoming attack. The article did raise questions of execution and motive, but Devon knew that the pieces of the alliance puzzle lay thousands of miles and many nations apart. It would take months for correspondents and statesmen in separate countries to gather rumors, facts, and sketchy reports. By that time, Lincoln and the British prime minister would have arrived at a mutual position on the affair. As for France, Devon was not sure how Lincoln would deal with the emperor Napoleon.

So the bold foray of the monkey fists had ended with ruin for the conspirators.

For herself, she had some personal triumphs to count. She had won kinship with the political ideals of her long-dead father; she had won a self. She had practiced an independence and bold freedom unimaginable in her life at Langley Place.

And she had merged her path with one man's, so briefly, so fiercely, that she would be forever marked by a love that had seeded deep and joyfully in her soul, beyond all reach of death's still hand.

Inside the tepee the flames of the night fire faded low and red. Gentry needed more wood. He rose and pushed aside the loose flap of buffalo hide. Outside, the night was cold and clear. Late December by white man's count, the Moon of Frost in Tepee by reckoning of the Sioux.

The Indian camp lay in a region of long, narrow lakes in Dakota territory.

In the distance the dimpled surface of Big Wing Lake bounced light from the stars. Gentry counted the cone shapes of twenty-eight tepees beside the lake. Only half were occupied. A devastating summer of smallpox had taken whole families; others of the clan had fled in fear of catching the spotted sickness.

Gentry gathered juniper sticks and fir logs stacked beside the tepee. He was in one of the most isolated tents. It suited him, and it suited Kai-ee-nah's father, Two Moons.

The old patriarch still blamed Gentry for the loss of his favorite daughter. And Gentry had not been readily welcomed by the clan leader, even though he had brought Two Moons many gifts, using most of the generous purse Pinkney Dobbs had plopped on a tavern table in Washington.

Gentry had endured lengthy interviews, but to his surprise, Dobbs didn't sit in on the questioning. "I'm retiring soon," he had said with a peculiar smile. "Time to let young fools grow wiser. Old fools just get older."

Gentry and Dobbs had reminisced over tall whiskeys, then Gentry had booked his train to St. Louis and outfitted a pack pony with supplies and gifts for Two Moons' clan.

That had been more than three months ago. Gentry had spent most of the time since quietly garnering acceptance, hunting hare and deer to replenish the meat drying on racks outside the tepee of his sister-in-law.

It was Ton-weya's acceptance that mattered most. The boy had followed Two Moons' example and withheld companionship from Gentry, doling out instead a taciturn presence, polite but reserved.

It was to be expected. Gentry had visited the tribe seldom in eleven long years: at times when he scouted the vast Dakotas for the cavalry, once after a winter in the mountains trapping beaver, once accompanied by a gregarious trader named Pa'ha John who was setting up a trading post on the Big Sioux River.

Gentry had treated Ton-weya as a detour, never a destination. The boy would have to decide whether to forgive him.

Gentry took the wood inside the tepee and fed the fire. High above, a bow hung from a crosspole, twisting with unseen currents on its string of sinew. Gentry had cut the bow from an ash sapling and scraped it raw and even. Now the bowed wood was seasoning in the heat.

He sat by the fire and waited. Ton-weya would come that night, as he had for the past four nights. He said he came to bring the food his aunt—Kai-ee-nah's sister—prepared.

But Gentry knew Ton-weya came to hear the stories. Gentry had begun to tell the boy of life beyond the village, of the places Gentry had seen, the life he had led.

Ton-weya came despite his anger and resentment, curiosity overpowering his pride.

The boy was wise, Gentry thought. Wiser than his father. Gentry's pride had given Teague Morgan no chance to atone for the anguished years of Calla Summer Sky.

When next he met Teague Morgan, Gentry would model himself on Ton-weya, let the curiosity rise and the pride fall. He would listen, and ask. Who was Teague Morgan? He did not know his father. Thus was he doomed, the ancients taught, for he could not know himself.

How was it then that she could know him? Devon, a woman reared in plenty, wrapped in a blanket of social grace, born with skin the color of angels' robes, the color of a race so rampant and rich and arrogant, they dominated tribes wherever they ventured. How could this woman grasp his soul and open it, let the ashes of his past fall to the wind like seeds of something new?

The resin in the fir logs crackled in the rising heat.

Devon. Her name was with him now. Next would come her voice, deep in his ear. Then the close, sweet scent of her skin. Then the feel of the fit of her body against him, and the blindness of the wanting.

Gentry closed his eyes to stop the hypnotic dance of flames.

There was a scratching on the lodge flap.

"Hi-yu wo." Gentry bid him enter.

Ton-weya stepped in silently, a wooden bowl in his hand. He hesitated, then offered Gentry the gruel. Sometimes Kai-ee-nah's sister sent strips of buffalo jerky, sometimes a flat-cake of maize. With the approach of winter came the gruel, a paste of prairie turnip and chokecherry flavored with bear grease.

"Sit," Gentry said, beginning the ritual that would allow Ton-weya to stay.

"I go to Two Moons' lodge," Ton-weya said.

"Two Moons tells good stories," said Gentry, crawling over his sleeping robes to reach a leather pouch close to the wall of the lodge. He withdrew a spoon of scooped horn.

"Perhaps tonight he will tell of the summer of the great flood."

"I have heard the summer of the great flood," Ton-weya said, sitting across from Gentry.

"Perhaps he will tell the year of such cold that the crows froze in the branches of the trees and fell dead to the ground."

Ton-weya grunted, an expressionless Sioux noise that meant nothing and everything.

"Or the season the Kiowa sent wife-stealers."

Ton-weya gave him a look of boredom. "My kinsman Long Claw tracked the enemy for a week and got his wives back. And he brought back one of the no-men who rode soulless like a white man, without clan or pipe or honor. And the chief ordered the worm, *wa-glu-la,* for such a creature."

Gentry nodded. The worm was not an honorable death. It was reserved for those who through deceit and disrespect had become no-men in the eyes of the Lakota. Only through bravery under torture could a no-man gain enough stature to enter the spirit world. He would be caged in a dark sheltered place and suffer greatly each day through loss of a limb. Then the avenger would leave so that the no-man could burrow back to the earth and seek the wormland where his spirit would do no harm.

"I have heard many of Two Moons' stories," Ton-weya said, impassive.

Gentry gazed across the fire at his son, a youth whose hair hung to his shoulders, without a feather. He had left his boy-seasons, but had not yet received his man-name.

He was already a good hunter and fine horseman. Fortunately, he would live to earn a man-name. The spotted sickness had left him thin, but with few pocks on his dark face. The potash salves of the white doctor had served him well.

The boy kept his eyes low, deferential, focused on Gentry's chest. His eyes were brown, set deep below a ridge of brow that was fine-formed and sharp, a delicate contrast to broad Sioux features. His brow and his height were the only traits attributable to the boy's Irish grandfather. Ton-weya had seen only thirteen winters, yet already his head reached Gentry's chin.

Gentry paused in his eating. "Has Two Moons told of the day I returned without his daughter?" he asked.

Ton-weya's eyes met his, briefly, boldly, then returned to the fire. "I have not heard of that day," Ton-weya said.

Gentry finished his meal and wiped the horn spoon clean. He held the long spoon as he talked, using one end to stir the fire when his words came slow. He spoke the past to his son, beginning with the day of Kai-ee-nah's death, revealing to Ton-weya what Gentry had not known at the time: The gunshot that killed Kai-ee-nah was fired mistakenly, by a woman kin to Kai-ee-nah by marriage, Teague Morgan's adopted daughter, Regina.

"I called and called," Gentry said of the evening he left Summer Sky with Kai-ee-nah's body on the poled travois behind the horse, "until my throat turned to fire and the wolves heard, and they answered. They led me to a distant place."

At dawn Kai-ee-nah's painted pony stopped by a clear stream, and Gentry knew it was a restful place for her. He cut four saplings for stakes and added branches to the travois to make a funeral scaffold.

There he raised the body of his beloved high, away from the scavengers, close to the Land of Many Lodges. No tribeswomen were there to keen for her, only the morning larks to sing. No drums to pound in anguish, only the click of squirrels cutting bark. "There was peace where her body lay," Gentry said quietly.

He stirred the ashes. The embers were fading to smoke, and Ton-weya scrambled quickly to get more wood.

Gentry was silent as the boy tended the fire. The quiet grew, and Gentry knew Ton-weya was uneasy.

"You need to rub more fat on it. It will crack," Ton-weya said of the bow his father was seasoning.

"It has been a long time since I made a good bow," Gentry said.

"It is a weapon for the patient," Ton-weya said gruffly. "A gun is more powerful."

The boy thirsted for a rifle, Gentry thought. "Do you speak English?" he asked.

"Two Moons taught me. He says we should know the enemy's tongue so that we know what lies he tells."

"How many *wasicun* do you know?"

"I see many. I have talked with only one. Pa'ha John, the trader on the river."

"Your grandfather is *wasicun,*" Gentry said quietly.

"And my father is more *wasicun* than Sioux!" the boy said suddenly, fiercely.

"I am more *wasicun* than I wish. I no longer fight what I am. But my spirit is with the Real People, the Cherokee. Do you understand?"

"I understand you are a man of many people. Where does such a man have his lodge?"

"In one moon's passing, I go to dwell in the lodge of my true father. If his blood is still bad with me, I will seek land by myself."

Ton-weya grunted.

"I would ask a favor," Gentry said carefully.

Ton-weya was silent, his eyes fixed on the fire.

"It is a long journey. Many days by land. Many days by a boat that travels with a giant wheel on its back. I need a good hunter with me. Two Moons says you do much meat-making for the camp."

Ton-weya remained silent a long time. "I would be a better hunter with a gun," he said finally.

"Pa-ha John has rifles to sell. I will see him on this journey."

"Perhaps I should practice with yours, so that I will be skilled when we reach the trading post."

Gentry suppressed a smile. "Perhaps."

"Now tell me," Ton-weya said.

"What?"

"How far you have traveled. What things you have seen."

In the request was a restless longing, and Gentry talked until the dawn rose on a foggy horizon. He spoke of the water-ship that crossed the river without banks, and the island of black faces, tiny lizards, and demon rain. And he spoke of a beautiful white woman, a warrior with hair the gold of rippling wheat. "Our souls have met, never to part," Gentry said.

"Why did you not make her woman-who-sits-alongside-you?" Ton-weya asked.

"We were small people lost in a great war. And I was hunted by a man who was a strong enemy."

"What wrong did you do to him?"

"I survived." Gentry met Ton-weya's gaze. "This man may someday seek vengeance on you for the same offense."

"Then we must kill him," Ton-weya said simply.

Gentry looked at his son, full of promise, full of Kai-ee-nah's curious questing.

"Yes," Gentry said.

THIRTY-SIX

A cold gust swept unexpectedly across the open ground. The mules lowered their heads and leaned harder into the wagon harness.

"That's Summer Sky, ma'am. Teague's place, straight ahead," the driver said, closing the collar of his coat against the wind.

Devon sat huddled in a flannel blanket on the open wagon seat. The ride from Independence, Missouri, had been long and bone-rattling.

Summer Sky, the house named for Gentry's mother, was a white-porticoed brick mansion, solid in construction, Greek Revival in facade. It presented an imposing front of brick pilasters, oversize columns, and a balcony with a cast-iron railing above the front door. The house rose starkly at the bottom of a river bluff that overlooked the town of Plain Shade. Bleak and leafless oaks were scattered across the yard. There were no plantings, no entrance gate, nothing frivolous to care for.

"We there yet?" Abby asked from her bundle of robes in the buckboard, her voice nasal with catarrh.

"Almost," Devon said. She let the warm blanket tenting her bonnet slide to her shoulders. She didn't feel ready to face Gentry's father. Teague Morgan's short note had said she was welcome to visit. Period. Devon tucked loose curls into her hat and clasped her hands in her lap.

"You all right now, ma'am?" the wagon driver asked.

"Yes, thank you," Devon said. She stared straight ahead, embarrassed. The driver had stopped twice so that she could empty the sour disquiet in her stomach. Both she and Abby had been ill during the train journey from Baltimore. Abby's croup had long since settled into a dry cough and cold. Devon's nausea and weakness had abated, until today.

The wagon passed under the portico but did not stop. It followed a cleared road around the side of the house to the back. Steps led up to an open-air gallery that connected an L-shaped wing to the main house.

The driver went up on the gallery porch and pecked on the glass of a paneled door.

From her perch on the wagon seat, Devon saw a bearded man emerge. A long white tongue of napkin hung over the front of his shirt. He jerked the napkin from his collar.

As he descended the steps, the tall man daubed the napkin across a thick salt-and-pepper mustache and beard. He wore a dark denim shirt that gapped at the neck to show a gray flannel undershirt.

Devon shrugged off the blanket as he neared. The wind blew into the bell sleeves of her loose coat, and she barely controlled a shiver.

"Miss Picard, I take it? Teague Morgan." His voice was gruff. He didn't extend a hand to help her down.

"I'm sorry to interrupt your dinner," Devon said.

"Stew's too hot anyhow," Teague said absently. He studied her, eyes crinkling at the corners, a sunburst of creases etched deep and careworn.

Finally, Teague held up a hand. "Better get inside." He helped her down.

Devon took the steps slowly. She felt unsteady after sitting so long.

Teague strode on ahead and opened a door onto a kitchen suffused with the aromas and warmth of dinnertime.

Abby followed Devon in.

"Have a seat. I'll help bring in your things," Teague said, and closed the door.

Devon and Abby were alone in a cozy kitchen of hard oak floors and a high, plain ceiling. A pie tin of dark, meaty stew sat steaming on the table. Beside it was a cutting board and three-quarters of a loaf of bread.

"That sure makes me hungry, Miz Devon," Abby whispered, looking at the fireplace. A round-bellied pot hung on a cooking crane. The contents sounded a thick, hollow plop as slow heat forced a bubble to break the surface.

"Be patient," Devon said weakly. The smell of red meat and cooked yams made her stomach threaten to rise. She sat quickly on a cane-seat rocking chair and bent forward, head on her knees.

She did not look up when she heard Teague and the driver shuffle past with bags and trunks.

"Sure you don't wanna stay for a quick bite o' somethin' warm?" she heard Teague ask the driver when they had finished.

"Naw, thank ya, Teague. Gonna go on into town. Surprise my boy. He works at the livery, ya know. Says it's warmer toolin' leather in the barn shop than helpin' his brothers slop hogs at our place. . . ." The driver's voice receded down the steps of the gallery porch.

Devon heard a stomp and scuffle as Teague wiped his shoes on a mat outside on the porch, then he came in.

"You're lookin' a little puny there, Miss Picard," he said after a pause.

There was barely a lilt left in his voice, and no Irish brogue in his syllables. His accent was as flat and direct as the land he had homesteaded.

Devon slowly drew herself upright. "I suppose I feel somewhat 'puny,' " she said.

"Want somethin' to eat? It's antelope. Fresh."

"No, thank you." She grimaced and held her breath. "I believe Abby is quite famished, however," she ventured.

Teague looked at the pretty mulatto girl who stood beside the hearth. "Abby, why don't you dish yourself some stew? You like blueberry crullers?"

"Ain't never tasted 'em, suh," Abby said, nervously clutching the collar of her new wool coat.

"Well, you'll like 'em. My cook, Mary Kate, made 'em before she left." Teague turned to Devon. "I'm here alone today. Let all my help off to see family. It's Christmas."

"Christmas?" Devon echoed numbly. She rose with difficulty.

Teague moved closer to steady her, but she sensed no sympathy in his gesture. He was distant, his tall body still emanating the crisp, cold air from outside.

"I'm afraid I need to rest, Mr. Morgan."

"Room's upstairs," he said, yet made no move to let her

pass. "I don't mind tellin' you that you don't look like the kind of woman Gentry would take up with."

"Perhaps your son changed, Mr. Morgan."

"I haven't. I doubt he would either."

Devon took a deep breath to hold her queasiness at bay. "He was away a long time. You don't know—"

Teague's hand on her arm tightened. "I know what I hoped, is all. And then your letter came, all black-and-white and done with."

"I thought it kinder to let you know he was—he . . ."

"You wanted me to share your misery! I got enough of my own." He dropped her arm.

Devon turned and left the kitchen, left its hearty stew and yeasty bread and its master whose rancor was blind and bitter.

She took the wide, creaking stairs with a hand on the banister, as if she were ailing and old. Her bags were in the second room on the left. She crossed directly to the four-poster bed and sat down. The room held the mustiness of neglected years. Sun rot had weakened the fabric of light, filmy curtains; a piece of scalloped lace trim gapped away from its seam on tenuous thread.

She heard his footsteps, leaden thumps.

He crossed the threshold, but neither spoke.

At last Teague cleared his throat, a raw, rough sound. "I've been dreadin' a letter like that for eleven years," he said.

Devon was silent.

"He's my only son."

"I'm sorry," she said.

"Why? Why did you come here?" Teague shook his head.

She looked at him, a man who held bits and pieces of Gentry in his memory, in his physique, in his dark, severe sadness.

"To bring you a gift from Gentry." She paused. "When Gentry and Kai-ee-nah came to visit you, they left their two-year-old son at home in the village."

Teague's eyes narrowed, their expression guarded.

"You have a grandson, Mr. Morgan."

He blinked. "A grandson?" he whispered. His hand covered his mouth, then slid slowly down his beard. "What's his name?"

"Ton-weya," Devon said, her voice strained, gone hoarse. There was silence.

"I have a grandson," Teague said. "But you. What do you have?"

She looked away. Tears rose like a permeable wall. She could not speak. She could not move.

Slowly, Teague came close.

Desperate, Devon leaned to his warmth, cried out for it, her fist pounding, pleading.

His arms fell around her, awkward as tree boughs, yet warm.

Teague was the first to hear Abby's timid footsteps creak on the stairboards. He stepped back and held Devon at arm's length. Then he left without word.

Devon rested. She woke long after nightfall when Abby tiptoed in with an oil lantern. She told Abby to change for bed, then put on a long dressing gown and brushed her hair.

"Miz Devon?" Abby began.

"Yes," Devon said, "you can sleep with me tonight to keep warm."

Abby smiled and crawled eagerly under the covers as Devon left with the lantern.

She found Teague in a worn armchair in the back parlor. Beside him on the reading table, a Weldon clock droned a quiet ticktock.

The room was warm. A big iron woodstove perched on claw feet near the wall, its long smokestack elbowing sharply through the wall to the outdoors. An aroma pungent as apple butter came from an earthenware pitcher on the stove top.

"Was hopin' you'd be down. Made some extra." He got up and went to the stove. "Hot cider and whiskey. Guaranteed to make you sleep like a baby."

"Or blather like a fool?" she said, accepting the cup.

Teague looked at her. "I'd prefer that, if you're up to it."

She sat in a chair opposite him. "I wouldn't care to be the only one talking," she said softly.

Teague pursed his lips; the great bush of beard drew upward. Then he sighed. "Deal, Miss Picard." He threaded a ribbon bookmark through the book on the arm of the chair.

"You may call me Devon," she said.

"And you may call me a liar. I told you wrong in the

kitchen. I've changed over the years. Lord knows every man changes, or dies a fool." He sipped the cider, staring thoughtfully at her. "I'm still a son of a bitch. But a more reasonable son of a bitch."

"I'm sure Gentry would have approved of such a vast change in character."

Teague didn't smile. "Gentry approved of nothing about me. And I, being a mite hardheaded, returned the feeling in spades. He blamed me for abandoning his mother in misery. I never told him any different."

"Why not?"

"Because he was right."

"But I know you looked for Gentry and his mother. You spent hundreds of dollars on detectives. Regina told me."

"I abandoned them for five years," Teague said, jaw set, eyes far away. "Came out here and sank all my money into the land. Lived in a log shack and spent every waking moment working, turning the money back to the land. Land paid me back, took care of me.

"But I didn't take care of her," he said softly. His words were difficult to hear. "Could've sent for her the end of that first year, when the baby was born. But I didn't. People out here don't like Indians. Too many homesteaders remember the raids. They don't try to understand tribes, or territory. They're all 'savages.'

"And I had bank loans pending. I didn't want to jeopardize my land by letting everyone know who I loved."

He paused. "That's a pitiful kind of cowardice. To this day, pitiful."

"You tried to make amends."

"After." He shook his head. "After good harvests. After the interest was paid. After I was so big no one could censure me. Then I sent out the search parties. Then I commissioned this house.

"It's like a Kentucky house Callie saw once in a magazine. Callie loved nice things. But she never once asked me for a gift, for jewelry, for anything. She never once asked me to marry her or take her with me. It was me, I offered her everything. And I gave her nothing."

"You gave her Gentry," Devon said.

"False hope, false love."

"Gentry said she always knew you would come back for her, for Gentry. She told him so, many times."

"She knew?" Frowning, he stood abruptly and poured more cider in his cup. "She knew." He remained standing, facing the wall. "Tell me what else Gentry said."

"He said he gave you a bit of trouble."

" 'A bit'? Aye, he did." Teague smiled and sat down. "Nothin' I didn't ask for. I didn't know the boy. Took him from the settlement camp. Skinny thing. Quiet boy. Couldn't get him to talk. That more'n anythin' else drove me to bedlam and back. Any male with Irish in his stones talks and fumes and drops more lies in a day than a buffalo does chips. Not Gentry. He knew that'd get me. Him being quiet, pretending not to understand, so all my white friends would think he was just a stupid Indian. Vicious sense of humor, that boy. 'Course Regina didn't help things much. She was so jealous of him."

"Why did you adopt her?"

He shook his head. "I was scared. I couldn't find Callie and Gentry. I was building my little empire here for the next generation. And there was none. Regina's dad was a friend from Ireland. A good Joe. Inept at makin' a livin' though. Packed his family and all his worldly goods in a wagon and headed out on the trail with a guide everyone knew was a drunk and a cheat. Some mad Sioux dropped by and Regina turned up on my doorstep an orphan.

"I adopted her as soon as I could. Gave her false hope, I guess. Guess I've done that to too many women in my life. Regina deserved better. She'll get a livable sum when I die. But not this place, not this business or my thousand acres. Prime farmland. River fed. That's my gift to Callie and Gentry. Was my gift. To be passed down through Gentry, and his tribe. People round here sure gonna be surprised when I die and the Indians take over." His eyes crinkled with dry humor. "You in your twenties yet?" he asked Devon suddenly.

"Almost. I'm nineteen."

"Kai-ee-nah wasn't quite eighteen." He shook his head thoughtfully. "It's hell getting past fifty years old with so many regrets on your back. Bends you right over some-times."

"When Kai-ee-nah died . . ." Devon began softly.

"That day Gentry died for me too," Teague said abruptly. "I went up on the hill. He was farther away from me than I could ever reach. I never wanted somethin' so bad in my life as for that girl to start breathin' again. She would've brought us together. I know she would."

Teague rose stiffly from his chair. "But it's too late now. It was too late then." He crossed the room and took the pitcher of cider off the stove. "Come on into the kitchen now. You need some grub. And I need to get movin' before the rheumatiz stiffens up my back. I'll fix you some sugar bread. And you can tell me how my boy ended up fighting for the Union. Gawd, that hurt me when he signed up with the slavers."

They sat at the kitchen table near the fireplace and talked through the night, Devon detailing much of what had happened to her since meeting Gentry.

With halting, haunted speech, she recounted Regina's story of the shooting of Kai-ee-nah and Miles's butchered delivery of the fetus.

She spoke of her aunt and uncle, the grand plan of the alliance, Miles's treachery, Gentry's escape from jail, and the night Gentry held her and asked her to make the long journey to see his father.

It was as if a dam of words had been broken inside her. She could not stop the flow of the past, and Teague listened without interrupting, saving his questions for another time.

But he had one question that could not wait. "You're sure Miles fired the shot that sent Gentry under?"

"Miles said he did. Boasted he did." Devon felt lightheaded with relief. To have someone listen, someone from whom she did not have to hide facts and feelings.

Her arms rested on the oaken table, and she laid her head down, her cheek feeling the cold in her silk sleeve like something fresh and new.

"Get on up and get your rest," Teague said. "I've got a few things to arrange in town. Mary Kate'll take good care of you while I'm gone." He pulled a short wool coat off a peg by the kitchen door.

"Where are you going?" Devon asked.

"To find my grandson. Just to find him. I'm not gonna yank him out by the roots like I did Gentry. Not sure the Sioux would be as reasonable about it anyway."

Devon stood up and nervously tightened the sash of her dressing gown. "Make arrangements for two. I'm going with you."

"Like hell," he said.

"I've already been through that, Mr. Morgan. I'm hoping for a less rigorous journey."

Teague gazed sternly at her. "You aren't kiddin', are you?"

She met his eyes. "I want to meet him. I want to see where he lives, make sure he survived the scourge, that he is well and happy. . . ."

"You want to see Gentry," Teague said not unkindly. "You want to see Gentry in an Indian boy. You want to see where he lived, what he ate, know how he stayed warm, hear words he said. Gentry's gone from all that. He's gone."

"He is not!" Devon's fist pounded on the table, clattering the spoons in the pie tins. "He is everywhere. Hints and clues, bits and pieces, a man I knew for so short a time. I have a right to seek him."

Teague was silent.

"You owe me," she said softly.

"Owe you what?"

"A present. A Christmas present."

"What?"

"I brought you a grandson."

"What in God's name do you want from me?"

"Memories, Mr. Morgan," she said raggedly. "I don't have enough."

" 'Lov-ve-ve, O love, O careless love-ve-ve . . .' " Mary Kate's gravelly contralto filled the kitchen.

She sang because the kitchen was too quiet. She was all caught up. Midday dinner simmering in the kettle. A pot of fresh coffee on the warming brick. Pan bread cooling on the table. She stopped humming at the sound of someone on the porch steps. Must be carrying something, she thought. Scuffle and thump, scuffle and thump, like a butter churn.

Mary Kate headed for the door, wiping her hands on her apron. She opened the door with a proprietary frown.

The man on the porch looked haggard, but his clothes were brushed and smart.

"Colonel Brant?" she asked incredulously. "My good Lord!"

"Nice to see you, Mary Kate," Miles said easily.

"Well, come on in." Mary Kate opened the door wide. Her gaze was glued to the polished cherrywood leg showing beneath the hem of his greatcoat.

"How's Miss Regina—I mean, Mrs. Brant? Must be, land sakes, more'n ten years since we seen her. She writes regular, though."

"More than you can say for Teague," Miles said.

Mary Kate paused, her guard rising. "Mr. Morgan don't make much time for writin', that's a fact," she said breezily, opening a cupboard to get a mug.

"Folks in town say Teague's not here."

"You only missed him by two days. They left—" Mary Kate stopped.

They, Miles thought. He was right. "Well, I should've told you all I was coming," he said. "Know when he'll be back?"

Mary Kate bustled about the hearth. She took her apron in hand to grip the hot handle of the coffeepot. "No, sir, I don't," she said cheerily. "You know Mr. Morgan. Not one for givin' a body fair warning about anythin'."

She set the steaming mug in front of Miles.

"Folks in town said he was going north," Miles said, "all the way to Lakota territory. Nothing much up there but Indians and trouble." He sipped and smiled.

"I reckon that's so. Would you care for some dinner, Colonel Brant? Pipin' hot," Mary Kate said in a rush.

"Don't mind if I do."

She pulled a good china bowl from the cupboard. "Been traveling awhile, have ya? Imagine it's kinda hard to get through with the war an' all."

"I just show my discharge papers," Miles said. Or Beque Trouvier's passport, whichever created less suspicion.

Miles sat at the table with his back to the hallway, listening to the sharp tap of the wooden spoon as Mary Kate filled his plate from the pot on the hearth. "Thought Teague would've got you a good cookstove by now, Mary Kate."

"Well, Colonel Brant"—Mary Kate rose and turned—"I ain't no fancy cook. I been doin' it this way for forty—" She stopped, her eyes wide. Over Miles's shoulder, she could see

Abby, backed against the wall of the hall like a gnat on flypaper, her terrified eyes on Miles.

Before Miles could turn around, Mary Kate hurried forward and set the plate smack in front of him. "Get on outta here!" she yelled. "You'll have to 'scuse me, Colonel Brant," she added as she swept past him. "There's a range dog gets in through the chute and tramps dust all over. Shoo!" Mary Kate was gone through the doorway, peeling Abby off the wall as she went.

She pushed Abby ahead of her to the front hall. "Get on down to the cellar. Now!" she whispered, and gave Abby's shoulders a quick hug.

Mary Kate bustled immediately back to the kitchen. "Critters," she sniffed. "How's the stew?"

"Excellent," Miles said, chewing slowly, thoughtfully. "Teague will miss your cookin' on the trail, I imagine. It's a good month to get up to Sioux country. That's where he's going, isn't it? Up to see Gentry? That little wife of his was Teton, if I remember right."

Mary Kate looked at Miles. "We got word Gentry died, Colonel Brant. Killed in some battle somewhere, I guess. Mr. Morgan never told me much."

"Miss Devon bring you the news?" Miles sank his teeth into a chunk of potato.

Mary Kate was silent.

"Did you know Devon Picard is my cousin?" Miles cut himself a square of bread from the cast-iron skillet on the table.

"Never would've guessed." Mary Kate busied herself at the sink.

"Cultured young lady. But headstrong. Real headstrong."

The pump handle grated up and down. Mary Kate said nothing.

"She took one of my slaves. Strong, young, light-skinned girl. I'm sure it was an oversight on Miss Devon's part."

Mary Kate whirled around and dried her wet hands on her apron. "There aren't any slaves here, Colonel Brant. Mr. Morgan ain't never allowed it. You won't find a one on this property."

Miles nodded politely. "I understand, Mary Kate." He stood. "Thank you for lunch." He walked toward the door with a swaying, graceful limp that minimized the thump of his wooden stump on the kitchen floor. "Sorry I missed Teague. But it was only by two days," he said pensively. "I'll be seeing him, Mary Kate. Let him know that for me, will you?"

"Sure will, Colonel Brant." She frowned with sympathy. "And I sure am sorry about your leg."

"Me too, Mary Kate," he said evenly. He opened the door and turned to her. "I've learned to look at it philosophically, though. There are lots worse hurts that can be visited on people."

THIRTY-SEVEN

A warm, wet snow began to fall, large flakes that settled like lace on the ponies' dark manes.

To Gentry's left were the banks of the Big Sioux, a muddy-brown rush of river. Within sight was the outpost of Pa'ha John, a Jesuit priest turned trader who had once been Gentry's tutor at Summer Sky.

"That is the trading place?" Ton-weya asked, drawing his sorrel pony closer to Gentry.

Gentry nodded, aware of eagerness in the boy's voice. Ton-weya would soon have the gun Gentry promised.

With an imperceptible pressure of heel, Ton-weya urged his pony forward through the heavy flurries to ride beside the two Sioux warriors ahead. Long Claw and Rain Falls were respected hunter soldiers and had pronghorn hides and beaver fur to trade for guns and metal-head axes.

As the party drew near the cabin, Rain Falls and Long Claw slowed to let Gentry lead. Gentry knew the ways of the *wasicun*. He would bargain for them.

A lean-to shed was tacked onto the back of the barn behind the trading post; it was used as a shelter against wind and snow for animals. The two warriors stayed there to tend the ponies.

Before he opened the door to the trading post, Gentry took off his hat and dumped the snow. He brushed off his shoulders. Ton-weya did the same. Both wore leggings and long ponchos made of buckskin.

Inside, a woman sat alone near a squat-bellied, cast-iron stove, a hoop of needlework spread across her lap. She was

Indian, and looked up at Gentry and Ton-weya but did not greet them.

"I wish to see Pa'ha John," Gentry said.

She waited a long while before answering. "We are not open for trade right now."

"Pa'ha John is not here?" Gentry asked.

The Indian woman pulled a long-nosed revolver from under her sewing. "He is not here," she said quietly.

"I'm an old friend."

She was silent.

"Gentry Morgan."

The name registered. "Your father?" she asked.

"Teague Morgan."

"You are dead."

"You are pronouncing sentence?"

"I say what your father thinks," she said.

"My father wrote Pa'ha John?"

"Your father was here. He stayed two nights. He and the woman."

Gentry paused, gathering his thoughts and his hopes. "Yellow-hair woman?" he asked.

She nodded.

"She seeks me."

"She mourns you. They seek your son."

"Why did we not pass them?" he asked.

"You came by Snake Ridge?"

Gentry nodded.

"Pa'ha John feared the weather and took the trail across the valley."

"When did they leave?"

"Two days ago." She paused, then lowered the gun. "The others left yesterday morning."

"What others?"

"Five men, tracking your father. One *huste.*"

One lame. Miles. Gentry heard an undertone of anger in the woman's voice.

"*Ka-ki-sni-ya-pi?*" he asked. Did they torment you?

She looked down, sliding nervous fingers along the barrel of the revolver. "You will help my husband?" she asked finally.

"We need guns, fresh horses, food."

She nodded and left to prepare a pouch of meat.

They traveled until nightfall, then wrapped themselves in buffalo robes to wait out the snow flurries. When the snow stopped, Gentry found the north star, and the band continued on through the crystal cold night. The sky was vast black, rich as the pelt of an otter.

Ton-weya urged his pony beside Gentry's. *"Ah-te,"* he said. The boy was slightly out of breath.

Father, Gentry thought. It was the first time since his return that the boy had addressed him with the term of honor. Gentry stopped, realizing that he set a harsh pace for horses and men alike over steep terrain. It was a torturous shortcut, but Gentry wanted to reach the forested valley sooner than Miles. He had to.

"Hau, mi-cun-ksi." I listen, my son.

"The *huste* we hunt. His hand drew the blood of my mother and pulled my too soon brother from the womb?"

"Yes."

"Have you told Long Claw?"

Gentry looked ahead. Long Claw had disappeared over a rise, his new Sharp's rifle in a sling across his back. Rain Falls was far behind on the trail with the packhorses. He would catch up at the next resting place.

Gentry shook his head slowly. "Do not tell Long Claw yet. Anger will make him strong, but foolish."

The weather held through the night, and the next day they descended to more level ground and picked up the day-old trail of four horses, one with heavy packs. Gentry's father and Pa'ha John were half a day's ride ahead, moving slowly across open country, unaware they were tracked by enemies.

By nightfall of the second day Gentry knew where Pa'ha John would choose to camp—near a ravine at the fork of a creek, a spot Gentry had found when they'd traveled together years before and where he had first taught Pa'ha John to make a wickiup. Gentry pressed on, leaving Ton-weya with Rain Falls. Long Claw had long since struck out on his own path.

The temperature dipped suddenly during the night. Gentry feared a storm would rise. The northwest wind gusted more sharply, whistling through stark trunks of trees and leafless boughs. Gentry felt his face freezing. From a waist pouch he drew the white grease paint the Sioux used for protection from winter cold. He smeared it across his nose and cheeks and huddled deeper in the soft fur of his buffalo robes.

When the sun rose, he saw the smoke of Pa'ha John's morning fire in the distance.

Gentry advanced warily, scouting the perimeter of the area, looking for signs of Miles and his four hired guns.

He found still-warm ashes and fresh horse dung—and the prints of five horses heading toward Pa'ha John's camp.

Gentry mounted his tired pony and galloped as close as he dared. After tethering the pony by the fork of the creek, he checked ammunition in his rifle and pistol and secured a long knife to his calf under his leggings.

The top of the creek was frozen, but he could hear the trickling rush of the deep, icy stream beneath the surface. He crept away from the creek and up through the still forest toward the ravine. The only sound was the howl of the wind when it rose, and the scratching of branches as it fell.

Gentry belly-crawled to a boulder at the crest of the hill. He could hear Miles's drawl before he could see him.

". . . sorry to be dropping in so rude and unexpected, Teague," he was saying.

Gentry peered around the boulder.

The ground sloped sharply, then leveled and ran to a deep, craggy ravine. Two of Miles's men stood on the slope not far from Gentry, their guns drawn.

Miles was much farther down, on level ground, next to Teague Morgan and Pa'ha John.

And Devon. She was real. She had come. She stood farthest from Miles, by the ravine, shrouded in blankets to break the wind.

Gentry pressed his cheek against the cold granite stone. She had come.

He knew he should wait for Long Claw to whistle a sign that he was near. At this distance, Gentry could easily drop one of the two gunmen on the slope, but the unknown whereabouts of Miles's other two hirelings made him uneasy. Gentry kept himself flattened against the rock, breathing deeply to keep his heart pounding low and even.

". . . so you see," Miles was continuing, "I had some business in St. Louis and stopped by your place. I imagine Devon's told you how much your place means to me,

Teague. And this one question got stuck in my head. Made
me crazy, matter of fact." Miles stepped closer to Teague. "I
was wondering why, if you thought Gentry was dead, you'd
traipse through snow and godless country to get to his old
Indian village."

Teague didn't answer.

Miles walked past him, limping badly toward Devon. "I
got to thinking, what if Gentry had a child when he was
little more than a child himself. Child could be twelve, thirteen, fourteen years old by now." He stopped ten feet from
Devon, his gun drawn. "And that's what I was about to ask
you on the ship, Devon, before you so promptly incapacitated me." He extended his cherrywood stump. "What do
you think of your handiwork, by the way?"

Devon met his gaze. "I'm sorry you did not die," she said.
"Living is your hell. I could have saved you much misery."

"Oh, and you, my dear," he said, smiling as he started
toward her again.

Gentry tensed and sighted the rifle. The *huste* must not
touch her. And he must not die. Yet.

Gentry's rifle cracked. One of the gunmen on the slope
fell, hand to his chest. The other gunman dropped to one
knee and fired blindly up the hill toward Gentry.

Gentry reloaded fast and ducked to the other side of the
boulder. He fired again.

The second gunman on the slope fell.

Gentry rolled away from the big rock to get a new position.

A bullet chipped the rock face where he had been. Then
another ball of lead stung the ground near his foot.

The other two men Miles had hired! Now Gentry knew
where they were, in the woods behind him, in field position
to pick him off.

Gentry crouched and scrambled toward a stand of trees.
A bullet stung bark.

His only chance was over the hill and down into the
camp. He dashed across the crest of the hill and hunched
down, bringing his rifle to sight on Miles.

The shot went deliberately short. Gentry was afraid of
hitting his father or his friend, both standing too close to
Miles.

Miles sank stiffly to one knee and fired. Gentry rolled left, discarding the rifle and drawing the revolver, rising to run a cut-and-shift pattern, bearing down on Miles.

But in the split seconds of Gentry's approach, Devon moved forward. Two trancelike steps that brought her closer to Miles.

She did not take her eyes off the advancing man, his ghostly face streaked fierce with white. "Gentry?" she whispered.

Miles heard her. Immediately he pointed the gun at her and cocked the hammer.

"No!" Gentry's cry was long and guttural, echoing in the raw chill. He halted, heaving breath that left clouds of white in the freezing air.

"Damn if she isn't right!" Miles said, narrowing his eyes. "I'd kill her in a minute," he added to Gentry. "You know that, don't you? Drop your gun."

Gentry did.

Miles eased the hammer gently to the strike plate.

Gentry released a long, slow breath. He felt the eyes of his father and of Devon on him, but could not stop looking at Miles's face, his small, sharp nose reddened by the cold, the raw windburn on his cheeks, the lean and hungry smile, and his strange, pained eyes, burning, gloating.

"Hold your fire but keep your guns up!" Miles yelled to his two gunmen on the rise. "What we got here is a family reunion." He gestured for Gentry to join the others.

Gentry walked slowly toward his father.

How much older he looked. The lines around his eyes etched too deeply, his long body sinewy, the shoulders curving forward, inward. The man who had never bent to Gentry's will bowed to the weight of time.

Gentry paused. *"Ah-te,"* he said softly in greeting.

Teague pressed his lips tightly together. After a long moment he cleared his throat and nodded. "Son."

They looked at each other, appraising the passage of years, how mellowed the mien, how forgotten and forgiven the injustices, imagined and real.

"Mi-cun-ksi." Teague said the word haltingly. "Son. Kai-ee-nah taught me. But it's been a long time."

"She had much to teach, if we had listened," Gentry said.

"Speak up, Gentry," Miles said with a mock-peevish drawl. "I want to be touched by all this."

Gentry ignored the taunt and went to Pa'ha John. The garrulous trader had no niceties. "How many you got with you?" he asked roughly in Lakota dialect.

"Two men and a boy," Gentry said.

"Well, we've still got two men with guns and the mouthy bastard to take care of." Pa'ha John glanced beyond Gentry. "Afraid your side's got one less than ya think, my friend. Look up there." He nodded toward the top of the hill.

Miles's gunmen were walking down the slope, leading their horses. One pushed a boy in front of him.

Ton-weya was gagged, his hands tied behind his back.

"What have we here?" Miles said as Ton-weya approached.

The boy's moccasins soundlessly cracked the surface of the frozen snow. Gentry looked at his son. There was no fear in Ton-weya's eyes, only disdain for the *huste*. Did that mean Long Claw and Rain Falls were near?

"Stop right there," Miles told the boy. "I'd wager this little redman's about fourteen years old, wouldn't you, Gentry?"

"Ten and three winters," Gentry said, still gazing at his son.

Miles took off the gag to look at Ton-weya's face. "I think I detect a little Morgan in the woodpile there. Go say hello to your granddad, boy. Make it quick. I've got to make you the first one I shoot."

Gentry tried to stop the pounding in his ears, the overpowering need to hurl himself forward and smash Miles in the face.

But he would be shot. Then there would be one less to fight for his family when the time came.

One less to fight for Devon.

He turned to her, finally, as if just recognizing who she was, as if they had not been speaking to each other since he'd entered her camp. This place was hers. The still, silent woman's. She who had thought him dead, who had watched the water swallow him, who had fought Miles's trap and dealt evil a painful blow. She who had kept her word and sought out his father, and his son.

She who knew him. They need not speak. But they must hope. When he looked at her, he saw that she was numb to hope, so often had Miles fouled her faith in what would come.

Gentry began to walk toward her.

She let the blanket fall from her head, and he saw her hair, hanging down over her ears to her shoulders, drawn back at the sides like a child's.

He smiled.

Her face warmed.

The slip-click of Miles's gun hammer sounded behind him.

"Hold it!" Miles said. "You think I'd allow you two one maudlin minute of comfort after I've come so far? Touch her and I'll drop her where she stands, I swear. Wheedlow!" Miles called behind him to one of the gunmen, who had mounted.

The man reined up beside Devon. "Pack her up on your saddle and hold her tight till we get through here," Miles said.

Wheedlow reached down and jerked away the two blankets draped across Devon's shoulders. She wore a long, thin wool cloak underneath. The gunman pulled her up in front of him.

Gentry watched, blood pounding in his temples. "She will be cold," he said.

"She'll be warm enough when I get through," Miles said. "Now shut up while I enjoy the opportunity God's given me. The whole blessed family, right here. I guess God's saying pain pays, right?"

Miles smiled humorlessly at Devon, then turned to Teague and the Indian boy beside him. "Now I have one question for you, Teague. About your will."

"I wouldn't leave a red cent to an aberration like you. Or your heirs," Teague said. "I changed my will before I left town. Regina gets some spending money, but her trust is endowed only on your death. My land is forbidden to you, in explicit language no one's gonna mistake. If I don't have any direct surviving heirs, the land goes to the Cherokee nation, Summer Sky's people."

"I can challenge that," Miles said calmly. "You're not of sound mind. You've been misled by a strange, histrionic Englishwoman."

"My lawyer knows my mind. The people of Plain Shade

know my mind. And I made it clear in a deposition tacked to my will that I don't want a slaver cutthroat like you profiting from my death."

Miles gestured theatrically. "Smugly, self-righteously delivered. Seems you've got my hands tied. But not for long. Never for very long. I always find a way out. Not you, though. You're stuck here, Teague. And you're going to watch the grandson you don't know die yelping like a pup."

"Miles!" Gentry said harshly, hearing the erratic balance of sanity in Miles's voice. "Give me the truth before I die."

"Truth? What makes you think I owe you one stinkin' grain of truth?"

"Because you're a man of great vanities. You're proud of that day. And we're the only people you can ever tell."

Miles's lips stretched in a grudging smile. "True enough, you bastard. True enough. Well, let's talk about that day on the hill. Let's add a little poignancy here. Very little. I don't want to stay too long. That wind shoots through like a knife sometimes. I'm freezing. Are you freezing, Devon?"

Miles spoke to her but continued to look at Gentry.

"Not really much to tell," Miles went on. "That story about my hand-to-hand knife fight was made up, of course. I saw your wife in her pretty blue dress up on the hill, and I went up there to take care of my inheritance. I was a highly eligible man in Wilmington, you know. I didn't have to marry a plain Jane like Regina. I did it for my future.

"But there was K'eenah, all swelled up with Gentry's future. Bullets banging all around us, ricochets pinging off trees below us. Good cover. I was just beneath the knob of the hill when I saw Regina getting scared and trying to pull out a gun. When she turned around, I shot K'eenah.

"I came up and took the gun and said, 'My God, Regina, look what you've done.' Regina hated that little Indian girl, and she took over the guilt without once questioning whether her gun had done it."

"You let Regina carry that burden? All these years?" Teague roared. He started toward Miles.

"*Ah-pe, Ah-te!*" Gentry's arm shot out to halt his father. "You cut your own hand for an alibi," Gentry said quickly to Miles.

"A little too deeply, I might add. A surgeon learns more

from his mistakes than his successes. Like that bit of surgery with K'eenah. Didn't hurt her a bit. She was already dead."

Gentry closed his eyes a moment, breathing deeply. "Then she did not ask you to save the child," he said, his voice strained.

Miles frowned. "Of course not. I birthed that unborn thing for the sheer finesse of the experience. What harm was there? Don't you understand?" He ran his hand through his hair, exasperated. "I have a highly curious intellec—"

"Wicasasni! Huka hey-ey-ey!"

Gentry wrenched the war cry from the dark madness deep inside himself and signaled the world with a shrill, unearthly howl. He rushed forward, his only thought to choke the breath from the no-man demon before him.

Miles quickly raised his gun, but Gentry flung himself against Miles's outstretched arm, and the shot went wild.

Simultaneously other shots rang out from atop the hill. Then Teague picked up Gentry's revolver and began firing.

Gentry did not hear the guns. He knew only the tensile yielding of Miles's neck. His hands had an unbreakable grip; they formed a noose that tightened; pressing deeper into Miles's windpipe, choking the breath of his lungs, rupturing the path of his words so that he would never again be able to speak of that day.

Miles flailed, losing strength, his face swelling red.

"Father!" Ton-weya called. "The *wasicun* takes the yellow-hair woman!"

THIRTY-EIGHT

Gentry looked up.

The hired gunman Wheedlow was escaping with Devon on his saddle. Dodging a shot from Long Claw's rifle, Wheedlow disappeared over the hill.

Long Claw had already killed the other gunman. There was only Wheedlow—and Miles—left alive.

Gentry released Miles, took his gun, and whirled around.

"I'll cover him," Pa'ha John said. "Get going."

Gentry looked quickly at his father and Ton-weya. They were safe. Teague had a hand wound; Ton-weya was bandaging it.

Gentry loped up the hill and mounted a horse. Rain Falls was on the crest of the rise. He signaled. "They cross the creek."

The ice. It was too early for the creek to freeze solid.

Gentry could not urge his horse faster across the icy snow. His quarry was already a hundred yards ahead, approaching the creek. Devon's long cloak billowed like a dark wing.

Gentry shot once in the air, trying to warn the gunman. Wheedlow only whipped his horse faster as he rode out across the frozen creek.

Devon struggled anew, trying to break the man's brute hold. Then she heard a tinkling, like an ominous chime.

The ice broke through before they reached the middle of the creek.

The horse squealed and fell sideways. Spidery webs scurried across the ice toward the bank, then the center fell through with a hollow crunch. A sharp-toothed crevasse opened with the floundering horse and freed the rushing water.

Devon screamed as the frigid shallows washed over her. Gasping, she was immersed to her neck. She flailed for a handhold on the ice. Righting herself, she finally found her footing on the slippery rock bottom.

She stood, streaming water. Her sodden skirts tangled around her legs. She could hardly move. The water was at her thighs, hardening, the freezing rush like a palpable thickness. She forced herself forward, toward the solid ice close to the bank.

She heard a shot and turned.

Wheedlow fell in the snow on the opposite bank.

Looking ahead again, Devon saw Gentry at the edge of the creek. He lay on his stomach and crawled outward, testing the ice with his rifle butt.

He crawled close and extended his hand.

Devon stretched and reached it. She was shocked that she could not feel its warmth.

He pulled her toward him, then helped her roll up and onto the ice. He crawled backward to the solid ice at the bank, sliding her with him. Then he grasped her around the waist and drew her upright on the bank.

Her wet hand trembled as she tried to touch his face. "Gen-tr-trr—" She could not say his name through the chattering of her teeth, the quivering of her chin.

Together, she thought. They were together. Why did he look at her with such sadness? Why didn't he hold her, make her warm, still the quivering in her arms? He could make it stop. He could hold her still.

"We have to hurry," was all he said. Choked words. He was afraid. Of what? she wondered. They were together. But even she did not feel the happiness. Too much of her body felt heavy and numb.

Gentry lifted her to his horse and mounted swiftly behind her.

He held her at last, arms around her waist, but she could not lean back against him. Shivering began in her shoulders and arms, and she bent forward to contain the shaking, but it only worsened. She was racked by uncontrollable tremors by the time Gentry pulled her to the ground beside one of the long, low wickiups Pa'ha John had built the night before.

"Ton-weya!" he shouted as he stripped the soaked wool cloak from her body. "More robes inside and across the roof. Quickly. Then build a fire beside us."

"Holy mother, she's dripping wet," Pa'ha John said.

"Those wet things have to come off her, Gentry. Quick," Teague said.

"D-d-d-don—" Devon tried to tell Gentry not to take her clothes off in front of all the men. He laid her gently down on a buffalo robe outside the wickiup and pulled off her boots. He threw them aside, then began to slit the sodden garments plastered to her skin.

Teague knelt nearby with a blanket, shielding her from interested eyes and the chill wind. He covered her as Gentry methodically cut along sleeve and bodice, petticoat and leggings.

Her body was blanched and white, her blood retreating inward to husband its warmth. Gentry worked quickly through the layers of her garments, finally laying open the underskirts along her abdomen.

He stopped, paralyzed by what he saw.

There, above soft corn-silk curls, rose a tight and burgeoning mound. Small yet, but protruding firmly, just beginning to add girth to the small pad of her abdomen.

No. Gentry could not speak.

"Keep going, Son. You've got to keep going!" Teague commanded.

Gentry heard nothing more. He focused intently on slitting the last remnants of her clothes, peeling them away, aware only of time, time past, time lost on a windy hill, time promised in the woman growing ever colder before him.

He wrapped Devon tightly in the blankets Teague held.

"She stopped shivering," Teague said. "Her body's giving up to the cold."

Gentry picked her up, his face like stone, for Devon was growing stiff, her muscles rigid.

He did not look at her. He sought his father's face, reassurance. "Make the fire bigger," Gentry said hoarsely, desperately.

Teague put a hand on Gentry's shoulder. "Fire's not going to help her, Son. Warm skin will."

Gentry lay Devon in the wickiup on thick robes of buffalo fur, deep in shadowed darkness, far from the light at the mouth of the small hut. No drafts of cold air came through the double covering of skins Ton-weya had draped across the shelter. There was little headroom. Body heat would quickly be trapped.

He tucked the robes around her chill body, then cut pads of buffalo fur to tie around her feet.

Once, her body jerked in sudden spasm.

He worked quickly, alarmed, his senses warming to the musky scent in the fur, the pungent sap in the rough thatch of cedar above them, the terrible silence in the small space. He edged backward to the entrance.

Outside, Rain Falls had gathered the horses.

Pa'ha John stepped forward. "We'll leave you alone now. Going on to Two Moons' village." He cleared his throat, awkward. "She's young. She can make it."

Gentry slipped off his moccasins and stood barefoot in the snow.

"We'll send someone with food and a lodge," Pa'ha John added.

"I'll return, *Ah-te*," Ton-weya said to Gentry.

"He's going to introduce me to Two Moons," Teague said. "I think it's about time the granddads got acquainted."

"It's time," Gentry agreed quietly. He drew his poncho over his head.

"What you want done with him?" Pa'ha John asked. He pointed at Miles.

Miles sat in the snow. Long Claw stood beside him, resting the point of his lance in Miles's belly.

Miles looked at Gentry. He moved his lips, but made no sound. Grimacing, he held his hand to his throat and tried again.

Gentry had taken his voice. "You will not be heard," Gentry said quietly, looking at his enemy, a man whose cold gray eyes were still open and scheming, while his beloved's warm ones were closed as she slept a dangerous sleep.

Gentry turned to Ton-weya. "Did you translate the *huste*'s story for Long Claw?"

"I told him," Ton-weya said.

"Then I ask Long Claw to pronounce punishment."

Long Claw looked at Gentry. *"Wa-glu-la,"* he said strongly. The worm.

There was silence.

"Serves the bastard right," Pa'ha John said uneasily.

Ton-weya grunted approval of the ancient torment.

Gentry turned his back and took off his buckskin shirt, and Long Claw jerked Miles upright.

Miles faltered, trying to gain his balance. Long Claw's lance prodded him forward, up the hill. Miles refused to go. He fell and scurried down toward the white men and the Indian boy.

Long Claw's lance pierced his arm.

Miles could not scream. He struggled to stand so that he would not feel the bite of the lancehead again. Then he limped up the hill, Long Claw prodding him.

Gentry gave no more thought to Miles. Looking up, he saw the sky was clearing, but the sun was still weak. The wind hit his bare chest with a gentle shear.

"We go, *Ah-te,*" Ton-weya said.

Teague and Pa'ha John were already trudging up the hill.

"I hope the yellow-hair woman grows well and warm," Ton-weya added.

"She is not yellow-hair woman," Gentry said. "She is *mitawin.*" My wife.

"I will tell the women of our lodge. When you return with her, we will make a feast."

"Pi-la ma-ye," Gentry said softly. Thank you.

Ton-weya ran to join his grandfather.

Gentry untied the waist thong of his soft tanned leggings and let them fall. He placed his clothes inside the entrance to the wickiup, then threw more wood on the fire outside to keep it alive.

He crawled into a darkness that was soft with the combed shaggy fur of the great *pte,* the buffalo, the life-giver of all the Indians on the Plains. Pray God, it held life for his beloved also.

He lifted the robes that covered her and lay with his body next to hers.

Gentry groaned aloud. She was still so cold, so rigid. He gathered her to him, closing his arms around her in an embrace he knew she could not feel. She could not know how her velvet skin chilled him, frightened him, how coldly her breasts pressed against him, how unyielding her back when he tried to hold her closer.

Frantic, he rolled on top of her, blanketing her with his body while the robes kept his warmth trapped around them. He held his weight lightly against her abdomen. Against the child. His child. Rising new from a woman who had yet to sit by his side as wife, who had sought the remains of his spirit and his world when she thought he was dead, so she could fill the child with knowledge of him. He understood why she had braved such an arduous journey. She was stronger than he. He would not have had the courage to explore her world if he thought she was lost to him.

If she were lost. Devon. *"Mitawin,"* he whispered. *"Mitawicu. Mitawicu,"* he said to the darkness, though no one could hear.

He could. He could hear.

"I take this woman for wife. I take—" He stopped, fear trapping the breath in his lungs. He laid his head close to hers. "Devon." He waited silent, unmoving, for her to warm and hear him.

She did not stir.

Chill imprisoned Devon's senses, isolating her awareness so that she could not respond, could not speak, could not command her hands to touch him. But she could hear him, the grief in his voice. And the hope. She wished she could say words to comfort him. Words to ask forgiveness for bringing his unborn child to such a barren place. Not widow, not wife, could she explain the zealous, burning need to know his living son? To see Gentry in a body young and skilled? To not be cut off from her love's past, so alien from hers, so far from the world in which she would rear his child? Could he know her fear of being alone, orphaned again, the water claiming all that was warm and wanted in her life? The fear had blinded her to danger, blinded her to all except the need to step in his path, walk in his shadows.

But the shadows grew warmer now. She knew he was near, knew that his cheek lay against hers. Gradually, she became aware of his long hair lying soft across her neck. And his hand, stroking her arm, awakening her skin, restoring memory of love's touch, a warming palm pressed to her breast, seeking a heartbeat, seeking assurance.

Devon felt herself grow lax under his weight, her flesh

tingling and pliant. Her chest molded to him, her hips and legs slowly losing their leaden cast, feeling his hard thigh aligned to hers.

Gentry waited as her warmth returned, enclosing her, basking her, as if his heart were a small, ambitious sun drawn to earth only for her, restoring promise in a cruel winter.

Though he had dreamed of her for months, through hardened, lonely nights, he felt no desire for her now. Nothing so earthly held sway alongside his fear of living without this woman.

He desired her closeness. Her laughter and wit. Her contentiousness, her strong will. Her fierce courage and graceful talent. He desired the glistening of eyes like windowed passages only he was allowed to enter.

He kissed her cheek.

"Tay-chee-khee-lah," he whispered. I love you.

He felt her hands rise, touching him tentatively, one to each side of his hips. Slender fingers, ice-cold, glided up his side, under his arm, and touched his mouth. He felt their numbness and made a gentle cup of his hands, breathing warmth into the mold.

Her hands trembled in the cocoon and he loosed them, knowing that they awakened with vengeance, the flesh burning with pain, seared by needles of splintered ice.

Devon gasped, her hands outstretched before him like petals straining to break, untouchable.

He rejoiced silently, for the pain meant life returning.

He grasped her wrists. Chill, but growing supple. He shifted his weight to lie beside her and embrace her, stroking her back and buttocks to warm the smooth skin that would bloom young and pink by the light of the fire in his lodge.

Slowly, her fingers calmed and bent. They traced his face, his throat, the scars on his chest.

"It is you," she said.

He gathered her hands and kissed them.

"And who did my wife expect?" he asked.

"Husband," she whispered.

He placed his hand on the mound where his seed flourished. "Soon a father."

She placed her hand atop his. "I was alone. Even with the child growing. So alone."

He held her. "The strong are always alone, *mitawin*. You paid the price of purpose. And you owe nothing more. Nothing. It is time to rest." His voice was a hoarse whisper. "Rest, so you will grow strong to fight and dream and—"

"And draw," she said. "This land. It's an artist's dream, so bold in form, in its people."

He kissed her lightly. "First draw my village, so that I'll remember it. And draw my son, so that we can keep his presence in the house of his grandfather, and draw—"

She placed two fingers to his lips to interrupt. "I could not draw you. Your face was empty on the page. I could remember you only in my heart."

"I will offer my spirit to your pencil now, *mitawin*. On the island, I kept my soul from yours out of fear. I was afraid you would take my soul back to your world and forget it there. And it would die. I would die."

"Do you still fear?"

He smiled. "No. Are you afraid, *mitawin?*"

She caressed him in answer.

"Then I must say the song to fix the loneliness of souls. It is Yu-we-hi, sacred formula of the Cherokee. So powerful that a man can say the song but once to a woman. Are you warm enough to listen?" he asked, molding her to him as if she were shield to his heart.

She kissed him. "Yes."

And he spoke the words into her ear, a vow soft but so strong, he need never repeat it, letting the words flow from a deep and gentle place inside him.

"There in Ela-hiya you rest, O white woman. No one is ever lonely when with you. You are most beautiful. Instantly, at once, you have rendered me peaceful. My path shall never be dreary. I shall stand erect upon the earth. Instantly, you have caused it to be so with me.

"Now make I the path peaceful for you. No one is ever lonely when with me. I am most handsome. I stand with my face toward the Sun Land. I am covered by the everlasting peace. Your soul has come into the very center of my soul, never to turn away."

"Never to turn away," Devon whispered, her hands touching him tenderly, strong with promise.

AUTHOR'S NOTE

For inspiration and information I gratefully acknowledge the writings of Thomas Henry Tibbles, Civil War scout, newspaperman, preacher, and Indian activist; the memoirs of James D. Bulloch, naval affairs expert, who worked in secret service overseas to acquire and arm ships for the Confederate Navy; the work of Dr. James Mooney, historian, who carefully collected and documented Cherokee myths, traditions, and sacred formulas; Ruth Beebe Hill, whose sensitive, persevering search for the Sioux spirit was uniquely rendered in *Hanta Yo*.

For constructive comment through many drafts, I thank Professor Edward Dreyer and writer Deborah Roffino. For foibles and errors of fact the author assumes responsibility.

For their forbearance, love, and encouragement, I thank my family.

L.A.W.

A riveting tale of passion and love

A LASTING FIRE
by Beverly Byrne

In the midst of the passions tearing Spain apart stood the House of Mendoza -- a dynasty whose brilliant men and clever women had amassed immense wealth and enormous power. Threatened from within and without, the Mendozas intrigued against one another and against mighty political forces...and lived in fear of disaster should love for the forbidden god of their forebears be exposed.

One extraordinary woman would shape the destiny of the Mendozas...Sofia. Snatched from the jaws of death and raised by Gypsies, she has boundless courage and the voice of an angel. She becomes *la gitanita*, the most beloved woman in all of Spain. But death, madness, and betrayal stalk her. Then, one miraculous night, fate and her mysterious past collide....

A LASTING FIRE by Beverly Byrne. Available in July wherever Bantam Fanfare Books are sold.

AN 234 -- 5/91